THE WITCH OF HEBRON

JAMES
HOWARD
KUNSTLER

THE WITCH OF HEBRON

A World Made by Hand Novel

Atlantic Monthly Press
New York

Published simultaneously in Canada
Printed in the United States of America

FIRST EDITION

ISBN-13: 978-0-8021-1961-2

Atlantic Monthly Press
an imprint of Grove/Atlantic Inc.
841 Broadway
New York, NY 10003

Distributed by Publishers Group West

www.groveatlantic.com

10 11 12 13   10 9 8 7 6 5 4 3 2 1

This book is for my wing men
Adam Chromy and Duncan Crary

*Be watchful, and strengthen the things which
remain, that are ready to die: for I have not found
thy works perfect before God.*

—Revelation 3:2

In the not-distant future . . .

First, gasoline became scarce and expensive, and now it is simply gone. The automobile age is over. The electricity has flickered out. The computers are all down for good. The great corporations have fallen. Paper money is worthless. Two great cities have been destroyed. Epidemics have ravaged the population. The government isn't functioning. There may be a president and he may be in Minneapolis, but it's little more than a rumor.

The people of a little town named Union Grove, in upstate New York, endure, living very locally in a world made by hand.

The world beyond Washington County has become an unknown country. . . .

ONE

Now it could not have been a more beautiful mid-October day in upstate New York in the year that concerns us, which has yet to come in history. Long jagged Vs of honking Canada geese winged their way toward the Hudson River over Pumpkin Hill, where the crowns of the suffering maples blazed red and orange as if on fire, and the birch leaves glowed like golden coins, and the line of sumacs at the edge of Deaver's hayfields ran as vivid as blood against the darker margin of the woods, as though Pumpkin Hill were a living thing itself, with a pulsing interior. Some people in the nearby town of Union Grove might have said it was, since the habits of thought having to do with old, deadening certainties were yielding to another way of seeing and feeling the world that, instead, brought everything to life.

Two boys and a yellow dog made their way up a dirt path along the Battenkill River, a tributary of the Hudson. In the low water this time of year, some gravel bars lay exposed, as bright and clean as the beaches on desert isles, and many fine trout lurked unmolested in the dark runs of cold water between the bars. Indeed, far fewer people were to be found angling there in these new times on a fall afternoon when there was a harvest to get in. The boys, both eleven, were Jasper Copeland, son of Union Grove's only doctor, and Ned Allison, whose father, a doctor of philosophy, not medicine, and once vice president of a now defunct college, ran the town's livery stable—as good a livelihood as medical doctoring in an age when cart and saddle horses were in short supply.

Up ahead across the river the two boys spied a rude shack made of castoff, salvage, and flotsam between the abandoned railroad tracks and the river. It was not without charm, having a deck cantilevered out over the riverbank with a rustic railing composed of fancifully shaped driftwood balusters, and behind all that, several generous, vertical windows, none of them matching. Two beaver pelts and one of bobcat were tacked up along the upstream exterior wall. The boys could smell them from where they came to crouch behind a clump of stately bracken.

The shack was the home of Perry Talisker, known around town as "the hermit," who did not altogether shun his fellow human beings but led a solitary existence there beside the river some distance from town. He trapped animals and traded their furs for necessities. Earlier in life, he had worked as a butcher for a supermarket chain. He could skin a rabbit in five seconds flat. He made his own corn whiskey and consumed just a little less than he made every year. It was reputed to be as good as or better than the whiskey made by Stephen Bullock, the wealthy planter. Perry Talisker made regular visits to Einhorn's store in town and was capable of polite conversation about the weather and conditions on the river. But he smelled as ripe as the pelts tacked to his house, and his conversational partners tended to cut it short. When he left the store with his sack of cornmeal and jug of seed oil, Terry Einhorn would have to light a candle to defeat the lingering odor.

"I think he's in there," Ned whispered. "I saw something move. C'mon, let's get closer."

The two boys crawled farther up the path along with the dog, which was a five-month-old puppy, a sweet-faced mutt named Willie with feathered fur on his legs. From their new position just opposite the shack they were afforded a clear view within.

"I see him," Ned said.

"Spying isn't right," Jasper said, but he kept looking anyway.

"Crazy people bear watching."

"My dad says he's just odd."

"Odd folks can turn crazy," Ned said.

They watched the hermit silently for a minute from their hideout in the bracken.

"What the hell is he doing?" Jasper muttered.

Talisker appeared to be sitting in a chair fighting with what, across that distance and through the glare on the windowpanes, appeared to be a snake in his lap. A little while later he subsided, dropping his arms to his sides and throwing his head back. The defeated snake lay inert on his lap. Then his chest heaved and the boys heard what sounded like an elongated sob above the noise of the river. A train of racking, descending sobs followed.

Jasper shuddered. He clutched the puppy close to himself there on the hard-packed dirt path. It licked him on the chin and he murmured, "Stop it, Willie."

"Listen, he's crying now," Ned said. "Jesus."

The sobbing continued. Whatever they thought they had witnessed—and neither was altogether certain what it signified— they knew at least that these were the sounds of a grown man in anguish, and it made them more uncomfortable than anything else they had seen him do.

"Let's get out of here," Ned said. He cut out up the path. Jasper lingered another moment in a sickened thrall, watching the hermit and listening, then quit their hiding place and caught up with his friend. Willie shadowed him. They didn't discuss what they had seen. Each in his own way was embarrassed by it, sensing the dark mystery it represented and the indecorum of watching it. Eventually, the path took them up the riverbank at Lovell Road by the ruins of the old power station. There they burst up from the glowing golden tunnel of the river into the starker late-afternoon light. Jasper carried a wicker creel on a leather strap diagonally across his body. The creel contained two heavy trout. In his right hand he carried his father's carbon fiber fly rod, a miraculous artificial material that might never be seen on earth again, his father said, now that things had changed so much for the human race.

Jasper had little recollection of what the old times were like except for a vivid sense memory of riding in an automobile all trussed up in a special seat designed to immobilize small children. He remembered the speed of objects rushing past a window, and the brightly illuminated signs of commerce, and his own discomfort in the strangely aromatic plastic seat, even the mood of desperation in the sharp, terse exchanges between the adults up front. That was all. Everything else beyond that memory was the familiar world of Union Grove and Washington County and the people in it he had known, including the sad and disgusting hermit.

The boys walked silently an eighth of a mile to where the road came to a T at old State Route 29, with its fissures and potholes and stretches where there was no pavement at all anymore.

"What the hermit was doing," Ned said as they walked back toward town, "that's nature's way."

"What was he crying for, then?" Jasper said.

"Nature's harsh and strange," Ned said.

In a little while, they came to the edge of town, marked by the ruins of an old strip mall. All that remained of the Kmart sign were the letters that spelled *art*. Though his mother and father had explained these things to him, the strange idea persisted in him that this had once been some kind of great bazaar at which objects of art were bought and sold. He knew that in the old times everybody had a lot more money and things. He knew that there had been many machines besides cars that ran on a liquid called oil that, for various reasons, had become impossible to get in the new times. The sharp break between the old times and the new times was something his parents carried with them constantly like a wound that refused to heal.

The rusty skeleton of an old car squatted deep in the poplar scrub behind the remnants of the Kmart building. The interior had long been burned out. Its steel roof was peeled back like the tongue of an old shoe, saplings had grown through holes in the floor, the hood was a tangle of raspberry canes, and blazing red Virginia creeper struggled up an empty wheel well along the rusty door. Somehow the car had escaped the Great Collecting that had occurred years before when the nation was hard up for steel to prosecute a war in the Holy Land. Jasper hardly remembered that. The boys sometimes visited the car, regarding it with the same morbid awe as the skeleton of a large mammal that had crawled into the woods to die.

"You want to go see the old car?" Jasper asked as they came to the strip mall.

"No," Ned said. "I have things to do."

"You want to visit the stallion over at the New Faith?"

"No," Ned said. "We've got all the horses I need to see. I have to rake out their stalls before supper."

"You want one of these trout?"

"I'll take a trout. Thanks."

"Get a stick."

Ned got a green stick and ran it through the gills and the mouth, twisting the ends like a handle. He didn't have a fishing rod. They weren't making them anymore. He was too proud to use an alder branch.

"I think I'll go visit that stallion," Jasper said.

"I wouldn't tell anyone what we saw out here today," Ned said.

"I wasn't going to."

"They'll ask why we stayed around and watched."

"I know."

Ned took off down the road for his home in town. Willie followed him for a few steps, then returned to Jasper's side as the boy cut behind the strip mall, past the ghost of the car, and took a shortcut through the woods around the town reservoir to the edge of the old high school property on the northern edge of town. The high school, which was abandoned after the epidemics that winnowed the town population, had been sold the previous June to a group of seventy-seven wayfaring Christian Evangelicals from Virginia who called themselves the New Faith Brotherhood. Fleeing the disorders of their home state, they had found peace and tranquillity in Union Grove, decided to settle there, and had worked sedulously to renovate the high school for their own purposes. The old football field had been transformed into a magnificent garden. The crop rows were mostly laid up for the winter now except for table greens and winter squashes. They had converted the old school bus garage into a stable. The other grounds and ball fields had been fenced up as pasture. One paddock held the group's prize stallion, a liver chestnut half Morgan named Jupiter. Not many people outside New Faith had been inside the main buildings of the establishment, and their ways remained mysterious, even threatening, to many townspeople of Union Grove.

As Jasper came out of the woods into a stubble field of recently harvested corn, he was struck by the low angle of the sun and the long shadows of everything on the landscape, the brilliant color in the trees behind the school and the perfection of the air temperature as the afternoon merged into evening. A warm nugget of profound contentment at the center of himself welled into a deep gratitude for being. He could see the beautiful stallion grazing in its paddock a hundred yards away. As he set out across the stubble field, a brown blur darted from behind a hummock of cornstalks in the direction of the paddock. The groundhog made desperately for his home in a hole behind the run-in shed. Willie lit out after it.

"No, Willie," Jasper hollered at the dog. "Get back here!"

Two

About the same time that fine fall afternoon, three men made their way around the construction site that was the old Union-Wayland box mill, which had shut down in 1971, decades before the U.S. economy imploded altogether in the aftermath of the banking collapse, two terrorist nuclear strikes, the Holy Land War, and the sharp decline in oil supplies that shattered everyday life in America. The three men, all of middle years, were the Reverend Loren Holder, minister of the town's congregational church and part-time town constable, Robert Earle, mayor of Union Grove and journeyman carpenter (formerly a software company executive in the old times), and one Brother Shiloh, a member of the New Faith order, who had much useful experience for the task at hand, having once served as a civil engineer with the Roanoke Water Authority.

Loren and Robert wore beards in the town fashion while Brother Shiloh was clean-shaven in the custom of his sect. His handmade black broadcloth frock coat, wheat-colored linen trousers, and white shirt would have also distinguished him from the townsmen, who mostly dressed in whatever garments they had leftover from the old times. Robert wore a threadbare tartan flannel shirt with patches on the elbows and canvas overalls hand-sewn by the young woman who had come to dwell with him after his wife died, while Reverend Holder favored a well-worn blue sweatshirt bearing the faded seal of Middlebury College (defunct) and corduroy pants with frayed cuffs.

The old mill building, which had been established in 1894 as a sash-and-blind works, had been successfully gutted over the summer. Robert had directed the reconstruction of the roof, repairing it with slates that came from the quarry in Granville, twenty-two miles away by the Vermont border. The joists and floorboards of both levels had been replaced, too. The materials were paid for with three and a half ounces of gold from jewelry collected among the townspeople. The labor was volunteered. The general idea—Reverend Holder's inspiration—was to construct a community laundry. American society, at least as those in Union Grove understood it—since news of anything outside Washington County was sketchy at best—had changed drastically from one in which every household ran laborsaving appliances such as clothes washers to one in which certain tasks were better done communally. The last spasm of electric service had shuddered through town for less than a minute in August, and for practical purposes everybody now assumed it was off for good.

As a business proposition, the laundry was conceived as a three-way partnership between the town, the New Faith organization, and the two "proprietors," Robert and Loren. They hoped to have it in operation by spring and expected to employ ten people. Brother Shiloh's job was to design a system for lifting water from the adjacent Battenkill River and directing it to a heating tank driven by a wood-fired furnace, then to a series of copper kettles where the washing and rinsing would occur. Wastewater would be directed into a sand and gravel leach pit excavated in the old parking lot, now overgrown with sumacs. In theory, the sand-filtered water would seep back to the nearby river hardly less clean than it came out. The excess heat from the furnace would be ducted into the capacious second-floor loft, where a network of drying racks could be used in place of the outdoor clotheslines when the weather was bad.

"It'll be hot work," Brother Shiloh remarked as they navigated a steep temporary stairway down from the loft. He appeared to know what he was doing, technically, but he always managed to put a little added negative spin on things, both Robert and Loren noticed, as if he didn't really want the project to succeed. It was an annoying note to what was otherwise shaping up to be a very positive development in a town that had known little but hardship and loss for years.

On the whole, the New Faithers had proven to be a valuable addition to the community. They possessed a broad array of practical skills, from metalworking to animal husbandry. Just weeks after moving into the old school building, they'd helped repair the town's crippled, gravity-fed water system. Though ardent proselytizers, they were careful not to push too hard among the townspeople, in the interest of good relations. They even proved valiant in the face of danger: Some of the brothers were veterans of the Holy Land War, and four of them, along with Robert Earle, had carried out the daring rescue, in June, of Stephen Bullock's trade-boat crew, who had been held in a hostage-and-ransom racket run by the boss of the Albany docks, Dan Curry. Several of Curry's gang had died in that venture—not least their boss, who received a bullet between the eyes from the expedition's leader, Brother Joseph. Shortly after that, a party of New Faith brothers brought to justice the local bully Wayne Karp, whose cohorts and kinspeople ran the old landfill as a salvage business, took apart abandoned buildings for their materials, and pushed around anyone outside their clan with whom they disagreed. In a reckless act one very hot day in June, they'd murdered a young townsman named Shawn Watling up at the landfill's general supply depot, where salvage was sorted and sold. Robert Earle had been on the premises when the murder happened, though he did not witness it. The courts were not functioning and no one was prosecuted. In the wake of that incident, Robert happened to take Watling's widow, Britney, and her daughter, Sarah, into his household, a decision that raised more than a few eyebrows around town, though the fact of the matter was that the young widow's choices were extremely limited. New Faith had tried to recruit her, but she would not go their way.

Now, as the summer turned the corner into fall, and the remorseless heat yielded to temperate days and cool nights, and the hills and hollows of Washington County lay ripe with the harvest, the people of Union Grove settled into a deferential amity with the pious newcomers. But suspicion about the group, and its odd ways, persisted quietly among the "regulars," as the townsfolk now distinguished themselves from the New Faithers.

The three men crossed the first floor to the riverside end of the mill building, where a waterwheel would go. There was a hole in the brick wall there, awaiting the hub and the machine linkages and gearing that would run off its axle. The site was a good one. The river ran through a natural rocky flume that channeled the water tightly and concentrated its power.

"It looks like you got about twelve foot of head going to that old millrace," Shiloh said, speaking loudly above the whoosh of water in the flume outside. "The way she lies, I recommend an overshot wheel. Lifting water up here will be the least of it. We can fabricate a serviceable pump. It'll be a little crude but give you all you need. You'll have a good deal of power left over for a takeoff to run the mangles and agitators and whatnot. Probably mill some corn while you're at it," Shiloh couldn't resist adding. "Pity to run those raggedy clothes you-alls wear through this fine new setup, though," he said.

"Maybe we'll dress up more when it's going," Loren said.

"No disrespect, Reverend, but why wait?" Shiloh said. "That beat-down look can't be good for the town spirit. And those beards are downright primitive."

"If we all dressed alike, how could we tell our folks from your bunch?"

"Oh, we'll all come together by and by," Shiloh said. "You'll see."

"All drinking from the same Kool-Aid bowl?"

Robert could see where this was leading. His good friend Loren had an instinct for the last word, and he had been in prickly spirits for many months, especially where the New Faithers were concerned.

Robert ventured to change the subject. "Do you suppose we might get some electric running off of this waterwheel setup as well as all the other stuff?" he said.

"In theory, sure," Shiloh said. "Question is scrounging up anything like a suitable generator or finding enough scraps to piece one together, not to mention the right size copper wire, plus your step-down transformers and whatnot."

"Mr. Bullock has a little hydro unit running at his place, you know."

"I've heard. Shows it can be done. . . ."

Their attention was diverted by a commotion at the street end of the big building. Brother Jobe, minister and chief executive of the New Faith Covenant Church of Jesus, clamored up the crude plank ramp that substituted for steps at the front entrance. He was incapable of entering a place quietly. He never simply moved from point A to point B—he bustled. Today he was accompanied by one Brother Eben, a slight, red-haired Carolinian, who scribbled with a pencil into a pad of foolscap even as he tried to step over heaps of scrap lumber and stacks of brick and buckets and other hazards in his path. Brother Jobe appeared to be issuing directives and Eben wrote them down as rapidly as possible.

". . . and I'm serious as all get-out on this hog business," he said to Eben. "We are going to raise us some commercial-grade pork next year, and I think we can show these folks hereabouts a thing or two about hams. It's the feed and the cure both. We going to finish ours on acorn, and this here allotment is thick with sweet white oak. Ah, gentlemen, I thought I would find you down here."

"Evening," Robert said.

"We've just acquired twenty-two acres adjoining our holdings to the north."

"Who from?" Robert asked.

"A Mr. Kelvin Lochner."

"He's dead," Loren said.

"Yes, I'm aware of that. Mr. Murray is seeing to the title issues," Brother Jobe said. With the legal system in tatters, Attorney Dale Murray affected to act as the town's chief conveyer of land deemed to be in ownership limbo, with the heirs and assigns scattered to the four winds. But with the registry of deeds at the county seat in Fort Edward having burned to the ground two years previously in a suspicious fire, it was unclear what he pretended to accomplish, other than collecting a fee now and again. A drinker and Robert Earle's predecessor as Union Grove's mayor, Murray had "sold" the vacant, decaying high school and all its property to the

New Faithers in the spring for what amounted to a promissory note.

"Anyways, we're looking to put in a hog operation there," Brother Jobe said, grinning broadly.

"Pigs smell bad," Robert said.

"That's true. Pigs ain't house cats, for sure. But these are the new times and things got to be done a little differently. I think you'll agree that the niceties of single-use zoning is over and done with. Now imagine the taste of barbequed baby back ribs melting in your mouth. Not to say country sausage. And did I mention anything about Virginia-style hams?"

"I think our folks might object."

"Object to ham? I never heard such nonsense. Half your folks in town here got goats and we all got chickens. A pig is a noble beast. Only thing smarter than a pig, I hear, is a human being or a ding-dang dolphin, if there's any left out there. Besides, we ain't going hog wild, no pun intended. We going to start real modestly and work up. Your folks will get over it. Now look here," Brother Jobe changed the subject, "it appears like we missed a case of this here corn smudge."

Washington County had been afflicted with a formerly unknown crop disease that blackened the corn kernels on the stalk. It prompted the town trustees to vote in an emergency law requiring the destruction of affected crops. The disease had appeared on three farms so far, including that of trustee Ned Larmon, where it was first discovered. He'd sacrificed five acres of standing corn back in September.

"Who is it this time?" Loren asked.

"This fellow, Corey Elder, on the Center Falls Road."

"He's a hard one."

"I'll depend on you to talk sense to him."

As constable, it was Loren's job to ask the affected farmer to voluntarily comply. So far, no one had refused. They had been promised fair compensation.

"You tell this farmer he can get it back either in corn or direct in silver, his choice," Brother Jobe said. "But he's got to act. We can't have this corn sickness running rampant. And if you're nervous about going over there, you can have some of our boys for backup."

"That won't be necessary," Loren said. "I'll go talk to him."

THREE

As Jasper Copeland raced through the stubble field after his dog, he caught a shoe on the butt of a cornstalk. It sent him sprawling facedown against the hard ground. As he got up and resumed running he saw the big brown stallion rear back on its hind legs, whinnying wildly. He was aware of his heart pounding, and not just from the dash across the field. As he drew closer to the paddock, he saw Willie dart in and away and around the bigger animal, nipping at its fetlocks and even leaping up at its muzzle, barking the whole time.

Jasper cried "Willie, stop it!" and "Willie, come!" and "Willie, no!" over and over but the dog would not stop harrying the stallion. The stallion reared repeatedly. Jasper's heart sank as it pounded in his chest. He banged up against the split-rail fence, where he continued to yell at Willie. And then as the horse came down again and its hooves seemed to miss Willie by inches, Jasper ducked inside the fence and ran toward the horse, brandishing his father's fly rod as if it were a carriage whip. The horse reared again and Jasper tried repeatedly to beat it across the head with the rod without effect. This time when the horse came down, its hooves found some part of the dog's body. There was more than one scream. The stallion bolted away, leaving Jasper alone with the dog lying at his feet.

He gaped down at Willie in disbelief. The dog was still alive, eyes open, panting shallowly, but otherwise not moving. He lay on his side with a drop of blood forming a bubble at one nostril. With mounting terror, Jasper scooped the dog into his arms, ducked through the fence, and began loping toward what had been the old main driveway to the high school where Salem Street turned into the North Road at the edge of town. He ran all the way home with Willie cradled in his arms, though the dog weighed thirty-eight pounds. When he finally got there and cried out for his father, he felt like his heart was going to burst.

Dr. Jerry Copeland rushed out of his lab behind the room where he saw patients. Jasper had laid Willie on the padded examination table and was screaming, "Daddy, please, save him!"

"What happened?"

Jasper explained about Willie chasing a groundhog into the paddock where the stallion was.

Dr. Copeland grabbed a stethoscope and found a heartbeat, but in doing so he realized that he knew almost nothing about canine anatomy, other than that they had the usual array of mammalian organs and that he was unlikely to be able to do anything to save the dog. There was one other remote possibility.

"Go run over to Mr. LaBountie's place and ask him to hurry over here as quick as he can," the doctor told Jasper. Jason LaBountie was Union Grove's veterinarian. The boy blinked and nodded. He shifted his attention to Willie on the table and ran his hand along the dog's side, from his ears, which were still very warm, all down its flank.

"Don't, Son," the doctor said. "He's in shock. Better not to touch him."

Jasper was well acquainted with the meaning of shock, being the son of a doctor in a time and place where there was no longer any access to hospitals. Everything came to his father's doorstep these days. He often assisted his father with patients after school and in the evenings, even in surgeries, and had already acquired as much knowledge as a first-year medical student might have in the old times, though available remedies were much sparser and advanced technologies no longer existed.

"Go, quickly now," the doctor said.

The boy nodded again and ran out of the office.

The doctor began to systematically examine the dog's body to try to assess its injuries. There were no obvious wounds on the surface. Its abdomen seemed distended and he suspected that the animal was bleeding internally. There was some blood mixed with fecal matter around its rectum and a small discharge at the nose. Through the stethoscope he heard the rales and crepitations that signified fluid in the lungs. The heartbeat was accelerating and the dog's panting was noticeably quicker and shallower than minutes before. He was quite sure the dog was not going to make it. He thought of his internship out in Madison, Wisconsin, years ago, those rotations in the emergency room, the incredible destruction of the body in a car crash, the moment when life left the body and all the wonders of modern medicine did not avail to make sense of that awful moment. These days there were no more car crashes, at least.

A movement across the room brought him out of himself. His wife, Jeanette, closed the door behind her. She had a handsome dish-shaped face with very large, questioning eyes. Her family had moved to America from France when she was nine years old. He could see her size up the situation immediately. She was a nurse.

"Oh, Jerry . . . ," she said.

He could only offer a sigh and a pained glance.

Then Willie convulsed and gave out a strange little strangled bark that resolved in a sickening gurgle. Jeanette flew across the room to the doctor's side. After another moment, the dog lay still with its eyes wide open and their own anxious breathing was the only sound in the room. Jeanette buried her face in her husband's shoulder as her eyes filled with tears. The doctor took her in his arms. Looking over the top of her head, he could not help but observe what a beautiful dog Willie was. The dog population was way down in these new times. Most people had little surplus meat to feed them and manufactured pet foods no longer existed. The doctor had gotten Willie as a puppy in barter for treating the daughter of Lloyd Hokely, the sawmill owner up in Battenville. She had been bitten by a copperhead snake. There was not much the doctor could do. There wasn't even any ice to be had out that way on short notice, so icing the leg was out. He ran a saline IV drip into her, gave her some willow extract, and that was about it. The bite of such a snake was generally not fatal, and the girl was nearly full-grown at fifteen, so she recovered fully. The doctor left the Hokely place with the puppy in his lap in payment for services as he drove his cart back to town behind a horse named Mac. He fell in love with the puppy right away.

"Where's our boy?" Jeanette asked, turning around. The doctor told her. Just at that moment, Jasper's little sister, Dinah, five, stepped warily into the room. Jeanette watched her attempt to take in the scene.

"What's wrong with Willie?" Dinah said.

"Nothing," the doctor said, at once ashamed and angry with himself for lying.

Jeanette hurried across the room, swept the child off her feet, and made for the door. The doctor heard Dinah break out bawling as they left the office.

When they were gone the doctor poured himself a glass of 100-proof pear brandy, which he kept in a fine glass-stoppered decanter on the steel cart beside the examination table. He often administered a dose of strong spirits to patients who came in, just to calm them down enough so he could proceed with treatment. He'd run out of advanced analgesics years ago and was otherwise reduced to using opiates and other herbals.

The brandy warmed the doctor's stomach. He soon began to feel it move through his stomach lining into his bloodstream and brain. He sat down in the padded chair beside the cart to wait for his boy. The beauty of the dog's still body brought tears to his eyes.

Four

Jason LaBountie, a large specimen of a man, sweating even in the cool evening air, entered the doctor's examination room like an ox coming into a stall. He had cornbread crumbs in his beard and the doctor imagined that he'd been dragged away from the dinner table. He came right to the exam table and bent so closely over Willie's body that he appeared to be sniffing it. Meanwhile, Jasper entered the room.

"This dog's passed on," LaBountie said.

"Yes," the doctor said. "I'm afraid we've lost him."

"Isn't there something you can do?" the boy asked.

LaBountie shook his head. "The life has gone out of him."

"I've seen my daddy start up people's hearts. Can't you try?" the boy said, almost yelling. "Either of you?"

"He's beyond that, even if we tried," LaBountie told the boy. Then he turned to the doctor. "He was stomped pretty good, looks like."

"Well, apparently so," the doctor said.

LaBountie addressed the boy: "Severe internal injuries. Hemorrhage. Shock. It's a bigger deal than just an arrested heart, young man. Awful sorry."

Jasper recoiled into a far corner of the room, sank on his haunches, and began to sob in a high keening manner. Darkness crowded the windows and the room seemed to dim moment by moment. The doctor turned to the steel cart behind him. Among the items on it was a fat three-wick candle to which he struck a match. He turned back around with the candle on its brass saucer.

"I told the boy I was strictly a large-animal man, Jerry," LaBountie said. "I haven't worked on dogs and cats since the old days in vet school. We don't have a dog ourselves."

"It's moot now. Thanks for coming, though."

"There's damn few dogs around the county these days."

The doctor grunted in affirmation.

"Who can afford to feed a dog now?"

The doctor realized it was self-evident that he was able to. "Hell, Jason," he said, "you must take some pay for service in meat, given your line of work."

"Sure I do. But not enough for a dog."

"Is trade in kind okay with you on this call? Or are you looking to get paid?"

"Well, I doctor my own family," LaBountie said.

"I thought you were strictly a large-animal man," the doctor said.

"My kids are large enough. Anyway, I ran like hell to get here."

"We appreciate it."

"You can send over a ham sometime, Jerry. You'll do that, won't you?"

"Of course I will, Jason," the doctor said.

The two men had locked eyes, while the boy remained sitting in the corner with his knees drawn up and his face buried in his crossed arms. Just then a gust of cold wind rattled the door and then seemed to blow it open. The figure of a short man in a dark suit with a broad-brimmed hat stood framed within it.

The doctor and the vet turned to take in the intruder. Jasper looked up, red-eyed.

"I'm starting to feel the goldurned chill of winter already," Brother Jobe said, stepping over the threshold into the office, "and it ain't Halloween yet. I think I found something belongs to you."

LaBountie excused himself and almost shoved Brother Jobe aside in making for the door.

"What's with him?" Brother Jobe asked.

The doctor didn't feel like trying to explain. Meanwhile, he noticed that Brother Jobe was holding the two pieces of a flyfishing rod in his right hand. It looked familiar to the doctor and it also looked broken. He was about to ask to see it when Brother Jobe held it up and read an inscription on the nickel silver butt-end cap.

To Jeremy
On his graduation
May 18, 2001
From Dad

"Must be your daddy gave you this here pole," Brother Jobe said, handing it over.

The doctor took it. It was a very fine graphite fiber rod made by the Orvis Company, nine and a half feet long, designed for a number 5 line. The company no longer existed as far as the doctor knew. The carbon fiber represented the height of synthetic material engineering from the golden era of technology that was no more. The doctor saw that the rod was smashed about six inches above the rosewood reel seat. Shattered carbon fibers stuck out like unkempt hair. The reel itself was also crushed. Gazing at the rod, the doctor realized it could never be fixed or replaced.

"I found it in the paddock where we keep our stallion," Brother Jobe said. "Sorry about the dog."

The doctor looked up slowly. "Jasper, would you go in the house, please?" he asked the boy.

"I want to sit up with Willie."

"He's passed away, Son."

"Just because he's dead doesn't mean I can't sit with him."

The doctor went to the corner of the room where his son sat on the floor and he squatted down to his eye level.

"You go inside right now," he said quietly, suppressing a roiling surge of emotion. "Brother Jobe and I have some business here and you have to go in the house."

The boy did not fail to perceive the tremor in his father's voice and the striking paleness of his face in the meager light. It unnerved him enough to obey this command, and just then he remembered leaving his father's wicker creel in the stubble field where he'd cast it off to follow Willie into the paddock. He choked back a sob and left the room, leaving the door open. When the boy was gone, Brother Jobe gave the door a little shove shut with the toe of his boot. The doctor lay the broken fly rod on the table with the dead dog.

"It's a right dreary situation," Brother Jobe said. "Ain't it?"

"Drink?" the doctor asked, ignoring the remark.

"Sure. What's on tap?"

"Pear brandy."

"Make it yourself?"

"I got it in trade."

"You do well in trade, I suppose."

"I've got my share of patients who can't pay anything."

"Of course. Not being critical, mind you. Just an observation."

The doctor poured a generous drink for Brother Jobe in a cobalt blue pony glass that was more than a 150 years old. Brother Jobe appeared to admire it.

"You like fine things, don't you?" he said.

"I'm what used to be called a cultured person," the doctor said.

"At least you're plain about it. I admire that. You're a man of science to boot."

"Yes, I am," the doctor said, refilling his own glass. "That's why I feel a little queer about what I'm about to ask you."

"Fire away, Doc."

"That dog died less than ten minutes ago. I've got a notion that you might be able to bring him back."

"Where'd you get that idea?" Brother Jobe asked.

"I think you know."

Events of the summer just past had led many in town to wonder if the chief of the New Faith brotherhood possessed abilities beyond the limits of ordinary experience. Robert Earle, who had come closer to knowing Brother Jobe than anyone else in Union Grove, once asked him flat out whether he was "a regular human being"—to which Brother Jobe replied, "I like to think so." The doctor, too, had seen evidence that Brother Jobe was, at least, something more than he merely seemed.

"We're frittering away precious time," the doctor said. "I'm asking you to try to bring this dog back."

"I can't do that," Brother Jobe said.

"Can't or won't?" the doctor said.

"Don't you think I would've brought my own son back if I could've?"

In July, Brother Jobe's son, named Minor, had been killed by the miscreant Wayne Karp, who himself died less than twelve hours later under mysterious circumstances in the town jail. The bodies both came into the doctor's "morgue"—his spring house—where he was obliged, as the official coroner, to assess the causes of death. Brother Jobe's son had sustained fatal gunshot wounds to the head, the bullets entering through the eye and the mouth. Wayne Karp had died of wounds that appeared to be identical. The difference was that Wayne Karp had neither exit wounds nor any lead bullets in his head.

The doctor knocked back what was left in his glass and gave the dog a long look.

"My boy loved that dog very much, and I did, too."

"Of course you did."

"I can't shake the feeling that you've got something going on."

"Some kind of what?"

"Something outside what's normal," the doctor said.

Brother Jobe smiled thinly, and the small features of his round, beardless face seemed to crowd together as if his thoughts pained him. The silence in the room was so profound, squirrels could be heard scratching somewhere in the soffits.

"This here's excellent poteen," Brother Jobe finally said.

"Come on. What's your deal?" the doctor said.

"Okay, this here's my deal," Brother Jobe said. "I can't bring anything that's dead back to life. I can go the other way, though."

"Go the other way?"

"You ain't stupid, you know what the other way is."

"You mean you can kill?"

Brother Jobe cocked his head a degree. "So to say. Take life away from something that has it."

The doctor reflected a moment.

"How does that make you anything more than a common killer?" he said eventually.

"Just a moment, there, sir. We both deal in matters of life and death."

"I've never deliberately taken somebody's life," the doctor said.

"What makes you think I have?"

"I saw what you did to Wayne Karp."

"What makes you sure I done that?"

"You were the only other one there."

"Robert Earle was there."

"Robert Earle was asleep in the next room," the doctor said. "When the bodies came in here, I measured the wounds both on your son and on Karp with a micrometer. They were identical down to the millimeter. On each one, the same tooth sheared off at the same place, at precisely the same angle. Quite a coincidence if you ask me. I'd come to the conclusion that you were trying to make a point."

"Well," Brother Jobe said, puffing out his cheeks, "there's whatever I do in the common world, and then there's the Lord's justice."

The doctor poured himself another drink and proffered the bottle toward Brother Jobe, who shook his head and put a hand over his glass. "Not that there was anything wrong with it."

"Wrong with what you do?" the doctor asked.

"No, with your hooch," Brother Jobe said. "I best be on my way."

"One more thing."

"What'd that be, Doc?"

"I'm not a religious man, really."

"I suppose I know that."

"But sometimes I wonder—"

"Anytime you want to come to the Lord—"

"What I wonder is, which Lord do you really serve? Or think you serve?"

"Now, whatever do you mean by that?"

"There's a Lord of light," the doctor said, "and we're given to understand that there's a corresponding Lord of darkness. Right?

Consistent with the nature of our world—male and female, night and day, yin and yang, whatever you want to call it."

"That's mighty interesting, sir," Brother Jobe said, "but the ding-dong of the ying-yang is a bit beyond my country education. I'm sorry I can't help your dog. A dog is a great comfort, especially in these here times. I hope you can find another good one and raise it up to have some respect for critters bigger than itself. Good night to you."

Five

Robert Earle was spading manure into a raised garden bed behind his house when he looked up from his work to see a familiar figure standing ten paces away in evening light beside the old refrigerator he used as a meat smoker. It was Jane Ann Holder, wife of the congregational minister, Loren Holder. Jane Ann had been Robert's lover until that summer when the young widow Britney Watling came into his household. Robert was Loren's best friend. Loren had been unable to perform in a conjugal way for some time, and Robert had been a widower for some time, and in the course of things an arrangement found its way between the three of them, not without tensions, resentments, and complications. Then, suddenly, Robert had discontinued his relations with Jane Ann when Britney, wife of the slain Shawn Watling moved in, at first to become his housekeeper, but then becoming, in the parlance of town gossip, his new woman.

Robert stopped digging and rested his calloused hands on the butt of the spade's long handle. He took in Jane Ann on a tide of longing and regret. She wore her long hair pinned up like a Gibson Girl's in their great-great-grandmothers' time. He recalled the many nights he'd watched her take out the pins and let her hair fall along her shoulders and down her breasts. He worried about Jane Ann and what they thought they had been doing in those years of tortured passion, and especially what a burden it had brought upon her. His part in what would become of her now pained him as much.

"Your table greens are looking very handsome, Robert," Jane Ann said.

"It's good to see you, Jane Ann."

"You're just saying that."

"I've got some nice lettuce here if you'd like to take some home."

"Trying to get rid of me already?"

Robert shook his head. "I know you're mad at me," he said.

"Let's not call it that."

"What would you call it?"

"Call it an unhappy woman who doesn't like the outcome of a certain situation, and has to wear a mask of benign serenity going around town, and who worries incessantly about her missing son who has been gone for two years, and sometimes despises her husband as much as she loves him, and misses you terribly."

This was the point at which Jane Ann's shoulders hunched and she dissolved in tears. Robert jammed his spade in the planting bed and went to her, but when he tried to comfort her, she shook him off. He stood by helplessly, watching her weep.

"I miss you, too," he said. "But I needed someone like a wife."

"Is she *like* a wife, your little kitten?"

"There's nothing wrong with her."

"Unlike me," Jane Ann said. "There must be a lot wrong with me."

"There's nothing wrong with you, either."

"Then why can't I get on with my life?"

"I could guess, but it would only upset you again."

"Try."

"You'd never leave Loren. You know it. I know it. You and me, we could never be together like a man and wife. Especially in this town, in these times."

Jane Ann shook off a final sob and then straightened her shoulders resolutely. Looking up at Robert with damp, red eyes, she touched his arm and then batted at his shirtsleeve.

"I could find another lover, I suppose," she said.

Robert didn't offer a comment on that.

"Do I sound like a calculating slut?"

"You're a fine person living in circumstances you never expected."

He put a hand to her cheek.

"You smell like manure," she said.

Just then, Britney Watling, Robert's housemate, came through the back door into the outside summer kitchen that would soon be dismantled for the winter. A candle burned behind her inside the house. Wood smoke curled above the roof where low purple clouds hung in a pumpkin-colored sky. For a while, the three of them stood silently, triangulated in the darkening garden as leaves fluttered to the ground in the breezeless air.

"Supper's on, Robert," Britney said. Her voice was surprisingly husky for such a petite woman. "Hello Jane Ann. Would you have some cider with us?"

Jane Ann declined, though she thought it was kind of Britney to ask.

SIX

Jasper Copeland cried all the way to the stubble field and found his father's wicker creel with the trout in it. The stallion was still out in his paddock, as if nothing had happened. He wondered why the Jesus people hadn't punished him, at least shut him up in a barn where he couldn't harm another living thing. The world that, an hour earlier, had never seemed so filled with loveliness, now seemed hopelessly cruel, faithless, and ugly. The orange sky streaked with low purple clouds looked like a sickness sweeping over the land. It looked like the things his father removed from human bodies in surgeries, terrible things he'd had to burn in a wood-fired incinerator to make sure they would cause no more trouble in this world. Jasper recalled the words of his friend, Ned Allison, about the filthy hermit, that *nature was strange and harsh*. The reality of Willie's death assaulted him over and over with shocking freshness each time. The thought of the dog's warm fur against his cheek brought a surge of anger and hatred that he had never known before. He sobbed all the way home.

It was dark when he got there. His mother was just getting supper on the table. His father, the doctor, entered the large kitchen that was the heart of the house carrying a candle in a brass saucer. He'd been in his study reading history, Wheeler on the Battle of Chancellorsville, with yet another glass of pear brandy. The boy and his father seemed embarrassed to encounter each other back in the normality of suppertime in the kitchen. Nobody spoke. Even Jasper's little sister, Dinah, waited silently behind her chair, eyes downcast, for the others to come to the table. Jeanette, at the stove, ladled a blood-dark rabbit stew into four porcelain soup plates decorated with Chinese dragons.

Jasper put the creel on a counter. Muttering "I'm not hungry," he brushed past his father and headed upstairs to his room.

The family sat down to supper without him, an absolutely silent meal at which their collective pain seemed to occupy the empty chair like an uninvited guest who monopolized their attention. When they were finished, the doctor put a generous square of corn bread on a little plate and went upstairs to his son's room. Jasper lay on his bed facing the wall with his clothes on and a candle burning on his night table. The doctor sat at the end of the bed, but the boy didn't stir or acknowledge his father's presence.

"You awake, Jas?"

The boy groaned lowly.

"I brought you some corn bread."

"I don't want any."

"I'll leave it here on the table."

Jasper didn't respond.

"We can get another dog," the doctor said.

Jasper flipped over so quickly the doctor recoiled.

"Willie wasn't any dog. He was like a person."

"All dogs seem that way after a while."

"It's not fair. Why did he have to die?"

The doctor felt a restless anxiety run through him at a question he could not possibly answer.

"You can always get another dog. I'll never get another fly rod like that one," he said, regretting it instantly.

"That damn horse stomped on it just like he stomped on Willie," he practically shouted.

"What the hell were you doing in the paddock with it?"

"I was trying to save Willie."

The doctor cursed the brandy that had compromised his self-control, making him sound less like a father than a child.

"I know . . . I know," he said.

"You're the one that let him die."

"That's not true. You heard what Mr. LaBountie said."

"You could have made that Brother Jobe bring him back."

"He can't bring things back."

"Then how come you asked him to?"

The doctor didn't know what to say. He could only assume that the boy had managed to overhear his exchange with Brother Jobe, so there was no denying it had taken place.

"Sometimes grown-ups are like children and they confuse their wishes and prayers with what they know is real."

"You think he has powers, too. Don't you?"

"I don't really know what kind of powers he has," the doctor said, "or if he has any powers at all. It's not so hard to pull the wool over people's eyes."

"You know what I think?" Jasper said.

"What?"

"If he's anything, he's the devil. Or something like a devil."

"He's just a blowhard," the doctor said. He realized that his head had begun to throb. "We'll get another dog for you," he said wearily.

"I don't want another dog. I want Willie."

"I know," the doctor said, "but you have plenty of love left in your heart to give to another dog. When the time comes."

Jasper flipped back over, facing the wall.

The doctor blew out Jasper's candle.

"You shouldn't fall asleep with an open flame in the room," he said. "It's not evil, it's just very unwise."

Seven

Jane Ann Holder took her time going home. Everything about the night was fraught with memory and emotion. The sensations infused her as though she had become little more than a vehicle driven by them. She plied the town streets like a wraith in a ghost story, seeming to glide unnaturally past houses where, here and there, a candle burned, or voices could be heard against the quiet absence of machines, or a piano tinkled a Chopin etude in a minor key. Turning onto Van Buren Street, she saw a three-quarter waxing moon rise over Deeds Hill, which defined the town at its southern compass point as Pumpkin Hill did to the northeast, so that the town seemed to lie in the cupped palm of an immense benevolent being that cherished it. In the tumult of her sadness she was reassured by the thought that she belonged to a great network of souls and living things that were all cared for by something like God.

She roamed the streets of town until the growing chill made her shiver, and then she went home to the rectory beside the Congregational church where she lived with Loren. Approaching it from way down Salem Street, she saw candles glow in several windows on the first floor. Loren would be going back and forth between the kitchen and the dining room, where he liked to keep his work at hand—an elegy, a community calendar, or a manual on pickling meat, now that it was the season for slaughtering animals.

Loren enjoyed cooking, and fall was the great season for cookery; it was harvest time, when there was plenty of everything, so much that it often felt like the old times. Back then you merely nipped into the supermarket after the workday and picked up anything you wanted: short ribs, lamb shanks, duck breasts, mangoes from the faraway tropics, artichokes from California, aged vinegars from Sicily, Mexican chipotles, Belgian chocolate, French lentils, black pepper, curry powders, English Stilton cheeses, and delicious coffee—Kona from Hawaii, Jamaican Blue Mountain, Brazil arabica, Sumatra, Kenya. All gone, all gone.

Jane Ann first met Loren at a drug-saturated fraternity rave at Middlebury College, back in the previous century. She had transferred there after a disappointing stint as an art major at nearby Bennington, which was run like a seedy carnival. Middlebury was a step up—a compact, erudite, outdoorsy little college for rich kids who didn't get into Harvard, Yale, or Brown. In those days, Loren was quite the party animal, as well as captain of the lacrosse team. He was a big, handsome, shambling fraternity boy with taped-up loafers, a goofy smile, and an interest in poetry. After the rave, they went at it in his choice fourth-floor turret room of the rattletrap fraternity house. Five, six times before morning. The room was painted Chinese red. Loren had a beautiful silk Oriental dressing gown that he let her wear to the bathroom down the hall. He also had a hookah the size of a double bassoon and a Jeep with a ragtop. Soon she was his girl. The popular drug Ecstasy was what led Loren into theological studies and eventually the Congregational ministry. His first assignment was Glens Falls, where they spent eleven years, but they eventually came to Union Grove, twenty miles to the southeast, when the position opened. It was a sweet, quiet corner of the upper Hudson Valley, at the time a bedroom community for people who drove to well-paid jobs as far off as Albany, the state capital. Here they'd raised their son, Evan, who had gone off with Robert Earle's boy, Daniel, two years ago to see what happened to the rest of the United States after the tribulations. The two young men hadn't been heard from since.

Loren was sautéing chanterelle mushrooms at the big wood-fired cookstove when Jane Ann finally came inside. Fall was also the great season of wild mushrooms and Loren had many a woody glade scoped out where they came up reliably after a rain. He appeared to be well into a bottle of Jane Ann's own wine. It was made from the local wild grapes that grew rampant over fences and around the roadsides. She flavored it with sweet woodruff to cut the foxy edge.

"Where have you been?" Loren asked, not irritably. "I was worried about you."

"I made some calls," she said, and this was true, for in her capacity as the minister's wife, she often stopped in to see the sick or the bereaved or just to visit with friends. Most townspeople were members of the congregation since all the other structures of socialization had fallen away. "You?"

"Me? Gathering wilds. Before that, down at the old U-W Mill, with Robert and that engineer from the Kool-Aid gang," Loren said, referring to the New Faithers. "This new laundry will be the greatest project the town has ever seen. I know, you don't think it's any great shakes, but it will accomplish a couple of very important things. It'll free up people's time and it'll give folks confidence to go forward and make other improvements, maybe start other businesses."

"But nobody has any money," Jane Ann said.

"Laundry is the housework people hate most," Loren replied obliquely. "Did you know that?"

"Not scrubbing floors?"

"No," Loren said. "Laundry."

"How do you know that?"

"I read it somewhere," Loren said.

"On the Internet?"

"Ha ha," Loren said. The Internet had unraveled years before the electricity flickered out altogether in the summer. "Facetiousness is often hostility in disguise," he observed. "Are you angry at me?"

"No," she said. Shame was now added to her cargo of regret. "You know how I get sometimes."

"I know," he said. "And I know you know I know."

"I apologize for inflicting it on you," she said.

"That's what I'm here for. But okay, apology accepted." Loren put great store in apologies and in the resolution of disagreements. "You look very beautiful in candlelight. Do you know that?"

"Thank you for the compliment."

"You're welcome."

Jane Ann got a stemmed wineglass from a cabinet and emptied the remains of the bottle into it.

Later that evening, after a supper of mushroom and kale omelets and fried potatoes and what would be some of the last of their fall lettuce dressed in buttermilk, honey, and cider vinegar, and the last of a three-day-old rye bread with plenty of sweet butter from the Schmidt farm, Jane Ann and Loren retired to read in their bedroom. His bedside book, as opposed to his downstairs reading, was a biography of Theodore Roosevelt. He loved the period of the early twentieth century, before the World Wars, modernity with all its hopes intact, its visions of the coming industrial Golden Age, the benevolent New World machine empire of muscular virtue! And he loved the confident, buoyant figure of TR, who seemed to embody all of that so well. Jane Ann had been working on *To the Lighthouse* by Virginia Woolf for more than a month without getting past page 50. It had more value for her as a soporific than as literature.

Jane Ann wore a faded silk nightgown that had long ago been canary yellow. Loren wore a plain cotton nightshirt. The room was cool. They only fired up the little parlor wood-chunk stove in the corner on the bitterest winter nights. The bedroom was just above the kitchen and its more massive cookstove. Beneath the practical ceremonies of bedtime, an insistent tension prevailed between them. Something had gone wrong with Loren's anatomy or psychology—he really couldn't be sure which—but try as he might, he couldn't perform anymore. The pharmaceutical remedies for his condition, once ubiquitous, were no longer available, and Loren did not know what else to do except endure it. But his sympathy for Jane Ann was such that he'd encouraged the arrangement with his best friend, Robert Earle, for Jane Ann and Robert to discreetly spend a conjugal night together every week—with the understanding between the three of them that their household assignments would not change. The consequences of such an arrangement were not necessarily subject to mandates. They all went along with it out of a combination of sympathy, necessity, and desire, knowing it might not end well. It could have ended worse, but it had created strains between them, and within themselves, that would persist indefinitely.

Now, as Jane returned from a trip to the bathroom, Loren put aside his book and watched her navigate in candlelight across the room, around the bed, noticing the way her breasts swayed within the nightgown, the targetlike nipples visibly shifting this way and that way. He was always moved by the sight of her, whether or not he was able to do anything in the service of it. But this evening, having consumed more wine than usual and more than a dram of applejack after dinner, Loren was stirred to attempt an act of love with his wife.

"Would you take your nightgown off?" he said as she slipped between the sheets. She looked a bit surprised at his request.

"I'll be cold later," she said. "You know how I am."

"You can put it back on later."

She pulled the garment over her head in a single deft movement and hung it on the bedpost, then slid down into the sheets, regarding him warily as she did. Loren struggled out of his nightshirt. He was a large man and had put on a good twenty pounds over the bountiful months of the year, but he still had the physical grace of a varsity athlete. He flung off the nightshirt, slid back under the covers, and sought out her lips. He kissed her for a very long time. Eventually, her lips and tongue responded with something like the passion of years earlier. His hands explored the once-familiar curves of her hips and bosom like a sojourner who had returned to a beloved place after a long absence. Then he slipped down below her waist and kissed her intimate places in such a way that she came to heave and arch her spine and finally gasp in a rapture that had her clawing the bed sheets.

In the aftermath of that act, Loren maneuvered back up so as to hover over her. He pressed his cheek to the fragrant damp place where her forehead met her hairline and attempted to guide himself inside her with one hand while she drew her knees way up to become more accessible. But despite everything, he was still not functioning normally. He fumbled more than once and soon an acid pain spread through the muscles in the arm he had propped himself up with, and finally he rolled onto his back beside Jane Ann while her knees slid down and she brushed a strand of damp hair off her face.

For a long time, neither of them spoke. Loren now fought a tumult of emotion—amazement, shame, fear, anger, self-pity. He thought in the midst of it all to curse God but then remembered that he had given up on God some time ago—that he now believed only in the divinity of the human race—so he struggled mightily to forgive himself and whatever fate had driven him to this predicament. Jane Ann observed his inarticulate torment in the candlelight. Finally, she turned toward him and buried her face close up against him and said, "I will always love you."

Eight

Much later, when the house was still, Jasper Copeland, who had not slept a moment since his father's visit, put on his clothes in the moonlight that streamed through his dormer window. He retrieved the backpack he had stuffed and hidden in the closet after his father left. It contained a few articles of clothing. He'd cinched a rolled-up blanket to the keeper rings at the bottom. He threaded the leather sheath of a hunting knife to his belt. It had a six-inch blade. The knife, like the fly rod, had been his father's. Finally he jammed a pillow and a wad of clothing under the blankets on his bed and, satisfied that it resembled the shape of a sleeping boy, stealthily made his way downstairs. He knew all the creaky steps on the staircase and took extra care to tread lightly on them.

Down in the kitchen he mixed a handful of rolled oats in a plastic bowl with a few spoons of sorghum syrup until it formed a gummy mass. Then he spooned it into a flannel rag from the box of rags his mother kept under the counter. When he'd completed that task, he collected some food items—six inches of hard sausage, some cheese, the leftover corn bread from supper—and some useful articles—a small steel saucepan, a fork and spoon, a plastic tumbler—and packed them up with his clothes. Then he exited the house through the back door and went to the old carriage house that constituted his father's offices, lab, and the upstairs infirmary he had set up for patients too sick to be home.

Willie's body still lay on the examining table. Jasper was shocked all over again to see the dog and struggled to understand exactly what had gone out of him to reduce him to nothing more than a stiff, inert object. When he buried his face against the dog's flank, he was horrified to realize how cold it was and that this was the last time they would ever be together. Though he knew could depend on his father to give Willie a proper burial, it was little consolation. He blubbered a while, then proceeded to his father's lab behind the examination room.

The doctor kept his supply of opium in an old cookie tin in a drawer under the counter where his microscope stood. Jasper knew exactly where to look. He easily pried off the top. Inside were several balls of raw opium gum. The doctor obtained them from farmers who grew poppies for him, more or less as a public service. The doctor prepared the tinctures of opium there in the lab, in order to have some idea of what he was dosing his patients with. In the absence of the manufactured wonder drugs of the old days, this laudanum was the only useful analgesic he had.

Of the several balls of opium, Jasper selected one that was the size of a crabapple. He got out the rag that contained the oats mixed with sorghum syrup, pushed the opium into the center of the sticky mass, and molded it until he had something that resembled a popcorn ball. Then he rewrapped it in the rag, stuck the whole thing in his pocket, and put the tin back in the drawer. Last, he took three of his father's beeswax candles—the ones with no tallow in them—and stashed them in his pack along with a dozen of the matches his father bought from Roger Hoad, who sold them in little bundles tied with hemp cord.

He stroked the dog one last time on his way out of the building and took care to close the door so the latch didn't so much as click. Then he was out under a yellow moon and a sky exploding with stars. The clouds of early evening had dissipated. The air was sharply colder now, and it boosted his confidence that he'd had the foresight to pack a wool cap and gloves. He did not know where he would be going, exactly, but he knew that the nights would only get colder in the days ahead.

The streets of Union Grove lay perfectly still at this hour, which was just after three in the morning, though Jasper did not have a timepiece and knew only that it was very late. He passed the Allisons' house on Van Buren Street and was sorry that Ned was not coming with him. Where Van Buren met Hill Street, Jasper made his way to the old water treatment plant, now defunct without electricity or manufactured chemicals to run it, and entered the margin of the woods there. It was both a shortcut and a way of keeping his movements concealed. The woods frightened him and he moved rapidly, at the edge of panic, until he saw the reassuring contours of the old high school ahead. The New Faith people were said to keep watchmen posted. He couldn't see anyone at this distance, so he left the woods to traverse the same stubble field he'd run across so desperately hours earlier trying to save Willie. He felt exposed but he didn't want to run now for fear of scaring the horses.

He stopped at the split-rail fence, his lungs burning and his breath visible in the moonlight. The stallion, Jupiter, stood at the far end of his paddock, very still with one rear leg jacked back a little, resting on the edge of its hoof. His big head drooped. Jasper moved along the fence line until he was as close to the stallion as he could get without going inside the paddock. He clicked his tongue a few times. The stallion jerked up his head. Thinking to make sure the animal remained calm, Jasper begin humming a tune. It was "Row, Row, Row Your Boat." The stallion gave out a little whinny and dashed twenty yards toward the center of the paddock. There, he wheeled as if taking in his entire surroundings and then ran the rest of the way to the opposite perimeter. Jasper continued the song, now softly singing the lyrics. Soon the horse began making his way around the fence line at a trot, fully awake, as if challenging any interloper. He came directly toward Jasper, who continued to sing evenly. Jupitar replied with a snort, his big eyes flashing, and stepped up boldly to the fence where the boy stood on the bottom rail so that horse and boy were, for that moment, at eye level. Jupiter dipped his head as though playing a game and made another half-circuit around the perimeter, ending up again on the far side of the paddock.

It occurred to Jasper that nothing might induce the stallion to come to him. But he was not afraid to go inside the paddock and try to go to him. He reasoned that Jupiter was used to being handled by the New Faith men. He set down his backpack against the post and climbed through the fence rails, then walked deliberately toward the horse. It sidestepped warily to the left. The boy countered, steadily clicking his tongue. Jupiter stepped back into a corner where the fence met the side of the old schoolbus barn and finally submitted to the inevitability of being approached by a human being. Jasper felt sorry, momentarily, for the stallion's dumb domesticity. When the unwelcome notion that the stallion was a beautiful creature intruded, the boy remembered what a beautiful creature his dog Willie had been and how carelessly this stallion had stomped the life out of him.

Twin clouds of steam blew out of Jupiter's nostrils. Jasper slowly reached in his pocket and retrieved the lumpy rag from it. He carefully opened the rag, took out the sticky ball of oats, sorghum syrup, and opium, and held it out in his palm. The stallion looked at him fiercely. Jasper remained in position, motionless, arm extended, perfectly still. The stallion took a tentative step in his direction, sniffed the sweet gummy ball, snorted at it, and touched it with his prehensile lips. Then, at last, he took the whole thing delicately out of Jasper's upturned palm. The boy watched the horse chew the sticky mass as he lowered his arm and felt the tension flow out of his muscles. Then he about-faced and hurried back to the rail fence, where he collected his backpack and made off into what remained of the night, thrilled by the horror of his prospects and by what he had done.

NINE

Habitually a poor sleeper, Perry Talisker lay alone on a thin mattress in his shack by the river listening to the endless tragic music of the water rushing over its own hard bed. Sometimes, Perry's loneliness cocooned him in such a tight place that he cried out against God's mysterious wrath, and he wondered what he had done to become the object of it.

He missed his wife, Trish, who had left him years ago when times had just started to get hard and the Hovington Supermarket chain closed down, including the one at Union Grove Plaza, because the truckers could not make their deliveries, and no meat came in for Perry to butcher and sort, and the local farmers had not yet come to realize the necessity of raising meat for more than themselves, and the whole equation of chain retail failed. In the store's last weeks, the electricity was still on, but the cooler and freezer shelves were bare. They'd run out of everything they needed to get the job done anyway, including foam trays, shrink wrap, and self-adhesive label blanks for the check scale.

More than a few people died that first year without heating oil, mainly the old. Perry had barely gotten himself and Trish through the winter by jacking deer and ice-fishing at Cossayuna Lake. Then the house burned down during a particularly vicious late-season cold snap when they ran the woodstove all out and a chimney fire got into the old laths in the walls. It was March. A few weeks later on Easter, the temperature reached eighty-six degrees and the last remnants of the winter's snow melted into something like a banana daiquiri. The world was turning upside down, Trish said. They moved into the abandoned Hi-Dee-Ho Motel while Perry tried to figure out what to do next. The plumbing was shot, the electricity was shut off, and April being what it was, some nights they froze in there. That was when she left. In those last days of the old times, with gasoline getting scarce, a few jitney buses were still running for people who wanted to go somewhere. Now even they were bygone. That May after Trish left him, Perry started to build the shack on the river to get on with the business of living off the land. It seemed more and more evident that the economy was not coming back to anything like it had been.

Trish didn't say where she was going, but she had a brother in Plattsburgh, a hundred miles north on Lake Champlain, and Perry suspected she was there. He sometimes entertained notions about venturing up there to bring her back—*back home,* he put it to himself, as if to suggest he would be doing her a service—but it sure wouldn't be a matter of just driving up some afternoon and stuffing her in the car. At best, now, he might rent a horse and cart from Mr. Allison and it would take maybe two weeks up and back, and he worried about what kind of hazards lurked on the roads. There was talk of pickers (bandits) in the places between towns that had gone back to near wild, and the roads themselves were in miserable shape after years of frost heaves and neglect. Hardly anyone went anywhere anymore. In less sober moments, Perry also dreamed of tromping all the way up to Plattsburgh in winter on snowshoes like some kind of mountain man from the pioneer days, and he imagined the impression he would make when he got there: a hunk of avenging muscle, fur-swaddled, with blood in his eyes, come to claim his woman!

That was where the fantasy fell apart. His brother-in-law, Randy, was the type to take an aluminum baseball bat to somebody when only mildly annoyed, and he was a large fellow, much bigger than Perry. And besides, why would he want to force Trish to be with him against her will? That wasn't love. Perry was overwhelmed suddenly with sorrow for his own stupidity. If only he'd cleaned that damned chimney out.

In despair, he got out of bed, threw some pine chunks into the potbellied stove, which stood across the single room of his shack, and sat down in the chair beside it. He'd made the chair himself out of cedar roots. It was as solid as a throne. On the adjacent table was the bottle of corn whiskey he'd been working on earlier in the evening, along with his lap dulcimer, also made by hand out of spruce and cherrywood, with strings taken from a ruined piano he'd come across in a church basement out on the Spraguetown road. He poured a glass of the whiskey, which was a 150-proof straight distillate filtered through charcoal and flavored with artemisia (wormwood), which gave it a taste weirdly reminiscent of marshmallows.

The whiskey drove the panicky edge off his despair and left him with the more familiar and manageable feeling of pure loneliness, which he was able to channel into the simple tonic chords he had learned to produce on his dulcimer. His pluckings formed a sound track that allowed him to comprehend and bear what he had become. They were also, it seemed to him, a defense against God's apparent plan to heap hardships upon him, though he was not altogether certain that it was God behind his tribulations. Perhaps it was God's eternal opponent, the fallen angel, the Dark One. He sometimes thought of his music as an attempt to call out to God, in the grammar of God's own beauty, to rescue him from the devices of the arch fiend. What should he make of God's failure to answer him?

The yellow light of the resiny pine chunks and the purer white rays of moonlight shining through the treetops, reflecting off the water, and then faintly on his ceiling played through the dwelling with patterns evocative of either heaven or hell, depending on which direction Perry looked. On the wall above his bed hung a large old print of a painting, circa 1862, by Arthur Fitzwilliam Tait, of an Adirondack hunter surprised by a mountain lion. The animal was about to spring and the hunter seemed late in swinging up his rifle. Perry loved the picture, apart from its artistic qualities, for the fact that the tale was never resolved. He could imagine any outcome.

He poured himself four fingers more of the whiskey and knocked back half of it in a gulp. The burn pleased him. Perhaps there was something of the devil in it, he thought, and in him, too. His sleep deprivation combined with his loneliness and the whiskey and his anxious ruminations about the supernatural forces at work upon him, causing his head to swim. Looking at the picture on the wall, he realized he had killed many animals in recent years. Had he affronted God by doing so? Yet hunting for sustenance was the human race's oldest occupation. Then it came to him very suddenly, as though beamed down on the moonlight: He needed to hunt down and kill a mountain lion, or catamount, as they were called in Washington County. This would be his challenge to God. The act would determine who exactly was the directing persona behind the predicament of his life. Even if the quest killed him, he would leave this world knowing the answer. The clarity and authenticity of this idea, in his gathering drunkenness, seemed absolutely ineluctable as he hobbled across the room and collapsed back on his bed.

TEN

At seven-thirty in the morning, Brother Jobe was summoned to the east paddock where the body of Jupiter, his half Morgan stallion, lay motionless on its side. Beads of dew glistened in the sunlight on the horse's dark flank just as it did on the cropped grass he lay upon, prompting Brother Jobe to suppose his prize stud had had some time to cool off where he lay. He examined the horse from a dozen different angles and heights, even crouching a few inches off the ground to look into its big unseeing black eye.

"You got any idea what fetched him down, sir?" asked Brother Enos, the person in charge of the morning feed. At sixteen he was barely a man, with carrot-colored hair and a port-wine birthmark that ran up his jawline to the vicinity of his left earlobe. He fidgeted with the bucket containing the stallion's uneaten morning ration of oats.

"I thought you might venture a clue," Brother Jobe muttered, prying open the stallion's jaws with both hands and examining inside the mouth.

"I don't have no idea, sir."

"Hmmmph," Brother Jobe said. "We'll see about this."

Minutes later, he was in the central chamber of the new construction that had filled the courtyard between the two wings of the U-shaped modernistic high school. Twenty-four other new rooms surrounded this chamber. It served as the summer quarters for Mary Beth Ivanhoe, originally of Lynchburg, Virginia, who was known within the New Faith order as "Precious Mother," and sometimes "the Queen Bee." Two things had happened to Mary Beth Ivanhoe at age nineteen as a result of being struck by a sport-utility vehicle driven by a drunken undergraduate from Radford University: She developed an unusual form of epilepsy that seemed to enable her to perceive events beyond time and place, and she grew convinced that she was able to speak to God directly. That was back in the period now referred to as the old times. She'd come into the New Faith a year after her release from the hospital, spellbound for Jesus. She had joined the group as just another initiate seeking a structured community life at a time of great turmoil and uncertainty in America. But her peculiar abilities had led the New Faith order to rapidly elevate her to an exalted position within the organization. She used her gifts to guide the people of New Faith in their journey to find safety and peace that had led them to the town of Union Grove, New York, the previous spring. A retinue of handmaidens almost constantly attended her, and her physical condition was such that she spent all her hours in bed.

The chamber was dim. The only daylight came from the windows in a cupola at the center of the room. The air was close and warm, though at this hour of the morning the outside temperature hovered not much above freezing. It bore a sharply sweet odor of fecundity that might have put off anyone not already acquainted with it. Five women in smock dresses bustled about a large bed in the center of the room that held the corpulent object of their attentions. She was propped up on a mass of pillows, her skin unnaturally pale. She wore a distempered expression beneath a black silk turban that made her head look small. Physical pain of one sort or another had been her intimate companion for many years. Somewhere in the distance, babies cried.

"Mebbe you sisters could excuse us for a few minutes," Brother Jobe said, and the women fluttered out of the room like moths until the only sound was the heavy breathing of the room's chief occupant.

"Get thee behind me, sumbitch!" Mary Beth said to her visitor, punctuating the command with a screechy laugh that resolved into a coughing spasm.

"Morning to you, too, Precious Mother," Brother Jobe replied. He pulled a wooden side chair up to the bedside. "You full of vinegar today."

"I don't feel so good."

"What else is new?"

"You got a dead studhorse lying under the cold dew is what."

"A little birdie tell you that?"

"You don't need no TV special reports with a mind like I got," she said. "It's half exploding as I speak."

"He wasn't a day over nine years and was in the very pink of health last time I laid eyes on him. I give him a good look-over just now. There ain't a mark on him, nor no sign of colic or founder. I'm stumped out loud."

"Everything you are is out loud," she muttered, and coughed again.

"What's got you so cranky, then?"

"When you moving me to those new quarters? I get cold in here these days."

"It's like a durn steam bath."

"Not for me it ain't. I chill easy."

"Soon as the carpenters are done."

"Hurry 'em along, why don't you."

"You can't lean on men that do fine custom work. We'll get you in there soon enough. Can we get back on track here, Mary Beth?"

Her eyes rolled up under the lids, briefly, as they always did when her emotions rose and the visions streamed in.

"I can tell you it wasn't no natural death," she said.

"I already figgered that out. Why don't you help me a step further. Tell me who done it and how."

"Not one of us," she said.

"Ditto what I said before. Pay out some."

"A little lost soul."

"You holding back."

"Mebbe you should just let this one alone, BJ."

"Not on your life," Brother Jobe said. "There's hell to pay."

"I'm hungry."

"Alls you do is eat."

"I eat for more than myself. Since when you become a ding-dang diet doc, anyway, you sawed-off, baby-faced, vengeful little sumbitch?"

"Aw, hell's bells, girl, alls I want to know is who done this deed. You'll tell me or I swear I'll put all your girls to work out in the fields forking compost and you can just do for yourself in here."

Mary Beth Ivanhoe's eyelids fluttered, her teeth clenched, and her back stiffened. A gob of foamy spittle bubbled from one corner of her mouth and she issued a series of strained grunts. Brother Jobe merely watched from his chair. Mary Beth suffered dozens of these fits every day. Not much could be done about them. Those who spent time in her company had learned to patiently endure them. The spell subsided after a minute and left Mary Beth gasping among her heaped pillows. Beads of sweat glistened all over her waxy face.

"Have . . . mercy," she gasped. Eventually her breathing resumed its labored normal rhythm. "You been here all along?" she asked Brother Jobe.

"I ain't moved a muscle," he said.

"You got any idea what this takes out of a body?" she asked wearily.

"Yes I do. Your curse is our blessing."

"We're all cursed when you get down to it. The innocent as well as the wicked. That's the tragic heart of the matter, and I'm sorry about it."

"I daresay you speak the truth there, Precious Mother."

"Listen up then. Here's what you wanted to know."

ELEVEN

About the same time that morning, the doctor appeared at the door of his friend, Robert Earle. Robert's housemate, Britney, answered the door, a petite woman of twenty-six, hard-muscled like the gymnast she had once been. Her tough, wary expression softened when she saw it was the doctor, a trusted figure in town. Behind her, and clinging to her ankle-length linen skirt, stood Sarah, her seven-year-old daughter by Shawn Watling. The child fled shrieking at the sight of the doctor. She had last seen her father's body in the doctor's spring house, an impromptu morgue, after he was murdered at the General Supply, as the town landfill was called since it became a salvage operation for useful articles. Shortly, Robert emerged from deeper within the house holding a chisel and a sharpening stone.

"Everything all right?" he asked. Britney went to see about Sarah, leaving the two men alone in the front parlor.

"My boy's run away," the doctor said.

"Are you sure about that?"

"He stuffed a pillow and a bunch of clothes under the covers to make it look like he was sleeping late. But he's gone."

"Did you two have a fight?"

"I wouldn't call it that, exactly. His dog got killed yesterday and he's very angry because I couldn't save him."

"How'd that happen?"

"He got in with a horse and, being a puppy and all . . ."

"I'm very sorry."

"I could use some help looking for Jasper, if you're not too busy."

"I can take a day off."

"I'd appreciate it."

Robert had been doing a job of very exacting finish carpentry for the New Faithers, something beyond their skills. He offered now to see about rounding up some of their more capable men who had been rangers in the Holy Land War to come along and help search for the boy. They were skilled trackers, he said.

"I don't want them involved in this," the doctor said. He explained how it was one of the New Faith horses that had stomped on the dog, how Brother Jobe appeared mysteriously at his office just after the dog died, and the strange business that had transpired between them there.

"I feel stupid even telling you this," the doctor said. He ran his fingers through his beard and his hair. "I asked him to try to bring the dog back to life."

Robert absorbed the statement but didn't reply.

"Shows how desperate we get sometimes," the doctor said. "Even someone like me, a man of science, who ought to know better."

"Well, Brother Jobe, he's got something going on," Robert said. "I don't know what to call it, but it's something out of the ordinary."

"I feel like a fool," the doctor said.

"What did he say when you asked him that?"

"He said he couldn't bring things back to life. He could only go the other way."

"The other way?"

"That he could bring on death. Kill things. Something like that."

"Well, I don't want to seem mentally backward, Jerry, but between you and me, based on what we've seen around here, there seems to be something to that."

"I don't like to think so."

"I don't know that it depends on what we like or don't like to think."

"For all we know it's some kind of hocus-pocus, like a magician on stage. They don't do magic. They just very artfully distract your attention away from their trapdoors and devices."

"What he did with Wayne Karp wasn't smoke and mirrors, Jerry. It was flesh and bone."

"Then maybe he's just a garden-variety killer."

"I think the truth is we don't know what Brother Jobe is or how he does it. But for the moment, wouldn't you rather have it on your side than against you?"

"Well, I feel like a damn fool asking him to bring that dog back from the dead. And for now I'd just like to keep him and his people out of this," the doctor said. "You still willing to go search with me?"

"Sure."

"I'll stop by Tom Allison's and arrange to get a saddle horse for you. I can ride old Mac."

"Okay."

"Come by the office when you're ready to head out. And thanks."

"Sure."

Neither Robert nor the doctor knew, just then, that Jupiter the stallion lay dead in his paddock, nor how he met his end.

TWELVE

Jasper Copeland woke up in a field of golden bracken off the Battenville–Cambridge Road, a byway so untraveled even back in the old times that it had never been paved. He'd slept in his clothing with his father's ancient wool hunting shirt over his sweater, his wool hat and gloves on, bundled in a blanket. His breath hung in a cloud on the cold, still air. Sparkling frost dusted the fronds of the bracken ferns. The dazzling sunlight that poured through the treetops, with the leaves at the height of fall color, filled him with an exhilarating terror. He was at large in a world that had made itself beautiful again, as free as a wild animal.

And then, as the reality of his situation rushed back at him, he remembered the woeful particulars of the life he had suddenly left behind: his beloved companion, Willie, who was now dead, the desperate scene in the paddock where Willie got hurt, then listening outside the window of his father's office to his father bargaining with Brother Jobe, and the ghastly deed he had done to Brother Jobe's stallion. His moral sense informed him that grave and terrible things had been set in motion that could not be undone and would change his life. He was not yet lonely for his family. If anything, he was still angry at them, especially his father. He supposed that the discovery of his foul deed would turn even them against him.

His backside was damp from sleeping on the spongy ground and his neck hurt. It occurred to him that he did not have a plan for what to do next and that it might be a good idea to come up with one. His lack of foresight frightened him, but he recognized that this moment required him to stand apart from his feelings, to simply act, and that his first order of business should be to just get going—that the act of getting himself into motion would stimulate him to begin to make a plan. So he stuffed his father's hunting shirt into his backpack to give himself more freedom of movement and set off down the Battenville–Cambridge Road.

His footsteps warmed him up quickly, but after a little while hunger and thirst crowded out his more desperate thoughts, and he looked for a suitable place to stop and eat some of the provisions he'd brought with him. One side of the road was a set of fields and pastures belonging to farmer Ben Deaver, an airline executive in the old times. The fields were separated by hedgerows and low walls of granite stones worked up out of the ground every year in the relentless frost heaves. The corn, barley, and oat crops were reduced to stubble now that the harvest was over, and piles of fragrant manure lay up and down the rows waiting to be harrowed in. A final hay crop in one field was mowed and laid out in windrows, soon to be stacked or carted off to the barns. A substantial percentage of crop land had to be devoted to animal feeds in the new times.

The ownership of the land on the other side of the road was in limbo, since the family who had last lived and farmed there had all been taken by the Mexican flu some years earlier. What had been crop fields and pastures were now overgrown with sumac and poplar scrub. Adjoining parcels were second-growth woods from a previous era of abandonment when dairying had collapsed back in the 1980s. The casual observer might think it was mature old-growth forest. The flu and the encephalitis scourge that followed the flu had reduced the population of Washington County to less than half of what it had been at the turn of the millennium. A great deal of property now existed in legal limbo, since not only were its freeholders dead but communications had fallen off so severely that their far-flung relatives, heirs, and assigns could not be located. Nor were the courts functioning to adjudicate claims. Nor were the old computerized title records accessible. Nor were many people traveling anywhere. Houses and other buildings of all kinds stood vacant around the county. The people who ran the General Supply—inhabitants of Karptown, the former trailer park named after their fallen leader, Wayne Karp—enjoyed a lively business in the disassembly of these derelict structures and the resale of fabricated building materials that were no longer manufactured. Even old nails and screws had value. After farming, salvage was the town's leading industry.

Farther down the road, Jasper spied a horse and cart as it came around a bend, perhaps a quarter mile ahead. He reacted quickly, slipping into the trees on the wooded side. He hid behind a blown-down locust tree and watched the rig pass by. The driver was an older man he recognized, but he could not attach a name to him. So many people came through his father's office with their illnesses and injuries that over the years Jasper figured he'd seen everybody who was still alive in Washington County, though he never learned all their names. The driver hummed a tune to himself and the horse walked briskly, as if both were enjoying the crisp sunny weather. Jasper thought to himself that he would like a job driving a horse cart if he were ever allowed to rejoin society again after what he'd done. The sorrow attending that thought was shoved aside by his renewed awareness of hunger as he observed that the cart was filled with potatoes, freshly dug, still coated with earth. Potatoes were his favorite food, after apple pie. His mother made a kind of pan-fried cake of shredded potatoes cooked in butter in a cast-iron skillet that was about the tastiest thing he knew of. It came out of the pan upside down, all one piece, with the top brown and crispy. He was sorry that he had not brought a frying pan with him, but he knew how to roast potatoes in the coals of a wood fire, something his father had taught him on the overnight fishing and camping trips they sometimes made when the doctor needed to get away from his obligations. These memories of food sent him foraging in the pack for the corn bread, sausage, and cheese he'd brought with him. He told himself it would be smart to save some of it for a meal later in the day, but his hunger was so extreme that he couldn't resist eating all of it.

When he was finished eating, he set forth carefully up the road in search of the field where that cart full of potatoes had come from. He didn't have to go far to find it. From a distance, he saw half a dozen figures laboring there: hired men in rough clothes, forking up the earth and laying up the potatoes on the ground, where others came along and put them into willow baskets. Jasper stole around a hedgerow and crept up against a wall of old fieldstone, where he peered through the thicket of blackberry canes. He waited there for more than an hour, watching, sometimes slipping off to sleep from boredom until the gentle creak and clatter of the horse cart alerted him. When the cart came into the field, the laborers brought baskets of potatoes to it and dumped them in until the cart box was full again. Then the horse and cart went off down the road. The laborers gathered up their tools and departed. Jasper waited until he was sure they were gone and would not return. Down in the field, he found more than enough potatoes left for his purposes. He took enough for his supper and breakfast but not so many as to weigh down his backpack and slow his progress.

The way the sun was slanting, he knew that evening was not so far off. There were few clouds in the sky and he sensed that it would be a cold night. Feeling the urgent need to move on, he set off down the road again in a direction that he judged to be northerly, where the shadows of the trees pointed. North of here was the tiny hamlet of Hebron, where he had been a few times with his father, and farther north lay a place called Glens Falls, where he had never been but where his father had once worked in a hospital. It called itself a city. It was much larger than Union Grove. The words *Glens Falls* sounded musical, and he imagined it a handsome, lively place, full of bustle and enchantment, where a stranger, even a boy, could make himself useful in exchange for a warm place to sleep and regular meals. There were quite a few orphaned children in Union Grove, taken in by kind families. Hadn't the shopkeeper, Terry Einhorn, taken in the dim-witted Buddy Haseltine, who swept the floor and stacked wooden crates and washed the windows? Or perhaps there was somebody like Stephen Bullock up there, a rich man of property who had a whole community of souls living on his plantation and was always looking for new blood. Jasper was not so keen on becoming a common laborer, like the potato diggers he had watched that day, but even at age eleven he had skills that full-grown men did not have. He had assisted his father and knew enough about illness to dispense useful advice. He had helped his father perform many routine surgeries, knew how to sew up wounds, and had once attended at the amputation of a man's leg, hopelessly shattered by a falling barrel of flaxseed oil. It occurred to him that he could possibly find a position doctoring people.

With these thoughts in mind he made his way up the road. Not much farther he came upon the edge of an orchard. He reasoned correctly that this was the extreme corner of the property because there was not a person or a building in sight. It was planted with Northern Spy, a late-harvest apple, and he put six nice ones in his pack on top of the three that he ate then and there.

THIRTEEN

Brother Jobe enjoyed the gliding gait of his mount, a mule named Atlas. He was fond of telling people that a mule rode much more smoothly than a good saddle horse, and was smarter, and could stand up to heat better, and was not stubborn but rather sensible and disinclined to follow obviously foolish commands that might discommode or injure it. A mule was a superior animal, and he felt positively superior riding one, despite what others might think. And once he got his mule-breeding business up and going next spring, he was confident that folks would begin to see the advantage of mules. Of course people still wanted horses, and he aimed to keep breeding them, too, but for now he was out a perfectly good stallion.

Though it was a pleasant, crisp fall afternoon, and despite his enjoyment at being out on the road riding Atlas, Brother Jobe suffered in a personal globe of perturbation knowing, as he now did, that the doctor's boy had poisoned his studhorse, Jupiter. He was further vexed by the knowledge that the boy had eloped from Union Grove and was on the loose somewhere in the county. He was reluctant to pursue the boy, fearful of roiling relations between his people and the townspeople if and when the boy was found. If the boy happened to come back on his own, well, that would be another matter. All politics aside, he wanted to flog the boy within an inch of his life, or maybe beyond that.

Brother Jobe was on a journey to Steven Bullock's plantation, several thousand acres of fruitful bottomland and upland five miles outside town at the place where the Battenkill joined the Hudson River. He had business to discuss with Mr. Bullock, the grandee of the county, with his vast holdings, his many faithful servants, and his personal hydroelectric outfit. To start with, there were certain urgent matters of the law that required the attention of Mr. Bullock as

Union Grove's elected magistrate. But mostly, Brother Jobe wanted to inquire about getting a stallion to replace Jupiter. Bullock was raising big German Hanoverians for the saddle. America was dearly short of horseflesh, so rapid had been the descent out of the old times into the new. Wasn't it odd, then, Brother Jobe mused to the soft rocking gait of Atlas the mule, that his daddy had owned the leading Ford dealership in Scott County, Virginia, back in the twentieth century?

Brother Jobe had come about halfway to his destination when, lost in musing about back home, he saw a lone figure up ahead on the road. As he drew closer, the figure began to wave its arms in a broad gesture that reminded Brother Jobe of a railroad grade-crossing signal from the old times. He instinctively reined in Atlas. The lone figure strode forward confidently. The closer he came, the more his appearance resolved from that of a grown man into something more like a gangly, overgrown boy. He was perhaps twenty, with curly yellow hair and a scraggly blond beard that, if he ever took to shaving regularly, would hardly require the razor twice a week. His cheeks were sunken as if he had not been getting regular meals. He was carrying a bulging leather shoulder sack, which he now took off and tossed aside to the edge of the road.

"What's up, stranger?" Brother Jobe said.

"And good afternoon, to you, too, sir."

"A fine day to be rambling."

"I'm a rambler and a gambler—you've got that right."

"That so? Are you knowing the Lord, son?"

The young man dipped his whole upper body in a guffaw. "Not yet," he said.

"Would you like to?"

"I hope not to meet up with him for some time yet. I like it here on earth, rambling and gambling as I do."

"You can be born again in this world and know the Lord."

"I've had enough of birthing, sir. I'm enjoying my prime. Would you like to hear some of my song?"

"Your song . . . ?"

"Yessir, the 'Ballad of Billy Bones.'"

"That'd be you? Billy Bones?"

"Yessir. The very same."

"Well, I don't have time for no song and dance, son."

"There ain't any dance to this. Not yet, anyway."

"Mind if I pass on the song, then?"

The boy unbuttoned his brown leather coat and drew it open to reveal the butt of an automatic pistol tucked into the waistband of his striped trousers and something that looked like a two-foot-long brush knife in a scabbard on his other hip.

"Give it a chance, sir. You won't regret it."

"Along about now the only thing I regret is not bringing a firearm to entertain you with."

"So much the better then, because neither of us will get hurt. Are you ready for my song?"

"Fire away."

"Here goes:

"When first I came to New York State
My fortune here to find
I followed reg'lar upright ways
Was always nice and kind

But as I rambled round the state
A bandit I became
I plied the roads with gun and sword
And plundered many a man. . . ."

He sang these verses in the style of a mournful dirge. During the second verse, he drew the automatic pistol out of his waistband and held it aloft in an emphatic manner.

"I think I get the picture," Brother Jobe said.

"I ain't done. There's lots more verses."

"I heard enough. If you got yourself a ding-dang ukulele, folks might stand it better."

"You know where I might find such a thing?"

Brother Jobe felt his patience melting away. "Lookit here, son, I don't carry no cash money. This here's a waste of your valuable banditry time. Anyways, you are a durn sorry excuse for a minstrel and a worse robber."

"You think so? Well, maybe I'll just have that horse of yours. I'm sick of pounding this road."

"This here's a mule, you dumb ass."

"Mind how you speak to me or someone might get hurt after all."

"Look right here, boy." Brother Jobe held an index finger to the outside corner of his right eye.

"Huh?"

"That's right. Look right in."

"Think you can run the snake eye on Billy Bones?"

"I already done it. As we speak, I can see inside your mush-filled brainpan at a throbbing vein within. I'm surprised you can't feel it."

The young man cried out in pain and visibly drooped while his gun hand fell to his side. "Sweet Jesus," he moaned.

"Well, look what you found after all."

The young man staggered to the side of the road and squatted into his haunches. "What are you doing to me, mister?"

"I'm calling a halt to these monkeyshines and giving you something to reflect on."

"My head's splitting open," the boy said, and vomited between his dusty shoes, a thin stream of yellow green puke, as if he had been eating grass for his breakfast.

"You'll be all right in a while, long as you quit the vicinity and don't never show your sorry face here again."

At that, Brother Jobe gave Atlas some heel and the big mule resumed his stately walk. As he left Billy Bones on the roadside, the young man was weeping loudly in the sunshine.

Fourteen

The Reverend Loren Holder ventured onto the old steel-truss railroad bridge that spanned the Battenkill, thinking he was leaving his last footsteps on solid earth behind him forever. The notion to end his life had seized him in the night with a force comparable to true love, something sudden and irresistible. He'd worked out all the details mentally in the hours before dawn. Though his mood now was such that he seemed to be viewing the whole world through a narrow culvert, he retained enough presence of mind to see the despair that consumed him as a kind of object narrative, so that his life seemed like a story unspooling to this inexorable destination. The bridge. The river. The beautiful day. The end.

When he got to the middle of the bridge, he dawdled on a girder that supported the rusty old track and its half-rotten ties. He carried a length of rope looped over his shoulder like a mountaineer. It was a very good machine-made nylon rope of the kind that was no longer manufactured or sold, another useful remnant of the old times. It occurred to him that whoever found him ought to be sure to keep the rope for some better use than the one he intended it for.

He peered over the edge of his precarious perch on the girder. It was a good forty-foot drop to the water. The river was low this time of year and he could see trout finning in the shallow pool down beside the central bridge abutment. These very trout, he thought, had been preceded by how many millions of generations of fish, and how many more would come after? And how many more seasons would revolve in the future history of this mysterious world before all the generations of everything would exhaust themselves? And then what? Would all the worlds and worlds and worlds of worlds fold in upon themselves to nothing? And what could prevent more worlds from emerging out of nothing after that? And might he,

Loren, emerge new and whole out of the nothing he intended to enter this beautiful afternoon? He hardly dared hope to find out. A moment of vertigo left him trembling.

He felt a tear start down his cheek and quickly wiped it away, chiding himself for being a coward in the face of the infinite. He noted also that his strange view of things this day did not include a glimpse of the putative character known as God. He had given up on that personage some time ago, preferring to see a divine spark in his fellow human beings, who had, after all, dreamed up this great Lord and protector to avoid the lonely burdens of their own sanctity. And so, Loren reasoned, it was a more responsible thing to deny the existence of the deity to the very end than to succumb to the fairy tales about him and his celestial kingdom. That was Loren's theory, and he was oddly satisfied with himself for having summed it up so concisely in his own mind, especially at this moment. It would allow him to enter the cosmic interstices between this life and whatever lay beyond it clear-eyed and honestly. He took the coil of rope off his shoulder, looked up into the truss work of the bridge, and tried to calculate which structural member above would be the most suitable to tie up to. This took his mind off metaphysics.

When he'd chosen a particular horizontal beam, he attempted to lob his coil of rope over it, not a hard trick for someone who once had a pretty good layup shot on the basketball court. Except that, in his tremulous state, he forgot to hold on to one end of the rope, and the whole rope sailed over the beam in a clump and arced down into the river, where it landed with a splash, spooking many large trout. He watched it catch the current and float away past a tangle of blowdown around the next bend.

"Reverend," somebody said softly behind him.

Loren wheeled around to find Britney Watling standing on the tracks with pack basket slung over one shoulder. He regarded her with a combination of wonder and horror.

"I was over there." She pointed to the far end of the bridge. "I couldn't help noticing."

Loren was struck, at that moment, by an incongruous recognition of the young woman's beauty in the autumn sunlight, her caramel hair piled up halolike, her small mouth slightly open, her upper lip an inquisitive pink V, and the soft flesh just beneath her collarbone heaving slightly with each breath.

"Do you remember a more beautiful day?" she asked.

Loren's throat was so dry he could not even croak out an answer.

"This is the kind of day you think God is in everything," she added.

"Of course," Loren said.

"Are you feeling okay?"

Loren nodded.

"You're all shaky."

"I slipped for a second. Lost my footing."

"You could break your neck falling off this thing. I always stay over here in the middle, where you can't fall off. Why don't you step away from the edge and come over by me."

Loren nodded and stepped off the girder and came over beside her.

"Thank you," Britney said. "You were making me nervous."

As Loren quietly hyperventilated, the staggering beauty of the world flooded his senses. His heart raced.

"Robert and the doc have taken off," she said.

"Taken off where?"

"The doc's son ran away. They're looking for him."

"Why did he run away?"

"His dog got killed by a horse."

Without speaking further, Britney reached out and took Loren's large hand in her small one. He was shivering as though he had just survived a plunge in an icy pool. Together they walked off the bridge back toward town.

Fifteen

Jasper Copeland stayed off the roads for the remainder of the afternoon as he moved north from Union Grove in the direction of Glens Falls. He'd traveled seven miles through woods, fields, and orchards since his adventure in the potato field. His mood, however, had devolved from ebullient that morning to dejected as the day wore on. His pack seemed heavier and his prospects for the coming night seemed increasingly uncertain, and a longing for the familiar things of home began to stir dimly in a remote sector of his consciousness. He dragged in his footsteps, searching now for a place to spend the night, until he came upon a ruined fieldstone foundation that was little more than a pentimento on the landscape of an earlier society—in this case, the house of one Benjamin Rodney, an early settler of Washington County, who laid the stones in 1762 and whose grandson had deserted the homestead for the Ohio frontier in 1817. Mixed hardwoods had reclaimed their fields and pastures except for this rectangle of stones, in the corner of which Jasper found the skeleton of a human being.

He approached it warily, as though it might spring to life and attack him if he was not careful. The bones were draped in frayed and shredded gray nylon pants and a torn grayish green sweater. A broad ashen smudge along the neckline and diagonally down the front suggested that the garment, and the person in it, had been subjected to flames. Jasper did not fail to notice that a foot was missing. But the skeleton was so twisted where it lay quasi-upright against the rocks that it took him a moment to understand that the tibia and fibula were gone as well. He wondered whether an animal had made off with them or the person had lost his leg in the process of losing his life. Study it as he might, crouching among the pungent dead leaves, he could not determine whether it was the skeleton of a man or a woman.

He eventually realized that he would learn no more about the skeleton by studying it and that the evening seemed to be falling like a curtain in the woods. So he plodded on, thinking he might be better off finding his way onto a road again. He knew that abandoned houses were plentiful in the county and he reasoned that it would be nice to find one for the night. The temperature was dropping and he retrieved his gloves and hat from his pack. A three-quarters moon was rising through the treetops against the purple sky when he came upon a decrepit mobile home, as such dwellings were once called, at the end of what had once been a quarter-mile-long driveway into the woods. The driveway was overgrown with poplars. The hulk of a pickup truck stood on bare rims in a thicket twenty yards from the trailer. Nothing remained of it but rusted metal suggesting it had been set on fire some years ago. Vines crawled in and out of its openings.

Jasper set down his pack beside the truck and got a candle and a match. The sheer physical relief of setting down his load lifted his mood. The door to the trailer hung open and askew on one hinge. He ventured inside, waited until his eyes adjusted to the dimness, and then searched for a surface to strike his match on. He could not afford to waste one. The wall surface, he noticed, was some kind of plastic material embossed with a stuccolike texturing. He ran his match over it and the head flared, illuminating the building's interior so brightly for a moment that it hurt his eyes. He lit the candlewick and carefully cupped his hand around the flame until he was sure it was going.

The light revealed a small table with a plastic bench on either side of it. He dripped a little wax onto the table and stuck the candle on the spot. The place looked pretty well stripped. The plumbing fixtures were gone from the tiny galley kitchen opposite the table. He rummaged through the cabinets and the drawers, thrilling a little to be acting like a burglar, but found absolutely nothing. He retrieved the candle and ventured into the next room where he found a plywood box platform for a double bed. The mattress was long gone. There was nothing in the two small closets except a couple of plastic hangers, one of them broken. A little bathroom crammed between the galley and the bedroom was also stripped of plumbing and fixtures. There was a hole in the floor where the toilet used to be. But next to the hole Jasper found the front half of a child's stuffed animal. There was little stuffing left in it, except for in the head, and it was all dusty. He was at a loss to understand what kind of animal it represented—it was nothing that he recognized—but it had a cheerful expression, big eyes, and a snout full of nylon whiskers. Jasper dusted it off and, thinking that he'd found something like a new companion, tucked it tenderly into his sweater, determined to keep it from further harm.

He'd already decided to spend the night in the trailer. In the meager twilight emanating from the last red streaks in the sky, he gathered up some of the plentiful dry twigs lying around the trailer's clearing and started a fire with them, the light of which allowed him to find some larger branches to feed the fire. Soon he had a majestic blaze roaring. He ate two apples from his pack while he watched the fire burn down enough to rake a bed of embers apart from the main fire with a stick. He placed his three largest potatoes on these embers and tended them carefully—rolling them this way and that way—for half an hour until he judged that they were cooked. Then he stabbed each with the sharpened end of his stick and put them on a rock out of the heat. Though blackened on the outside, they were yellow and creamy within. He was so hungry that he burned the roof of his mouth devouring the first two, and only while consuming the last one did he think how much better they would have been with some butter and salt.

When he finished his meal and had no more room for even another apple, he tossed more wood on his fire and hatched a scheme for begging provisions at some farmhouse door the following day. He was far enough from home, he reasoned, to not be recognized by anyone. He could make up a story about who he was and where he was going, and ask for whatever he needed to sustain him—corn bread, eggs, butter, cheese, maybe even meat—as he made his way to Glens Falls, where he would find a place for himself.

In a little while he retired to the trailer. The door to the little bedroom was still on its hinges and the deadbolt on it worked. The plywood bed was hard, but he was glad to feel sheltered and secure. He stuck the six inches of candle to a blob of hot wax on the night table and retrieved the stuffed animal from his sweater. He could put his hand a little ways inside and hold it up like a puppet.

"What's your name?" he asked it.

"I don't know," he said on the animal's behalf.

"Do you mind if I call you Willie?"

"No, that's a nice name."

"I'm going to take care of you now. Nothing bad will happen to you anymore."

"I'm tired of laying on that dirty floor."

"You're with me now," Jasper told it. "Everything will be okay."

When he said that, the tears gushed out of his eyes as he thought about his home, and his family, and town, and dear friends, and the other Willie, whom he had been unable to keep out of harm's way.

Sixteen

Brother Jobe rode up into the driveway of Stephen Bullock's plantation house, dismounted, approached a man standing at the mouth of a great gray barn—one Dick Lee, an insurance claims officer in the old days and now the chief stable hand—and inquired about the lord of the manor. Dick Lee gazed at the visitor with bewilderment.

"The head honcho of this outfit," Brother Jobe explained. "Mr. Bullock. I'm here to see him."

"And who would you be?"

"I'm the head honcho of the New Faith outfit back to town. You heard of us?"

"I guess I have."

"Do you know the Lord?"

"I don't think about it much."

"Is that so? What about the extraspecial select moments when you do?"

"I don't think about it much even in those moments when I do think about it."

"It just passes through your noggin like the morning breeze?"

"No, it's more like when I'm going at it with the wife. She always yells 'Jesus Christ' when I hit her sweet spot." Dick Lee enjoyed a laugh. "Anyway, Mr. Bullock isn't around."

"Is he on the property somewheres?"

"He's over to the sorghum mill just now, I think."

"Well, if you'll just maybe send and fetch him, I'd be grateful."

Dick Lee seemed to weigh this a moment. Then he yelled into the dark mouth of the barn to his back: "Eddie Flake!"

A boy about sixteen with a lopsided head and a touch of palsy came limping out. He was directed to fetch Bullock. Brother Jobe watched him lope off down the grassy wagon lane that connected the house and barns to the other parts of Bullock's vast acreage.

"You send a cripple boy all the way over there?"

"It's what he does," Dick Lee said. "I'll take your mount."

"Mind how you handle him."

Dick Lee's demeanor had settled into one of not-well-concealed condescending amusement. Brother Jobe, at five foot six and plump, with facial features that seemed crowded together in the center of his face, and dressed in his severe black frock topped off with a broad-brimmed straw hat, presented a figure that others seemed to find risible, sometimes to their later regret.

"Never rode a mule myself," Dick Lee said.

"It's the coming thing," Brother Jobe said.

"It isn't coming here," Dick Lee said as he vanished into the barn with Atlas.

"Our Lord rode an ass into Jerusalem, you know," Brother Jobe called after him.

Brother Jobe waited a good half an hour by the soapstone horse trough under a blazing orange old maple between the house and the barn. The waiting irritated him, as there was really nowhere to sit except the rim of the horse trough, which was not comfortable. It also irritated him that no one had invited him into the house, and his gall reached such a pitch that he almost went into the barn to retrieve his mount when Bullock appeared in the wagon lane in front of Eddie Flake, who was more than forty years younger and struggled to keep up. Bullock, with his Roman nose, longish white hair, tailored trousers, cotton blouse, and fine polished boots, looked something like Buffalo Bill, Brother Jobe thought, lacking only the flowing mustache and goatee.

"You take tea?" he asked Brother Jobe rather brusquely.

"When poteen ain't available," Brother Jobe said.

"Follow me."

Like the crippled boy, Brother Jobe, too, found it hard to keep up with Bullock's long strides. He followed him around the graceful old white clapboard house to a pavilion beside a pond. Inside, the pavilion was furnished with a low table between two substantial cushions on a tatami mat. The west wall was open to the pond.

"Have a seat."

"You mean on that pillow?"

Bullock didn't even reply. He removed his boots and sat down on the cushion to the left, Indian-style, and Brother Jobe did likewise to the right. He took off his straw hat and placed it on the table.

"Don't put that there," Bullock said, and Brother Jobe snatched it back.

Just then, Mrs. Bullock swept into the pavilion bearing a tray with a rough-looking ceramic teapot and two matching cups without handles.

"Why, Mr. Jobe," she said. "What a pleasant surprise."

Brother Jobe struggled to stand up.

"Sit down," Bullock said.

"Afternoon, ma'am."

Sophie Bullock, a signal beauty at fifty-eight, wore a russet-colored full skirt and a golden silk shirtwaist with long gathered sleeves and ruffles in front. An alluring topaz pendant dangled below her collarbone. While she kept busy directing the daily operations of the household on the large plantation, looking after the many needs of the families who lived there, she rarely undertook physical labor. To Brother Jobe, she looked like a goddess of autumn. As she bent to place the tray on the low table, he got a good look down her décolletage, exercising his senses to the degree that he silently invoked his Savior's name. He was still enjoying the view as she poured him a cup.

"Why this here's real ding-dang tea," he said.

"Of course it is," Bullock said.

"Where all do you get it?"

"We get a lot of things."

"Do you get any coffee?"

"Sometimes. These days we get tea. And we like it."

"Well, there ain't nothing wrong with it."

"We hear your group is making great strides reviving Main Street over in town," Mrs. Bullock said as she filled her husband's cup.

"Why, yes, ma'am. We've done opened a barbershop and a haberdash already, and I aim to get a tavern room going sometime this winter."

"Really? How is it your denomination goes along with ardent spirits?"

"Well, ma'am, our spirits are ardent for the Lord."

"She means how come you let your people drink liquor," Bullock said. "Most religious people we know of take a dim view of that."

"We ain't Baptist or Methodist, Your Honor. We got our own ways. Lookit here, the pope of Rome and his bunch are all for drinking the blood of the lamb, ain't they? And their outfit is ongoing in bidness some two thousand years now. In these hard times, folks need a spot of life's comfort. We're all for music, dancing, and poteen in moderation and in its place. It don't conflict with love of Jesus. And the town needs a place where all folks can meet and mix, theirs and ours. There ain't any such facility in town. Everybody stays all buttoned up in their households after sundown. It ain't healthy."

"You don't have to call me 'Your Honor,'" Bullock said.

"You are the elected magistrate," Brother Jobe said.

"Don't remind him," Mrs. Bullock said with a girlish laugh as she withdrew from the pavilion. Brother Jobe craned his neck to watch as she retraced the flagstone path back to the house.

"I'm sorry, but I have to remind you," Brother Jobe said, turning back to Bullock, "we still got the matter of that killing back in June. Young man, name of Shawn Watling. We attended his funeral not two weeks after we got here. I'd expect by now that you would have called for an inquest, got started convening a grand jury and such."

Bullock's irritation increased visibly. He shifted on his cushion, put down his teacup, and took it up again. "I've had my hands full here on the farm," he said.

"I expect you have," Brother Jobe said. "Believe me, I know what it's like to run a big outfit. But you and you alone represent the rule of law around here. And forgive me for saying it, you've been neglecting your duties."

"Are you lecturing me?"

Bullock's eyes met Brother Jobe's directly for the first time and their gazes locked. Apparently Bullock saw something in there that made him wince.

"All right," he said. "I'll order that young man's body dug up and we'll have a look."

"I'll be grateful if you'd get hopping on that," Brother Jobe said.

"I don't think we're going to learn anything," Bullock said. "Anyway, Mr. Wayne Karp himself is no longer with us—thanks to you, rumor has it—and I'm inclined to think that he or one of his people was the trigger man in that incident. As long as you're here, I'd like to ask you: How'd you manage to kill that tough little bird?"

"I didn't have nothing to do with Mr. Karp's death."

"Come on. Just between the two of us."

"The Lord's wrath took him down."

"I guess the Lord works in mysterious ways."

"You got that right, sir. Somebody poisoned my studhorse last night."

Bullock gagged on his tea and fell into a coughing fit.

"You all right there, sir?"

"Poisoned?" Bullock said, recovering.

"That's right."

"Then I suppose you have some idea who's responsible."

"We're working on it."

"If you don't know who might have done such a thing, then what makes you so sure the animal was poisoned in the first place?"

"Don't you worry. We know."

"Do you have a vet amongst your people?"

"We have more than a few that served in the Holy Land," Brother Jobe said, referring to the war years earlier that closed down oil imports from the Middle East and brought the industrial nations to their knees.

"Not army vets. I mean horse doctors."

"We got several fellows that knows everything there is to know about horses."

"Horses sometimes do just drop dead, you know."

"This here horse was as healthy as you or me."

Bullock poured himself another cup from the teapot.

"Do you want to tell me who you think did this?" he said. "Just between the two of us."

"It wouldn't serve no purpose. I don't know as we could prove anything at this point."

"So you say you know who did it, but you can't even prove that the animal was poisoned."

"Yessir. That's it in a nutshell."

"I must say, it doesn't quite add up."

"Well, it adds up to this: I need another stallion."

"Oh? I can lend over ours. Darwin. He's just hitting his prime."

"I'd be grateful for that. But I was wondering if you might have a spare stallion for purchase outright."

"Not just now. But I've got some pregnant mares."

"Is that so? We could stand new blood."

"They're Hanoverians. Wonderful, big, strapping, all-around brutes. First-rate behind either a combine or a carriage. And excellent saddle horses, too."

"My Jupiter was a half Morgan. Sumbitch was fruitful and multiplied like all get-out, but I castrated all his male offspring. Rest his poor soul."

"Do you think horses have souls, Brother Jobe?"

"I hope to think so. Why not? They're better than we are. Look what we done to our world."

Bullock reached for his boots, slipped back into them, and got up from his cushion.

"It's been a pleasure, as usual, passing time with you, Brother Jobe."

"Always uplifting to share in your bounty, sir," Brother Jobe said, pulling on his boots and rising likewise. "When do you suppose those mares of yours are liable to foal?"

"Late March, I expect."

"You let me know if there's a colt amongst them. And don't rush to cut his balls off, sir."

"You can depend on me."

"I know I can, sir. By the way, that's a handsome pond you got. Any bass in there?"

"Bass?"

"We're all about bass where we come from. Why, this might surprise you, but you're looking at the two-time consecutive winner of the McDonald's Big Bass Splash."

"What's that? A fishing contest?"

"One of the big tournaments back in the day. Paid out half a million and I won the ding-dang thing twice in a row. Set me free to pursue my own interests instead of selling cars off my pappy's Ford dealership."

"No kidding?" Bullock said.

"I'm a regular fish hawk, sir. It ain't bragging if it's true, right? You must have some big old honkin' hawgs in that pond."

"Gosh, no," Bullock said. "The only thing in there is native speckled brook trout. It's spring-fed. Probably too cold for bass."

"Too bad. The bass is a noble creature."

"Well, up here we consider them trash fish. This is trout country."

SEVENTEEN

Robert Earle and the doctor walked their horses steadily north up old Route 29 in the low afternoon sunshine, scanning the road, fields, hillsides, and ridgelines for a glimpse of Jasper. A wonderful perfume of the season hung in the air, a combination of ripe apples, burning cornstalks, and the rot of fallen leaves. The landscape they traversed came alive intermittently with figures laboring at one thing or another: stooking up barley sheaves, forking hay, digging potatoes, spreading manure, harrowing fields behind a team, repairing walls. It looked, at times, the doctor thought, like a scene out of Van Gogh, complete with one weary figure napping sweetly up against a haystack on a back quarter of the Schmidt farm. The two often stopped to inquire if anyone had seen a boy of eleven making his way on the roads or fields. No one could say that they had seen such a boy.

By late afternoon, some twelve miles northeast of Union Grove, with the sun kissing the voluptuous summit of Lloyd's Hill and the temperature dropping, they came upon a well-kept homestead, a cottage in the gothic style surrounded by an extensive compound of beautifully tended gardens. The garden closest to the house was planted mostly with herbals, the doctor noted—sprawling borage, stately angelica, blue green wormwood, drifts of mint, shaggy humps of cannabis, burdock, tansy, rue, lovage, as well as other things that he couldn't identify. Behind the herb garden, hops climbed up a twenty-foot tepee of saplings, and chickens strutted in a little hen yard surrounded by a wattle fence. There were several outbuildings, including a substantial barn. It looked like new construction, Robert noted. A brindle horse grazed in a paddock beyond the barn and a cow in a pasture behind that. White smoke curled out of a fieldstone chimney at the back of the house. Twilight was settling over the property like a soft velvet cloak.

"We might inquire about spending the night here," Robert said. "They look like clean, decent people."

The doctor thought about the alternative, camping out in the cold. "All right," he said.

They dismounted, tied their horses to some lilacs growing by the stone wall along the road, went up the porch steps to the front door, and knocked. A woman of startling appearance soon answered. Her hair was silvery, but she had an ageless unlined face that did not match. Upon seeing the two men, she offered a reserved, mysterious smile, as if, perhaps, she was pleased to discover that a package she'd expected had been delivered. She looked to Robert like a ghost of something from the lost world of movies or magazines—an actress, a model, the girl in a vodka ad in a *Vanity Fair*. It rocked him for a moment, but her magnetic presence soon brought him sharply back to himself. She wore a full patchwork skirt of vibrantly colored satin pieces, arrayed in sweeping diagonals according to the ranks of the spectrum, like a sash made of rainbows descending from her hips. Above she wore a black long-sleeved tunic, belted so that her figure was on display. An herbal perfume radiated from her: notes of rosemary, tansy, bee balm.

"Afternoon, uh, ma'am," the doctor said, with something catching in his throat. He proceeded to explain who they were, that they were searching for his eleven-year-old son who had run away from home down in Union Grove, and he asked whether she had seen the boy.

"No," she said.

"The thing is, ma'am," Robert said, "we're going to continue our search tomorrow."

"Of course," the woman said.

"We were wondering if we could possibly put up for the night here. Maybe sleep in the barn."

"We can pay," the doctor said.

"Silver coin," Robert added. Paper money was disdained in the new times. Hard metal currency was preferred, though scarce.

She looked each of them up and down, sizing them up, apparently comfortable with what she saw. Her poise was as striking as her costume and demeanor.

"All right," she said. "You can stay here tonight."

"We're upright and straightforward," Robert said.

"You better be. I imagine you'd like a hot supper."

The doctor and Robert spoke simultaneously:

"You don't have to trouble yourself," the doctor said.

"That would be kind of you," Robert said. "We'll pay for that, too, of course."

"It'd be my pleasure," the woman said and turned to the doctor. "You must be terribly worried about your boy."

"I am," he said.

"You can turn out your horses with mine back there," she said, pointing behind the house. "You'll find hay and oats in the barn, and some feed buckets. Help yourselves."

"Why, that's very generous, ma'am," Robert said.

"I'd like to improve your chances of finding what you're looking for. Besides, I could stand some company," she said. "My name is Barbara Maglie." She held out a hand to each of them in turn and shook firmly as they introduced themselves. Her hand was long-fingered and delicate but red from work in the garden and kitchen. Her touch was warm and vaguely electric.

"When you've settled your horses come to the back door. I'll be in the kitchen."

Robert undressed the horses while the doctor fetched two buckets of oats and a big wad of hay from the barn, which was immaculately kept. Out in the paddock there was a hand pump beside a wooden trough. The horses seemed relaxed and content there. After the men stashed their tack and gear in the barn, they reported to the back door of the house, as instructed. The exterior had been painted recently, a rich buttery yellow with white trim. Commercial paints of that quality had not been available for years and Robert wondered how she had accomplished it.

Barbara Maglie admitted them to the rear addition to the house, which comprised a large kitchen. She had set more than a few beeswax candles around the big room against the failing daylight. They cast a soft glow on what was clearly a hardworking production center but also a place of striking charm and style. A substantial soapstone sink occupied the near window wall, with a red-handled brass hand pump at one end. A long library table ran perpendicularly to it, opposed at the other wall by a claw-foot cookstove with bright nickel handles and appointments, and an attached hot-water reservoir. Robert had been searching for such a stove for years. It was the sort of thing that was no longer manufactured anywhere in the vicinity of Washington County. A cat snoozed on a fleece beside the hot-water reservoir. On a large ceiling rack above the stove hung a formidable array of pots and pans, many of them heavy-gauge copper, all polished and gleaming in the candlelight. Half the library table was occupied with small pumpkins, Turk's head and butternut squashes, and large globe onions with traces of garden soil on their skins.

"I've been canning," Barbara Maglie said, tossing a chunk of maple wood in the stove's firebox. "Have a seat."

She gestured beyond the library table, at the center of the big room, where a comfortable old sofa was grouped with a wing chair, a couple of spindle-back rockers, and a drop-leaf coffee table on a red and gold Oriental rug. Several large books lay stacked on it, with a picture history of New York City on top. The darker side of the room behind the seating contained two more long tables, one with a marble pastry slab. Shelves full of glass jars, bottles, bins, and books filled the entire far wall, except for a gothic window at the center. Strings of garlic, onions, and red chili peppers hung from the ceiling beams along with some drying crookneck gourds that were destined to become birdhouses, and a collection of baskets. A wonderful buttery aroma emanated from the stove. Some additional pots stood on the stovetop. Robert wondered at their contents and his stomach growled.

"Listen to you!" Barbara Maglie said.

"Sorry, ma'am."

"Call me Barbara. Do you like chicken pie?"

"That sounds too good to be true, Barbara."

"Oh it's true. You must be thirsty, too."

They agreed that they were. She disappeared down a stairway into the cellar with a candle, returning shortly with a plastic gallon jug of cider and a small wheel of cheese. She brought these items to the coffee table before the sofa and then brought over a bottle of brandy, a candlestick, some glasses, a wooden cutting board, and a knife, which she stabbed into the cheese.

"It's like a Queso de Aracena," she said. "Goat's milk. The rind is edible."

"Did you make it yourself?"

"No, I traded for it. I can't do everything myself."

She poured them each a bolt of the brandy with a cider chaser, and a cider for herself, and left the brandy bottle on the coffee table.

"Oh lord that's good," the doctor said.

"This is a lovely place," Robert said. "Do you mind my asking, is there someone else in the picture here?"

"Besides the two of you?"

"A husband."

"No," Barbara said. "There used to be. Before."

"Children?"

"A grown daughter. She was last in San Francisco as far as I know. It's been more than a few years now. I worry."

Robert told her about his son, Daniel, who had gone off to see what happened to America when he was nineteen, two years ago, how he'd set off with the teenage son of his good friend, the congregational minister, and that they hadn't been heard from since.

"I keep expecting him to walk in the door any day, though," Robert said.

"Well, maybe he will," Barbara said.

They all addressed their cider glasses a quiet moment. Barbara poured the two men another shot of brandy.

"It must be difficult for you out here all alone," Robert said.

"I like it. Do you remember what Georgia O'Keeffe said? No, of course you don't. Why would you? She said the cure for loneliness is solitude."

The doctor smiled slightly. "That's good," he said.

"You don't worry about pickers and vagabonds out here?" Robert said.

"My cats protect me," she said, then made a fierce face and held up her hand as if it were claw-filled, and let out a growl. Even the doctor laughed.

She adjourned to her stove and, in a little while, called the men to the cleared end of the library table, where she set three places with antique bone-handled flatware and napkins in silver rings.

Her chicken pie came to the table in a big copper pan with about a third of it already missing."

"Leftovers," Barbara said. "Hope you don't mind."

"It's magnificent," the doctor said, his hunger excited by the brandy.

She set down a big wooden salad bowl full of rocket and sliced pears dressed with vinegar, bacon fat, and fresh thyme, then went back to the stove to fetch a pot of collard greens braised in butter, onions, and cider. A basket of corn bread with a ramekin of butter arrived last. Her table reminded Robert of a particular restaurant he had loved back in Boston in the old days. It used to boast that all its ingredients came from within a hundred miles of the city. Now there was no other option.

"Grace," she said. "There. Let's eat."

"You don't stand on ceremony, do you?" Robert said.

"Ha!" Barbara said, heaping chicken pie and collards on their plates.

"You're not from here, are you?" Robert said.

"Neither are you, I'd guess," she said.

"Boston area," Robert said. "Can I ask how you happened to end up here?"

"Well, sure," she said, dandling her fork, the silver tines gleaming in the candlelight, which, in turn, reflected in her dark eyes.

"We lived in New York. This was our country place. I'd done some modeling. I met Albert, my husband, on a Grey Goose shoot—"

"Grey Goose vodka?" Robert said, struggling to speak with his mouth full.

"That's right. One of Albert's accounts. It was his agency. After Nine/Eleven I wanted a place outside the city. I mean really far outside the city. This place is really far. In the old days it took us four and a half hours to get up here in a car. Except I came here alone, mostly. Albert wanted to be in the Hamptons. I guess you could say our interests diverged. I'd accumulated some real estate in the city over the years with my modeling money, in Chelsea and the West Village. I had my own income from rentals in them. After the Wall Street crash, New York got very depressing. I spent more and more time up here. By then, Andrea, our daughter, was off in Berkeley. Of course the place was a wreck when we first got it."

"The barn out there looks new," Robert said.

"It was built last year."

"You do it yourself?"

"God, no."

"Who renovated the house?"

"I had some help."

"They did a fine job."

"Outstanding," said the doctor, who had been eating with single-minded intensity. "The whole place is charming as hell. Amazing really, considering."

"What happened to Albert?" Robert said.

"I put a spell on him."

"What kind of spell?"

"I turned him into a rat."

"I see," Robert said, though he didn't see at all.

"His whole identity was wrapped up in the agency, and when that went, well . . . I haven't been back in the city for eight years now. My property is still there, I suppose, but the rents don't come in anymore. I haven't heard from anyone in New York since the phones went out. When was that?"

"Five years ago," the doctor said. "What were your friends still doing there?"

"Waiting for things to return to normal."

"I knew people like that back in Boston," Robert said.

"They must have been very disappointed," the doctor said.

"I miss the electricity," Barbara said.

"Don't we all," Robert said.

"Ever try to set a compound fracture by candlelight?" the doctor said. "Sorry. I guess that's not really table talk."

"Your boy will come back home," Barbara said.

"You think so?"

"I know it."

"How so?"

"Just a feeling."

"We'll find him," Robert said.

"He'll come home even if you don't find him," Barbara said.

"What do you mean by that?" the doctor said.

"He'll find you again when the time comes," she said.

The doctor gazed at her a long moment, then sighed and drained his cider glass.

"More chicken pie?" she asked.

She served a sweet pudding of walnut and quince afterward. They lingered at the table, drinking cider and brandy, talking about the old days, three people of middle age whose lives had turned upside down and inside out, who remembered cars and television and paying for things with plastic cards, and the great thrumming engine of modernity that history had driven into a ditch. Eventually the men found their eyelids drooping as fatigue and drink overcame them. Instead of the hayloft, Barbara offered them each a regular bed in the house.

"I have rooms galore."

"You're very kind," the doctor said. "You run a tab on us. I've got enough silver. People pay me real money now and then."

"There's nothing wrong with money," she said.

She took the men upstairs and steered each to a well-appointed room with a full bed, crisp clean linens, and lofty feather quilts. It was chilly upstairs and the men fell asleep as if drugged.

Much later that night, Robert dreamed that Barbara Maglie came to him under a ceiling of summer stars in startling unclothed fullness, smelling of fragrant garden herbs, with flowers in her silver hair, offering the wet and yielding center of herself, and promises of open-ended delight in a secret realm. The dream went on and on and he woke up panting with the light of dawn pouring through his east-facing window, wondering if Barbara Maglie had actually stolen into his room during the night. Otherwise he could not remember an erotic dream as vivid and prolonged as this one. Had she put a spell on him? How was it possible that such a woman did not have a man? As his mind reeled, Robert remembered the young woman who had come to share his own house and bed back in Union Grove, and who, with her seven-year-old daughter, comprised his family now. He shook his head at the dangerous thought that lurked at the margin of his consciousness and prepared to pull his pants on.

In the room next door the doctor had a dream as powerful and confusing as Robert's. Barbara Maglie came to him as the most intimate companion he had ever known. He woke up short of breath on a damp spot in the sheets, at once amazed and embarrassed at the first wet dream he'd had since med school. Had she put something in his food or cider? Some hallucinogen, a fragment of mushroom or scraping of toad, a sprig of wormwood? Or maybe she had not employed any chemical artifice at all, and the dream was merely the product of her magnetism. How could such a woman not have a man, he wondered. He got up and caught sight of himself in a mirror over the chest of drawers. The gaunt, bearded figure there was a stranger to him.

The men came downstairs a few minutes apart to find Barbara busy at her stove frying potatoes in bacon fat and preparing to scramble up a half dozen eggs to go with them and last night's corn bread. They ate gratefully but abashedly, speaking only of the boy they were searching for and how to recognize him in case he wandered by. In the chance that Jasper did come by her place, the doctor asked Barbara not to tell the boy that they were out searching for him, and she said she understood perfectly.

When the doctor went to the outhouse, Barbara brought a refreshed teapot to the table and sat down across from Robert.

"Did you sleep well?" she asked.

"Like a box of rocks," he said.

"Any dreams?"

"Sure," he said, working to avoid her gaze.

"Men pay me for what they see in their dreams," she said.

Robert looked up at that. "Excuse me?"

"How do you think I get by?"

"I wondered, frankly."

"Did you like your dream?"

"Was it an advertisement?"

"It was your dream. You'd be joining a very select group. Only silver coin when you come, no paper."

"It's a long ride up here from Union Grove."

"Some come from farther away than that."

"I don't know what to say."

"You don't have to say anything now. Just don't tell anyone—not your companion, the doctor, not anybody. This is just between the two of us."

"All right," Robert said.

When the doctor returned, he said it was time for the two of them to push on and that he was going out to saddle his horse. Robert took a turn in the outhouse. When he was done there, he saw the doctor and Barbara Maglie in the paddock behind the barn. They appeared deep in conversation and seemed to stop suddenly when they saw him coming up the path. Robert wondered, naturally, whether Barbara had tendered an offer to the doctor, too. He went straight to the barn to fetch his saddle and things. When he was ready, they both mounted up and bade farewell to Barbara Maglie, thanking her for her kindness and hospitality and reminding her what the boy looked like, in case he should turn up—while trying to avoid the mutual recognition that each now carried a secret.

She walked with them as far as her vegetable garden and, brushing loose strands of hair out of her face in a rising chill breeze, watched as they turned out past the leafless lilac bushes, up the open road.

EIGHTEEN

Ned Allison turned up early at the Congregational church school knowing that this time of year his teacher, Jane Ann Holder, came in a half hour before class to fire up the woodstove. School was far from what it had been in the old times. Mrs. Holder managed a classroom with children ranging from seven to fifteen. Formal education in Union Grove ended there. Young people sixteen and older with ambition entered apprenticeships or the few family businesses like the Allisons' livery and Einhorn's store, while the dull ones went to work as farm laborers. As far as anyone knew, college had been discontinued entirely in this region of the United States. The local colleges—Greer, a four-year liberal arts school in Excelsior Springs, twenty-five miles to the west, Bennington College, an equivalent hike to the east, and Washington County Community College—had all closed years ago. One heard as little about higher education in America as about the doings of the putative president, Harvey Allbright, who supposedly headed what remained of the federal government, now relocated to Minneapolis since the bombing of Washington, DC. No young person in Union Grove was prevented from improving his or her mind beyond what the church school offered. The town library was still a going concern, open six days and five nights a week under the care of the polymath Andrew Pendergast.

Ned Allison found his teacher feeding splints to the stove and actually startled her when he stole over and touched her on the shoulder.

"You're here early," she said, blinking. Her breath was visible.

"Robert Earle and the doc went out looking for Jasper," Ned said.

"Yes, I heard," Jane Ann said.

"They didn't come back last night, though."

"I suppose they'll ride around the county until they find him."

"I don't know if they will," Ned said.

"They'll find him," Jane Ann said. "Or maybe he'll come back on his own."

"I'm real worried. Someone should know what we saw."

"What did you see?"

"The other day, down by the river, we were spying on the hermit."

Jane Ann knew who the hermit was and where he made his home.

"You shouldn't spy on people."

"The hermit, he was doing something . . . bad."

"What was he doing?"

"I don't know how to say."

"Try."

Ned rolled his eyes.

He had his . . . thing out."

"His . . . male thing?"

"Yes."

"Where were you when he did that?"

"On the riverbank across from his shack. We had a real clear view through the window. He was weeping and carrying on."

"Did he see you?"

"That's what I'm worried about. I went to leave, but Jas he lagged behind a while longer. I wonder if the hermit saw him."

Jane Ann fed more splints into the woodstove and stood up.

"I wonder if maybe he snatched him on his way to school," Ned said. "Or something like that."

"Snatched him?" Jane Ann said, taken aback. She knew quite a bit about the imagined fears of children, and she had assumed that the hermit, Perry Talisker, was harmless despite his isolation from the life of the town. What if her assumptions were wrong, she wondered.

"What would he do with him?" she heard herself wonder out loud.

"I don't know," Ned said. "That's what I'm worried about."

NINETEEN

Perry Talisker locked up his shack on the river and set out in God's radiant morning light to hunt down a catamount. He was outfitted lightly, for peak efficiency, in a waxed canvas coat, with a thin wool blanket slung and tied over one shoulder. Over the other he carried a lever-action Marlin rifle chambered for the .30-30 cartridge, of which he had many boxes, stockpiled during the last months when he still received a paycheck from the Hovington supermarket chain, just as the country was heading straight into the tank. He was pleased this morning also to be wearing the tracker moccasins he'd recently finished sewing himself, with cow leather soles and fringed deerskin uppers that rode above the top of his powerful calf muscles.

In daylight, the Dark One he suspected of corrupting his spirit and lurking in the hidden corners of ordinary life did not maintain its maddening pull over him. But he felt no more comfortable thinking that God was watching over him and judging his every thought. So what did it matter whether you gave your bond to the light or the dark? Each was a despot in its own way, he thought.

Preoccupied as he was, Perry did not fail to notice the spectacular beauty of the river, the golden leaves shimmering in a breeze, trout dimpling the pool upstream of the house, the flight path of a barred owl winging home silent and ghostly after a night of mousing, the rich perfumes of the autumn woods and living water, the eternal music of the rushing stream. All these sensations filled him with a joy that transcended the quarrels of his mind. For the moment, then, he settled on the notion that he was venturing out in defiance of both spectral forces, bringing to his task a nascent third force with its own lonesome sacredness of human will. He would make his way across the country in their full view and he would act as he had prepared himself to act.

He intended to scour the rugged rural township between Hebron and the place where the Hudson River looped west toward Glens Falls. The human population in that corner of Washington County had dwindled away to almost nothing in the years since everything went to hell. The high rocky ridge of hills known as the Gavottes made farming difficult there. Hebron itself was nearly a ghost town now, having been especially hard-hit by the encephalitis that traveled in the wake of the deadly Mexican flu. The remaining deer herds found refuge from jackers in this empty part of the county— few people respected the idea of hunting season in the face of universal hardship. It was there, in the rugged Gavottes, living off the deer herds, where the big cats denned up, raised their young, and hid from their dwindling human adversaries. Now and then one would range down into the farming townships, including one big female that had reportedly killed a four-year-old boy in the parlor of a house in the glen behind Vail Hill.

Whatever his relations with the hidden entities who animated the world, Perry Talisker felt fully alive and keen for the hunt, a healthy animal in his own right, ranging wide-eyed and alert into the glorious autumn landscape.

TWENTY

Jasper Copeland slept well in the ruined mobile home. His body heat alone had brought the temperature up ten degrees in the small, tight bedroom. After roasting and devouring all but one of his remaining potatoes, he had set out on the road again eager to walk off the morning chill and determined to get to the shining city of Glens Falls as soon as possible. He had traveled six miles up the pot-holed and fissured county Route 30 since he departed.

Jasper was practiced in the art of telling time by the position of the sun in the sky. He knew it rode lower above the horizon at this time of year and he calculated that it was about noon. He was hungry again. He stood now on a little rise in the road surveying a farmhouse a quarter mile in the distance. Behind it was a pasture dotted with tiny specks of animals—goats or sheep—too distant to make out. Smoke rose out of one of several chimneys. He decided to venture down and ask whoever was in the house for some articles of food that he was unlikely to glean from the fields and orchards—corn bread, cheese, butter, jam, perhaps some ham or sausage. Minutes later he presented himself at what he presumed to be a kitchen door, since the little porch to it was full of cabbages and squashes, and red peppers hung from the disintegrating fretwork around the roof. A thin, blowsy woman who was older than his mother answered his timid knocks. After opening the door to reveal the large kitchen within, the woman wiped her hands on a soiled apron and regarded him with suspicion. Beads of perspiration glistened on her forehead and upper lip as though she'd been exerting herself. She drew a spray of auburn hair out of her eyes.

"You by yourself?" she asked.

"Huh?" Jasper said. He thought it was obvious he was by himself. "Yes, just me, ma'am."

"Sometimes pickers work in teams," the woman said.

"I'm not a picker," Jasper said.

"What are you then?"

"I'm just a boy."

"What do you want?"

"Nothing."

"Then why did you knock on the door?"

"Just wondering if you could spare some food."

The woman gazed at him a long moment as though trying to figure him out.

"Where are you from?" she asked.

"Not from around here."

"Give me a straight answer."

"I'm from Bennington," Jasper said, mentioning a town he'd heard of many times but never been to.

"My brother Ellis lives there," the woman said. "Ellis Lovejoy. Do you know him?"

"I might have heard of him."

"He's county magistrate."

"Then I must have heard of him?"

"Sounds like you're not sure.

"No, I surely have heard of him."

"What are you doing so far from home?"

"I'm going to Glens Falls."

"By yourself? On foot?"

"Yes."

"How come?"

"My family all died. I'm an orphan."

The woman recoiled.

"What'd they die of?"

"Mexican flu."

"That was some years ago."

"Yes. I lived with my aunt and uncle for a while after that."

"What happened to them?"

"They died, too."

"What of?"

"Uncle died of ulcerative colitis and Aunt killed herself."

"What do you know of ulcerative colitis?"

"You get bloody diarrhea and vomiting."

"How do you know all this?"

"I was studying to be a doctor."

"Who with?"

"My father."

"He was a doctor?"

"Yes. Trained in a college, with the license and all."

"He must have started you out young."

"When I was practically a little tiny baby."

"And you say he let the flu get him?"

"He was with patients who had it."

"And how come you didn't get it?"

"Lucky, I guess."

"Well, I'm sorry you lost your folks. Do you have more people in Glens Falls?"

"Not that I know of."

"Then why are you going there?"

"They need doctors there."

"Oh?" She glanced furtively within. "We could use one here."

"You have a sick person here?"

"My father's unwell." The woman's turned her penetrating gaze back to Jasper, but this time she nibbled the inside of her lip.

"I'll see him," Jasper said.

"What's your name, boy?"

"John Hopkins," Jasper said, trying to invoke the place where his father went to medical school, the only doctorish-sounding name he knew.

"You wait here."

The woman withdrew inside the house, leaving Jasper on the kitchen doorstep worrying that he would be exposed as a fraud, while gnawing hunger vied equally for his attention. She returned quickly.

"He wants you to come in," she said.

She ushered Jasper inside. The woman had been preparing cabbages for sauerkraut on a big folding table. She had half filled a plastic tub with cabbage shreds, and many other heads waited to be sliced up. The kitchen was a chaotic operation. Baskets, sacks, pans, vessels, peelings, husks, and assorted garbage cluttered the counters. A steel sink was piled high with dirty dishes. Cabbage debris littered the floor around her workplace.

From there they passed through a formal dining room, also disorderly, with jumbles of items piled around—old electric appliances, a television, big audio speakers, obsolete power tools, a computer monitor, things that vehemently proclaimed their own uselessness. Eventually they arrived at a dimly curtained bedroom. A large older man sat there in a battered plush chair. He wore a filthy old shirt that had once been white and a pair of equally shabby drawers with lobsters printed on the fabric. The room smelled of decay.

"Here he is, Papa."

"So you're the doc."

"Yessir."

"A child doc. Aren't I the lucky one?"

Jasper didn't reply.

"I'm told your papa was a doc."

"That's so."

"How could you really know anything?"

Jasper reflected a moment. "I've seen a lot," he said.

"I don't know that I trust you to know what you're doing."

"I can just be on my way," Jasper said.

"No, wait," the woman said. Jasper hadn't actually moved. "He's got boils."

"Is that so?" Jasper asked the man.

"Yes it is."

"You can show me."

The man took off his shirt with some difficulty. He had a boil the size of a pullet egg beside a saggy, milk-colored left pectoral, another in the region of his left underarm, two in the region of the right.

"There's two more down around here," he said, indicating his groin.

Jasper asked the woman to throw open the curtains. As she did, mild north light flooded the room.

"Do you want me to treat them?" Jasper asked.

"I guess I do," the man said.

"I'll need some things," Jasper said. "A lighted candle, a pot of boiled water, a pot of regular water, some strong soap, a needle, and some jack cider or whiskey or brandy with a glass. Also some clean rags, and please boil up a couple of them with that water. Can you gather up those things?"

The woman said, "I'll try," and left the room.

"You ever seen a case like this before?" the man said.

"Yes," Jasper said.

"It hurts."

"I would think so."

They remained in a globe of silence for some time after that. The man emitted occasional grunts of discomfort. Jasper stood before him trying to fix his gaze on anything but the man. Through the window he could see a pasture with six Nubian nanny goats grazing in it. He was half sorry he had chosen this house to stop at, but another part of him was eager to treat his first patient. Eventually, the woman returned with all the things he'd asked for, though she had to make several trips.

"This is plum brandy," she said. "Will it do?"

"Is it strong?"

"Very. I made it myself."

"Okay."

Jasper scrubbed his hands in the pot of regular water, then fished the boiled rag out of the hot water. He made a lather with the soap and the rag and very gently washed the surface of the boils on the man's upper body. Then he asked the man to remove his drawers and he washed the boils on his groin and thigh. He observed an eczematous rash around the man's nether parts as well.

"Ma'am," he said.

"Yes?"

"Fill that glass about half full with the brandy."

She did.

"Give it to him."

She did.

The man held the glass up before his face and looked at it angrily.

"Drink it down, mister," Jasper said.

"What for?"

"I don't have any laudanum."

"I don't believe in drinking before sundown."

"You only have to do it this once."

He raised the glass and drank the contents in five large swallows, then sucked in a lungful of air. Jasper twisted up one of the clean rags and proffered it to the man.

"Bite on this."

He took it and did so, making an incongruously high-pitched gleep of dread as he bit down. The woman started to leave the room.

"I'll need you to stay and help," Jasper told her. She returned to her place behind him. "Light that candle you brought in." He poured brandy all over his hands and rubbed them. Then he poured on some more, lavishly.

"Lord," the woman muttered. "What a waste."

"Do you have that needle?"

"Yes," she said.

"Hold it in the candle flame. Then pour some brandy on it."

Jasper soaked one of the rags in brandy and carefully swabbed down the boils.

"Hand me that needle," he said, and then systematically set about piercing the white head of each boil and draining it. Then he swabbed them all down with brandy again, which caused the man to squirm and make noises that sounded like cursing with the rag clamped in his mouth.

"Okay, that does it," Jasper said.

The man spit out the rag and drew in a series of sharp, pained breaths.

"Do you know how come you got like this?" Jasper asked.

"God don't like me, I suppose."

"I don't know whether that's so or not," Jasper said. "But boils come from being filthy. You have to wash more regularly than you do. You have to change your clothes once in a while."

"You a professional scold, too?" the man said.

Jasper didn't answer. He turned to the woman and said, "You should fetch him some clean clothes. Swab him down with brandy again before supper. And see to it he changes his underwear twice a day at least for the next week or he'll just get infected again. If you do that, these ones might heal up and he won't get any more."

"All right."

"I'm done then."

Jasper dripped more brandy over his hands.

"Jesus," the woman said.

They left the old man in the dim bedroom and returned to the kitchen.

"I suppose you want to get paid," the woman said when they got there.

"I wouldn't mind," Jasper said. He'd seen his father negotiate the difficult issue many times, with people who had little to give in trade for services.

"I can't give you any money," the woman said. "We don't have any."

"I'll take food," Jasper said. "I could use some cheese and sausage."

"Don't have any."

"You've got six nanny goats out there. How could you not have cheese?"

"You're a little smart-ass."

He asked about corn bread, butter, and honey. She said they were out.

"What else have you got?" he asked.

"I've got cabbage."

"I'll take a cabbage.

"Take two."

"I can't carry two."

"That's a pity. I've got cabbage all day long."

"Is there anything else you can spare?"

"I've got some apples."

"I can pick all the apples I want along my way."

"Isn't that nice? You steal from folks?"

"What about those butternuts in the basket over on that counter?"

"They're all we have. I can't spare any."

"Are you sure you don't have any cheese?"

"Goddamn it!" she shouted back, rising visibly out of the heels of her shabby shoes. "What's the matter with you? You deaf? We don't have any damn cheese."

"I'll take the rest of that brandy, then."

"I'm not giving brandy to a child."

"It's for doctoring."

"I can't spare any."

"I don't believe you don't have cheese."

"Are you calling me a liar?"

"No."

"Of course you are."

"I'll just take a cabbage and be gone, if you don't mind."

"I don't know that I care to give you anything now, you little smart-ass. Calling me a liar."

"I didn't call you liar."

The woman glanced furtively around, grabbed a weeding hook off an empty curtain rod where it hung, and brandished it at Jasper.

"You get out of here right now or you're gonna have to doctor yourself. Get out!" she shrieked.

Twenty-one

Billy Bones perched hungrily on a large glacial rock that anchored one corner of a forsaken rural cemetery along old Route 30. He felt a gaping emptiness in his midsection and cinched up the tired old belt that held up his filthy striped pants. He had eaten nothing but apples all day and he was sick of them. They hurt his stomach and made him vomit. The previous night he'd had only acorns for supper. But they required too much preparation, and he could barely gag them down.

He'd passed several farmhouses along his way and had more than half a mind to venture a burglary, but he lacked the patience to stake out any house long enough to determine how well defended it might be, and he didn't want to rush into a situation where someone might cut him a new rectum, or worse. He imagined—but didn't know for sure, lacking good orienteering skills—that he was still more than a day shy of his objective: Madam Amber's fancy house in Glens Falls, which he considered his base of operations. Madam Amber let him stay there and even fed him in consideration for doing odd jobs, some of them rather unsavory. And if he returned from an outing on the roads with any takings in cash money, she let him enjoy the girls, of course. A number of the girls would have consorted with him free of charge, since he exerted a certain peculiar charm, but Madam Amber ran a disciplined enterprise and didn't allow giveaways. She would even punish a girl if she found out about it.

Billy Bones now huddled against the afternoon chill, listening to the dry oak leaves rustle overhead and longing for a plate of Madam Amber's fried trout and eggs, a house specialty, when down below his perch, he saw Jasper Copeland round a bend in the road. Jasper trudged along with his eyes downcast, since it was so easy to trip on the broken pavement.

Billy Bones was both thrilled and disturbed to see what appeared to be someone ripe for picking. Being nearsighted, he thought for a moment that the approaching figure was a small man, perhaps even a dwarf—in any case, a person capable of defending himself, perhaps desperately and viciously so, since it was unusual even in these hard times for a solitary child to wander the byways. But as Jasper drew closer, Billy Bones quickly sized up his quarry as a boy indeed, and slipped off the back of the rock when Jasper had trudged past. He skulked around the weed-filled graves through a gap in the ancient cast-iron fence and presented himself to Jasper's back.

"A good afternoon to you, little vagabond." he called out.

Jasper wheeled around stoically.

"By yourself, then?" Billy Bones asked.

"No," Jasper said.

"You look alone."

"My brothers and uncle are not far behind me."

"Is that right?"

"Are you a picker?" Jasper asked.

"I'm more than that. How far behind would they be?"

"Who?"

"Your people."

"Just a little way. Can't you hear them?"

Billy Bones cocked his head and perked an ear in the direction Jasper had come from.

"I don't hear anything. You must be weary, boy. Cast off your sack and rest a while."

Jasper didn't respond.

"I said drop your sack!" Billy Bones repeated. Then he opened his leather coat to reveal his weapons. Jasper put his backpack down gingerly on the pavement and backed away. Billy Bones came forward and squatted down to rummage inside it. He almost instantly found Jasper's one remaining potato, held it up triumphantly, and took a big sharp bite as if it were a less than perfectly ripe pear. He turned it over in his hand, regarding it while he chewed, as though struggling to unravel its mysteries. "Where all's that supposed family of yours, then?"

"They're almost here," Jasper said. "I can hear them."

"You keep saying that. Where all's you going to today?"

"We're going home, just up the road. Less than a mile. Mom and Dad and three uncles and my five older brothers."

"No sisters or aunts in the family?"

"Just men."

"Is that right? Your mom a man, too?"

"Of course not."

"Where all's you been?"

"Union Grove."

"That's a pissant town."

"It's all right—"

"Don't contradict me! I say it's pissant. Full of Jesus jokers and he-shes. I don't give a good goddamn about that town. I curse it."

"What did it ever do to you?"

"Never mind. And one more thing: You don't have any family coming down the road here. You're by your lonely, I'm quite certain."

Jasper did not reply.

Billy Bones chewed up the rest of the potato.

"I hate a raw potato," he said.

"Then why didn't you roast it up first?"

"I don't have time for cookery. I got places to go and people to see."

"You are a picker."

"I'm a bandit, goddamn it. That's several steps above your picker, understand?"

"I don't see any difference."

"A picker doesn't have a song. You want to hear my song?"

"You're going to sing a song?"

"You're goddamned straight I am. Listen now."

Billy Bones shoved the backpack into the pavement and stood up. He sang his introductory verses and then two more stanzas in his customary nasal drone:

"The ladies know young Billy Bones
Whose kisses are like candy
And when they see what's in his pants
It makes them good and randy.

They moan and groan and shake it up
And love him till they're weeping
But Billy is too smart to stay
In any one woman's keeping."

When he was finished he asked, "You like how I made those rhymes up?"

"Is it about yourself?"

"Well, hell, it's my song. 'Course it is."

"What do you need a song for? The people you rob don't care to hear about you."

"Well, they got to hear it whether they like it or not. That's how a legend is born. Imagine how they go and tell their people they came upon this audacious bandit that sings about his exploits, and the tale spreads. I'm known far and wide."

"I don't see why you'd want to be known. Sooner or later, men are going to hunt you down."

"They can try. I guess it hasn't happened yet. I'll stand my ground with the best."

"Are you done robbing me?"

"I haven't robbed nothing but a damn potato. And there's no one coming up the road behind you. Why don't you just tell it straight?"

Jasper rolled his eyes and shifted his weight from one foot to the other but did not reply.

"Am I boring you?" Billy Bones asked.

"No, this is the most fun I had all day except when I had to treat this old man for disgusting boils and then his daughter cheated me out of my pay."

"What do you know about boils?"

"I'm a doctor."

"I never heard such a tale. A boy doctor?"

"My father is the doctor of Union Grove and I help him all the time. I know medicine and I'm setting out to be a doctor on my own."

"Had enough of childhood, then?

"I guess I have."

"What about your homefolks?"

"They're home and I'm here."

Billy bones chuckled with admiration.

"You must not like that pissant Union Grove much yourself," he said, "if you're striking out on your own at such a tender age."

"I had to go. I've done deeds as bad as yours."

"Such as what?"

"I'm not going to tell you."

"You kill someone?"

"Something like that."

"Aren't you a doozy! Well, I'll tell you what. I'm not going to rob nothing more of your things. See, this is the main difference between a picker and bandit, besides having a personal song. A picker is a low-down cowardly parasite like a rat or a bug. A bandit, he's a gallant soul with a sense of fun and honor, too. I don't rob little children. In fact, I could use a sidekick with your accomplishments and experience, especially if you're such a dangerous desperado as you say. How'd you like to be the sidekick of the bandit Billy Bones?"

"I just want to be on my way."

"Goddamn it, I've got a proposition for you. You say some people cheated you? I say, let's go see about that. I'm at your service, my young friend, along with Blast'em and Slice'em." Billy Bones held open his leather coat again and gestured toward the pistol in his waistband and the brush knife that hung off his belt. "Now where'd this happen with the boils and all?"

"Just back up the road a bit," Jasper told him.

Twenty-two

Billy Bones and Jasper Copeland watched the house from a thicket in the woods above the farmhouse. A witch-hazel shrub there blazed yellow in its strange fall flowering. Jasper recognized it from foraging botanicals with his father. He cut off some switches with his knife and stuffed them in his pack.

"What the hell are you doing?" Billy said.

"It's a medicine tree."

"Where'd you get that knife?"

"It's mine."

"Let me see it."

Jasper handed it over.

"Nice," Billy said, turning it over in his hand. "I'll let you keep it, long as you don't try to stick it in me."

"I won't stick it in you."

"You bet you won't, little desperado. Now lookit here. . . ."

Billy instructed Jasper to go down to the kitchen door while he, Billy, sneaked around to the blind side of the building where the old garage stood along with a small barn and a half-collapsed corn crib.

"Go on now. Go down there."

"What am I going to say?"

"Ask her to have pity on you and give you some food. Tell her you're an orphan."

"I already tried that. She said she'd carve me up with a weeding hook."

"We'll see about that. I'll be right behind you."

"I'm scared."

"No you're not. Not really. You just think you are. I can tell what a plucky young vagabond you are, deep down. If you play your cards right, I might make you my protégé."

"I don't want to be a bandit. I can doctor."

"Who says you can't be both? Especially when you practically have to rob folks to get paid these days. You get along now and do what I told you."

Jasper trudged down the hill, through a ragged field of winter squashes and pumpkins, and climbed the steps up the porch to the kitchen door. He waited there for a moment, feeling exposed and panicked before rapping on the door's glass pane. When the door swung open, the same blowsy woman presented herself. She stood with her hands on her hips and her mouth open in an expression somewhere between consternation and horror at the sight of Jasper.

"You again! What do you want?"

"Please ma'am. I'm an orphan and I'm very hungry. Surely you can spare a little cornmeal and bacon."

She glared at him a moment, then softened slightly.

"All right, damn you. But don't you come inside this time. Wait out here."

As soon as she turned back inside, Billy Bones tiptoed up the porch steps, slithered around Jasper, and entered the kitchen like a weasel entering a poultry house. Jasper heard a sharp cry—the woman—and then Billy calling for him to come inside, too. Jasper entered the house and found Billy red-faced, brandishing his big pistol before the woman, who stood quivering against the sink.

"I knew you were a picker, you little shit," she said to Jasper, practically spitting.

"Pickers?" Billy cried. "Goddamn it, we're bandits!" He proceeded to explain the distinction before offering to sing his ballad.

"Keep your song to yourself, you scum," she said.

"Scum?" Billy said. "Us? My protégé here doctors you up and all he asks is a little supper and you threaten him with a weed hook? A goddamn child! Don't you have a motherly bone in that ugly carcass? I got half a mind to gut-shoot you."

He waved the pistol closer to her face. The woman screamed. A commotion down the hall signaled the arrival of the father. He had barely stepped into the room when Billy Bones shoved the muzzle of the pistol up against his face. The terrified man, in obvious pain, had changed into different clothing that was not much cleaner than the outfit Jasper had found him in earlier. Billy Bones appeared to swell upward like an orchestra conductor summoning a momentous chord and then brought the butt of his pistol crashing into the side of the man's head. He hit the floor like a grain sack. Blood poured out of a gash above his ear.

"Guess who won't be getting doctored now?" Billy muttered. "Too damn bad." The woman continued screaming. "Shut up!" he said. "Or you'll be down there with him!" Then to Jasper: "While I sing my song, see what you can find in these cabinets. Go on!"

Jasper brought a wobbly chair over to the cabinets and stood on it as he rummaged through them. The woman fell into sobs while Billy sang half a dozen quatrains of his song and the man remained motionless on the floor. Jasper found two jars of cider jelly in one cabinet and a jar of dried lima beans in another. A ceramic jar decorated like a keg contained coarse-ground cornmeal. He emptied a quart jar of dried rose hips onto the floor and scooped the jar full of the meal. Wild rose hips were rampant this time of year. He jammed the box of shelled butternuts into his backpack. All he found in the remaining cabinets was a small jar of honey.

By this time, Billy Bones concluded his song. He asked the woman where she kept her cheese and meats.

She pointed to a door and said, "Cold room," before resuming her sobs.

Jasper didn't have to be told to look in there. On an otherwise bare shelf he found a jagged cake of hard cheese under a brown bowl and two onions with the field dirt still on them.

"No butter," he said, stuffing the cheese into his sack.

"We don't have a cow," the woman said between sobs.

"Any hams or bacon in there?" Billy yelled across the room.

"None that I can see." On a pantry counter on the other side of the cold room, among stacks of old soup plates, platters, tureens, and other items for table service, Jasper spied the same bottle of plum brandy that he had used as a disinfectant a few hours before. It was still half full. "There's a bottle of brandy in here."

"You don't say! Hot damn."

"I don't have room for it in my pack."

"You let me worry about that bottle. Bring her on out."

Jasper came back and handed over the bottle. Billy held it at arm's length, regarding it with a look of incandescent satisfaction. He pulled the wooden stopper and glugged down three big swallows.

"Ah!" he said. "That's what I call medicine!" Then, to the woman, he growled, "Where's the money?"

"What money?"

"The money you got."

"There's no money here," she said.

Billy dipped his upper body in a guffaw.

"Do I have to tear the place apart? I will."

She did not answer, so he set the liquor bottle on the table among the cabbages, dragged her out of the room, and down the hall. While they were gone, Jasper searched through the kitchen drawers, finding little besides a jar of red chili pepper seeds. Somewhere vaguely overhead, he heard things bang around along with muffled voices and cries and sobs. The man on the floor stirred once and groaned but did not get up. Soon Billy Bones returned to the kitchen without the woman. Thumping sounds above suggested to Jasper that Billy had locked the woman up.

"Feel this here," Billy said, indicating a lump on the side of his pants. "Go ahead, touch it."

Jasper fingered the lump. He surmised it was a pocketful of coins.

"Bunch of silver coin and one gold half eagle," Billy said. "I'm rich! How's the old mister doing?"

"He moved."

"He's lucky I didn't kill him," Billy said, directing his voice to the body on the floor. "And if he knows what's good for him, he'll lay low right there for the next half hour or so, or sure as my name is Billy Bones I will put a bullet in the back of his head."

With that, Billy used hand gestures to tell Jasper that they should go. Jasper slung on his pack and followed Billy out the door. Billy led him around the house to the other side where the goats were browsing in a nubbly paddock.

"Take this and wait here," he told Jasper, handing him the brandy bottle.

Billy let himself into the paddock through a gate of battered steel pipe and rusty chain-link. The goats came to him as if they knew him. He stooped to pet them. Jasper didn't really apprehend the exact moment when Billy caught one of the smaller goats in a headlock, drew the bush knife off his belt, and slit the animal's throat. The goat kicked two or three times and made a gurgling noise. The other goats skittered across the paddock and then went about their browsing, insensible to what had happened. Billy stooped to the carcass on the ground. When he was sure it was dead, he separated the little goat's head from its body in a few deft strokes. Jasper took it all in with a sense of paralyzing despair. He watched as Billy picked up the goat's head, held it above his own, and ran across the paddock to where the other goats browsed, as if to gambol with them. They scattered. He seemed to lose interest in this game almost instantly and chucked the goat's head among the other goats. He returned to the dead goat, gutted it, butchered off its hindquarters, and left the rest in a red heap. Finally, holding each hindquarter like a club, he left the paddock and shut the gate behind him.

"What'd you do that for?" Jasper asked.

"You like meat for your supper, don't you?"

Jasper did not reply.

"Don't look at me like that," Billy said. "That's what it takes to get meat in this world. Something has to give up its life, you know. I don't relish doing it. You eat meat, don't you?"

"Yes."

"All right, then. Come on, let's get out of here. I left my sack in those woods up the hill. We'll find a hideout for the night and have a fine supper and get warm and I'll school you in the ways of the road."

They proceeded together back across the field of pumpkin and squashes.

"What did you do with the woman?" Jasper asked halfway up the hill.

"I tied her to a bed frame. The old geezer'll untie her."

"What if he doesn't wake up again?"

"He'll be all right."

"We don't know how bad he's injured."

"What's it to you if he ever gets off that floor?"

"Who'll untie that woman?"

"What do you care?" Billy said, slinging his bag over his shoulder. "She was going to take a weeding hook to you. Come on, let's get out of here."

TWENTY-THREE

Robert Earle and Dr. Jerry Copeland rode southwest on the Coot Hill Road, watchful and glum in the fading daylight. They had been crisscrossing the roads between Hebron and Argyle all day long, using an old topo map from the U.S. Geological Survey that had been folded and unfolded so many times over the years it barely hung together. They had seen many curious things since leaving Barbara Maglie's house that morning—a red-tailed hawk eating a pine martin, a man being flogged in an apple orchard while nine other men on his crew looked on, a dead ox rotting in a locust grove off the Goose Island Road—but they encountered no sign whatever of the doctor's son.

Robert and the doctor had ridden most of the day in silence, each lost in observation and thought. Now the doctor became aware that his horse was walking just a little off its customary gait. He dismounted, took a position at the horse's forequarter, and hoisted up its leg.

"He's lost a shoe," the doctor said.

Robert knew what that meant but also knew that it was the doctor's call. He remained silent in his saddle.

"We'll have to go back," the doctor said. "For now."

It was eleven miles back to Union Grove. Leading their horses on foot, they knew they would not get back to town before dark.

The silence persisted as they marched into the low-hanging sun.

The tiny hamlet of Argyle still had a store, an ancient establishment offering a scant array of local trade goods: grain, honey, eggs and milk, bacon, dried fruit, sauerkraut, candles, jack cider, old and new furniture, and tinware. The proprietor, one Miles English, was a man of fifty with a head too small for his body, like a chicken's. He was just closing for the day, locking the front door of the old brick building, which had been a store since the time William Henry Harrison occupied the White House. For a while in the twentieth century it had even featured a pair of gasoline pumps out front. They were long gone now. When Robert and the doctor came by, Miles English was not altogether pleasant about seeing to their needs, but he grudgingly reopened the store for them. The doctor bought a pint of 100-proof jack and took a long pull from the bottle as soon as he got his hands on it.

"Don't drink in the store," English said.

"We've come a long way."

"I don't care where you come from or where you're going. Just don't drink in the store."

"Do you have any corn bread made up?" Robert asked.

"Meal only."

"Any cheese?"

"No cheese today."

"Sausage?"

"None today."

"A hard-boiled egg?"

"None."

"You got any food made up that doesn't require preparation?"

"This is not that kind of store."

"Dried fruit?"

"I've got dried apples."

Robert bought two pounds of dried apples wrapped in a cone of old yellowed newspaper that carried the headline ACTIVISTS PUSH TOUGHER RULES FOR TAPPING GROUNDWATER. The local section of the Glens Falls *Post-Star* was dated April 20, 2009. The price for the apples was 150 paper dollars or a dime in silver coin. The jack was 500 paper or a silver quarter. The doctor paid for all of it in silver. Robert wolfed down apple rings as English examined the coins in the meager light of a window until he appeared satisfied.

"If you eat too much of them, you'll get the shits," the doctor said.

"Mind your language in here," English said. "Anything else you need? I'd like to get on with closing up."

"We're looking for a boy," the doctor said.

"A boy for what purpose?" English said. "Sport or labor?"

The doctor glared at the storekeeper for a long moment as if trying to puzzle something out. Then, having come to a certain conclusion, he reached across the counter and seized English by the frayed collar of his threadbare flannel shirt.

"My son ran away from home some two days ago and we've been searching the county for him," he said.

"I ain't seen him."

"Are you carrying on some kind of trade in wayward boys?"

"Take it easy," English said. "You're hurting me."

"I can hurt you a lot more if you don't give me a straight answer."

"I don't trade in boys."

"Then why did you say that?"

"I don't know."

The doctor tightened his grip.

"You can explain better than that."

"Just playing the joker card," English croaked.

"It wasn't very funny."

"Okay, I'm sorry!"

The doctor let go of English's collar with a little shove so that the storekeeper bumped against the back counter, rattling a row of glass jars.

"I'm the doctor down in Union Grove. If you see a wayward boy of eleven years old around here, you send word down to me immediately. His name is Jasper Copeland."

"Yessir."

"I'm going to ask around about you in the meantime. If it turns out you're selling wayward boys out of here, you'll be a storekeeper in this county no longer. Do we understand each other?"

English nodded vigorously.

Robert, still chomping on his dried apples, followed the doctor out the door and they resumed their march homeward.

TWENTY-FOUR

The Reverend Loren Holder, sitting at the table of his spacious rectory kitchen, studied the sun going down over Pumpkin Hill until it vanished with a little orange flash. Not long afterward, his wife, Jane Ann, came in from foraging mushrooms behind the reservoir at the edge of town. She put the basket on the kitchen table where her husband might admire them, being an enthusiastic cook. But he seemed lost in thought.

"I came back from school at noon," she said, "but you weren't here or over in the church, either."

"Charles Pettie's father passed away. I was called over there to help make funeral arrangements."

"I didn't know he was ill."

"He wasn't. He was old. Anyway, I was over there."

"How come you didn't fire the stove?" she asked.

"I don't know," he said.

She got up and stuffed some pinecones, birch bark, and splints into the big cookstove's firebox and set a match to it. When she was satisfied the splints were going, she shoved some larger split logs in, returned to the table, and sat down.

"Are you all right?" she asked.

"I'm all right," he said.

She wasn't so sure.

"Ned Allison told me something disturbing this morning."

"What's that?"

She described what Ned thought they had seen Perry Talisker doing in his shack by the river, and she tried to convey the boy's anxiety that the hermit might have had something to do with the disappearance of Jasper Copeland. Loren seemed to come out of himself.

"I never thought the hermit was a danger to anyone," he said.

"What do we really know about him?" she asked.

Loren shifted heavily in his seat. "Nobody has ever complained about him."

"The boy is still missing," she said. "And you're the acting constable."

"This kind of thing can lead to a witch hunt," he said. "You put sex in the picture and people get hysterical."

"Somebody should at least go over and talk to him."

Loren hesitated a moment, then said, "Okay. I'll go talk to him in the morning."

"Thank you. And one more thing."

He turned to look at her directly for the first time and was struck by how beautiful she was in the sparse purple light. "What?" he asked.

"I want to apologize," she said.

"What for."

"The time with Robert."

Loren sighed. "Well, we all agreed on the arrangement," he said.

"We made a mistake. It ended up hurting both of us."

"If Robert didn't have a girl of his own now, you might still be there every Thursday night."

"Does that mean you won't accept my apology?"

"No, I will, I will," Loren said and, bringing a hand up to his brow, began to cry quietly.

Jane Ann reached across the table for his other hand, took it in both of hers, and kissed it. The fire in the cookstove was beginning to heat up the large room.

TWENTY-FIVE

Brother Jobe and five New Faith brothers stood near the edge of the woods in drizzling rain over a large hole in the ground. On the other side of the hole lay the dead stallion, Jupiter. A mule team had dragged his bloated body there from the pasture where he was poisoned. Four locust fence posts were levered under his body over the fulcrum of a thick pine log. Brother Jobe spoke a homily about how Jesus was born in a stable, a house for horses, and how the newborn king was laid in a manger, a box that horses eat out of, and how the horse therefore is imbued with the power of Jesus by the act of eating from the manger. Next he offered a prayer for the soul of Jupiter and another prayer for a fitting replacement, and then four of the brothers levered Jupiter over the edge into his grave. With tears disguised by the drizzle, Brother Jobe left them filling the hole, and returned to his quarters in the former high school.

Brother Jobe's personal quarters consisted of what had once been the high school principal's suite of offices. The outermost, where the secretary once sat, now served as his study and sitting room, while the innermost became his bedroom. The suite contained furnishings that were familiar and comfortable to him, carted all the way to Washington County, New York, from the far reaches of Virginia—a tulipwood bed, a chest of drawers that featured a bas-relief Indian head carved by his great-grandfather, an Enoch Woodard–made shelf clock that once graced the mantle of his childhood home, and a large framed photograph of his mother and father taken in the lot of their Ford automobile dealership. There was no kitchen in the suite, as Brother Jobe took his meals with the others in the school's cafeteria. He did, however, enjoy a private bathroom. He was quite satisfied with his new living arrangement.

A small sheet-metal stove had been recently installed in the bedroom, and when Brother Jobe came in from the sad chore of burying Jupiter, he found Brother Boaz laying a fire. Brother Boaz served as Brother Jobe's manservant, though he was not formally referred to as such. He simply made himself as useful as possible and was not assigned to any other duties required in such a large operation as the New Faith brotherhood. If anything, Brother Jobe referred to Brother Boaz simply as "my right hand."

A beeswax taper burned on the bedside table, throwing eerie shadows on the wall. The splints flaring in the little stove put Brother Jobe in mind of Nebuchadnezzar's fiery furnace. Sometimes, he reflected, the Lord wants to see if you can stand the heat. He remembered the night a few months earlier when the flesh of his flesh, Minor, was shot dead by the miscreant Wayne Karp. He pictured the sweet-faced visage of his wife, Hannah, who had been killed in an automobile crash before the Holy Land War put the kibosh on oil and the whole grisly spectacle of the USA carnival on wheels unraveled. He didn't miss the NASCAR, that embodiment of wickedness and foolery, one bit. Gazing into the flames, he marveled at the miraculous survival of himself and his people in the fiery furnace of the new times and wondered what further travails awaited them all. Just thinking about it all brought on the peculiar feeling of being uncomfortable in his own skin.

Shuddering, he poured himself two fingers of corn whiskey from a crystal decanter on the chest of drawers and sat gingerly on the edge of his bed. He felt a dull ache in his lower abdomen and wondered if it was something he ate. The squash pudding? The collards? The mashed turnips? They hadn't served meat in a week. A fugitive thought: Scour the countryside for piglets! Maybe, he thought further, they should have stewed poor Jupiter instead of burying him. But there was the matter of what had poisoned him, and he didn't want to poison the whole ding-dang New Faith outfit. And there was the matter of *who* poisoned him. Dwelling on the problem accentuated his feeling of dull, creepy unease.

"Anything else you might need tonight, sir?" Boaz asked.

It took Brother Jobe a few moments to come out of himself.

"You might send for Sister Susannah," he said. "There are some verses I'd like to have transcribed for Sunday."

"I'll fetch her right away, sir."

Boaz left the room. Brother Jobe peeled off his clothing, hung his black frock coat and trousers on pegs beside the chest of drawers, tossed his suit of underwear in a basket hamper, and donned a long cotton nightshirt. He wearily drew back the bedclothes and inserted his legs between the sheets as though he were filing a bad memory of himself in a folder that might be mercifully lost and forgotten in the cosmic bureaucracy of sleep. The wind was picking up outside, rattling the windowpanes in their old industrial sashes.

By and by, Boaz returned to Brother Jobe's quarters alone.

"It's Sister Susannah's time of the month," he said.

"Is that so."

"Apparently."

"Transcription of holy verse will have to wait then."

"Maybe I can help with that—"

"I'll work on accounts instead," Brother Jobe said. "Fetch Sister Annabelle."

When Boaz left, Brother Jobe reached for the small mouth harp on his bedside table and began blowing a medley of songs remembered from his Virginia homeland: "He's Gone Away," "Poor Wayfaring Stranger," "Barbara Allen," and a full-out, especially lachrymose rendition of the inevitable "Shenandoah." His performance brought tears to his own eyes. He was weeping loudly when Sister Annabelle entered the chamber.

Sister Annabelle was a stately young woman of twenty-three with a lithe figure and the dark hair and eyes of her Greek American parents who had run a chain of pizza shops from Norfolk to Richmond in the old times. She had excellent business sense and was in charge of the clothing store—the "haberdash"—that the New Faith order had recently opened on Union Grove's Main Street. She moved into place at the foot of the bed, across from the pink-faced figure weeping in his nightclothes, her strong-featured face clouded with concern.

"You sent for me?"

"I thought we might do figures," Brother Jobe said between sobs.

"Are you sure you're up to it?"

"I don't know. I'm so sad."

"I see you are."

"I could stand some consolation, I guess."

"All right, then," Annabelle said, kicking off her calfskin slippers.

"We just now laid him to rest out in yonder meadow."

"He was a beauty," she said unhooking her full skirt and allowing it to fall to the floor. Of course the news of the horse's untimely death had thundered through the community within minutes of discovery. She untied the ribbon at her throat that secured the top of her shirtwaist. With a little shake, the garment fell open at her bosom. She crossed her arms and pulled it over her head. Brother Jobe emitted a little gasp.

"I hear you know who did it," she said.

"Maybe I do."

She shinnied out of a petticoat, leaving her absolutely without clothing.

"Not one of ours?" she asked.

"Mercy, no."

"One of . . . them?" she asked, meaning an outsider, a townsperson.

Brother Jobe sighed, a rattling sigh full of phlegm and despondency.

"What are you going to do about it?" Annabelle asked, reaching behind her head to let down her long black hair.

"I can't bear to dwell on it."

She shook out her hair so that it fell over her shoulders and flowed down her breasts.

"Maybe it's better you didn't just now," she said.

TWENTY-SIX

"That just screams home sweet home to me," Billy Bones declared as he and Jasper Copeland beheld an impressive wreck of a house that was denoted on its tilted, rusted mailbox as 2438 Goose Island Road in the drizzly murk of day's end. The house had been built at the height of the real estate "bubble" years back, in a mélange of styles executed so poorly that it made no particular statement beyond the incompetence of the builders. An excess of roof articulations clearly did not define volumes of space within but rather expressed only a wish to appear more complex than necessary. But it was very large, in the manner of houses built in the final years of the old times. A charred gaping hole on the gable-end roof to the left side, along with the weedy skeletons of milkweeds and mulleins in the yard, and the darkness within, suggested that nobody had lived in the house for more than a little while.

In the old times, people of means built their houses anywhere they pleased. It was not necessary to live close to a town. It was not necessary to follow any rural way of life in the rural places. In the old times, even the few farmers who remained did not put in kitchen gardens. It was not necessary when the supermarkets overflowed with food from all over the world, and a dizzying extravaganza of foodlike products poured out of America's own factory labs, and the back roads were full of cars taking people effortlessly to indoor jobs that were also effortless, if tedious, and paid princely cash-money salaries. Houses like the one on Goose Island Road were the first to be abandoned when the times rolled over.

Billy Bones and Jasper Copeland were not the first wayfarers to sojourn in the grand house at 2438 Goose Island Road. The deadlock plate on the front doorjamb had been kicked in, the wood shattered. Billy gently shoved the door inward. It swung open with a creak to reveal a foyer more grandiose than grand. The marble floor tiles there lay cracked and broken, with several missing altogether. Water had infiltrated the Sheetrock wall from somewhere upstairs, scattering little heaps of loose gypsum on the tiles. The door blew shut and the room instantly went dim. Jasper fished a candle stub out if his pack and lit it.

"Aren't you the clever one," Billy said.

"Lighting a candle in the darkness?" Jasper said. "That's just common sense."

"Billy Bones is a creature of moonlight and starlight. What's common sense to others doesn't have any magic in it."

"There's no moon and stars tonight."

"Since when you become such a mouthy little bastard?"

"I'm tired and hungry."

"You'll have your supper soon enough. Let's have a look at the accommodations, shall we?"

Squirrels had built a nest in the chandelier that still hung in the foyer, a vulgar thing of dangling mirrored-glass rectangles, colored plastic disks, and swooping arms, overcomplicated like the house itself. To the left of the foyer, in what had been the so-called great room, with its soaring two-story ceiling, a yawning hole admitted the gray purple twilight. The broken skylight frame that once occupied the hole in the ceiling had been tossed into a far corner. Previous sojourners had built fires on the concrete slab floor under the hole in the roof despite the obvious presence of a modernistic fireplace across the room. A ring of charred rocks on the floor surrounded the carbonized remnants of the last fire.

"Nice facilities," Billy Bones said, setting down the two goat haunches. He went over to the hearth, stooped down low with his head inside it, and looked up the chimney.

"Why did they make a fire in the middle of the room?" Jasper asked.

"Trying to find out," Billy said. He worked the flue damper back and forth. "Can't see any daylight up in there," he said.

"It's pretty dark out."

"You'd see something if the chimney wasn't stopped up. I say, when in Rome, do like the goddamn Indians. We'll make our fire on the floor."

Nothing was left in the kitchen. Even the counters and cabinets had been ripped out. Animals had been visiting the master bedroom on the first floor. The slate-blue carpeting reeked of musky urine and dark shiny scats lay here and there.

"You can have this one," Billy said.

"It smells horrible," Jasper said.

"Just kidding."

They ventured upstairs. Two bedrooms on the back side of the house had been wrecked when a dead maple tree crashed through the eaves in a lightning storm, admitting the weather in a ten-foot-long gash where the wall met the ceiling. All the windows were broken. Weeds were growing in the carpet near where the light and water leaked inside. Both rooms stank ferociously. In a third bedroom across the hall, a shattered skylight had let in enough water for the hardwood floor to have heaved up its warped parquets. The bathroom was stripped of all furnishings. In what had been an adjoining dressing room the wall was splashed with something resembling great gouts of blood.

"I bet someone was murdered here," Billy said.

"Maybe the place is haunted."

"Don't say that."

"Are you afraid of ghosts?"

"I suppose you're not," Billy said, reaching into his shoulder sack for the bottle of brandy. He took a slug and proffered it to Jasper. "Have a nip."

"No thanks."

"It'll help you grow."

"I don't like liquor."

"More for me, then."

The last bedroom was dry and contained a carpet that didn't stink.

"Looks like this is where we bunk up," Billy said, tossing his sack into one corner. "That'll be my area. No trespassing, hear? Meanwhile, my belly's touching my backbone. Go get some firewood while you can still see out there and meet me back in that big room downstairs."

"All right."

When Jasper returned with a double armload of different-size branches suitable for a cook fire, Billy was carefully hanging strips of goat-leg meat over a curtain rod and skewering them on a couple of unwound wire coat hangers.

"You know how to make a fire, don't you?" he said.

"'Course I do."

Jasper had a miniature cabin of twigs alight on the floor in short order and carefully laid a succession of larger sticks on it until the fire was going strong. The smoke drafted up out of the hole in a straight column.

"Feels nice," Billy said, taking another pull from the brandy jug. "Good job. Now, what all'd we get from those folks we stopped in on?"

Jasper rummaged in his pack, took out the jars of cornmeal, lima beans, honey, cider jelly, the hunk of cheese, the box of butternuts, and the two onions.

"What a haul!" Billy said. "Seems I remember you had a little cook pot in there."

"I do."

"Get her out and do like I say now. You know how to cut up a onion?"

"Of course I do."

"Of course you do! Would you mind not taking that Mr.-know-it-all tone of voice with me? Can't you tell I'm trying to be nice to you?"

"I don't know—"

"You don't know! Here I go making you my protégé, and collecting your doctor pay from those low-down, chiseling, land humpers, and what kind of thanks do I get? A lot of mouthy back talk? Now you and me are going to prepare a feast for ourself and bed down in a nice dry place, and I would like to be treated with a little more friendly respect, if you don't mind."

"You didn't give me any of that money."

"Well, I'm holding it for you, aren't I?"

"How do I know you're not just keeping it for yourself?"

"Oh, for God's sake!" Billy reached into his pocket, took out a fistful of coins, and slapped them on the floor. He pushed the gold half eagle to one side along with eight silver quarters and a dozen dimes and shoved the rest toward Jasper: two silver quarters and five dimes. "This here's yours."

"I doctored the old man's boils. How come you get to keep the gold?"

"Are you crazy? Didn't we rob those folks?"

"You did. I was just there."

"Like hell you were. You're what's called an accomplice. That's a partner in crime of a lesser sort. Get it?"

"I don't want to have anything to do with you robbing."

"It's too late for that," Billy said. "And me being the chief robber —who, by the way, you wouldn't get none of your doctoring pay without—then this gold piece and most of the silver is my takings and the rest is yours, and believe me I'm being generous with you."

"It's not right."

"Lookit, I'm your teacher and you're my protégé, goddamn it. How many times I got to explain the situation? Banditry is much more demanding and dangerous than doctoring. Accordingly, it ought to pay better. Nobody puts their life at risk tending boils."

"I'd like to see you try it."

"What in the hell's eating you anyways?"

Jasper hesitated

"My dog got killed," he said.

"Your dog? How so?"

"Stomped to death by a horse."

"I'm sorry to hear that."

"I went and killed the horse," Jasper said.

Billy recoiled slightly and regarded Jasper with a curious glance in the flickering firelight.

"You killed a horse? All by yourself?"

"It isn't that hard to do."

"Who all's horse was it?"

"A man in town. Nobody you'd know."

Billy searched the firelight a moment and then looked Jasper in the eye.

"You really are a desperate little character, aren't you?" he said.

"I'm a lost soul," Jasper said.

"Not anymore you're not. You're Billy Bones's compadre. You and me, we're going a long way down the bold road of banditry and legend, and we're going to start with a nice square supper. Now, do like I tell you. . . ."

Twenty-seven

It was a few minutes to midnight when Loren Holder heard a rapping on the door below his bedroom. He stumbled downstairs in the dark and worked his way through the parlor to the parish house door. He opened it to find Dr. Jerry Copeland on the portico hunched within an oilcloth raincoat. Water dripped from the wide brim of his straw hat and from the portico roof behind him.

"You up?" he asked.

"I am now. What time is it anyway?"

"It's late. Can I talk to you?"

"Certainly. Come in."

The doctor followed Loren into the kitchen. Loren shoved some splints into the firebox of the cookstove, where they flared in a residue of live embers, and put a teakettle on the steel surface above it.

"Have a seat," he said. "Peppermint tea all right?"

"Thank you."

"Did you find him?" Loren asked.

"No," the doctor said. "Didn't come across anyone who'd seen him. I don't even know if we were searching in the right direction."

Loren spooned mint leaves from a jar into a teapot and got two mugs out of the dish drainer. He could hear the doctor crying softly behind him. Eventually, steam whistled out of the kettle, then billowed. Loren brought the tea things over to the table and joined the doctor there, taking the seat at the end so as to sit closer to him. He dandled a spoon in the honey jar, waiting for the tea to steep. The doctor snuffled.

"This is breaking my heart," he said.

"It must be hard," Loren said. "I wonder sixteen times a day if my boy Evan will walk through the door again. It's been almost two years. I wish I'd stopped him from going."

The doctor gave an inconclusive grunt.

Loren poured the tea into two mugs. "Something's come up while you were gone," he said. "You know Tom Allison's boy, Ned?"

"Of course I do."

Loren laid out the story Ned had told Jane Anne about the two boys spying on Perry Talisker and Ned's fears that the hermit might be behind Jasper Copeland's disappearance.

The doctor listened with his mouth open, clutching the warm mug of tea close to his chest.

"I never saw him as a danger to anybody," the doctor eventually said.

"I didn't either," Loren said. "And I'm not even sure what to make of it. But maybe it's time you turned this thing over to some people who could help track down your boy."

"If you mean Brother Jobe, I don't like the son of a bitch."

"You don't have to like him."

The doctor pressed the mug against his forehead and resumed crying quietly.

Loren reached over and squeezed the doctor's left forearm. "I'm here with you," he said, falling into his familiar role as pastor and counselor.

"I have to tell you what happened," the doctor said. "It's eating me up inside." He proceeded to tell Loren about the night Jasper came home with his injured pup, how there was nothing he could do for the animal, nothing the vet, Jason LaBountie, could do, how Brother Jobe materialized out of the darkness, like a baleful spirit, how he, the doctor, begged Brother Jobe to work whatever powers he might possess to bring the dog back to life, how Brother Jobe said his powers only worked one way, meaning toward death, how the doctor both hated and feared him, and how he was ashamed of even thinking that the little tyrant possessed any kind of magical abilities, but he had seen things that made him very uneasy, and finally, behind everything, that the thought of his boy wandering somewhere through the countryside in the rain and darkness was killing him.

"I know it sounds crazy coming from someone with a medical education, a background in science, but am I the only one around here who wonders if there's something evil about the son of a bitch?"

"I don't think he's the devil, if that's what you mean."

"I can't even believe we're having this conversation," the doctor said.

"Well," Loren said, momentarily at a loss.

"Only two of us in town, myself and Robert Earle, saw the bodies of Wayne Karp and Brother Jobe's son—what was his name?"

"Minor."

"Right. Anyway, the wounds were identical. I mean, to the micromillimeter. I measured them very carefully. Robert witnessed it. Each was shot in the eye and the mouth. Same teeth sheared at exactly the same place and same angle. It was literally an eye for an eye and a tooth for a tooth. It couldn't have been coincidental."

Loren now grunted inconclusively.

"I'm telling you: Brother Jobe was sending a message," the doctor said. "And when all is said and done, and in spite of who I am, I wonder if he really is some kind of other-than-normal being with powers we can't account for."

"In my opinion he's just a mortal with a talent for pushing people around."

"Funny, you're the one who supposedly consorts with supernatural powers."

"You mean God?"

"Yeah, God."

"I'm not so sure about God anymore," Loren said.

"Have you given up on him, Reverend? I suppose many others have in these hard times. But I'd like to think you're hanging in there with him, or the idea of what he represents."

"Can I tell you something personal?" Loren asked. "Confidentially, between a patient and a doctor?"

"Of course."

"I've thought about doing away with myself more than once."

The doctor, who had been slumping in his seat, sat up straighter.

Loren continued, "I went out to the old railroad bridge over the river yesterday with a rope."

"Are you depressed?"

Loren laughed, heartily.

"Yes, I suppose I was kind of upset," he said.

"What happened?"

"For starters, I threw the fucking rope into the river. Not on purpose. I tried a hook shot over this steel beam about twenty feet up. I forgot to hold on to the other end of the rope. It was so fucking stupid it made me want to kill myself even more. But then the rope was gone and I was too chicken to throw myself off the bridge. I remember thinking how cold the water would be."

Loren's hilarity became so intense it doubled him up. The doctor was infected by it and couldn't help laughing himself. Loren laughed until tears came to his eyes. Their laughter subsided gradually while Loren poured them both more tea.

"You know what really pulled me out of it?"

"What?"

"Robert's little lady turned up."

"Britney?"

"She'd been gathering wild things up the tracks. Rose hips or something. I suppose she saw the whole stupid business with me and the rope. She was very kind about it. Didn't put me on the spot or ask any questions. Just took my hand and walked me home."

"She's a very sturdy girl."

"I don't know if she saved my life, but she kind of bolstered my faith in the human race."

"Why did you want to take your life?" the doctor asked.

Loren sighed and rearranged his bulky frame in the fragile-looking Windsor chair, as though trying to make himself look smaller. "I'm unable to have sex anymore."

"Can't get an erection?"

"Right."

"Is that a recent thing?"

"It's been a while."

"Depression often expresses itself that way."

"How do you know it's not the other way around—that I'm depressed because I can't get it up?"

"It could be vascular problems."

"You know what my blood pressure was last time you took it—a hundred and ten over seventy. You said it was perfect."

"Considering the amount of butter and cream we eat these days, it's remarkable."

"It's not like I don't get any exercise, either. I must have spent ten hours this week just forking compost into the garden. Not to mention walking here and there all over town. I'm wondering if there's anything you might suggest?"

"There's no more Viagra, of course."

"Is there anything natural that actually works?"

"Have you tried jerking off?"

"Actually, yes. Are you being funny?"

"No. It works for some people. I thought maybe you being a minister—"

"I was a frat boy before I was a minister. Do you know of any herbals that grow around here that might help?"

"There's nothing that I know of," the doctor said. But something about the candlelight in the room brought him back to the previous night at Barbara Maglie's house in Hebron—the startling, vivid dreams he had and what she had told him in the morning about how she made her living—and he wondered if perhaps she'd put something in his food or drink to stimulate those wild dreams, the longings they provoked, and the orgasm he'd apparently had in his sleep. It certainly would have been in the service of her livelihood, as she had made it clear to him—if he understood her correctly. He was not exactly sure he had, because it was all so strange.

"There's a woman up in Hebron . . . ," the doctor began, and he went on to try to explain who she was and what she might do for Loren.

"Is she a witch or a whore?" Loren asked when the doctor finished.

"Maybe some of both."

"Witches, devils. This is pretty wild stuff for you, Jerry."

"I don't know what I believe these days," the doctor said. "The world we know is slipping away and something weird is taking its place."

Loren made a face that suggested he did not disagree.

"She's an unusual woman," the doctor said. "I think she might help you. It can't hurt to go see her. If you can stand the journey."

"I'll think about it. I want you to think about going to see Brother Jobe about finding your boy."

"Aw, Christ," the doctor said.

"Who else can you turn to?"

"Nobody," the doctor said, finishing his tea. "There's one other thing bugging me: Robert and I passed through Argyle on our way. The shopkeeper there might be trading in young boys."

"Huh?"

"We stopped in to buy some food. I told him we were looking for a boy. He said, 'Labor or sport?'"

"What's that supposed to mean?"

"Like I said, trading in boys. Selling them for work or sex, I took it to mean. You ever hear of any such racket around the county?"

"No," Loren said. "But I'll ask. First thing in the morning I'm going over to Perry Talisker's shack down on the river to have a heart-to-heart with him. I'll let you know what I find out."

The doctor stood up and Loren did likewise.

"You've been a good friend and a good doctor," Loren said. "And I know you're a good father, too."

The doctor nodded while he choked with emotion, mumbled thanks, and headed back out into the cold rain.

TWENTY-EIGHT

Perry Talisker had come across more than a few abandoned dwellings on his journey to the uplands of the Gavottes. But as the evening sky clotted up with voluptuously malevolent clouds and his left hip began to ache, as it always did when rain was coming on, he determined to build himself a natural shelter rather than stay indoors. On his sojourns away from Union Grove, trapping and hunting, he avoided staying in empty houses, with their stinking carpets, mold, rot, and worse. He found himself a flat spot twenty yards back from a little freestone stream called Joe Bean Creek—named after a nineteenth-century farmer of Washington County who was killed at the Battle of Trevilian Station, Virginia, June 12, 1864—and built himself a lean-to. He made a fire a few yards from the mouth of his lean-to and very happily boiled himself a steel cup of "coffee" devised from his own recipe of roasted barley grains and burdock root, which he improved with a liberal ration of whiskey. He then placed two large white potatoes, a turnip, and three fat carrots (all gleaned from local farm fields) on a flat rock in the center of his fire and tenderly watched over them, turning them this way and that with a stick until he judged that the roots were well cooked. He ate them with minced jalapeño chili peppers macerated in vinegar that he had made himself and carried in a jar, and a big block of sweet buttery corn bread he'd packed from home. For dessert he ate some chunks of a homemade confection composed of crystallized honey and ground butternuts.

The rain came on gradually as the day's last light yielded to darkness—just, he thought, as if some superior intelligence were directing it to happen that way. He wondered which of the two powers competing for his attention and, ultimately, for his soul was behind it or whether they had worked out some regular schedule, like a protocol of battle, in which one took control from the other at set times. The whiskey inclined him to reflect with a certain pleasure that he had gotten through another day without falling captive to either the Dark One or his opposite, the all-seeing and ever-judging God. He drew immense comfort from eluding both of them and standing on his own, though he knew they were both out there. It occurred to him that if he got far enough from the realm of man—town, that is—and became more embedded in the natural world, perhaps the lords of darkness and light would forget about him and focus their attention on those who remained in society, with its endless varieties of wickedness.

He was snug, dry, and content in his little lean-to. The rain slid right off the layered pine boughs. He had inserted himself in a durable Mylar emergency sleeping sack bought by mail order years ago that had become one of his prize possessions in these times of hardship. It folded into an eight-inch-square packet, was apparently indestructible and entirely waterproof, and kept him warm inside with just one liner blanket in temperatures below freezing. He had laid a thick mattress of pine boughs on the ground under his lean-to, and they were as springy as the best factory-made mattresses used to be. As much as he feared and avoided human society, Perry reserved a wondrous respect for the manufactured outdoor adventure products of the old days, none of which was available anymore. He loved his little butane stove, which folded up into something the size of a hockey puck, but the minitanks of butane were no longer sold anywhere, so it was campfires now. He possessed an assortment of Swiss Army knives, folding multitools, and a military belt knife, which had serrated saw teeth on one side and a razor-sharp blade on the other. His steel Sierra cup was an old, treasured friend.

The food and whiskey and the many miles he had trod that day were dragging him now into sleep like a log to a hearth. He knew he was apt to wake up in the middle of the night, as he always did when the whiskey wore off and left his heart pounding, with his mouth dry, and his brain buzzing. But he also knew this first round of sleep would get him at least two or three good hours, and he rather looked forward to being alert later on when he could lie back and listen for animals in a place wilder than his shack on the river back in town. He wondered if one of the big catamounts might be among them. He laid his Marlin .30-30 rifle right next to his Mylar cocoon and sank back on the boughs. He pictured the earth turning on its axis through the dark ethers of space, and the face of his erstwhile wife flashed through his memory, which propelled him out of himself and the known world into the bonds of slumber.

TWENTY-NINE

"Put them onions there into the mush and mix them in good," Billy Bones told his protégé, Jasper Copeland, as they prepared their feast in the abandoned house on Goose Island Road. Billy had his goat-meat skewers jacked up on a couple of concrete blocks over the fire, and the meat juices dripped aromatically into the coals. "Keep stirring it," he said.

"The handle's hot."

"Well, get a sock or something out of your sack and use it like a pot holder."

Billy took the skewers off the fire and moved one of the concrete blocks to the side and set the meat on it to rest.

"Okay," he said, "now take them cheese crumbles and stir them in."

Jasper followed Billy's instructions.

"Now, take her off the heat and just keep stirring until the cheese gets melty."

A minute later, Billy declared the cornmeal mush with onions and cheese done. He took a spoon out of his shoulder sack and Jasper did likewise. Billy directed Jasper to set the pot down right between them and then laid the meat skewers on the concrete block beside it. Finally, he took a small jar of white crystals out of his sack and opened it with ceremony."

"Look here what I got."

"Salt?"

"You're damn right."

"Where'd you get it?"

"Won it in a poker game," Billy said. He sprinkled salt into the cheesy cornmeal mush and lifted a spoonful of it to his mouth.

"Mmm-mmm, that is goddamn tasty. Dig right in. And help yourself to meat."

Jasper obliged. He hadn't realized how hungry he was until Billy set all the food between them. He imitated Billy by sprinkling salt on his meat strips and then rolling them up to fit neatly inside his mouth. They ate silently until the ragged edge of their hunger faded.

"You know something, little desperado?" Billy said. "I don't believe I even caught your proper name after the better part of a day rambling together. What should I call you?"

"John."

"John what?"

"John S. Hopkins."

"What's the *S* for?"

Jasper had to think a moment.

"Sebastian."

"Aw, you just made that up."

"Did not."

"Well, it doesn't matter. John's good enough. Johnny. Johnny-on-the-spot. How do you like your supper?"

"It's okay."

"Just okay? I got news for you—this is about as good as it gets on a ramble. Fresh meat, a tasty side dish, and brandy to wash it down. We even got nuts and honey for dessert. Last night, alls I had was a pocketful of acorns."

"I had roasted potatoes," Jasper said.

"Well ain't you special."

"Every farm around here has got a patch, and lots are still left in the ground."

"I don't go for grubbing around in the dirt. Billy Bones is not any clod-scratching land humper. But tell you what. Since you seem to like it, and you're my protégé, I'll let you get all the potatoes for us while I get the meat on our rambles."

"They feed acorns to the pigs back home."

"That's all they's good for in my book. Anyways, tomorrow you and me will be up in Glens Falls at Madam Amber's house. Wait until you see what comes out of the kitchen up there. Katie Savage —she's the cook—she was a whore, but she got too old and ugly. She knows her way around the stove, though. Meat pies, trouts and viands, puddings of all sorts, fine cakes and sweetmeats, punches hot and cold. You ever enjoyed a woman, Johnny?"

"I don't know."

"I'd think you would know one way or the other."

"I kissed Susie Einhorn at the Battenville Grange."

"Did you? You get any further?"

"We kept it up for a while."

"Did you get your pecker wet?"

"No."

"You know how it all works, don't you?"

"I'm a doctor, aren't I?" Jasper said.

"You're a child is what you are."

"I've seen women that died in my father's office. Naked and laid out."

"Have you? Hope you minded your manners around them." Billy took a long pull from his bottle and wiped his mouth on his sleeve.

"I know what their private parts look like," Jasper said.

"Do you know how to work your own parts?"

Jasper picked silently at a strip of meat. He had defeated his hunger entirely and the gaminess of the roast kid was asserting itself unpleasantly.

"I guess that's just another thing Billy Bones'll have to teach you. Now that I'm rich, I vow I'll treat you to one of the girls when we get to Glens Falls tomorrow and your education in that department will be under way. Let's see them nuts over here."

Jasper shoved over the wooden box of shelled butternuts. Billy poured some honey into the lid of the honey jar and daintily dipped the nuts in it one after another, inviting Jasper to share. As the rain fell harder, more of it entered the hole in the ceiling, and the fire began to sputter. When the nuts were all gone, Billy got up, belched dramatically, and hung the remaining meat skewer from a wire that dangled off one wall where a lighting fixture had been ripped down.

"That'll be our breakfast," he said, "if the rats don't get it first." He kicked what remained of the fire, scattering embers across the concrete floor. "Grab your sack and that candle and let's go up to the bunkhouse," he added, then drained the last of the liquor, reared back, and pegged the bottle at the fireplace, where it smashed in a great fanfare of shards.

"What'd you do that for?" Jasper said. "That was a perfectly good bottle."

"Aw, shut up, you little scold!"

Upstairs in the one room that was dry, Billy claimed his corner and Jasper defaulted to one diagonally across. Jasper put on his extra sweater, his wool hat, and a second pair of socks and wrapped himself up in his blanket like a mummy, keeping his eyes on Billy across the room. Billy kicked off his boots and unbuckled his belt, took off his bush knife, and planted his automatic pistol on the floor right beside it. Weaving on his feet from the effects of the brandy, and belching, Billy unbuttoned the front of his striped trousers and took out an impressive appendage that seemed to Jasper like an alien being with a life of its own, bobbing this way and that way as though searching some indeterminate horizon for prospects.

"This here's what the ladies like best about Billy—the bone that made him famous. Big 'un, wouldn't you say?"

Jasper lay frozen in vivid revulsion.

Billy addressed his organ with a kind of ceremonial tenderness, squeezing, patting, and shaking it.

"Do you have to do that?" Jasper said.

"Just thinking about those girls up north makes me crazy with the itch. Tomorrow at this time, I'll be swimming in their sweet flesh. Titties and thighs. Wet lips. I'm gonna have each and every one of them in size order."

"At least blow out the candle—"

"Shut up, you might learn something."

"Learn to be disgusting—"

"Watch now. Here it comes. . . ."

He picked up the pace of his self-attentions, pumping and stroking with fierce animal commitment. Then he let out a howl as his back arched and he sent a few jets of his generative fluids against the wall of his corner. Afterward, he stood slumped and weaving in place with his shoulders hunched while his gasps reverted to simple breathing. Then, with a conclusive grunt, he shook out a few remaining drops and replaced the organ inside his striped trousers.

"Helps me sleep," he mumbled as he sank to his knees, wrapped himself in his leather coat like a bat in its wings, and pulled a thin blanket from his bag. "God, I'm tired."

He blew out the candle and within a minute he was snoring. Jasper closed his eyes, but his brain blazed with light. He thought of home and family and friends and town. But these thoughts only led to a recognition of how much trouble he was in and the impossibility of returning. He couldn't help worrying about the woman tied up in the farmhouse and whether she'd managed to free herself or was locked in an upstairs closet, desperate with thirst, praying for help. He also wondered whether her father, the old man Billy had coldcocked with his gun, was still lying where he fell on the kitchen floor. He even stole downstairs with the idea of possibly going back to the house to rescue the two of them, but when he looked outside the rain was pouring off the roof in a sheet. The night couldn't have been blacker, and he calculated that his chance of finding his way back to their house was close to zero, so he returned to the upstairs room and took refuge in his blanket again.

His thoughts now turned to the future, to his new life in Glens Falls. He determined to shake himself loose of Billy Bones as soon as possible once they arrived and to seek out opportunities to make himself useful in a doctoring way, perhaps attaching himself to a local physician, someone like his father, whom he might assist in exchange for a place to sleep and meals. In time, he thought, he would be able to set up on his own. These agitations finally subsided and he sank into a fervid sleep. He was dreaming about Willie when the lucid awareness that the pup was no longer alive provoked him back to waking. He had no idea what time it was. The rain had ceased and a big waxing moon shone through the skylight, illuminating the room more than the candle had. He sat up panting with fright and despair as the starkness of his situation came back into focus. It took a mighty effort to control his panic. He told himself that his chances of finding Glens Falls were better tagging along with the odious Billy Bones than striking out on his own in the dead of night. Anyway, this was possibly the only night he'd have to spend in Billy's company, and it was probably not long until morning, when they would be on their way.

The bandit snored musically across the room. Jasper's eyes fixed on the automatic pistol that lay on the floor beside him. He carefully untangled himself from his blanket and crept across the room to Billy's corner. Billy continued to snore. Jasper reached out for the pistol. He had handled rifles before. His father let him shoot the Weatherby .240 that he hunted with, but ammunition was hard to come by, even for a man in Dr. Copeland's position, who traded services for anything and everything. Ammunition in the county depended mostly on reloads these days, and the doctor was down to nine usable brass casings of the odd .240 caliber. His father also kept a Smith and Wesson nine-millimeter automatic in a drawer in his office. More than once, when he knew his father was off on a call around the county, Jasper took it out of its hiding place and handled it, though he'd never fired it. In fact, his father never showed it to him; he'd discovered it by accident below the counter where the autoclave sat, in a low drawer full of medical odds and ends. Billy Bones's pistol, a Springfield .45, was impressively heavy. Jasper hefted it, aimed through the sights, and was examining its many complicated parts, levers, and stops, when he happened to notice that the butt of the pistol was empty. There was no magazine. He wondered if Billy Bones kept it hidden somewhere or if he just didn't have one.

Billy stirred and groaned. Jasper froze, while his heart skittered. The bandit coughed, snorted, and flopped over onto his stomach. Jasper remained frozen just long enough to feel sure that Billy Bones had gone back to sleep. Then he replaced the pistol on the floor and stole back to his own corner, where sleep continued to elude him for hours while the moon sank out of view and the fetid room filled with daylight.

THIRTY

The last thing Stephen Bullock did before bedtime, in his capacity as town magistrate, was to sign a warrant directing Dr. Jeremy Copeland to exhume and examine the body of Shawn Watling and report his findings, the costs of which, labor included, were to be billed to the town of Union Grove, repayable in up to four dollars' silver coin. He gave the folded and sealed document to his chore boy, Roger Lippy, for delivery in person the following day. Then Stephen Bullock retired to the bedroom upstairs in the large manor house that was the beating heart of his four-thousand-acre holdings.

The spacious, cheerful bedroom was wallpapered in a motif that featured pink cabbage roses, with a flowery chintz-upholstered wing chair in one corner. His wife Sophie's dressing table stood between two large light-gathering windows, with curtains that matched the wallpaper. Two nineteenth-century landscapes of the upper Hudson Valley by the painter Hastings Lembert (1824–93), an ancestor, hung on the wall above a fine early Meiji (1871) *tansu* chest of drawers in *kiri* wood and chestnut. Bullock had picked it up forty years ago during his postcollege sojourn in Kyoto teaching English.

Sophie sat in bed reading by the light of her bedside electric lamp. Bullock's farm was the only establishment in the vicinity of Union Grove that still enjoyed electricity. It was thanks to a small hydroelectric generator where the Battenkill made one final ten-foot leap before it flowed into the Hudson River. It put out fifty kilowatts of power, enough to light the main house, the barns, the workshops, and the cottages his "employees" had constructed for themselves on his property. Finding replacement lightbulbs was a problem now that trade had fallen off so sharply. He'd laid in as many as possible during the hoarding times that followed the bombings in Washington and Los Angeles and the fall of the government, but his supply had run down so severely that he'd had to stop giving new ones to his cottagers—they were going back to candles—and lightbulbs were not the kind of thing he was equipped to manufacture on the farm, though his workshops did turn out many useful items from glassware to harnesses.

"You look very handsome tonight," Bullock remarked to his wife as he pulled off his blousy linen shirt and unbuttoned his riding trousers. She looked up over her reading glasses with a sly smile. She wore a silk nightgown that merely pretended to contain her abundant bosom. Bullock was observant enough to know that she tended to wear that particular article of clothing when she wanted his attention.

"Are you proposing to entertain me?" she asked.

"I'd be honored."

She put down her book, *Them,* by Joyce Carol Oates, a novel of mid-twentieth-century family depravity, and threw back the covers on her husband's side of the bed, patting the mattress to welcome him. He slipped between the cool, clean sheets until he was pressed warmly against the wife he adored. Soon he was kissing the little hollow below her ear where the wisps of silvery hair met her perfumed neck, as familiar a place to him as the wooded glens of his dreams, where he was forever young and on the hunt. She reached and turned out the light. His left hand ranged over the deeply contoured geography of her torso—as perpetually beautiful and interesting to him as the terrain of his own great farm—and she opened herself to him. Their ceremony was well practiced but no less pleasurable for its countless repetitions over the years. If anything, their comfort with each other only added to the pleasure they took together, along with their mutual wonder that they remained avid well into age. When their ceremony was complete, they lay panting, giggling, and whispering to each other in delight.

"Sleepy, now?" he asked.

"You know how I am," she said. Indeed, the transports of love acted on Sophie Bullock as the most potent soporific. It was a joke between them. Bullock himself always claimed to be reenergized by lovemaking, as if he had taken a shot of espresso.

"Would you like me to read a bit to you?" he asked.

"Sure," she said. "What have you got, darling?"

"*The Legend of Sleepy Hollow*, by Washington Irving."

She let out a delighted little yelp.

"Halloween's almost here," he said.

"You love holidays, don't you?"

"They're more important now than in the old days, when there were more distractions."

"Well, you go right ahead, but don't mind me if I slip off to dreamland."

Bullock kissed her damp forehead, reached for the lamp on his night table, and put on his reading glasses.

"*In the bosom of one of those spacious coves which indent the eastern shore of the Hudson,*" he began reading aloud, "*at that broad expansion of the river denominated by the ancient Dutch navigators the Tappan Zee, and where they always prudently shortened sail and implored the protection of St. Nicholas when they crossed, there lies a small market town or rural port, which by some is called Greensburgh, but which is more generally and properly known by the name of Tarry Town—*"

Bullock stopped reading at the apprehension of strange noises emanating from somewhere in the house, something banging, a dull thud, a squeak. The old house was alive in its own way, always heaving and groaning with the weather and the seasons. And there were the two servants who lived in the house, Lilah the cook and Jenny the housekeeper, who sometimes moved about downstairs late at night, getting something from the kitchen or the library.

But then Bullock heard a commotion on the stairs. He flung his book aside just as three figures crashed through the bedroom door and stopped in their tracks, apparently dazzled by the electric light. Bullock knew at once what they were. The three figures—bearded, bundled in close-fitting clothing, like soldiers, with trousers tucked into the boot tops, yet not in any discernable uniform—gaped in awe at what they had discovered and not just at the finery of the room.

Sophie Bullock, shocked into waking, had been prepared for a moment like this by her husband and by her own intelligence. She sat up in bed beside her husband and drew the bedclothes above her bosom. The Bullocks and the intruders stared squarely at one another in steely resolve during that interminable instant before one of them spoke.

"I've been expecting something like you for a long time," Bullock said.

"That's nice," said the tallest one, who wore a leather helmet leaking coyote fur, with an eagle crudely embroidered on a patch at the forehead. "It'll save us all a lot of bother. Just take us to where the gold is."

"What makes you think there is any?"

"Oh, come on. How could there not be in a place like this?"

While Bullock sized up the trio, he heard a scream from below and assumed it came from Jenny or Lilah.

"If you harm any of my people, you'll pay," he said.

"You're not calling the shots here just now," said the apparent leader, who brandished a very large revolver. He used its long barrel as a pointer, gesturing to reinforce his instructions. "Get out of the rack, Mr. Big."

Bullock threw back the sheets and sprang to the floor with an athleticism that surprised the intruders as much as his state of complete nakedness.

"Check out the missus," said another of the intruders, shorter and younger than the first. He wielded a sawed-off pump shotgun and sported a head rag that had once been a small American flag. A spray of blond hair leaked out from under it. "Nice-looking for an older gal."

Sophie Bullock didn't flinch.

The muffled screams continued from below.

The third member of the trio, black-haired and broadly built, with a tight-cropped beard and no visible weapon, approached the bed and seized the end of the blankets. Sophie resisted, but the burly man succeeded in yanking them off. She threw her arms across her bosom against the inadequacy of her nightgown.

"You come with me," the leader told Bullock.

"I'm not leaving my wife alone with your gorillas."

As though to emphasize the obvious, the shorter one unzipped his fly.

"These here boys are gentlemen," the leader said. "They just need some mothering."

The screams from downstairs had become sobs.

"Can I put my pants on?" Bullock asked.

"Go ahead."

The dark-bearded hulk fingered Sophie Bullock's silk nightgown. She issued a strangled cry of distress, while trying desperately to maintain her composure. The nightgown came away with a ripping sound. Sophie drew up her thigh in a posture of protection. Bullock calmly went to the wing chair in the corner where he had deposited his riding breeches. He pulled them on and fastened the buttons, keeping his eyes on the tall one in the leather helmet with the eagle on it. Then he reached casually beside the curtained window and pulled a braided cord, which set off a blaring electric klaxon on the roof.

"What the hell?" the dark-haired hulk said. The three intruders all shared a troubled glance. In that distracted instant, Bullock reached beside the wing chair into a bronze umbrella stand and withdrew from a sharkskin scabbard the twenty-six-inch-long *katana,* or samurai sword, that had been another of his acquisitions during his Japanese sojourn. The rigorous training he had undergone in those years returned to him unfailingly. He wheeled around and swung the weapon at the one who had been issuing instructions. The motion was so fluid and exact that for a moment a mere red line appeared between the man's beard and his shoulders. But then his legs wobbled and his body collapsed in a heap on the rug, while bright arterial blood gushed out of the stump of his neck and his detached head, still in its leather helmet, bounced on the floor and rolled up against the chest of drawers. The young, flag-headed accomplice barely had time to goggle at the spectacle before Bullock delivered a thrust of the sword cleanly through the young man's sternum, sectioning the heart from top to bottom and separating its owner from his life so efficiently that his brain was able to behold his own death for several seconds before he, too, crashed to the floor. The third one had the presence of mind to lunge for his companion's sawed-off shotgun, but he also presented the back of his neck so perfectly to Bullock that a minimum of effort was required to remove his head. The eyes could be seen rolling in the head as it became lodged between the legs of the dressing table.

When all three lay dead on the floor, with just the residual twitching of their shocked nervous systems, Bullock wrested the revolver from the dead leader's hand, grabbed the sawed-off shotgun from the floor, and hurried out of the room. Sophie remained naked on the bed above the fallen, bleeding intruders, her screams subsumed in the noise of the klaxon, which had succeeded in summoning the men from Bullock's village up the hill. They now swarmed around the house, barns, and workshops of Bullock's manor in the rain, rounding up nine other intruders at gunpoint in the electric floodlights which were part of the alarm system that tripped when Bullock had pulled the chord.

Bullock, shirtless and bloody in the stark glare of the floodlights, ordered the captured invaders to be locked in the enormous cold-storage locker that his grandfather had installed in one of the barns in 1965 for preserving his apple crop. Others attended to Jenny Ferris, the housekeeper, on the first floor of the big house, where she lay battered and misused, while Sophie Bullock, now dressed in her gardening denims, supervised the removal of the bodies from her bedroom and the mopping up of the blood that had spilled from their worthless hearts.

THIRTY-ONE

"Who can tell me why we celebrate Halloween?" Jane Ann Holder asked the pupils in the classroom of the Congregational church school. The twenty-seven children in her class ranged from six-year-old Robin Russo to fifteen-year-old James LaBountie. At her question, the teenagers in the room grinned, squirmed, and rolled their eyes to display their embarrassment at the childishness of the subject (despite their residual love for it). But the younger ones became avidly alert at the mention of a festival so close to their hearts. "What's the purpose of Halloween?"

"To share good things like sweets and cakes," said Kelly Wheedon, who was ten, "because not everybody is fortunate."

"That's true," Jane Ann said. "What else?"

"To honor dead people who can't be here among us anymore," said Ned Allison.

"Yes. To acknowledge them. Our memory of them, at least."

"I think that's where the idea of ghosts comes from," said Mary Moyer, twelve, a blossoming intellectual. "A mix of memory and imagination."

"Very good," Jane Ann said. "How many of you believe in ghosts?"

Several of the younger children raised their hands, a few tentatively, while checking around the room to see whether they had company in their belief.

"There's no such thing as ghosts," said David Martin, fifteen, a cynic through and through.

"Maybe the boundary between memory and imagination isn't as firm as we like to think," Jane Ann said.

"What is is and what ain't ain't," David Martin said.

"Isn't, not ain't," Jane Ann said.

"Whatever."

"No, not whatever. Isn't, not ain't," Jane Ann said.

"Well ghosts ain't, as in there ain't no such thing."

"Isn't!"

"That too."

"I don't want to hear 'ain't' come out of your mouth anymore, David."

He slumped in his seat, defeated, more cynical than ever.

"Any more ideas about why we celebrate Halloween?" Jane Ann asked.

"To get rid of rotten eggs," said Darren McWhinnie, thirteen, the class wit, to a smattering of laughs.

"Don't worry, we've got plenty for your house," cracked Barry Hutto, fourteen, an instigator. "I'm saving 'em up, personally."

"Like to see you try it—"

"All right, that's enough of that, thank you," Jane Ann said. "Who can tell us where the 'tricks' part of trick or treat comes from?"

"Tradition," said Carey Allison, nine, Ned's little brother.

"Last year we put Mr. Stimmel's rooster up in the church tower," said Albert Hoad, twelve.

"He didn't stay there long," said Billie Gasperry, twelve, a tomboy who followed along with Darren McWhinnie's gang. "Its wings were clipped and it fell out and broke its neck."

"You probably ate him, too," said Barry.

"I wished I did," said Billie. "I bet all you get is possum over at your house."

Jane Ann stepped in. "Let's cut out the quarreling and baiting, shall we?"

"He started it—"

"I don't care who started it. I'm tired of it. Who has an idea for a costume this year?"

"I'm going around as a flu victim," said Darren McWhinnie, who added some ghoulish sound effects.

"That's not funny," Jane Ann said. Hardly a family in town was untouched by the visit of the deadly flu three years earlier, and some of the children in the class had lost a sibling or a parent.

"I'm dressing up as Brother Jobe this year," said Arthur Shroeder, ten.

"My mother says he's the devil," said Nina Pettie, thirteen.

"He's like a big black bug," said Darren McWhinnie. "If you dress up like him, we'll squash you!"

Jane Ann allowed the general hilarity at that crack to subside on its own.

"Can anyone else tell me what we celebrate on Halloween?"

"It's the harvest time of the year with all the pumpkins and cornstalks and giving out of treats and all," said Sally LaBountie, fourteen, James's sister, an inward-looking girl who loved books and animals equally and who often evinced impatience with the workings of the other childrens' minds. "It's a time of plenty."

"Very true," Jane Ann said. "Does anyone know where all these traditions come from?"

"The old times," said Jason Schmidt, nine. "When it was the USA."

"It's still the USA," Jane Ann said.

"My dad says the USA is finished," said Jared Silberman, twelve.

"No, it's still here," Jane Ann said.

"Then why don't the electric come back on anymore?" asked Ryan Arena, fourteen. "Where's the army?"

"Why *doesn't* it come on," Jane Ann said.

"The army's still bogged down in the Holy Land," said Corey DeLong, twelve, who had heard the last bits of news on the radio before the electricity went out.

"We might's well be on our own here in town now," Ryan Arena said.

"We are on our own," Sally LaBountie said. "Haven't you noticed?"

"My dad says it's good riddance about the government—"

"I heard there's Chinese now in California—"

"And Texas has gone with Mexico, or the other way around—"

"They landed a man on the moon, the Chinese did—"

"We already done that, America, ages ago—"

"Can we get back to Halloween, class?" Jane Ann said, asserting her dominion in the room. "Who can tell me the nation that had the biggest influence in bringing Halloween to America?"

After a lull, Sally LaBountie said, "England. The Salem witch trials happened after the pilgrims landed. They believed witches could take the form of an animal like a black cat."

"Actually it was Ireland," said Jane Ann, who occasionally lost patience with Sally LaBountie's grandstanding. "The Irish came to America in waves, first in the late 1700s and again in the 1840s and 1850s, when the potato famine struck Ireland."

"How can potatoes cause a famine?" said Albert Hoad. "It's a food."

"Maybe they didn't know how to cook 'em," said Ryan Arena.

"Nobody's that stupid," said Darren McWhinnie.

"That's enough, Darren," Jane Ann said. "The Irish were subject to very harsh living conditions. Many were tenant farmers on land owned by rich people who lived in England, some of whom never even set foot in Ireland. The poor Irish tenant farmers lived on just a few acres. It wasn't enough land to grow corn or grain crops. So they grew potatoes as a subsistence crop." Jane Ann wrote *subsistence* on the blackboard with a piece of chalk that was actually a fragment of salvaged gypsum board. "That means just enough to get by on."

"Sounds like life here," said Billie.

"Yes, these are hard times," Jane Ann said. "But we're not as poor as they were."

"Not yet," said Sally.

"What pushed Ireland over the edge," Jane Ann continued, "was the potato blight, a plant disease that came into Ireland, possibly from seed potatoes grown here in America, and wiped out all the potato crops for several years in a row. Roughly a million people died, many from disease that accompanied the famine, when people's resistance was lowered by starvation. Many of the survivors left Ireland and came to America. Do any of you have Irish ancestors?"

A number of hands went up around the room.

"The Irish had a very rich cultural heritage, which they brought with them to America," Jane Ann continued. "Halloween is part of that heritage. It is a combination of the Celtic festival of Samhain"— she wrote the word on the blackboard—"which is an old Gaelic word meaning summer's end—the harvesttime—and the Christian holy day devoted to all the saints, or all saints, which traditionally falls on November first."

"Isn't *holy day* where we get the word *holiday* from?" asked Kelly.

"Yes it is. Very good," Jane Ann said. "All Saints' Day came to include anyone who had died faithful to the church and its beliefs. Therefore, the night before November first, October thirty-first, is when departed souls come back and roam the earth, and we the living encounter them while we're celebrating our harvest fest. Another term for the dead of the ages was *all hallows*, whose souls were hallowed by entrance to heaven." She wrote *hallows* on the blackboard. "And the *een* part is a contraction of the word *evening*. So, you see we end up with this interesting combination of a harvest festival joined with a night of the dead returning to earth. And that is where Halloween comes from."

A stillness fell over the class. The sounds of hammer blows were audible in the distance behind a closer cawing of crows.

"I'm gonna dress up as a potato," said Barry Hutto, breaking the spell. His joke went over with all the children, from the oldest to the youngest.

"I'm sure that will be easy," Jane Ann said, happy for the release of tension that the laughter represented. "Just put a burlap sack over your head." More laughter. "Now I want to read you a wonderful story about Halloween written by a great American author, Washington Irving, who also happened to be the great bard of the Hudson Valley."

"This is the Hudson Valley," said little Sarah Watling, seven.

"Quite right, Sarah," Jane Ann said, taking a seat at her desk and opening a very old edition of Irving's collected works.

"*In the bosom of one of those spacious coves which indent the eastern shore of the Hudson* . . . ," she began reading aloud.

THIRTY-TWO

Around sunrise the day after his home was invaded, Stephen Bullock decided to hang the rest of the intruders. He drew up a warrant of execution for the nine men during his breakfast and determined, before hanging them, to interrogate whoever was next in command after the three he had killed in his bedroom.

A little after seven in the morning, he entered the old apple storage cooler where the men were held. He went in alone. Five of his own men, well armed, remained outside the cooler. The captives inside recoiled at the light of the candle lantern when Bullock entered. They all shivered visibly in one corner of the large chamber, where they huddled together in hobbles with their hands tied behind their backs. The room stank of animal waste and fear.

"Three of your men are dead," Bullock told them. "I suppose you've figured out who they are by now. Who among you has the authority to speak for the rest of this gang?"

The men swapped glances.

"Don't be shy," Bullock added.

"We don't have no official ranks, if that's what you mean," said one, a large man with a shaved head, perhaps thirty years old.

"It seems you speak for the rest."

"Just for now," the shaved-head man said.

"Okay, I nominate you spokesman. And second it. All in favor? Aye. See, you're elected. Get up and come with me."

"Where are we going?"

"You're going to have breakfast and we're going to talk."

The man got up off his haunches and glanced back at his companions. He was rangy, gaunt, and hollow-eyed but obviously very strong. The tendons in his neck stood out like wires.

"Come," Bullock said.

The man shuffled in his hobbles, which only allowed him to take tiny steps. Bullock and his five men, armed with rifles and pistols, walked him to the manse. The clear morning was already blooming into a spectacularly warm Indian-summer day with many stimulating aromas in the air: fresh cut hay, burning brush, sorghum boiling down to syrup at Bullock's new cane mill on the river, corn bread baking. Bullock led his prisoner into a sunny conservatory wing of the house and directed the man to have a seat at a glass-topped table. The cords that bound his hands behind his back were removed, though the hobbles on his ankles remained.

Bullock's chore man, Roger Lippy, a Chrysler dealer in the old times, laid a stiff white cloth on the table and set it with silver tableware and damask napkins rolled into silver rings. Bullock held up a sterling silver fork and examined it in a shaft of sunlight.

"Too bad you didn't get to rob the place," Bullock said. "We have a lot of nice things here."

The prisoner didn't reply.

Roger Lippy stood by the table with a tray at his side.

"What would you like for breakfast?" Bullock asked the prisoner.

"You're gonna give me breakfast?"

"Certainly."

"Why?"

"Aren't you hungry?"

"Not especially."

"Okay, I'll order for you. Roger, tell Lilah to make this fellow a four-egg omelet with some of that Duanesburg cheddar, bacon and sausage, hash browns, and corn bread with the blackberry preserves."

"Yessir. Yourself?"

"I'll just have tea," Bullock said. "Tea for you?" he asked the prisoner, who just grunted. "It's real black China tea," Bullock added. "None of that fruity herbal crap. It'll give you a real lift. Go on, give yourself a break."

"Okay," the prisoner said. Roger Lippy left them. Bullock's other men took up positions sitting or standing outside the conservatory, on display but out of earshot. Sparrows flitted in and out of the room through the ventilation louvers.

"What's your name?" Bullock asked.

"What's it matter?"

"It should matter to you. It's your name. You can't defend your honor without defending your name, can you?"

"It's Jason Hammerschield."

"You couldn't have made that up."

"It's my name."

"Where's this gang of yours from?"

"It's not my gang."

"I don't mean you own it. But obviously you're a member."

Roger Lippy brought out a tray with a teapot and two matching cups and saucers. Bullock poured for both of them.

"The cream's from our own dairy and the sugar's made from our own beets, though we're working up a sorghum operation now," Bullock said. "So, Jason, where do you and your associates hail from?"

"Waterbury, Connecticut. We been on the road a while."

"How are things back there in the Nutmeg State?"

"The what?"

"Connecticut."

"They sucked. Which is how come we took to the road."

"Have you had many adventures?"

"It's a hard life."

"You must not be very good at what you do."

"We're all right. But it's slim pickings out there."

"Then it's extra sad that you messed up here. We're living large. We've got full bellies, electric power, amber waves of grain, groaning orchards, a nice big house, first-rate furnishings."

"I can see."

"Oh, you only see a teensy-weensy bit of what we've got going. Want me to put on some recorded music? I've got it all—classical, Broadway musicals, old Bob Dylan—"

Roger Lippy reappeared with Jason Hammerschield's breakfast, with a basket of corn bread, a ramekin of butter, and a dish of blackberry jam. The prisoner stared at the steaming plate that was set before him.

"Put on some Debussy, would you, Roger? The first preludes."

"Sure thing, sir."

"Go ahead, dig in," Bullock said to his prisoner, who continued to stare darkly at his plate.

"How do I know it's not poison?"

Bullock laughed sincerely. "You moron, if I wanted to kill you, I'd have one of my men shoot you in the head. Go ahead, eat."

Jason Hammerschield looked up at Bullock, squinting with dull incomprehension.

"I'll be very cross with you if you just let it sit there," Bullock added.

The prisoner took a tentative forkful of his omelet, then ate more rapidly until he was fairly inhaling the contents of the plate in a fugue of deprivation. He reached into the basket for some corn bread, slathered it with butter, and spooned jam on top. "What I want to know," Bullock continued, "is whether you are part of some larger horde."

"Some what?" Jason Hammerschield said, spraying corn-bread crumbs as he spoke.

"You know, a larger unit of people like yourselves, an army of marauders, scavenging across the land like locusts."

Jason Hammerschield chewed ruminatively.

"No," he said eventually. "We're just who we are. A bunch of guys."

"What do you call your bunch?"

"Nothing."

"Really? I'd think you'd sit around the campfire at night memorializing your exploits."

"What our what?"

"Making up stories about yourselves. For your own amusement. Creating a myth for posterity."

"We just fall out and sleep. It's hard living like we do."

"All I can say is you boys are seriously lacking in imagination."

Jason Hammerschield mopped up the last remaining specks of egg, hash browns, and crumbs of bacon with a triangle of corn bread.

"Allow me to suggest a name," Bullock said. "The Nutmeg Boys. Or maybe just the Nutmeggers."

Jason Hammerschield made a face and snorted. "What happens now?" he asked, tossing his napkin onto his plate.

"Just some legal rigmarole," Bullock said. "Do you boys have a lawyer?"

"No."

"Want me to represent you? I'm a member of the bar."

"That don't sound right."

"These are rugged times, admittedly, for the machinery of justice. By a stroke of luck, though, there's a magistrate on the premises."

"Who would that be?"

"Yours truly," Bullock said.

"I see," Jason Hammerschield said. "You the jury, too?"

"Pretty much. I could appoint some of my people, but they'd just do what I tell them. So why bother?"

A green look came over the prisoner as the horizon of his future finally resolved into a featureless landscape of grievous futility. He puffed out his cheeks, his eyes rolled up into his head, and he vomited his breakfast back onto his plate.

"It's been nice chatting with you, Jason, but I have an awful lot to look after here. We're slaughtering some hogs today. It's the season for it."

Bullock left the prisoner staring blankly into the panes of the conservatory walls and went outside to where his men waited.

"Take all these fellows down to the River Road," Bullock told the versatile Dick Lee, "and hang them there at twenty-yard intervals."

THIRTY-THREE

Robert Earle took a seat in Walter McWhinnie's cobbler shop in the former family room of Walter's house on Salem Street. Robert had been savoring this moment since he came home from searching the hills with the doctor and found a note informing him that the winter boots he ordered in September were finished and ready to try on.

Walter brought them out from the workroom behind the counter and gave one to Robert, who examined it lovingly. It was midcalf length and lined with lambskin, with a ring of fleece along the top. The double-stitched brown leather was waterproofed with beeswax, and the combination of new leather and wax gave off a luxurious, spicy aroma. A small pine-tree symbol was stamped on the vamp of each boot, the maker's trademark.

"This is a beautiful piece of work, Walter," Robert said, turning it over and over.

"Should last you a lifetime, with regular repairs," he said. "Go ahead, try them on."

Robert took off the moccasins that he wore most days when it was neither blazing hot nor snowy. They were also Walter's work, four years old, on their second resoling, but otherwise sturdy. Walter took a stool before Robert's chair and held the left boot out. Robert's foot went in effortlessly. When both were on, he got up and strode tentatively around the room. The boots fit perfectly and the shearling foot beds were soft as pillows.

"It's like they're already broken in."

"Glad they please you," Walter said. "There's nothing like good handwork."

Robert admired the boots in a mirror that leaned against the wall while Walter stepped back behind the counter to get the bill of sale. Perfectly satisfied with the look and fit, Robert went over to

the counter and pulled a fistful of silver coins out of his pocket—
pre-1964 quarters and dimes. He made neat stacks of them until
he'd laid out seven dollars.

"Those Virginians are keeping you busy, I see," Walter said,
alluding to the New Faithers.

"It's been pretty regular work over there."

"At least they pay real money. What are you doing for them,
exactly?"

"Finish work. Wainscot. Inlay."

"Fancy work."

"Yeah. Pretty fancy."

"I hear they got some big fat woman in there who they bow
down to and worship. A real freak type."

"Something like that."

"You seen her?"

"Once. They brought me in to meet her."

"You allowed to talk about it?"

"Sure. She's plenty freaky, all right. Has fits and spells. Seems
to have the ability to read minds. Whatever else she is, she has a
lot of influence there. I'm not sure what to make of it. The room
I'm outfitting is for her."

"She must be special," Walter said. "She give birth to quadru-
plets, the other day."

"What? Where did you hear that?"

"That Sister Annabelle, runs the new clothing store they started
over on Main."

"I'll be damned."

"She says it wasn't the first time, neither. This fat lady pops 'em
out like a laying hen. That Annabelle, she's a firecracker. I'm trying
to get some footwear orders out of her. They got something like
eighty people over to there, including little ones. You know if they
have a bootmaker in the house?"

"Not as far as I know," Robert said.

"I hear they have workshops galore where the classrooms used
to be."

"They do. But the craftsmen are a mixed bag, skill-wise. They've got me training some of their carpenters on finish work."

"Well, ask around and find out how they're fixed for cobblers."

"I'll do that."

"You tell them where you got your boots. I could stand the business. By the way, somebody poisoned their stallion, Annabelle said. That Brother Jobe is hopping mad. He thinks it was one of us."

THIRTY-FOUR

The Reverend Loren Holder poked around Perry Talisker's shack on the river. He rapped on the locked door and salvaged windows, and peered inside, but didn't see any sign that the hermit was around. He had trouble imagining the hermit as the sort who would abduct a child. In the artistry of the shack's woodwork, and the dulcimer on the table, Loren saw evidence of a complicated personality. He wondered about the inner life of such a man, what had happened to him as the old times became these harder new times and what torments drove him into seclusion. He had no idea where else to look for him.

So, at nine o'clock that morning, in what was already becoming a beautifully warm Indian-summer day, Loren tramped the two miles back across town to the old high school where the New Faith order made its headquarters. He entered the building through the same front doors he had passed through so often as the parent of a school-age child in the old times and easily found his way to the former principal's suite where Brother Jobe lived and worked. He found the Virginian in the hallway, dressing down one of the younger men of his tribe, Brother Malachi.

"That's the last durned time I send you out for shoats, or any other kind of livestock trading!" he hollered at Malachi, who was just twenty-one. "Go on and git back down to the barn before I put you to cleaning stoves in the kitchen with the women!"

The young man hurried away, shoulders hunched in disgrace.

"Sumbitch bought a pig in a poke," Brother Jobe muttered as much to himself as to Loren. "Durned mule-foot, wattle-faced, prick-eared throwback of a sow. Cost me five dollars, silver. What can I do for you this morning, Reverend?"

"We've got a kind of situation in town."

"You think? We got more situations around here than you can shake a stick at. It's got me vexed all to blazes, I'll tell you."

"I'll just get down to it then," Loren said, and laid out the disappearance of Jasper Copeland, the suspicions that had been raised about Perry Talisker, and the unsuccessful search through the county by Robert Earle and the doctor.

"Sorry to hear all that," Brother Jobe said. "But where do I fit in?"

"You've got some men who know what they're doing in this sort of thing," Loren said. "Trackers and rangers. We'd be grateful if you got up a proper search party. What do you say?"

"Why doesn't the doctor come ask me himself?"

"I'm asking you, both as the Congregational minister and the duly appointed constable. Let's call it official business."

"That's all well and good, but I'd be a whole lot more inspired if the doc would ask me himself."

"We don't have to stand on ceremony."

"It ain't ceremony," Brother Jobe said with an irate edge to his voice. "It's just common politeness. Anyway, if I was to mount a search, we'd need a detailed description of this boy and some notion about his habits of mind and such. I wouldn't dream of setting out without talking to his father about it first."

It did not seem unreasonable to Loren. "Well enough," he said. "I'll go talk to him."

Brother Jobe made a pinched, jaundiced face as a cramp ran through his abdomen.

"Hell fire," he muttered.

"You all right?" Loren asked.

"All this vexation is giving me a bellyache."

"Maybe you ought to mention it to the doctor when he comes over."

"Mebbe I will," Brother Jobe said. "If he can lower himself to come see me."

Loren excused himself and hiked another mile back across town to the doctor's office in the carriage house behind his house. There was no one in the waiting room. Loren called out for the doctor, who replied from the back room, his inner sanctum and lab. He was sitting at his desk, which was cluttered with instruments, jars, a plastic model of the human abdomen, stoppered bottles of this and that, staring at a handwritten document. A pony glass with an inch of clear liquid sat close to his right hand.

"Look at this," the doctor said. "From Bullock. He's ordering me to dig up the body of Shawn Watling."

Loren took the warrant and read it.

"Why did he wait all this time?" he asked.

"How should I know? You're the constable. Did he inform you?"

"Well, no," Loren said. "Maybe he was waiting until the weather cooled down."

"It's warming up again."

"It's just Indian summer," Loren said. He handed the warrant to the doctor, who let it drop back on his desktop in disgust, reached for the pony glass, and knocked back the contents. "You drinking before noon, Jerry?"

"It's not noon yet?" the doctor asked, apparently without irony.

"No."

"I guess I am, then."

Loren took a seat in the naugahyde chair the doctor kept on the other side of his desk.

"You're not going to lecture me, are you, Reverend?"

Loren ignored the remark. "I went over to Perry Talisker's place on the river," he said. "No sign of him. I have no idea if he was gone for five minutes or two days. But he wasn't there early this morning."

"Hmmm," the doctor said.

"Then I went and paid a call on Brother Jobe. I think he'll put together a bunch of his boys to search for Jasper."

"You think?"

"He wants you to go over and ask him."

The doctor sighed and fondled the bottle beside his empty glass.

"Don't pour another one, Jerry. Please. He wants some details about Jasper, how he thinks, stuff like that. Frankly, it makes sense."

"All right," the doctor said, without further debate or indecision. "I'll go over directly."

"I'm glad to hear that," Loren said. "I'm thinking of going up to Hebron to talk to that lady."

"You should," the doctor said, getting up from his swivel chair. "I think she can help you."

"I want to ask you a couple of favors," Loren said.

"Sure."

"Can you draw me a map? And lend me a firearm?"

"Yes and yes," the doctor said.

Thirty-five

Billy Bones woke up Jasper by jiggling the toe of his boot lightly into the boy's rear end. Jasper wheeled around and squinted up at Billy, with sunshine pouring through the skylight beyond.

"Quit that!" Jasper barked.

"Rise and shine then, you damn slugabed! The lark is singing in the meadow! The cows are in the corn! Summer's come back! And we're bound for glory—or at least a fine supper with the ladies."

"What time is it?"

"How the hell should I know? And what the hell does it matter? Pack your sack and let's get gone."

They were back on the road in a matter of minutes. Billy gnawed the shriveled remnants of his roast goat meat as they marched west up Goose Island Road. It was already a warm morning, and their way was mostly uphill, with woods and overgrown fields on each side. When they stopped to fill their water bottles in a little brook that trickled out of the Gavottes, Jasper said, "Do you have any idea where we're going?"

"'Course I do," Billy said. "Anyway, we ain't in any hurry."

"The sooner we get there the happier I'll be."

"Don't you take no joy in life, Johnny? What the hell's the matter with you?"

Jasper didn't reply.

"I never have seen such a fine October day. Look at the color in these hills! The blue of the sky! The smell of the woods! It's a song of beauty in itself. How can a person not take some happiness from all that?"

"Nobody's stopping you from feeling happy," Jasper said.

"Ain't there nothing that would make you happy?"

Jasper sat down on a rock beside the stream and reflected a moment.

"Having my dog, Willie, back, alive again," he said and burst out weeping.

"Aw," Billy said. "I guess you really loved him."

"More than anything," Jasper wailed.

"I'll get you another pup. There's lots of stray pups in this world that need love."

"I don't want another pup." Jasper shrieked and beat his fists against his own ears. "I want Willie."

Billy let Jasper wail until his torments subsided.

"Say, maybe another gallant act of banditry would perk you up."

"There's nothing gallant about robbing people," Jasper said, getting up off his rock and swinging his pack on again.

"Sure there is. I'm setting matters to right. Do you know the ruin of this country of ours was brought about by the rich?"

"The folks you robbed yesterday were poor."

"Compared to who? They had a farm, didn't they? A big house. Goats. If they put more effort in it, they might get something out of that land. Fruits of the vine and whatnot. They's what's called slovenly farmers. Lazy good-for-nothing gomers."

"What if that woman you tied up can't get loose?"

"Quit wasting your worry on that old hag. I rigged her up with the Billy Bones special slipknot. It's ancient Chinese magic, showed to me by a Chinaman himself. Once you give up the struggle, you discover you were free the whole time. Remind me to show you how to do it as part of your training."

They resumed marching along the sun-dappled road, the maples so intensely red and orange that the color seemed to scream out loud. Presently they came to an elevation where they could see the road dipping and curling into a valley below, and in the distance, perhaps a mile away, they saw a wagon drawn by two horses climbing the road toward them.

"Looks like fortune has just fetched us up an opportunity," Billy said. "And alls we have to do is wait here for it."

Ten minutes later, the team of horses lurched over the last little rise ascending the road out of the valley. They were old swayback common quarter horses. The driver was a gaunt man of middle years with a concave face and a sparse beard that lent him a simian look. The wagon's cargo box was filled with dusty onions that sent up little brown clouds with each jolt of the journey.

The driver halted his team some ten yards from where Billy stood, hand on hip, in the middle of the road.

"A good morning to you, sir," Billy said. "Have ever you seen such a splendid autumn day?"

The driver replied only by leaning over and spitting down into the road.

"Was that a 'yes' spit or a 'no' spit?" Billy asked.

The driver smiled weakly.

"You have the honor of meeting up with Billy Bones, bandit of legend. Have you heard of me?"

The driver just glared.

Billy drew open his leather coat to display the weapons in his waistband. He cleared his throat and sang the two opening verses of his personal ballad. The horses shifted in their harnesses and the doubletree squeaked.

The driver's glare turned into a sneer.

"It's a shame the newspapers are no more," Billy said. "They would have celebrated my renown far and wide. This young rogue here is my partner and protégé, Johnny-on-the-spot."

"I'm just walking the same road with him," Jasper said. "I'm no bandit."

"Don't confuse the man, Johnny—"

With Billy Bones momentarily distracted, the driver reached under his bench seat and drew out a sawed-off side-by-side double-barreled shotgun. But just as he leveled it at Billy Bones's heart, the shadow of a passing bird caused the offside horse to shrink backward, which bumped the wagon shaft and caused the driver to jerk his shot off target. Immediately recognizing the danger he now faced, the driver dropped his empty weapon into the mudguard

and attempted to gee up his team. But the old horses were exhausted from their climb up the steep road and, despite the loud
gunshot, hesitated to start again, only milling nervously about in
their harness. In the interval Billy Bones sprang up to the seat and
commenced beating the driver about the head with his big blocky
pistol, striking him this way and that way—on the temple, on the
back of his head, squarely in the face, again and again—until the
driver sat limply in his seat like an effigy with a red stump for
a head. Finally, Billy Bones delivered a blow so extreme that a
cloud of bright arterial blood exploded from the red stump and
hung in the air as the driver's inert body fell out the other side
of the wagon.

Jasper goggled at the spectacle for another long moment before he turned and walked stiffly down the road, the whole of his
body shuddering, and then broke into a desperate run toward the
valley below. Billy jumped down from the wagon and sprinted after
him. It did not take long for Billy to collar him and drag him to the
ground like a roped calf. Then he was kneeling on Jasper's chest.

"Where do you think you're going?" he said.

"You . . . you . . . killed that man."

"I did not. He's just out of it."

"No, he's dead! You killed him!"

Billy seized Jasper's hair. "Lookit here, Johnny. Didn't you see
that son of a bitch empty both barrels of a shotgun right at me?
He tried to kill me!"

"You told him it was a robbery. What do you expect?"

"Jeezus Christ Almighty, it's only money, robbery."

"You're a murderer!" Jasper screamed.

"It was self-defense!" Billy screamed back, yanking Jasper's hair
on each syllable.

Jasper howled in pain.

"He woulda killed me!" Billy said. "And maybe you, too!"

"Get offa me!"

Billy let go of Jasper's hair and slowly lifted his knee off Jasper's
chest.

"Son of a bitch had to defend a load of goddamn onions?" Billy muttered to himself as Jasper sat up and coughed strenuously. "Stupid bastard. No wonder they put him to driving the damn onion wagon. Too goddamn dumb to do anything else. Go on. Get up now."

Billy grabbed Jasper's shoulders, hoisted him to his feet, and made as if to brush the dust off Jasper's shirt and backpack, but Jasper slapped Billy's hand away.

"Come on back there with me. I aim to take a few of them onions with us."

"I don't want any onions."

"Well, I do, and I order you to stick by me. No more of this running off."

Billy fairly dragged Jasper by the shirt back up the road to where the horse and wagon remained.

"Put some of them onions in your pack," Billy said. He went around the far side of the wagon to check on the driver, who lay still, facedown in the weeds that grew up through the cracked pavement.

"I told you, I don't want onions."

"And I told you I do, goddamn it."

"They're heavy."

"Just take three or four. We got to bring something up to the Madam tonight. They have a lot of mouths to feed in that house."

Billy rummaged through the driver's pockets. One contained a roll of five hundred paper dollars in fifties and three silver quarters.

"Stupid son of a bitch," Billy muttered as he struggled to remove his hand from the driver's left pocket, which contained a bone-handled barlow knife. "What'd you have to go and fire on me for? I don't relish hurting nobody."

With the takings now in his pocket, Billy came around the other side of the wagon.

"You pack up some onions, like I said?"

"Yes," Jasper said.

"All right, let's get gone."

"He's dead, isn't he?"

"I ain't any doctor."

"I can tell if somebody's dead," Jasper said. "Want me to look?"

"What does it matter one way or another? You sure ain't gonna tend to him here if he ain't, nor raise him back up if he is."

"You going to leave the horses there, too?"

"I ain't a horse thief, Johnny. Besides, if we ride off on them, somebody could connect us to this scene."

"You can't leave them harnessed up to two tons of deadweight with no driver."

"They'll be all right."

"No they won't," Jasper said. "They'll die a slow death of thirst, if the wolves don't get them." He pulled the six-inch knife from the sheath on his belt, marched a few steps up to the team, and began cutting their harness off—the traces, the girths, cruppers, the reins—and pushed the animals forward until he was satisfied that they were free. Billy stood by, allowing him to do it. The horses sauntered to the side of the road and began grazing where the weeds were thick and green from the night of rain.

"I thought you were the mighty horse killer," Billy said when Jasper was done. "What do you care whether these two live or die?"

"They didn't hurt anybody," Jasper said.

"I guess that's so," Billy agreed. "All right, let's get away from here now."

They hadn't gone a quarter mile when Billy noticed a certain irritation about his face and arms, and ran his hand on his cheek and realized he was bleeding. He peeled off his leather coat and discovered a constellation of seven blood spots going from his shoulder to his biceps, with a couple of extras just under his left cheekbone.

"Will you look at this?" he said. "I'm shot! The son of a bitch got me after all."

He dropped his shoulder sack and sat on a bank of weeds on the side of the road.

Jasper followed him.

"Take your shirt off," Jasper said. "Let me have a look."

Billy complied and Jasper examined him.

"You've got some birdshot in there."

"Son of a bitch shot me."

"I can get them out, but it'll probably hurt."

"Goddamn," Billy said. "Well, do what you have to."

"Too bad you drank up all that liquor."

"I can take it."

"I mean for an antiseptic."

"I heal up good. Get her done, Johnny."

Jasper cut Billy a green length of birch branch to bite on, knowing the layer under the bark had a pleasant mint-tasting sap, and picked the lead BBs out of Billy's flesh with the tip of his hunting knife while Billy groaned.

"Okay," Jasper said. "I think I got them all out."

Putting his shirt back on, Billy said, "How come you didn't stab me in the heart just now when you had the chance?"

"I guess you don't know the most sacred rule of medicine, do you?" Jasper said.

"I guess not. What is it?"

"First, do no harm."

"What rubbage," Billy said. "Doctors do all kinds of harm. Everybody knows that. Do you know the most sacred rule of banditry?

"I don't want to know."

"Well, I'm gonna tell you anyways, you little smart mouth: It's live to do your deeds another day. No gomer is ever gonna get the drop on Billy Bones, if I can help it."

THIRTY-SIX

Perry Talisker heard a gunshot as he made his way along the elevations of the range of hills known as the Gavottes. He jogged through the woods in the direction it came from and soon reached a place of observation among the rocks of a granite promontory a hundred yards from the scene. Below he watched a wiry towheaded man fight with a darker-haired man in the driver's box of a freight wagon. He retrieved his field glasses from a side pocket of his pack and focused the objectives. A week earlier the foliage would have been too thick to observe the scene from this lair, but the previous night's rain alone had stripped off many leaves and the visual path was clear.

He watched the beaten man's head seem to explode in a cloud of red mist and the ensuing argument between his attacker and a boy at the scene. Without consciously framing what he was witnessing as a crime, Perry Talisker sensed wickedness and carefully swung his Marlin .30-30 off his shoulder with the dim notion to bring down the man who had battered the wagon driver to a bloody pulp. But he hesitated, realizing that no one had appointed him executioner, and by then, the wicked man and his young companion had vanished over the crown of the road that ran steeply down to the valley.

Talisker slung the rifle back over his shoulder and waited in the sunny stillness of the morning. After a while, the two figures appeared as distant specks where the road curled back into view, way out of range now. Eventually, Talisker clambered down the boulder-studded slope to the road and the wagon. The beaten man's eyes stared up unblinkingly into the sky and Talisker stood watching him long enough to determine that he was dead. His pants pockets were turned out, empty. Talisker did not want to touch him. The horses continued to graze contentedly in the ditch up the road.

He supposed that they would eventually find their way back home. He felt helpless. There was no aid he could render to the dead man. Though he had as little to do with society as possible these days, he knew that its wheels of justice were hardly turning, that there was little in the way of real law to go to even if one was inclined to seek it. But he also knew that all-seeing God had witnessed the same act he had, and that his counterpart, the Dark One, was no doubt present at this scene, too—and perhaps both were sufficiently distracted to allow Perry Talisker, the hermit of Union Grove, to slip back into the woods unnoticed in pursuit of his quarry.

Thirty-seven

The doctor did not know his way around the New Faith head-quarters. The town had closed down the high school before his oldest child was ready for kindergarten. The very hum and bustle of the place made him uneasy, as though he were too close to the dangerous machinery of a sinister enterprise. But he made a few inquiries among the men and women coming and going down the hallway, neatly attired in their costumes of earnest piety, the men clean-shaven and the women smelling of soap, and he was eventually directed out to the mule barn in one of the former ball fields, where Brother Jobe had gone to oversee the shoeing of his favorite mount, Atlas, by the group's farrier, one Brother Zuriel. A third brother, barely a grown man, stood watching.

"Morning there, Doc," Brother Jobe said in greeting, not even turning his head to see who was there.

"How'd you know it was me?"

"Brother Enos here said it was you coming across't the pasture a moment ago. You always think we're up to something, don't you?"

"Sorry," the doctor said, swallowing his pride.

"Honey of a day, though, ain't it? I got a mind to go for a ride."

The farrier politely asked the doctor to step aside so he could attend to the mule's left front hoof.

"You know my boy's missing, right?" the doctor said.

"I heard."

"The Reverend Holder speak to you about it?"

"I guess he did."

The doctor told him about riding up and down the county for two days with Robert Earle, and how his horse went lame, forcing them to return.

"Mebbe you should let us shoe your horse next time."

"Anyway, we didn't come across the slightest sign of him," the doctor said. "Nothing."

"It's a big county," Brother Jobe said.

"I know you have some men who were rangers in the Holy Land, men who know how to conduct a proper search."

"Indeed I do."

"I'd be very grateful if you could put them out to search for my boy."

"I expect you would."

"And it's not necessary to play games about this."

Brother Jobe gave the doctor his full attention. "You're pretty quick to anger, Doc," he said. "It's not good for your blood pressure. I'm not playing no games with you."

"I'm asking you to search for my boy."

"I know you are," Brother Jobe said with a penetrating look, "and I will."

The doctor flinched slightly.

"I can pay you in gold or silver or medical services," he said.

"It won't cost you but a pound of flesh."

"That's not funny."

"What makes you think it was a joke?"

The doctor sighed in anxiety and frustration but decided not to continue dueling verbally with Brother Jobe.

"Don't be such a gloomy Gus, Doc. We'll find him. A boy can't stray too far in this day and age, now can he? He ain't gonna hitch a ride to Altoona on no beer truck."

"I thought maybe I'd ride with the search party."

"Think again," Brother Jobe said. "In the first place, it would wear me out dealing with all your ding-dang suspicions. In the second place, you'll only get in the way. In the third place, your folks need you here, so I say you stay."

"He's my boy," the doctor said, and his mouth began to quiver.

"I know what it's like to lose a child," said Brother Jobe. "Me and my men'll stop by your place on the way out, get some particulars. I don't suppose you have any pictures of the boy."

"I have a drawing made by Mr. Pendergast, the librarian." Andrew Pendergast, man of many talents, now filled the void once occupied by photography. "It's maybe two years old."

"Can we take it along?"

"I suppose so."

"All right, then."

"There's something else," the doctor said, moving closer and speaking with quiet urgency. "We've got this fellow in town people call the hermit. Antisocial type. Probably not all there, mentally. Lives alone in a shack by the river." He explained how Jasper and Ned Allison had snooped on the hermit and what Ned had told Jane Ann Holder, his teacher. "I don't know if there's anything to it, but there's an outside chance of some connection there."

"Some sort of foul play?"

"I don't know. The Reverend Holder went to the hermit's place this morning and there's no sign of him."

"I'll bear all this in mind, Doc."

He also told Brother Jobe about what had happened in Argyle, the storekeeper who appeared to be offering boys for labor or sport."

"What the heck did he mean by that?" Brother Jobe asked.

"I sure wondered."

"Sport? Sounds like some kind of wickedness."

"I took it that way."

"Argyle, huh? Maybe we'll have a look-see that way," Brother Jobe said. "Sometimes the vexations of running this outfit put me out of sorts. I need to get away into sunlight and fresh air. You couldn't ask for finer weather to ride around in, now, could you?"

"The fall is longer here than it used to be."

"Maybe the old-timey times weren't so great as they're cracked up to be, Doc. We'll come by your place in an hour or so before we head out."

"I'm grateful for your help," the doctor said. Then he left the barn, neglecting to offer a handshake.

Not a minute later, Brother Joseph, the second in command to Brother Jobe among the New Faith order, came by the mule barn to consult on a few things prior to the search party's departure.

"I see the doctor finally humbled himself to come over in person," Brother Joseph said.

"He don't see the world like we do, but he's all right," Brother Jobe told his trusted adjutant, who would be left in charge of things. "It wasn't necessary for him to grovel or nothing."

"Did you tell him it was his boy who killed our stallion?"

"I certainly did not. And don't you breathe a word of that to nobody else. Not even amongst our own."

"I suppose you know what you're doing."

"I like to think so," Brother Jobe said, his stomach still aching vaguely despite the fresh air and sunshine.

THIRTY-EIGHT

Tom Allison rented the Reverend Loren Holder his most trustworthy mount, a nineteen-year-old half Percheron named Lucky. It was a massive gelding, sixteen and a quarter hands high, all black, with a broad seat and a gentle disposition, perfectly suited to Loren, who was a large man and an inexperienced rider. He rode Lucky from Allison's barn over to the rectory to say good-bye to Jane Ann, who had come home at noon, when the school day ended during harvest season. He'd told her that he was taking advantage of the fine weather to make ministerial calls at the more isolated farms scattered out in the county, which was at least partially true. He had a map hand-drawn by Dr. Jerry Copeland, who had used his U.S. Geological Survey topo map as a reference. The topo map was too tattered and valuable to lend out, now that they weren't printing them anymore, but the handmade map was a good one. Loren had panniers filled with corn bread, smoked trout, dried fruit, nut cakes, two bottles of Jane Ann's wine, a waxed linen poncho, two woolen sweaters, and a Bible. He had a leather drawstring purse containing nine ounces of old silver dimes and quarters in his trouser pocket.

Jane Ann came out the rectory kitchen door and stepped lightly through the fallen leaves and purple asters in the yard to where Loren sat on Lucky in the Unitarian church's old circular driveway. A patch of sunlight fell on her white muslin shirt so that she seemed illuminated from within for a moment.

"Aren't you high and handsome up there," she said, hands on her hips. "My hero."

"You thought so once."

"I still do," she said.

Loren shifted awkwardly in his saddle. The leather creaked. The burden of his secret objective weighed on him, while the sight of

Jane Ann filled him with both longing and anxiety. He felt as if he were embarking on a journey to some terrible self-knowledge that would alter him, that he was saying good-bye to things comforting and familiar without any promise of consolation. The thought made him shudder.

"When will you be back?" she asked.

"A day or two, I should think."

"I'll worry."

"There's nothing out there to worry about."

"James LaBountie said his father saw a panther on the road to Shushan."

"This is a mighty big horse," Loren said. "If I was a panther, I'd steer clear of him."

"I'll miss you."

"I carry you right here," he said, pointing to the center of his chest.

Jane Ann reached up for his hand and kissed it. He kissed hers back, then reined out Lucky, and clip-clopped up Salem Street toward Hebron.

THIRTY-NINE

Brother Jobe stopped in on Mary Beth Ivanhoe in her queenly quarters before he and his men departed. She lay propped up on a pile of satin pillows in her ornate bed with a baby in each arm, watching them nurse noisily, beads of sweat making trails from her forehead down the complex topography of her face. The pale flesh of her upper body fell in so many fatty folds that it was difficult to discern which was a breast.

"Somebody come and git these runts off of me!" she said. Brother Jobe wheeled around in the rush of Mary Beth's swarming handmaidens, who swooped away the squalling infants, helped the mother with her gusseted silk pajama top, and proffered a tray of fried chicken and cornmeal tidbits along with a tumbler of sweetened sumac and vinegar tea.

When the infants were out of the way, Mary Beth reclined with an arduous sigh and stared at the food in her lap.

"My titties are killing me," she said. "I got to run split sessions with these critters, there's so many of 'em."

"You done us a great good turn," Brother Jobe said. "Our folks is delirious with the little ones."

"Can't none of the sisters do a little gittin' with child? I could use a wet nurse around here."

"We're trying—"

"This is taking every last ounce of energy I got. Don't none of you men got the right spunk?"

"Tell you the truth, I think that ding-dang bomb in Washington all but sterilized this outfit. We took a chance passing so close to that city."

"It didn't appear to hurt me none."

"You're special, Precious Mother."

"Get me some damn nipple-end bottles, then, and milk the cow, why don't you?"

"The little ones need them antibodies and mother things."

"Well, I don't like it how all the actual work falls to me," she said, gasping a little, eyes fluttering in their sockets. For a moment Brother Jobe feared she would lapse into one of her seizures. He reached over to stabilize the lunch tray. Moments later, she seemed to come out of it.

"You all right?" Brother Jobe asked.

"I ain't been right since that sumbitch sideswiped me at the Hunter's Ridge Mall in 2006."

"Of course. We know your ailments and burdens—"

"You don't know the half of it."

"Well, let me get down to bidness—"

"This here ought to be your bidness," she said, seizing a drumstick.

"Mary Beth, I know you're vexed. We're both a bit sore beset this morning. I got two men waiting out there for me—"

"I know what you're up to."

"I'd appreciate it if you'd focus your mind and tell me what you know about this fellow they call the hermit."

"He's an odd one," she said, stripping the drumstick to the bone and reaching for her tea.

"Has he ever hurt a child?"

"Lord no. Where he goeth, the light shineth."

"Where's he at right now?"

"He's up north somewheres. Not far."

"Where exactly?"

"The hills. Hell's bells, I can't give you no coordinates. This ain't the U.S. missile command sittin' here. Sometimes I don't receive too good, you know. You tell them to put more salt to these hush puppies when you get a chance. And I'd like some pepper jelly, too."

"Is the boy with him?"

"The boy's with somebody. Not that hermit. Another boy. Older. They're up north, too. A valley. A bend in the river. What's that sourpuss face all about?"

"I got a bellyache."

"Alls you do around me is bellyache. Take some fennel tea. I know the sisters got some. They give it to me. Peppermint works, too. Taste this here and tell me if there's a damn bit of salt to it," she said, stabbing a fried corn tidbit with her fork and brandishing it in Brother Jobe's face.

"What all's the matter with you today, Mary Beth? Didn't I just say I got a ding-dang bellyache? I can't eat no fry-up!"

"Don't you yell at me, sumbitch. You'll give me a damn apoplexy."

A baby broke out crying in an adjoining chamber. Then another.

"Look what you done now!" Mary Beth said, sputtering cornmeal crumbs on Brother Jobe. "They'll put two more of them little monsters on me and I ain't even finished my chicken."

"Oh, Lord," Brother Jobe muttered and got up. "You want anything else today, you send for Brother Joseph. He's in charge while I'm gone."

"Last time you left him in charge around here I nearly starved to death!" Mary Beth said, but by that time Brother Jobe was out the door.

FORTY

Dr. Jeremy Copeland was brooding over Bullock's writ of exhumation when Brother Jobe stopped by on his way out of town with Brothers Seth and Elam, both of whom had served in the Third Ranger Battalion during the Holy Land War and more recently participated in the rescue of Bullock's boat crew at Albany the previous summer. Seth, a kind-eyed half-Cherokee from Chance, Oklahoma, was a skilled tracker famous for surviving a five-day trek across the Negev Desert without water after escaping the massacre at Ein Yahav. Elam, whose family went back in the Appalachians eight generations to a Scottish horse thief named Fyfe Persons, had been a North Carolina wildlife officer when the war broke out in the Holy Land. His company had parachuted by mistake behind Syrian Chinese lines at Hatseva and fought their way back to the American-held town of Dimona, losing half their number on the way. Now he was in charge of the New Faith's experiments with catfish farming. Both men were mounted on horses, a blue roan and a bay, while Brother Jobe rode Atlas, his big brown mule.

The doctor pushed out the squeaky screen door of his office holding the writ aloft as he approached Brother Jobe.

"Look what I received this morning from Mr. Bullock."

Brother Jobe took it and held it out at arm's length where his eyes could focus.

"This is about that young man you all laid to rest in June?" he asked.

"Right. Did you know about this?"

"First I heard of it," Brother Jobe said and handed the paper back to the doctor.

"You meet with Bullock now and again, don't you?"

"We ain't exactly bosom buddies. But it's good to see the wheels of justice finally aturning. Looks like he come to Jesus, so to say, on his elected duties."

"Can't we just let this boy rest in peace?"

"It's a murder outstanding, Doc, a serious breach of the social contract that absolutely nothing has been done about. The killer's still running free in our community. The rule of law is being flat-out snubbed."

"We know who did it."

"Maybe. But we still have to go through the proper procedure. You want me to send these two boys up to Karptown and do a summary execution? Believe me, they could get her done."

The doctor and Brother Jobe exchanged stares for a long moment. At length, the doctor shagged his head as if trying to shake a painful idea out of his skull.

"It'll work out for the best this way," Brother Jobe said.

"How about you lend me some manpower to dig up the coffin," the doctor said. "It says here Bullock has allocated some money for it."

"You apply to Brother Joseph while I'm gone. I'm sure he'll oblige."

Meanwhile, the doctor's wife, Jeanette, came out of the house with a tattered manila folder.

"I have those pictures you asked for," she said in a breaking voice and handed them to her husband.

"I'm right sorry about all this heartache with your boy," Brother Jobe said. "But I'm confident we'll run him down in short order."

"Run him down?" Jeannette said.

"Find him, I think he means," the doctor said.

"Yes, find him," Brother Jobe said. "You bet."

"Please do," she said, becoming teary. "I'll be so grateful."

She turned on her heels and went back inside, where she had been putting up hard sausage.

"She's suffering," the doctor said.

"Of course."

The doctor opened the folder and handed a photo up to Brother Jobe.

"Jasper was only three then," the doctor said. "Couldn't get printer cartridges after that."

"Jasper," Brother Jobe repeated. "I had a great-uncle Jasper. Biggest moonshiner in Scott County, Virginia. He did a volume business—"

Just then, a commotion down the drive between the office and the main house sent the horses and Brother Jobe's mule sidestepping nervously. Four men rushed forward bearing a fifth on a crude stretcher.

"He's hurt bad, Doc," one of the men said. All were townsmen, laborers on the Schmidt farm two miles north of Union Grove on the sunny side of Pumpkin Hill.

"You take those pictures and you find him," the doctor said to Brother Jobe as he turned to see about the injured man. It was Bruce Sauer, the stonemason, who had fallen forty feet off a scaffold while repairing the chimney cap on Bill Schmidt's house. "Bring him in the office," he told the stretcher bearers and disappeared inside after them.

"Lord have mercy," Brother Jobe said. He was about to mention his nagging bellyache to the doctor, but now it seemed trivial.

He and his men reined out the animals and turned down onto the quiet street.

FORTY-ONE

The town of Glens Falls, some two hundred miles north of New York City, nestled in an elbow of the Hudson River where that waterway quit its stately northward progress and shifted to a twisting, uncertain course before disappearing altogether in the dark mystery of the Adirondack Mountains. Billy Bones and Jasper Copeland entered it from the valley to the east, along a state highway where the chain stores once overflowed with plastic goods made in distant lands, and cars plied the multiple lanes ceaselessly, and the clownish tilt-up buildings dispensed the staple fried foods of the multitudes under their pulsing banners of light. All lay in ruins now, with the town's population reduced by disease, out-migration, and assorted hardships until it fell to sixteen hundred souls that were concentrated in the blocks of the old town center. They devoted themselves in the new times to a sparse trafficking in cordwood from the nearby forests and a trade in the meager wares that came on infrequent boats down the Champlain Canal from the workshops of Montreal. Not a few of the former inhabitants had scattered to the countryside, where they farmed or worked for farmers or cut the timber that became cordwood.

Jasper marveled at the vast, empty parking lots between the gutted strip malls, the shells of the bygone discount palaces, and the broad, broken highway itself, all of it encompassed by a tragic silence that was more a mute scream of history than an absence of noise.

"I think I was here before," he said.

"These type of places are everywhere," Billy said.

"It was different."

"One ain't no different than another anymore than one cornfield beats another."

"No, we had a car then. It *was* different."

"Damn, you must remember when you were a tiny baby."

"I do. Where did everything go?"

"America went to the dogs. All this went with it."

They plodded on, past the shattered plinth of a Honda dealership sign and the wreck of a Friendly's franchise sandwich shop and the bare concrete outline of a Stewart's convenience store and the skeleton of a Best Buy and a dozen other former landmarks until the highway necked down to two lanes. This led to a half-mile stretch of houses that had been converted inelegantly to business establishments at the end of the previous century, displaying their hideous frontage additions in materials not found in nature, and freestanding signs for chiropractors, opticians, and martial arts studios.

"What's a sheeropractor?" Jasper asked.

"Some kind of doctor. A foot healer, I think. Isn't that something you might know, Mr. High-and-Mighty Doctor Boy?"

"I must have forgot."

"*Sheero*, that's Latin for 'foot.' My sheeros is goddamn tired of pounding this road, I'll tell you that."

"Mine, too," Jasper said.

Only a few of the houses along this stretch appeared to be inhabited now. A column of smoke rose out of a chimney of one, a 1950s vintage bungalow. Two underfed children skulked without expression beside a broken fence. A woman in rough clothes dug in her dooryard potato patch while she sullenly eyed the passersby.

"Friendly types, huh?" Billy remarked as they passed, and he called out: "Don't worry, ma'am, we stole all our potatoes outside of town."

"Are you crazy?" Jasper said.

"Relax. We're almost there."

The stretch of miserable houses soon yielded on the river side of the street to the gigantic factory works of the defunct Finch-Pruyn Paper Company. Its wood pulp processing sheds were abandoned, its machines silent, its smokestacks idle, and the vast employee parking lot was given over to a cordwood-marshaling operation. Tumbled heaps of logs sprawled here, neater stacks of split logs there, and cribs of raw whole unsawn logs leaned up against the old factory walls. Gangs of grubby-looking men loaded wagons drawn by dray horses with the finished splits while others worked at cutting down the long logs on sawbucks in two-man teams. Another gang split these "rounds" with mauls and wedges. Yet another unloaded new logs just arrived off an ox-drawn wagon using block and tackle on a wooden crane.

"There's fools' work for you," Billy said.

"People have to stay warm."

"I'll stay warm this winter, you can be sure. But not by humping any old stove billets."

Not far from the factory grounds, Warren Street gave onto a burned-out district. Here once stood the fine homes of factory managers and executives, built in the paper company's heyday. Only a few shells remained among the weed-choked foundations after a catastrophic fire had leveled several blocks two Christmases earlier. This vacant quarter finally transitioned into the old center of town, which was composed of once-grand business buildings made of brick, limestone, granite, and even marble in the case of the preeminent bank, built during the era of national ascendance, ornamented exuberantly with turrets and bays and pilasters and swags. Now, only a few of the storefronts were occupied. Crudely painted signs on the windows denoted the various businesses: CANADA GOODS, GROCERY, CLOTHING ALL SORTS, HOTEL + MEALS and BATHS, and finally LIVERY. The rest were vacant, their shop windows blown out or boarded up and the upper stories occupied by birds and small mammals. The streets were nearly deserted as late afternoon edged toward evening. Not a single horse-drawn vehicle plied the carriageway.

Jasper gaped at the desolate scene in extravagant disappointment, his fantasies about making a new life in a bustling place dissolving.

"Is it always like this?" he asked.

"It's just a slow time of day," Billy said.

"Where are all the people?"

"Working in the cordwood yard or to home, I suppose. Madam's place is just a few blocks from here. Come along."

They trudged on.

"What's in there?" Jasper pointed at a seven-story colossus that loomed behind the business blocks on Glen Street, the town's main drag. The building had begun its existence in 1862 as the Glen National Woolens Company, making shoddy overcoats for the Union Army. After that, it housed companies that variously produced blankets, men's hats, rolltop desks, rifle stocks (First World War), bomb sights (Second World War), engine gaskets, and, in its final industrial incarnation, a company that fabricated stage sets for Broadway musicals, theme-park installations, and shopping-mall decor. It stood empty for twenty years after 1991. Early in the twenty-first century, three new floors were added to the original four and it was converted into luxury condominiums, of which only a few were sold before the project sank along with the economy.

"That's the Duke's castle," Billy said.

"They've got a duke here?"

"Not a real one. Just a damn boss grifter. There's lots of them around. Any town of size that's left has some boss grifter trying to run the show. I spit on them. They wanted me to join up but I told them to go to hell. Nobody's the boss of Billy Bones."

"What's this duke's name?"

"What do you care?"

"Just interested."

"Luke Bliss. Luke the Duke. He makes me laugh. He can barely run that cordwood concern, let alone rule a town. Don't stand there gaping like a fool. Let's go."

They trudged into another residential quarter, this one still intact, if run-down. The wooden houses were sturdy and dignified, in many fanciful styles, formerly the homes of businessmen and professionals in an age when the town's economy had dimension. Most were now in need of paint. In the oncoming twilight, candles glowed behind curtained windows.

"We're almost there," Billy said, "so listen up. Madam Amber, she rules the roost. You can't give her the high-and-mighty. She loves me like a son, so just follow my lead. There's eight floozies on board with her. One's a damn he-she, name of Angel. You steer clear of that one."

Soon they stood on the broken sidewalk before a large three-story building in the foursquare Italianate style with a cupola on top and a domed lantern on top of that. A wisteria vine clawed tortuously around the pillars and brackets of the front porch. The building had begun its life as Dr. Mortenson's Progressive Academy for Ladies in 1853, defunct in 1896. For decades after that it was a boardinghouse for single women employed on the Finch-Pruyn Paper Company's clerical staff. After 1959 it was a six-unit apartment house until the bottom fell out of American life and its present occupant bought it for two ounces of gold. Townspeople joked that it had come full circle to being a kind of ladies' academy again. The notes of a guitar were audible out on the street, something passionate and austere in the manner of Villa-Lobos.

"Here she is," Billy said.

A high-pitched laugh erupted somewhere inside, followed by the lower-register bellow of a man. Jasper detected the sweet smell of something baking on the mild evening air. His stomach growled.

"Don't do that around Madam," Billy said.

"I can't help it," Jasper said.

Forty-two

Brother Jobe and his two companions rode north in fine mild weather, inquiring, as they went, among workers in the fields and orchards whether they had seen a boy on the run. They received no useful intelligence about him whatsoever. They came across a few suspicious holes dug in a remote potato field that suggested food theft by someone desperate. They did not dig any potatoes for themselves, being well provisioned and bound by the ethics of their sect to pay for anything they needed. By late afternoon, riding along the fissured and broken old County Road 30, they arrived at a hill overlooking a lonely farmstead. Seth, who had sharp vision, detected something out of order from a distance.

"I see something dead, yonder, BJ," he said. "Blood on the ground."

"Let's have a look, then."

They rode down through a squash field to the little goat enclosure behind the house and found the mutilated carcass of a Nubian goat, its head cut off and hindquarters missing. The remains were stiff and flyblown, at least a day dead. Seven other goats milled about them bleating raucously. Their pasture was eaten down to dust.

"Elam, go have a look in that barn, see if there's any hay or grain. And fetch some water. I saw a hand pump in the dooryard. These critters is suffering."

Brother Jobe and Seth secured their mounts and went around to the kitchen door. For a house that was not abandoned, it was eerily still. They shared a glance and entered through the kitchen door, almost tripping over the body of an older man that the flies had been enjoying. Brother Jobe pulled a rag out of his coat pocket and held it up to his nose as he stooped to examine the body. He could tell by the disposition of things—the bloating, the blood pooled darkly in the back of the neck where gravity settled it—that the man had been dead for some time.

Seth jerked his head to indicate that they should venture farther within. They searched the downstairs rooms, finding nothing but the general state of clutter and untidiness, and crept carefully upstairs. In one of the bedrooms they found an unconscious woman of middle age tied to a steel bed. Her exertions had caused her to slip off the bed itself so that she was suspended by her bonds just short of a sitting position, semicrucified. Blood had dripped from the abrasions on her wrists all the way down her arms and seeped into the filthy bedsheets. The room stank of her eliminations. But Brother Jobe quickly determined that she was still alive.

Seth cut her bonds and Brother Jobe helped her slump the rest of the way to the floor. She groaned but did not wake up. They heard footfalls on the stairs. Seth drew a hog-leg Colt Bisley .45. The door squeaked open with a push from without. Seth cocked the hammer with his thumb.

"Expecting trouble?" Elam said when he found himself staring down the barrel of Seth's pistol.

"We found plenty," Brother Jobe said. "A wickedness without mercy come this way."

"I saw downstairs," Elam said.

"Put that ding-dang iron down!" Brother Jobe barked at Seth. "You two bring her outside in the fresh air. Find a clean blanket if you can. And move that man's body out of the house. I'll get her some water."

Minutes later, they had the woman outside on a blanket. Seth propped her up while Brother Jobe carefully held a glass of water to her lips. Some residue of instinct prompted her to take a first swallow. Then reflexes took over. A pint of water later, she opened her eyes, but didn't speak. Brother Jobe added a few spoonfuls of whiskey and some honey to her glass from his own rations and in a little while she began to cough and sputter. When she cleared her air passage, they let her lie back on the blanket with her head on a lumpy pillow.

"What's your name?" Brother Jobe said.

"Martha."

"Who done this to you?"

"I'm filthy," she said and began weeping.

"It's all right. We don't mind."

"I mind, goddamn it," she said.

"Seth, go fetch something clean for Martha to put on."

She continued to weep. Elam went inside and made a fire in the cookstove and heated a bucket of water. He found some soap and tore a bedsheet into rags and carried a chair outside. Seth returned with clean clothes. He and Elam hoisted Martha onto her feet and held her up. Brother Jobe unbuttoned her soiled shift and began swabbing her down with soapy rags. She cried through the entire procedure.

"Don't worry, ma'am," he said. "I worked in a nursing facility in my younger days. I done this a thousand times."

He dried her off with the remaining rags and helped her into the clean outfit: an old pair of green polyester pants and a rose-colored sweatshirt printed with a cartoon roadrunner and a word balloon saying *beep beep*. They set her back down on the blanket. With the late-afternoon temperature dropping, Seth found her a quilt from inside. Brother Jobe took a seat in the chair beside her blanket while Seth and Elam retired to the kitchen to make supper.

"Where's my papa?" she eventually asked.

"I'm sorry to tell you," Brother Jobe said, "but someone killed him. We got him out back now."

Martha cried some more but not as energetically as before, and she stopped rather abruptly. Brother Jobe suspected she was less than shattered by the news.

"We'll bury him after supper," he said. "You can choose the spot."

"All right."

"You going to tell me who done this?"

"Two boys. One about eighteen, twenty. The other younger. A child."

"You sit tight while I fetch some pictures."

Brother Jobe returned with the manila folder and handed her the pencil drawing of Jasper Copeland.

"He was older than this."

"That there's an old picture."

"It might be him then."

"He's the son of the doctor down to Union Grove."

Martha dropped the drawing.

"He claimed to be a doctor," she said. "Imagine that."

"Looks like he doctored you folks to a fare-thee-well."

"I'll tell you what: You ought to shoot him on sight. Him and his cohort both."

"I intend to bring them to the law."

"I wouldn't take the trouble."

"Yes, well, we're for due process and all that."

"They robbed me and left me for dead."

"What'd they take?"

"What do you think? Money. The older one, he violated me up there."

She broke down in tears again.

"I'm sorry," Brother Jobe said and proffered the water glass. She drank deeply as if trying to wash her insides clean. He waited until her weeping subsided before resuming his questions. "What did he look like, this older boy?"

"Fair-haired. Very skinny. And crazy, too. He made me listen to a song about himself."

"You don't say?"

"Oh, he's very proud."

"Matter of fact, he crossed my path not a few scant days ago, this selfsame singing bandit."

"Did he rob you, too?"

"Tried to. I give him a little taste of the Lord's wrath. In hindsight, I should have served up a man-size portion."

"If you see him again, you put a bullet in his head."

"We'll see about that. Tell me: Do you know the Lord, Martha?"

"What the hell are you talking about?"

"I'm talking about Jesus."

"You find somebody else to talk about him with."

"I know you've been through a tribulation, ma'am—"

"God doesn't care when we suffer. I know that now."

"We have a community down Union Grove way. We're building a New Jerusalem there one soul at a time. Oh, it's a sweet corner of the country in this time of hardships and travails. You're welcome amongst us, if you'd like to come."

"No thank you."

"You don't have to love Jesus right off."

"I'm not interested."

"You can think it over, Martha."

"I thought about it as much as I ever will. You tell me: If your Jesus has power over anything, why don't you ask him to turn the electric back on and make the world like it used to be."

"That world is no more, I'm sorry to say. But we can offer fellowship, warm hearts, busy hands, good eats, a place of refuge in the world."

"I got my own place right here."

"You can't stay here now, all alone."

"Of course I can."

Brother Jobe drank some of his own whiskey out of an old Lexan expeditionary bottle he carried it in.

"What sort of church man drinks whiskey right out of the jar, anyway?" she said.

Brother Jobe shrugged.

"You'll be called down to testify," he said. "Robbery, rape, and murder is serious business."

"First you got to catch them."

"We aim to."

"He's got a gun, that older one."

"I know."

FORTY-THREE

At the end of a long afternoon in the saddle, the Reverend Loren Holder rode around the back end of Lloyd's Hill in the northern reaches of the county and, just as the doctor's map indicated, came upon the cottage of Barbara Maglie with its gothic trimmings and aura of mystery. He had the odd notion, looking around, that he no longer knew what time he was living in, whether it was today or yesterday, or some temporal space apart from his personal experience of the world.

Upon his first glimpse of her, she was bent over at the waist picking rosemary stems in one of the several fenced gardens that extended around the cottage like formal outdoor rooms, each with its own geometry of beds, paths, plantings, colors, and scents. He sat atop Lucky watching her for a long moment, feeling light-headed, as if his blood were carbonated. The horse shifted its weight and the saddle creaked just loudly enough so that Barbara Maglie lifted her head and then her upper body, balletically, with a pronounced curve to her spine. She found Loren in her field of view and returned his gaze.

Panic seized Loren as her eyes met his. A chill pulsed through his inner fluxes, urging him to call off what suddenly seemed a foolish adventure, to rein out his horse and return to Union Grove as quickly as possible. But he did not yield to the panic. Instead, as though he were watching himself in a movie, Loren dismounted and led the horse down the path between the house and the sequence of gardens. Barbara Maglie waded through drifts of herbs and late-blooming asters, goldenrods, and cornflowers, and finally stepped through a garden gate fashioned fancifully out of twisted tree limbs.

Loren introduced himself, explained that he was the minister of the Congregational Church in Union Grove, and stated flatly that he had come to see her at the suggestion of his friend Dr. Jerry Copeland, who said that she might be able to help him with a problem of a delicate nature. Barbara Maglie appeared to understand exactly why he was there. Loren felt that she could see completely through him, as though he were one of those plastic models of human anatomy in the science museums of yore, only instead of his heart and liver, his sensibilities were on display and clearly labeled.

"Did he find his boy?" she asked.

"Not yet. We've got more men on the search now. Men who were soldiers in the Holy Land, who know what they're doing."

"They'll find him."

"How do you know?"

"How far can he go in these times?"

Lucky nickered. Barbara Maglie ran her hand along the horse's big jaw muscle and down his velvet nose. The horse did not flinch at her touch.

"It's terrible to lose a child," she said.

"I know," he said.

"You look healthy."

"I'm glad you think so."

"Did you bring silver?"

"I did. What are you going to do to me?"

"I'm going to help you."

"You sound very confident."

"I am."

"Do you ever fail?"

"May I call you Loren?"

"Please."

"Be easy, Loren."

"I'm trying."

"You don't have to try. I'll take care of you."

Her smile radiated an essentially female mystery that thrust Loren back to the sublime terrors of sexual awakening he had nearly forgotten: age fifteen, a summer night at a big house on Lake George, New York. A girl named Debbie Darrow, of advanced experience, who smelled like a strawberry and insisted on skinny-dipping in a thunderstorm. His excitement had reached such a pitch that he couldn't stop shivering, even after they got out of the water and made love on a sleeping bag in the room above the boathouse while lightning crashed all around and shook the flimsy rafters. She had a pack of menthol cigarettes and afterward lay smoking, whispering things to him in French, which he pretended to understand. The world never looked the same after that night. She dumped him a week later for seventeen-year-old Chad Moyer, who had a yellow Mazda Miata sports car of his very own.

"You can put your horse in the barn," Barbara said, startling him out of memory. "There's hay in the loft. I'll be in the kitchen."

Loren settled Lucky in a stall with a bucket of water and a manger full of hay and left his damp saddle pad drying on a half door. Then, traversing the yard between the barn and the house, he became acutely conscious of his fears, hopes, worries, and not a small degree of shame in selfishly seeking his lost carnal appetites. He felt hopelessly awkward in his own skin, a physically large man trespassing awkwardly in a female realm, like a Minotaur who had contrived to enter a bower. Meanwhile, the sun had dipped behind Lloyd's Hill, putting a bite in the smoke-scented air. He paused at the window in the kitchen door and watched Barbara Maglie move gracefully between her stove and various counters, hutches, and tables, the way her long skirt swayed and her hips shifted, the way her arms moved and her hands held their implements, the way the tops of her breasts heaved with her breathing in the shadows cast by the candlelight. She seemed purely representative of what was universally female and human, unknowable without being frightful. He knocked on the window. She signaled him to come in. Trembling, he entered her world.

FORTY-FOUR

Perry Talisker didn't bother making a supper for himself. Bundled in his blanket and Mylar sleeping pouch on a mattress of balsam boughs, he watched a single bright star emerge against a lustrous blue green twilight sky streaked with rose-bellied clouds. He knew now, as surely as he had ever known anything, that his days were numbered and that the number was a low one. He could sense, too, as vividly as anything he ever knew, that he was drawing close to his quarry: the big cat that left tracks the size of a child's mitten in the low, damp places and the bracken flats. He felt himself drawn to this climactic moment of his life like the man in a riptide being swept out beyond sight of land, and he was oddly relieved at the prospect of leaving the shore behind.

Lying on the fir-scented bed, reflecting on the end of his days, Perry Talisker's hunger pulled his train of memories past all the wonderful meals he had enjoyed across a lifetime, many of them dishes he had not tasted for years and never would again. He could imagine in all his senses, for instance, the gigantic batter-dipped, deep-fried sweet onion he used to order on weekend nights in the old times when he and his wife, Trish, splurged at the Outback restaurant at Aviation Mall outside Glens Falls. What a marvel that thing was! A gigantic sweet Vidalia split open by a cleverly designed patent device so that the onion layers formed petals like a great flower, allowing an eggy batter to penetrate every crack and fissure and then puff up magnificently when it met the hot fat in the Fryolator. The sublime crunch of the batter contrasted with the yielding sweetness of the onion and the smoky piquant dipping sauce that was several notches better than plain ketchup. He could never finish a whole one, but he'd still follow it with a rack of baby pork ribs, slow-cooked until they were nearly falling off the bone and then finished on the grill, offset with a dish of creamy coleslaw, which he regarded as a vegetable, something good for you.

Being in the food business himself back then, as head of the meat department in Union Grove's Hovington's Supermarket, Perry had standards. He wouldn't go to McDonald's—he didn't especially go for mustard and a dill pickle on his hamburger and he didn't trust their meat. He patronized only the better chains, where you could sit down on something soft and the lights were not fluorescent and the meat was a cut you could at least identify, a rib, a T-bone, a drumstick. But he also made a point, in those days, to seek out the few mom-and-pop places that remained in the backwaters. The Miss Ann Diner in Fort Ann was one of these. They offered home-made chicken and biscuits that Perry would drive twenty miles out of his way to eat. The gravy was made with real cream, the biscuits were wonderfully flaky, the chicken all white meat, and the portions heroic. They had a way with desserts, too: a bread pudding studded with chunks of bittersweet chocolate and saturated with bourbon whiskey; a many-layered coconut cake with supertart lemon filling; and, in summer, a toasted-almond peach cobbler.

For straightforward meat, he preferred his own cuts on the home grill. The steaks, of course, he butchered himself at the shop, his first choice being the porterhouse or New York strip with A-1 sauce and Tabasco, so tingly on the tongue. The hamburger he ground personally on the big Hobart machine at work, using a mix of sirloin, brisket, and chuck with the number 52 grinder plate. He always molded his burgers around a butter patty so that when they came off the fire, the butter perfectly saturated the hefty beef patty and then seeped out into the toasted kaiser roll. And, of course, there wasn't a better, meltier cheeseburger cheese than Velveeta. Toward the end of the good old times, before his credit cards went bad and the trade in electric appliances dried up, he bought his own personal home French-fryer machine so he could have fries whenever he wanted, and not those lame, limp oven fries from the frozen box—the real thing: thick-cut fresh Idahoes with a Russian dressing he made himself.

He held pizza in high esteem, though he had to admit that there was nothing wrong with good old macaroni and cheese. . . . This was Perry Talisker's last thought before the currents of sleep swept him away from himself onto the starry shoals of night.

FORTY-FIVE

Robert Earle worked a full day on the special room of inlaid wood paneling at the center of the former gymnasium of the old high school, where the New Faith order had framed in a multileveled warren of rooms resembling something like a beehive or, Robert sometimes thought, a maximum-security cell block. The room, he'd been told, was intended to be the winter quarters of Mary Beth Ivanhoe, the eccentric clairvoyant revered by the group as though she were its queen bee. Robert was also charged with instructing several young brothers in the finer points of finish woodworking and marquetry. What a contrast they were to the demoralized younger townsmen of Union Grove, he thought. The young men of the New Faith were positively buoyant with their situation in the world, eager to learn, and attentive. They didn't seem to miss the old times at all. They loved to scorn and disdain the absurdities of the old times in their workaday chats, cutting veneers and piecing together the complex patterns designed by Sister Zeruiah, who was chief among the women who attended Mary Beth Ivanhoe. Even with the high spirits of his students, Robert was not altogether comfortable laboring within the New Faith compound, but Brother Jobe paid in silver.

It was already dark when Robert returned home that mild Indian-summer evening. The woman he'd come to live with, Britney Watling, had had a long day of her own. She began it digging potatoes and onions, bedding them in straw in the cellar. Then she mucked the barn where she kept Cinnamon the cow, next door to the burned skeleton frame of her former home a block away from Robert's house. Then she forked the stall bedding into the compost heap for the following spring's planting. Then she worked on a set of ash-splint sorting baskets ordered by Mr. Schmidt, the wealthy farmer who had employed her murdered husband as a laborer and who, since Shawn's death, was always making little gestures of caretaking with her. Amid all this activity, she put together a supper of "fall pudding," a casserole of leftover corn bread, bacon cracklings, kale, onions, milk, eggs, butter, and hard cheese for Robert and her daughter, Sarah. They ate it with a salad of late-season lettuce and rocket in buttermilk dressing.

After supper, Robert and Britney took advantage of the mild weather to break down the contents and equipment of the summer kitchen and move it indoors for the winter—the round oak table, which had to be unscrewed from its pedestal to get through the door; the pots, pans, tubs, jugs, and crocks; the screened cabinet where they kept cheese and sausage away from flies, the china and tableware. When they were done and bathed—thanks to Union Grove's still-functioning town water supply, gravity-fed by the ancient reservoir on a shoulder of Pumpkin Hill—Robert showed Sarah how to play the "A" part of a fiddle tune called "Angeline the Baker." When Britney put her daughter to bed, there was still much to do. Robert had to sharpen his saws for the next day's work, and Britney needed to repair the lining of Sarah's winter coat. They were about to return to their chores when somebody knocked on the front door. This was not so unusual since Robert had become the mayor of Union Grove and was occasionally visited and even pestered at odd hours by townspeople with complaints.

This evening it was Terry Einhorn, the red-bearded, barrel-chested proprietor of the town's only grocery and general merchandise store. He appeared agitated yet did not readily disclose the reason for his visit. Robert invited him in and offered him a glass of cider, Holyrood's clear white, a new cider from the current year's apple crop, at 12 percent alcohol. Einhorn sold it at the store. Robert sat Einhorn at the circular oak table they had just brought inside to the winter kitchen. Britney excused herself.

"Wicked warm today, wasn't it?" Einhorn said when he had settled in his chair and drained about half his glass. Robert noticed that Terry's hand was shaking.

"You didn't come here to talk about the weather, did you, Terry?"

Einhorn drained the rest of his glass and Robert refilled it.

"There are twelve men hanging on River Road," the storekeeper said.

"You mean hanging around?"

"I mean hanging by their necks, from trees," Einhorn said. "Ten of them, anyway."

Robert sat frozen, staring at him.

"Excuse me," Robert said after an awkward interval. "Did you say ten or twelve?"

"Twelve. But two of them are hanging by their ankles. With their heads jammed between their legs."

Robert struggled to put together a picture.

"I don't get it. Like some kind of contortionist thing?"

"Their heads were cut off."

Robert looked past the dining room to Britney in the parlor, where she sat very close to a pair of candles, sewing in a halo of yellow light. He pulled his chair around the table, closer to Einhorn.

"Have you told anyone else?"

"Robert, they're right down there on the road for all to see. Everybody will know about it by tomorrow, if they don't already know."

Robert chewed the inside of his cheek. "Do you have any idea what this is all about?" he said.

"I was on my way to Bullock's landing this afternoon," Einhorn said, "now that he's running that weekly boat to Albany again. His man, Dick Lee, was there at the landing. He said Bullock had them strung up."

Einhorn proceeded to tell Robert what he had learned from Dick Lee about the bloody home invasion the previous night and Bullock's decision to summarily execute the surviving invaders.

Robert poured himself another cider from the battered old plastic jug.

"How'd two of them get their heads cut off?" he asked.

"Bullock did that himself."

"Pretty rough justice."

"They busted right into his bedroom and threatened the missus," Einhorn said. "I don't hold it against him."

"He's our magistrate. He's supposed to stand for the law."

"His first task is protecting the community."

"He's not the police."

"There are no police, Robert."

Robert and Einhorn drank in silence for a moment.

"These bandits—were they part of a larger bunch?" Robert asked.

"Dick Lee said he thought not. They were just a small band, out on their own. From Connecticut, apparently."

"Is that so," Robert said, thinking that he was from Connecticut, too, a place that existed a long time ago, in a galaxy of men in suits on commuter-train platforms and mothers ferrying children to lessons and hauling enormous quantities of purchased goods around in gigantic cars. All gone.

"Dick Lee said they strung them up where any other pickers or bandits were most likely to see them," Einhorn said. "In case there *are* more of them out there."

Robert could see where this was all leading.

"Okay. I'll go over there tomorrow and ask Bullock to cut them down and bury them," he said.

"That would be a good thing, Robert."

They sat silently at the table for a long time. Einhorn reached for the jug and poured himself another glass.

"You come by the store sometime," he said. "I'll give you a free refill."

Robert noticed Britney glancing over her shoulder at him from the other room. Then she snuffed the candles she was working by and went up to bed. Moonlight streamed through the window on the staircase.

"Thanks, Terry. Was that pretty much it, then?"

"Well, not exactly."

"What else?"

"A bunch of us are thinking maybe the town ought to call off Halloween."

"Who?"

"Doug Sweetland, Tom Allison, Ben Deaver, Robbie Furnival, some others. Out of respect to the doc, with his son missing and all."

"The trick-or-treat or the grown-up ball?"

"Both, I guess."

"Maybe I should see how Jerry and Jeanette feel about that, first."

"I don't know as I'd bother them about it just now."

"You know how the people in town look forward to it. Even the folks out in the countryside come in. It would be like canceling Christmas."

"Just a thought we had."

Einhorn drank up the rest of his cider and said good night.

Robert carried a candle in a tin saucer upstairs, where Britney waited for him in bed, sitting up with a candle burning on her nightstand, wearing an old plaid cotton bathrobe. He told her what was going on while he undressed.

"Halloween is all the kids talk about now," she said. "They'll be very disappointed."

"I know."

"These times are hard enough."

"I'll have to decide what's right."

"I'm glad Mr. Bullock hanged those men," Britney said. "If it was up to me, I'd leave them hanging until the crows picked their bones clean, just to make sure that people who have no business around here get a good look."

"That's what they did in the Dark Ages," Robert said.

"Maybe they had the right idea."

FORTY-SIX

Jasper Copeland followed Billy Bones as they entered Madam Amber's Fancy House, as the owner styled it, through the kitchen door into a scene of busy festivity. Candles blazed in a six-light chandelier over a long work table, around the stove, and in wall sconces. The big room was warm and alive with savory aromas of a meal being prepared. Guitar music and laughter resounded distantly from the front parlor. Several of the girls who happened to be in the kitchen squealed at the sight of Billy and swarmed around him as he swung down his shoulder bag.

"Look at you! You're hurt!" cried Hannah, who was fair-haired, big-boned, and sturdy. She'd been icing a cake moments before.

"Some damn gomer got me with a load of birdshot."

"How'd that happen?" asked Cheyenne, who was petite, with sad eyes and a turned-down mouth.

"Poker game," Billy said. "The bastard was dealing aces from the bottom and I called him on it."

"Poor thing!" said Christine, who was half Korean and wore a kimono loosely, affording glimpses within.

"Who's this?" asked Cheyenne, pointing at Jasper.

"That's my protégé, Johnny-on-the-spot Hopkins," Billy said. "I rescued him from a burning house down by Durkeetown."

"Did not," Jasper said.

"Aw, shut up. Let me do the talking."

"I'm a doctor," Jasper said.

"You! A doctor!" Hannah said, and all the girls laughed.

Just then, Jasper noticed another of the girls, Megan, seated at the far end of the long kitchen table. Her robe was off one shoulder and she was nursing a yellow puppy dog at her breast. She had lost a baby of her own five days before. The others noticed Jasper staring at her with his mouth open.

"Someone killed the mother," Cheyenne said. "People will eat a dog around here."

"How could you know anything about doctoring?" Hannah said.

"I swear, he doctored me up when I got shot," Billy said. "Picked the lead pellets right out of my flesh with a dagger. His daddy's the doc down in Union Grove. Any of you girls know him?"

"My father doesn't come here," Jasper said. He was still staring at Megan, as fascinated by her big bare breast as with the dog suckling at it.

"So you say," Billy said. "Maybe he's upstairs right now."

They all laughed at that, even Katie Savage the cook, who was wrangling a large pan of roast rabbit and barley pilaf, redolent of rosemary and butter, out of the oven. The sight and smell of the food diverted Jasper's attention.

"Do any of you gals ever get down Union Grove way?" Billy said.

"We don't make house calls," Cheyenne said, and they all laughed again.

"How'd you happen to hook up with this rascal?" Hannah asked Jasper.

"Only just to get here," he said.

"Liar!" Billy said. "He already done crimes with me."

"No, I didn't. I was just there."

"He was just there," Billy said, making a wry face.

"Why'd a kid like you want to come here, to a house of pleasure?" Christine asked.

"I didn't know what this was," Jasper said.

"Do you know now?" Hannah asked.

"I guess I didn't spell it out for the little doctor boy," Billy said.

"It used to be a ladies' academy," Cheyenne said.

"It ain't changed," Billy said.

"I was looking to set up working for a doctor here in Glens Falls," Jasper said. "Till I'm ready to go out on my own."

For a moment the women stared at him in the utmost curiosity, as if he were some oddity from the depths of the sea dredged up in a net.

"Why not just work with your papa?" Hannah asked.

"Did you run away from home?" Christine asked.

Jasper didn't answer.

"Oh, he's a desperado of the first degree," Billy said. "Don't let his looks and his stature fool you"

Then a voice from the hallway said, "Who let this donkey in out of the pasture?" Madam Amber swept into the room and around the table and swaggered up to Billy. "I hope you came back with some money in your pocket this time."

The owner of the establishment was forty-six, fine-boned and full-figured. She wore a bead-stitched gown that draped shimmeringly down her pronounced curves. Her face was powdered. A silver streak curled out of her brown hair from the part at the center. She wore a large white flower behind her ear, made of silk and wire.

"Do I have money? Mama, I'm goddamn rich. Lookit here!" He dug into his pocket and pulled out a fistful of coins, and from these he extracted the shiny yellow gold coin he'd taken at the Lovejoy farm. "Do you see this?"

"Looks like a half eagle," Madam said, squinting closely.

"You're goddamned right it's a half eagle. And there's plenty of silver on top of that. So get ready for me, Mama. Billy's coming at you. And everybody else line up in size order outside the door."

The girls all laughed again.

"You want to give me that half eagle in advance, in case you get careless?" Madam said.

"Hell, no. I got plans. Tell me, is the duke still running his game?"

"I imagine he still is."

"Then those boys have a date with Billy Bones, too, is all I can say."

"You're a bigger fool than I thought."

"Think they can cheat me again? I learnt all their goddamn tricks. Just watch if the tables don't turn now. I spit on those gomer sons of bitches."

"When did I hear that before?" Madam said. "And by the way, you stink like a carp. You're not staying in my house another five minutes without a bath."

"What can I say? I've been out rambling and gambling."

"Hannah, take Mr. Bones upstairs right now and scrub him down. And burn those rags he came in with. Who's this kid?"

"That's my protégé, Johnny Hopkins. His daddy's the doc down in Union Grove. He trained for doctoring at his daddy's knee."

"You run away from home?" Madam asked, stooping down to meet Jasper eye to eye.

"Yes."

"How come?"

"I couldn't stay there anymore."

"He killed someone's horse," Billy said.

"Is that so?"

"Yes, ma'am."

"What'd you do that for?"

"It stomped my dog to death."

"How'd you kill the horse?"

"I poisoned it."

"That's some doctoring. You know about poisons?"

"Not so much."

"He done crimes with me since then, though," Billy said.

"Don't do any around here and we'll get along just fine," Madam said. She turned to the girls. "He stinks, too. Someone make sure he gets a bath when Billy's done."

"And somebody send a bottle of that sparkling cider upstairs to me, pronto," said Billy as Hannah tugged at the sleeve of his tattered, bloody shirt.

Before she could drag him out of the room, another voice resounded from the hallway: "Is that who I think it is?"

A tall figure with a shadow of a beard entered the kitchen, slinking and swaying in an exaggerated manner. She wore very abbreviated denim shorts and a puffy pink sweater. Her legs were strikingly muscular, her breasts unnaturally pointed, her eye sockets darkened with blacking, and the lids painted in lead white for emphasis. Her mouth was florid red, like a wound. "Look what the cat dragged in," said Angel, the transvestite. When she spoke, her jaw muscles rippled.

"You'd eat what the cat dragged in," Billy said. "In fact, you'd eat the cat itself."

"I'd eat you," Angel retorted. "But you'd have to pay me double."

"I'd pay you to move to Rutland if you promised to never come back here," Billy said.

"I live in a Rutland of the mind," Angel said.

"Except you're so far out of your mind you can't even see it from here."

"Oooooo," Angel vamped. "She's making me feel bad."

"I can make you feel a whole lot worse—"

"Both of you shut up right now!" Madam shouted in an impressively shrill register.

"Come on, Billy," Hannah said, tugging his arm.

"And send up something for me to eat, too," Billy said as Hannah led him away.

"Katie, you keep account of what he eats, hear?" Madam said.

"Yes, ma'am."

"You must be hungry, kid," Madam said to Jasper. He nodded. "Give him a nice meal, too." She then swept out of the room as grandly as she had entered.

Christine told Jasper to take a seat at the end of the long table. Katie slid a plate full of the rabbit and barley in front of him with a side dish of carrots cooked in honey and butter and two large buttered slices of bread.

"What kind of bread is this?" Jasper asked.

"Canadian wheat," Katie said. Cheyenne slid a tall glass of milk beside the bread.

"All we ever get is corn," Jasper said.

"All most people get around here is corn," Katie said. "We get this special."

"Do I have to pay you?" Jasper asked.

"Don't worry about it," Katie said. "It's on Billy Bones's account. You can carry in some stove splints for me when you're done."

At the other end of the table, while Jasper ate ravenously, Christine and Cheyenne carved a couple of pumpkins into jack-o'-lanterns. Megan had put the puppy on the floor. It was now exploring the nether regions of the big room, which contained shelves full of food stored in glass jars and tins.

Jasper mopped his plate with the bread and thought of asking for seconds, even though he was quite full.

"Here, try these," Katie said, setting a dish with two golden apple fritters dusted with powdered sugar in front of him. Meanwhile the puppy came over to him and began tugging playfully on his bootlaces. Jasper put down a fritter and picked up the puppy. As he held it against his chest and buried his nose into its soft fragrant fur, his eyes filled with tears. He tried to conceal his face, but the puppy squirmed so intensely Jasper had to put it back down on the floor. He rubbed his tears away on his sleeve and quietly finished his fritters, watching Christine and Cheyenne carve the pumpkins while Megan took over icing the cake. When she was finished, she shoved the bowl and the spatula down the table to Jasper.

"Go ahead. Lick them clean."

"Thank you."

"Are you sad?"

"I guess."

"Do you miss your home?"

"It doesn't matter."

"Sure it does."

"I'm a lost soul," he said.

"All of us here are lost souls," Megan said. "But we're happy together. I wouldn't hang around with that Billy Bones anymore if I were you."

"I'm not going to. I only came along with him to get to Glens Falls."

"He's not right in the head."

"I know," Jasper said, recalling Billy's assault on the driver of the onion cart, the blood flying. "Who's the cake for?"

"Margaret. She's upstairs with a date. Maybe we can save a piece for you."

"I wish you would."

After the fritters, though, Jasper was content. He felt himself growing sleepy sitting upright in the chair. The next thing he knew, somebody was shaking his shoulder. It was a young girl in the vicinity of his own age. She wore a long skirt and a purple jersey that read G.F.H.S. LIONS with the number 69 below that. Her big owlish eyes radiated intelligence while her small mouth suggested a prankish nature. A pile of caramel-colored hair was held on top of her head with a plastic tortoiseshell clip, though sprigs and wisps had escaped around her face and neck.

"You're supposed to come with me," she said as Jasper looked up, blinking.

"Where?"

"The bathroom."

"I don't need to go to the bathroom."

"You need a bath. You smell like something that died."

"I can wash myself."

"I hope so," the girl said. "If you couldn't do that by now you'd be too dumb to live. Come on."

Jasper grabbed his backpack and followed. Of all the others, only Megan remained at the table, enjoying a glass of blackberry brandy. She winked at Jasper on his way past. From the hallway, he could glimpse a little slice of the parlor and the front entrance. It was alive with candles and music and conversation. Someone came in the door, a large man with a handsome gray beard, a broad-brimmed hat, and a riding cloak. His entrance provoked a commotion among the others in the parlor and when he took off his cloak, the lining was shiny scarlet.

"Who's that man?" Jasper asked.

"He runs the town," the girl said.

The girl grabbed Jasper's hand and pulled him roughly toward a back stairway. In the rear of the second floor was a spacious bathroom. They entered and the girl put her candle in its saucer on a dressing table. On the other side of the room stood a long cast-iron claw-footed tub with two water pumps at the drain end. The girl worked them with each arm. One pumped cold water into the tub. The other was connected to a boiler in the basement, stoked morning and night by a man-of-all-jobs named Ernie who had been on the maintenance crew at the paper mill in the old times and now worked in the house for meals and a warm place to sleep in a room over the woodshed. Steam rose off the bath as it filled.

"See how I'm doing this?" the girl said.

"Yes."

"You take over and do like I'm doing until you get enough water in the tub. Then take your clothes off and get to scrubbing. There's plenty of soap and brushes and washrags in the brass basket. You don't have bugs, do you?"

"Not that I know of."

"You been itchy at all?"

"No."

"Wash good. I'll be back for you."

She was out the door before he could ask her name.

When the tub was filled to his satisfaction, Jasper folded his dirty clothes and left them in a pile on the floor across the room, between a sink and an unlit chunk stove. He climbed into the tub and sank slowly into the steaming water, marveling at the luxury of it. The soap was very harsh and the brushes very stiff. He worked to scrub the grime out of his fingernails, and everywhere else he could see, and when he was done scrubbing he ventured out of the tub to pump more hot water in. He had almost fallen asleep again, lying back in the warm, soapy water, when the door creaked and the girl returned. Jasper cupped his private parts in both hands and went rigid.

"Don't come in here," he croaked. "Please."

"It's nothing to me to see a naked person," she said.

"I'm not used to it."

"Lookit, I brought you a nice nightshirt," she said.

"Can you just hang it on the hook there."

"Madam told me to put you to bed."

"Okay."

The girl hung the nightshirt up on the back of the door, strode confidently across the room, and grabbed a white cotton towel off the table.

"I can get one myself," Jasper said.

She came over to the edge of the tub, dangling the towel.

"Here," she said. "Take it."

"I can't take it."

"Why not?"

"I'm covering myself."

"So, uncover yourself."

"Can't you just drop it on the floor next to the tub?"

"There's water on the floor. Look what a mess you made! You slopped water all over the floor."

"I'm not getting out with you in here."

"Fine," the girl said, and tossed the towel back on the table with the stack of folded ones. "I'll be in the hall."

She marched out of the room. The door shut with a resonant click. Jasper opened the tub drain, stood up, and cautiously climbed out. He was halfway to the table when the door opened and the girl came back into the bathroom. Jasper lunged for the towel and wrapped it around himself.

"You don't even have hair down there yet," the girl said and started to laugh, bringing a hand up to cover her mouth as she did. Jasper just cringed in place. The girl came forward again, took a second towel off the table, and began drying Jasper's hair and shoulders while he remained hunched in mortification. The towel smelled of strong soap. "How old are you, anyway?" she asked.

"Eleven," Jasper mumbled.

"I'm thirteen," the girl said. "I could have a child soon."

"That would make you somebody's mother," Jasper said.

"You're brilliant," the girl said.

She declared Jasper dry and retrieved the nightshirt from the hook on the door.

"Put your hands over your head."

"I can put it on myself."

"Okay, put it on yourself." She handed over the nightshirt. He took it in his left hand while he held the towel over himself with his right.

"Would you at least turn around?" he asked.

"I'm not going to look at you."

"Yes, you are."

"I'm not the least bit interested in you."

"Then turn around. Please."

"Oh, all right, you big baby."

She turned around. Jasper turned his back on her, too, dropped the towel and slipped on the nightshirt, which also smelled of strong soap. When he turned back around, she was facing him again.

"I saw your backside," she said.

"Did you enjoy it?"

"It's a nice little backside."

"Everybody has one."

"So true," she said.

"Even you," he said.

"I have a very nice one, thank you."

"Good for you."

"People have commented."

"Do you go around showing it off?"

"Not especially."

"Then why would anybody care?"

The girl smiled. It transformed her face.

"You really don't know, do you?"

"Why, is it some big secret?"

"You could say that," the girl said. "Pick up your boots and come with me."

"What about my clothes?"

"You'll get them back clean tomorrow. We do wash morning, noon, and night around here. Come now."

She scooped the candle off the dressing table. With his boots in one hand and his knapsack over his shoulder, he followed the girl farther down the back hallway to a small bedroom. It contained a bed with a few threadbare stuffed animals on it, a bookcase, a battered chest of drawers with a lace counterpane and little colored glass bottles and other small treasures on it, and a small doorless closet with a few dresses and coats hanging within. On the wall was an old poster in black-and-white of the New York City skyline lit up at night in the old times, viewed from under the span of the Brooklyn Bridge. The girl turned down the sheets and blankets and told Jasper to get under the covers. He did. She put down her candle and sat on the edge of the bed. Jasper lay back blinking at her.

"What's your name?" he asked.

"Robin."

"Are you somebody's daughter?"

Robin laughed ruefully. "Of course, silly."

"Who? Madam?"

"No one here."

"Why are you here?"

"I'm an orphan," she said. "I heard about who you are."

"I'm nobody," he said. "Whose bed is this?"

"Mine."

"I can't sleep in your bed."

"You're nobody, so there's nobody here."

"You're a girl."

"Thanks for noticing. Anyway, I have things to do still. We only get busy at night and I have to fetch and do for the ladies."

"Just give me a blanket and I'll sleep on the floor," Jasper said, but moments after the last word left his lips, he fell fast asleep.

"Good night, nobody."

Robin leaned forward and kissed him on the forehead, then reached for her candle and left the room.

FORTY-SEVEN

Brother Jobe gritted his teeth and grunted, gazing up at the star-strewn heavens, his gut aching and his mind roiled by disturbing notions. The pain in his belly had retreated during the day and then returned after his supper of mashed potatoes, fried cabbage, and salt ham with the inevitable corn bread. The pain started with the ham, and he had tried to quell it with whiskey, which he now regarded as a damn-fool boneheaded mistake, since the idea was growing on him that he had developed cancer of the stomach—weakness of the gut ran in the males of his line. His daddy had fallen ill back when the American car industry was collapsing and headquarters in Detroit called one day to say they had a mind to close down the family's Ford dealership. His daddy fought the higher-ups, but they had to consolidate, they said, to save the company. His father drank Pepto-Bismol by the crate that year and lost seventy pounds until he looked like a scarecrow in his old shirt collars. A visit to the hospital and a battery of tests sealed his fate. The doctors poured chemicals into his veins and aimed radiation into his gut for nine months, but it was an ugly, losing battle. The way Brother Jobe saw it, the Ford Motor Company had killed his daddy just as surely as if they'd stuck a tire iron in his heart.

It all happened so quickly. And then the United States itself got some kind of fatal thrombosis of the economy, and people all over Scott County lost jobs and couldn't pay their obligations, and the malls shut down one by one, and the oil stopped coming from Mexico and Venezuela and Africa and wherever else it used to come from until neighbor was fighting neighbor for it at the pumps, and then the goldurn pumps shut down. And then things really started going downhill. The lights went out. Folks started shooting. It was sickening. The whole Sun Belt was boiling over with gunfire and with animosities that everybody thought had been left behind in the old century. Boy were they wrong. By then, Brother Jobe was running his New Faith church in a tin-can Butler building that used to be a beverage store out on Highway 664. He never liked the building but it was all he could afford. To his way of thinking, the building itself was kind of an affront to the grace of Jesus. Anyway, before you knew it, Brother Jobe and his people had to get out of Scott County, Virginia, and they went north, where things were said to be more peaceful.

Now, as Brother Jobe looked up into the autumn night sky he thought that the constellation Pegasus traced the shape of a Ford F-110 pickup truck. He gnashed his teeth at the pain in his gut and cursed Henry Ford and the invention of the automobile, which had ruined his father as well as his beloved state of Virginia, with every meadow and pasture paved over for discount shopping and the NASCAR nonsense.

His two men, Brothers Elam and Seth, slept in their bedrolls a few yards away across the glowing remnants of their campfire. Elam snored like an outboard motor. They were tired from a long day in the saddle and then having to dig a grave for the old man. Brother Jobe was weary, too, but his gut hurt too much to sleep. He wished he could conjure a healing spell upon himself, but his gifts, such as they were, ran in other directions. They mystified even him, the possessor of them. But they were what they were.

Someone lit a candle in an upstairs room of the Lovejoy farmhouse. It couldn't have been anyone but Martha up there, he thought. How did she imagine that she could carry on alone all the way out here? And if, in the days or weeks ahead, with winter coming on, she realized the futility of her situation and set out from this desolate place to find family or loved ones elsewhere who might take her in—why, then, how would he, Brother Jobe, find her again when he finally took the vicious child he was after into custody, hauled him back to Union Grove, and sued for prosecution of his crimes? Not to mention the singing bandit. Martha's pigheaded independence galled him. As another spasm of pain sliced through his gut, Brother

Jobe wished he might strike a taste of his own pain into Martha, for her impudence, and in the process perhaps persuade her to come back to town with them. At that moment he thought he heard a groan from the vicinity of the upstairs room with the candle burning in it. It soothed him to feel his righteous powers in operation, and he turned his gaze away from the farmhouse window back to the stars above, whispering into the darkness: "Oh, Jesus, son of mercy, by thy wounds am I healed. I resist sickness and disease. Carry my sorrows and let me walk again in wholeness. All praise to thee, thy will be done, amen. . . ."

FORTY-EIGHT

The angles of the wall suddenly yielded to curves as Loren Holder tried to focus his vision beyond Barbara Maglie, who led him gently by the hand upstairs into a bedroom. She had fed him a supper of smoked trout chowder, little dumplings of acorn squash worked into cornmeal and fresh cheese in sage and butter, sausage sautéed with apples, and a pear pudding. It took her two hours to prepare the meal and he did not tire of watching her move about in her kitchen. He listened to her talk about her life, and he talked to her of his life, and they shared stories about the common life of their times and their country. She'd given him an especially fine delicate etched stemmed glass to drink from and she refilled it repeatedly with a reddish beverage she brewed herself. It was a potent infusion made with various amounts of monkshood, ginseng, *Turnera diffusa, Tribulus terrestris, Datura metel*—one of the nightshades—cardamom, Salvinorin A, hellebore, cherry root, borage, staghorn sumac (for color), and active agents from the resin of *Cannibis sativa*.

In the sparsely furnished but airy room above, Barbara lit beeswax candles on stands at each side of a low platform bed, which was covered with an intricate patchwork quilt in the design of a nine-pointed star.

"Did you make that yourself?" Loren asked.

"No," Barbara said. "Someone gave it to me."

"It's complex."

In one corner a little chunk stove stood with glowing embers visible through the window in its door. The room was quite warm, a novelty in these times, especially at this time of year.

"Are you comfortable?" she asked.

"My thoughts are racing."

"Don't worry. Soon we'll focus them."

One thought that raced through Loren's mind was that it might be better to flee the premises than go through with the ceremonies at hand. But he apprehended that it was only a thought, and no accompanying panic rose up in him to assist the impulse toward action. He was amazed at how easy it was to dismiss it and see it replaced by another thought: a recognition of how beautiful Barbara Maglie's face looked in the flickering light.

"Let me help you take those boots off," she said.

He looked around and, seeing no chair in the room, sat at the edge of the low bed. Loren watched Barbara pull off his boots as if she were bringing to conclusion a long ordeal in his existence. She took the boots and very deliberately arranged each before the window opposite the bed, with the toes pointing outward.

"What's that for?" Loren asked.

"You'll walk on moonbeams when you leave here."

"There was something in those drinks you gave me, wasn't there."

"A few things.

"I was a stoner back in the day."

"I know. You told me."

"I did?"

"Yes."

"I'm more than a little stoned."

"I would think so. I've got something else for you." She reached for an inlaid enamel box and held it open for him.

"What's this?"

"A little extra treat for your spirit."

"How did you learn so much about herbals," Loren asked and reached tentatively for a dark lozenge-shaped tidbit in the box, turning his gaze from the box to Barbara and back.

"I'm a witch."

He broke into a sudden gale of laughter. "Are you a good witch or a bad witch?" he said. "I'm sorry. I can't help it."

Barbara smiled radiantly, enjoying his intoxication.

"I'm a good witch," she said.

Loren recomposed himself.

"Okay then," he said. He placed one of the little tidbits in his mouth. It was sweet, fruity, with an undertone of turpentine.

"Be still and behold," she said.

She kicked off her slippers, reached down and pulled a drawstring at her waist that let her skirt fall, and, in a motion that seemed continuous, crossed her arms and drew her cotton blouse over her head so that she was left perfectly naked. Loren felt things shift drastically inside of himself, a long-lost feeling that was like the return of a familiar companion after a long separation.

"You can trust me completely," she said.

He nodded his head, believing her.

Turning this way and that in a manner that recalled both ballet and Oriental ritual, she allowed Loren to gaze at her while the chemicals intensified his wonder. She moved slowly, like a statue in a museum of living figures.

"How long have I been watching you?" he asked eventually.

"A while."

In fact it had been half an hour.

"I think I've lost track of time," he said.

"Good," she said. "Lift your arms up straight over your head." She drew off his shirt.

"I'm going to give you a massage now," she said.

"I'd like that."

"Lie back."

She unbuckled his belt and pulled off his trousers.

"Look at me!" he said, marveling at his own excitement as if at a great spectacle from a distant hilltop. "I'm the man in the room!"

"Ah! You're coming home to yourself."

"How did I get lost?"

"It doesn't matter anymore. Turn over."

Barbara went to get a little pan of clarified butter that she'd put on a trivet by the woodstove to warm, and began her ministrations by spreading the oil on his shoulders and then straddling his long back so that her breasts lightly met his oiled skin as she reached forward to press and release the large muscles of his neck and shoulders. She operated her charms and secrets on Loren well beyond that, deep into the night, working his arousal as though it were a project in the arts, a composition, a culinary venture, or an opus of chamber music, taking care to forestall his arrival at the ordained destination until his every cell aligned with her purposes and rang in harmony at the molecular level. To Loren, the witch of Hebron became the essence of all women, in a delirium of scent, warmth, wetness, hair, and yielding flesh that had him, finally, spinning on a blinding circle of light until he sobbed in a spasm of gratitude. The herbal agents in his system transformed what had begun as a physical experience into a musical one, carrying him from a suspended chord to a resolving seventh, like the conclusion of a hymn.

FORTY-NINE

It was much later that night when thirteen-year-old Robin returned from her duties and chores to her upstairs room in the back of Madam Amber's Fancy House. The rooms below still rang distantly with voices, laughter, notes plucked on strings, and fugitive strains of lovemaking. In the light of her candle, Robin found Jasper immobilized in the toils of sleep just as she had left him hours before. She slipped out of her clothing into an oversize faded green T-shirt printed with the likeness of a forgotten star of a forgotten musical fashion from a forgotten faraway place and the words RASTAMAN BUFFALO SOLDIER on it, and inserted herself between the sheets beside Jasper like a bookmark. He rolled onto his side. Robin pressed up against his back and curled an arm around his chest. He wheeled around suddenly.

"What are you doing?" he asked.

"I'm coming to bed," she said. "What's wrong?"

"I can't be in here with you."

"Of course you can. Why not?"

"You're a girl."

"So what?"

"I'll sleep on the floor."

"No, stay."

He struggled to get out of the covers, but she held on to him and he was effectively pinned between her and the wall.

"Let go of me."

"Wait," she said.

"Please!" he said, his voice breaking.

"Be still. Just for a little while. I won't hurt you."

He stopped struggling. They lay quietly together for several minutes.

"See," she said. "You're safe with me."

His breathing modulated.

She ventured to stroke the smooth skin where his temple met his hairline. "You're a beautiful boy," she said.

"I'm nothing," he said.

"Has nobody ever been kind to you?"

He dissolved in tears, thinking of his mother and father and their constant kindness, and his teacher, Mrs. Holder, and his friends, and all the people back in town, and his betrayal of their kindness in his many crimes. But as he sank into desolation, his body yielded to the shelter of Robin's arms and her fragrance of soap and lilac. Slowly, as the moon outside the small window moved from behind a chimney into the naked limbs of a locust tree, he melted farther into her embrace, becoming aware of her softness and her sweet breath against his ear, until at last, still hiccuping with broken sobs, he dared to reach around the surprising curve above her hip.

"Sweet, lost boy," she whispered.

"What will happen to me?"

"Don't worry," she said and kissed his lips.

Rather than shrink away, he submitted and was astonished to feel a thrill running through him, a thrill with the qualities of a metabolic awakening. She kissed him again and he kissed her back, wishing suddenly to drink her soft lips in, to consume her. The minutes moved the moon through the naked branches of the locust tree to a perch above a nearby rooftop as the two lay entwined, their breathing more rapid and their kisses ever more urgent, until Jasper kicked off the blankets. Robin wriggled out of her T-shirt, presenting to him a field of warmth and softness as astounding as a new world, and assisted him out of his nightshirt, so they were finally skin to skin, moving and rocking with each other in a tropism that led Jasper into a velvet rhapsody of stars and tides.

As he came back to himself, he lifted his body above Robin, the moonlight holding her nakedness, marveling at what he had just discovered.

"Something happened to me," he said.

She giggled shyly behind her hand. "It's what happens to people," she said.

"Do you know what I mean?"

"Of course I do."

"Did it happen to you, too?"

"Yes," she said. "More than once." She giggled again.

"More than once?"

"Girls are like that."

Jasper settled onto his back, his mouth open.

They lay quietly, head by head, watching the moon move behind a distant church steeple. She fished for his hand and he allowed her to hold it. The ambient sounds throughout the house had subsided into silence.

"I brought something for you," Robin said. She deftly rolled onto her feet, stepped over to the chest of drawers, and returned to bed with a plate of something, which she balanced now on the flat of her stomach beneath the shelf of her ribcage and her emerging breasts.

"What is it?"

"Birthday cake."

She gave him the fork. He rapidly devoured several mouthfuls.

"You have some, too," he said.

"I had a piece of my own already. This is all for you."

He slid the plate onto his own belly and finished the rest of the cake.

"Do you know the name of the doctor here in town?" he asked.

"Dr. Hankinson. He comes and sees the ladies twice a month."

"I want to go see him tomorrow."

"What's wrong?"

"Nothing. I'm looking for a position. Do you know where his office is?"

"Yes. Not far from here. What sort of position?"

"Assisting. When I grow a little more, I'll go out doctoring on my own."

"You should wait until your voice changes. People like their doctor to have a deep voice."

"People aren't so picky when they're sick or injured. You'd be surprised."

"If Dr. Hankinson takes you on, you can stay here."

"I hoped to get a room with my position."

"You can stay here until you do. Then I'll come visit you in your room."

"All right."

"You just stay away from that Billy Bones. He's no good."

"I'm through with Billy Bones. He's a crazy person. They should lock him up somewhere and throw away the key."

Robin took the empty plate and put it on the floor. She pulled the covers up over them and buried her nose in the place where Jasper's neck met his shoulder.

"Don't be sad anymore," she whispered to him. "You have me now."

The moon drifted below the distant silhouette of the old Finch-Pruyn Paper Mill's smokestack. Very soon, foreheads touching, they both fell asleep.

Gray daylight was gathering in the branches of the locust tree outside the window when a commotion downstairs woke Jasper and Robin. They bolted out of bed together, fumbling with their nightclothes, and followed the screams to the stairway. Someone was fighting on the floor below. Through the stairwell, they could see bodies moving and clothes flashing and something red spattering the carpet. More screams joined the commotion and the thuds of something hard striking flesh. Jasper and Robin crept down the stairs to see.

Billy Bones wrestled on the floor of the landing with a strapping figure in a negligee. He repeatedly brought down the barrel of an automatic pistol against his adversary's head. By now, several of the other girls had ventured from their rooms into the hall, along with a naked elderly male customer and Madam Amber herself.

"Oh my goodness," Robin whispered, gripping Jasper. "It's Angel!"

"You're killing me!" Angel shrieked as Billy brought the steel down on her again and again.

"That's exactly what I aim to do, you goddamned freak of nature. Try to rob me, will you!"

Madam saw Robin on the stairs and screamed up at her. "Run down the back stairs! Go get Mr. Bliss and his men!"

Robin reacted instantly and automatically and ran up to the third floor to get around to the back staircase. Jasper hesitated, in thrall to the blood and mayhem, gripping the balusters like prison bars.

Angel lay motionless. Blood ran out of her head off the edge of the stairwell and dripped down into the first-floor foyer below. Her pulse had faded and her organs were shutting down. Billy Bones hoisted himself up and wobbled in place, still drunk.

"Don't bother going to get Luke the Duke. I killed the son of a bitch an hour ago."

All the women shrieked again and ran off in different directions.

By this time, Robin was out the back door and running down the alley for help.

Billy glanced up and spied Jasper on the stairway.

"Get your stuff," he said. "We're leaving."

"I'm not going," Jasper said.

Billy Bones didn't waste a moment arguing. He sprang around the landing and up the stairs and caught up to Jasper in the doorway of Robin's room. He seized a fistful of Jasper's nightshirt, shoved him in the room, and slammed the door. He saw Jasper's backpack at the foot of the bed.

"Where are your clothes?"

"They took them to the wash."

Billy Bones rifled Robin's chest of drawers and found a red sweatshirt and a pair of denim overalls. "Here, put these on," he said, shoving them into Jasper's midsection.

Jasper just stood there holding them. "They're girl's clothes," he said.

Billy smacked him on the side of the head so hard that Jasper's ears rang. Trembling, he struggled into the shirt and then the overalls.

"Hurry up."

"I don't know how to fasten them."

"Goddamn you," Billy said, doing it for him. "You can doctor on people and you can't put a pair of bibs on yourself. Jeezus H. Christ. Get those boots on now."

"The legs are too long."

"Roll them up, goddamn it! Are you just pretending to be stupid all of a sudden?"

Jasper fished into his backpack for his spare socks while Billy tossed his boots at him.

"I don't want to go with you."

"Too goddamn bad. You're coming. Tie them laces up!"

When he was done, Jasper remained seated resolutely on the edge of the bed. Billy reached out and yanked him onto his feet.

"Grab that sack of yours. Let's go."

With a fistful of the hood on Jasper's sweatshirt, holding him like a dog on a short leash, Billy dragged Jasper downstairs, past Angel's body, which still lay sprawled in the second-floor hallway. Billy retrieved his own shoulder bag from Angel's bedroom and proceeded down to the kitchen on the first floor. None of the other women of the house, including Madam Amber, were still on the premises. Only the elderly Ernie, the man-of-all-work, remained, and he stood stunned in the kitchen, leaning on a broom, having just come up from firing the wood furnace in the basement.

"What are you looking at, you sorry old gomer?" Billy said.

"Where'd everybody go all in a hurry like that?" Ernie asked in a wheezy voice.

"The circus is in town. Get the hell out there and watch the parade before I cut your goddamn throat."

Ernie slunk out the back door while Billy plundered the cabinets for chunks of cheese and sausage and bread and stuffed them into his sack. Then, with Jasper still in tow, he ventured out of the house into the alley. The outside air had a shocking bite to it, nothing like the mild day before, and the sooty clouds scudded over the city rooftops on an ominous wind that stripped leaves off the trees.

"Why do I have to come with you?" Jasper asked.

"You're still my protégé," Billy said. "All the pains I took teaching you what I know? We got a special bond now, you and me. If you try to run off, I'll make sure you regret it."

Billy dragged Jasper forward and gave him a kick in the pants to urge him forward. They wended through the backstreets and alleys to the ragged edge of town, and before long they could look back and see the rooftops and steeples and defunct industrial smokestacks of Glens Falls in the distance.

FIFTY

Brother Jobe was dismayed to discover Martha Lovejoy stone dead in her bed that morning when he went up to persuade her one last time to give the New Faith a try before he and his men took their leave. Her refusal, he judged, was now complete and unalterable and her own stubborn fault. There was no obvious sign of what exactly had caused her death, though she was not young. Her recent injuries and deprivations may have taken some time to catch up with her, he reasoned further, taking a seat on the edge of her bed and studying her inert features, not so harsh and contrary as they had seemed in life, though her static demeanor now did not look exactly peaceful, either. He wondered if his own pain during the long, restless night had somehow affected the operations of his mind. In his distress, had he projected a wish of death her way, or had he imagined that? He simply didn't know. But it was yet another vexation to lose a valuable witness to what was shaping up as a pretty heinous crime spree by the singing bandit and his younger accomplice.

It happened that the pain in his own gut had abated again. It got bad every time he took a meal, he now realized. Perhaps he had grown an ulcer, not a cancer, due to all the annoyances and irritations that ceaselessly visited him. Consequently, he swore to lay off eating until they'd accomplished what they set out to do: find the boy—and his bandit cohort—and return to town with them. If some bug had got a foothold in his innards, he'd starve it out. He could stand to lose a little blubber, anyway. His clothes felt tight these days.

"Martha," he said quietly to the corpse, "I'm truly sorry it has come to this. But we got to push on. We going to lay you to rest beside your papa before we do."

He took up her hand in his. It was cold.

"The sting of death is sin, and the power of sin is the law," he intoned. "But thanks be to God! He gives us the victory through our Lord. Listen, I tell you a mystery: We will not all sleep, but we will all be changed. For the trumpet will sound, the dead will be raised imperishable, and we will be changed!"

He put Martha's hand back down on the covers, patted it, and went downstairs.

There, in the kitchen, Elam had fired the cookstove and was frying up a batch of cornmeal pancakes in a big cast-iron skillet to eat with apple butter and a pot of roasted dandelion root "coffee," a New Faith staple. Seth stepped in the door with an armload of stove splints.

"Looks like we got another hole to dig," Brother Jobe said. "Sorry, boys."

Elam glanced over his shoulder and Seth turned his eyes to the ceiling.

"Martha done up and died on us last night."

"Dang," Seth said. "After all that."

"She hang herself up there?" Elam asked and flipped three corn cakes expertly. "They tend to do that, I've noticed, when the man of the house is taken."

"No, looks like her heart just give out, poor thing," Brother Jobe said. "You two go ahead and eat, though. I'll turn out the animals."

"I'll save some flapcakes for you."

"Don't bother. I ain't hungry."

They buried Martha next to her father between two butternut trees behind the house. When Martha's grave was ready to receive her body and they lowered her down into it on a blanket, Brother Jobe conducted a brief ceremony. Then he went to the paddock behind the barn and saddled their mounts while the younger men filled in the grave. Before leaving the Lovejoy farm, they opened the gate to the goat pasture and set the animals free.

"Shame not to take them back with us," Elam said.

"We ain't the herder type," Brother Jobe said. "Anyway, how I see it, if I leave them in that there pen, by the time we get home and send someone to fetch them, they could all be dead. This way they at least got a chance."

The goats followed the mounted men as far as the road where, seemingly bewildered by their freedom, they stopped and turned to gaze back on the only home they had ever known.

FIFTY-ONE

The Reverend Loren Holder woke up from the most intense caval-cade of dreams he had ever known, in a room filled with light. He knew at once exactly where he was. The clarity of his mind amazed him, considering the substantial dose of chemicals he'd received the night before. Nothing about what he was feeling might be de-scribed as a hangover. If anything, he felt energized and confident, fully within himself and comfortable, completely and cosmically refreshed, younger. *Restored* hardly encompassed it. *Reborn* came closer.

All the particulars of his hours with Barbara Maglie, and the hours of dreams they melded perfectly with, seemed immediately accessible to him, without being overwhelming—the symphonic swirl of perfume, hair, yearning, and warmth that was woven against a tapestry of the highest pitched emotion. She was not in the room, but her scent lingered on the pillows, and so did some strands of her silvery hair. The things in his world assumed a satisfying congru-ent order that had been absent for as long as he could remember, even his knowledge of what had happened to his country and his people over the years. It suddenly seemed as ineluctable as gravity or the presence of love in the universe. He was tempted to think again in terms of God.

The smell of bacon frying prompted him to dress and go down-stairs, where Barbara Maglie attended to their breakfast. She wore a long skirt of bright silk patches and a thick gray sweater.

"Good morning," she said, lifting a pan of corn bread from her oven and cracking some eggs into a buttery skillet using one hand, as a professional chef might. "How do you feel?"

"Strangely marvelous."

"I would think so."

"Something happened to me last night."

"Yes, that's true."

"I think I even know what it was. But something tells me not to talk it to death."

"Your instincts are right," she said. "Come and have breakfast before you go."

He took a seat at the end of her long table. She brought over two plates, dishes of fresh butter and blackberry preserves, and steaming mugs of rose-hip and skullcap tea.

"Your wife is very beautiful," Barbara said.

"How do you know?"

"I had a vision."

"What kind of vision?"

"The far-seeing kind."

"She is beautiful," Loren said.

They ate silently for a while. Loren watched a red-tailed hawk alight on a fence post in the nearest of the several gardens. It carried a mole in one of its talons and reached down furtively to tear off bits of the mole's flesh, quickly returning upright again to survey the yard with its fiercely hooded eyes.

"You're very beautiful, too," Loren said.

"I know. I'm a witch."

"You kill me."

Loren finished his eggs and mopped the last of the yolks with a piece of corn bread.

"I have a feeling everything will be all right with me now," he said.

"It will," she said.

"What about you? Will you be all right, here, all by yourself?"

"Of course. It's how I live."

"Don't you get lonely?"

"Loneliness is a state of mind, not a state of being."

"I guess I should know that."

"You did. You forgot. Now you'll remember."

"Men," Loren said. "We have these protective instincts."

"I know," she said. "There's nothing wrong with that. But I'm a witch. We have our ways."

She placed her fork and knife on her plate in a conclusive gesture.

"I'd better see to my horse."

In a little while, Loren had Lucky saddled up and ready for the long ride back to town. Barbara came outside to bid him farewell. There was a bite to the morning air that was new. Wind bent the treetops and stripped away leaves. Clouds moved swiftly through the sky, while here and there patches of blue appeared, suggesting a weather front breaking through.

"The thing is," Loren said, "what if I want to see you again?"

"You can," she said. "But you'll be all right, anyway. You might imagine you're in love with me, but you're really in love with the world again."

"That's a good way of describing how I feel."

"By the way, I had another vision. I saw you with four children. Boys."

"Really? Doing what?"

"I don't know. Nothing bad. It was like you were their father."

"Do you have a lot of visions?"

"Not so many as you'd think."

"Can you tell me what this one means?"

"No. It was just a flash through the brain. I'm a witch, not a goddess."

"I don't know about that."

Loren took her hand and she allowed him to kiss her on the lips. Then he mounted his horse.

"You know something I really like about these new times?" she said.

"What?"

"You men look so good on your horses."

"Really?"

"Yes, much better than the old times, in a German car with the top down. A horse is better."

She laughed musically and turned back toward her house. Loren reined out Lucky and walked him up toward the road.

"Thank you for everything," he called out over his shoulder to her.

She waved without looking back.

FIFTY-TWO

More than once in the early going that day Jasper attempted to run away from Billy Bones as they hiked up another shattered road into the lonely highlands of Washington County on the east side of the Hudson River. Each time, Billy ran him into the ground, banged his head against the dirt or the pavement or a tree, and told him he would kill him if he tried it again. As their climb grew steeper, Jasper gave up trying to run away. He reasoned that sooner or later they would stop for the night and he'd find an opportunity to slip off and make his way back to the house in Glens Falls and take refuge with Robin, who would hide and protect him. All he had to do was be patient.

Around midday they halted at a little bridge over a nameless creek on the back side of the Gavottes.

"Take a seat," Billy said.

"Right here on the bridge?"

"I don't see any traffic around."

Jasper sat down with his back against the rusty old guardrail. Billy did likewise.

"Give me that hunting knife of yours."

"What for?"

"For my peace of mind is what for. Give it over."

Jasper did not respond quickly enough to suit Billy, so the bandit grabbed Jasper's backpack and began rooting around in it. "What the hell?" he said, extracting a potato. "You holding out on me?"

"I didn't know that was in there."

"Like hell you didn't."

"It's just a stinkin' potato."

"What else you got in here?" Billy asked. He felt around, found the hunting knife, and stuck it in his own sack. Then he came across the tattered remains of the toy stuffed animal that Jasper had rescued in the abandoned trailer. "What all's this?"

Jasper's insides ran cold. "It's nothing."

"It's some kind of puppet or dolly."

"It's nothing."

"You keep saying that. All right then." Billy lobbed it over the guardrail on the downstream side of the bridge. Jasper sprang up and rushed to the rail.

"What'd you do!" he screamed.

"Nothing," Billy said. "Don't you run after it and make me get up. Get over here and sit your ass back down again. I aim to eat my lunch now."

As Jasper watched the current carry away the stuffed animal, his helplessness closed a door to the room in his mind where his rage lived. He shuffled back and slumped next to Billy.

"Puppets and dollies is girl stuff," Billy said. "You got to man up."

He took out the victuals he had purloined from Madam Amber's kitchen and spread them out on his leather shoulder sack between them.

"Help yourself," he said.

"I'm not hungry."

"Aw, don't give me that. You just walked five miles without no breakfast. You got to be hungry."

Jasper shrugged.

"You going to give me the silent treatment now, like you don't like me anymore?"

"I never liked you."

"What? You lying little bastard—you worshipped me!"

Jasper couldn't help issuing a noise that was half laugh, half sob.

"You begged to be my protégé."

"You imagined that."

Billy glared at him as if a bad odor had come between them.

"Well, I'm hungry, even if you're not, so excuse me while I eat my damn lunch."

He devoured a half pound of Moses Kill cheddar and a hunk of hard sausage and battled the oppressive silence by making sounds of delectation as he ate.

"What's not to like about me?" Billy asked when he had put a dent in his hunger. "I got a sunny disposition, I got style, I'm colorful, I'm generous to a fault, I even got a song to sing. You won't meet a better companion in these hard times than yours truly. Answer me."

"You keep murdering people."

Billy recoiled as if stung. "I don't mean no harm by it," he said. Jasper laughed ruefully.

"Okay, maybe that don't sound right. Look, people get in the way and they don't have the sense to get out of the way."

"What about that man on the onion wagon? How'd he get in your way?"

"Is your memory impaired, boy? That son of a bitch emptied two barrels of birdshot at me. A man does that, and misses, he might as well write out his own death warrant."

"You were robbing him at the time."

"Yeah? Well, he should've been perfectly happy to part with a little bit of cash money and a pound or two of goddamn onions than to lose his goddamned life protecting them. But no, he up and decides to defend his onions. Jeezus Christ on a cracker! Would you pay four bits of silver to save your damn life? I sure would for mine, if it came to that. Let me tell you something, Johnny boy. There's a whole world of goddamn stupid gomers out there who make bad choices in life. You can't blame Billy Bones for that. Their fate is in their own hands."

"Why'd you kill that Luke the Duke?"

"You weren't even there!"

"I know that."

"You know everything, you goddamn know-it-all. You really want to know? I caught the son of a bitch cheating again at cards and I called him on it and he got all huffy and said his boys were going to teach me a lesson. And I don't take threats to my person lightly."

"You already knew he was a cheater."

"Well, I gave him another chance. Billy Bones is fair-minded and bighearted."

"Maybe you should have just stayed away from that card game like Madam said."

"Maybe you should just shut your damn mouth, since you're a child and don't know nothing about how the grown-up world works. Society's got a right to honest games of chance. If everybody cheated like that, there wouldn't be any card games at all in this world. And the world would be poorer for it."

"Were you trying to rob them, too?"

"Hell, no! Why would I do that? Then there wouldn't be any game."

"Because that's what you do. You're a bandit."

"I don't do it around the goddamn clock. You say you're a doctor. I don't see you doing that nonstop twenty-four goddamn hours a day."

"If you didn't drag me out of Glens Falls, I might be working for the doctor right now."

"I took you out of that hellhole for your own good, believe me."

"Why did you kill Angel, the he-she?"

Billy glanced this way and that way, as if searching the labyrinth of bare branches above for an answer.

"He, she, it," he mumbled. "That's a whole different story. There's no way a child would understand that."

"You sure acted like you hated her."

"'Course I do. Did."

"Then what was your bag doing in her room just before we left?"

Billy began to speak but hesitated and puffed out his cheeks, sighed, and shook his head.

"Look," he eventually said, "you don't want to eat none of this food, that's your business, but we got a ways to go yet today."

Jasper gazed at the remains of sausage and reached for it.

"That's right. You better eat," Billy said. "That's a good choice you just made, however you judge me for the moment. I want you to know, I ain't any wild-eyed crazy killer type. I ain't had a week like this one in, well, never. This is not my normal way. A lot of things seem like they got out of hand in recent days. When it rains, it pours. I vow to you that the next bunch of people we come across, I will be as nice as pie to, long as they don't pull a shotgun on us or try to cheat us or beat our ass. Does that sit all right with you?"

Jasper nodded his head, still chewing.

"Say it."

"Okay."

"Okay what?"

"It's all right with me if you don't kill anyone ever again."

"Okay," Billy said. "And it's all right with me if you don't kill no more horses, either. Come on. Let's go."

FIFTY-THREE

Not long after departing the Lovejoy farm, Brother Seth picked up some tracks in a muddy stretch of Goose Island Road leading north-west into the highlands of the county. They were the footprints of an adult and a child. They followed them through midmorning until, in the elevations of the Gavottes, they came upon the grisly scene of a body in a ditch near an abandoned wagon filled with onions. There was no horse in the vicinity.

Seth and Elam, who had seen plenty of death in the Holy Land, agreed that the corpse was about a day old. They agreed it was a man's body based on its size, remaining scraps of clothing, and the length of the hair on the skull. But much of the flesh had been consumed by animals, including the soft tissues of the face and hands. One whole leg was missing, and there was a black maw of blood and shredded cloth around the abdomen, where the organs had been eaten out.

They all held rags up to their faces not so much against the stink as the awful carnage it presented. Seth and Elam rolled the corpse over to examine the other side. It was as stiff as a cedar slab.

"Lookit here," Elam said to Brother Jobe, who squatted in the dust beside them. "The back of his skull's all bashed in. That ain't the work of any wild animal."

"I got to suppose that this mischief was done by our quarry, the boy and the other," Brother Jobe said.

"Their tracks lead right to it," Seth affirmed.

"What a terrible wickedness that child walks in," Elam said.

"A sorry amen to that," Brother Jobe said.

"What do you want to do with these here remains, BJ?" Seth asked.

"I say we load him in the wagon, hitch it up to a couple of horses, and follow where the road leads. Maybe inquire along the way if this poor soul belongs to somebody. Try to find the law hereabouts, if there is any."

"That suits me," Elam said. "I'm tired of digging graves for strangers."

Seth took a map out of his jacket and looked it over.

"Looks to me like these two are heading straight for this here town of Glens Falls, about seven miles up the road."

"All right," Brother Jobe said, "then that's where we'll go. Hoist that body aboard, boys."

"You want us to put him right up there on them onions?" Elam asked.

"Didn't I just say so?"

"It's disgusting."

"Well, you can't throw all them onions in a ditch in times like these," Brother Jobe said. "This here must be a thousand-dollar load. Folks can always peel a onion. Go on, heave him on in."

They covered the body with a blanket and lifted it into the wagon's box. The blanket happened to be the one rolled up behind Seth's saddle.

"Dang," Seth said. "That blanket was like an old friend to me."

"You can warsh it out," Elam said.

"Not after a dead man slept amongst it. You can never warsh that out. And Halloween's coming, too. It gives me the chills just to think of it."

"Well, let's get him to where he's going before he turns into a durned pumpkin," Brother Jobe said.

"I wish he would turn," Seth said. "He'd smell a whole lot better."

Elam carried a small repair kit of waxed thread and an awl with a number 5 needle. He stitched back the girth, collar, and traces of the wagon harness. Then they hitched the horses to the wagon, leaving Brother Jobe aboard Atlas, the mule. Seth and Elam tossed their saddles into the wagon box with the onions and the dead man, and the trio set out once more, down from the highlands into the broad Hudson River valley below.

An hour later they came upon a white farmhouse set a hundred yards from the road. It was a tidy establishment with an orchard in the front yard whose trees were heavy with apples. Fields of neatly stooked cornstalks rolled out on the land beyond the house. Elam and Seth hung back on the road with the wagon and the corpse while Brother Jobe rode up to the house, dismounted, and went to the door. A woman in an apron answered, wiping her hands, and spoke briefly with Brother Jobe. Then he withdrew with a tip of his hat and swung up onto Atlas again while the woman went back inside.

"Our man don't belong to this outfit here," Brother Jobe reported. "Nor has she heard any of her neighbors say they're missing nobody. She ain't seen any sign of the boy and his cohort either."

They stopped at three other farms along the way. Nobody knew where the dead man was from and no one had seen Jasper and Billy Bones. They did learn, however, that the closest thing to constituted law in Glens Falls was a gentleman named Luke Bliss, whom people spoke of as "the Duke" in a generally ironic way. The town, one old farmer told them, was a pitiful remnant of its former self. In his childhood, he said, the town was so lively and fine that a national magazine called it Hometown USA.

"It don't look like we're going to locate who this fellow belongs to," Seth said.

"Maybe we'll be keeping these onions, after all," Brother Jobe said as they continued on.

"And the wagon to boot," Elam said.

"Long as we don't have to keep the corpse," Seth said.

FIFTY-FOUR

Robert Earle walked the four miles from Union Grove to Stephen Bullock's plantation. For most of it, he enjoyed the bracing autumn air and the tranquillity of the landscape away from town and the bustle of the New Faith headquarters where he'd been working for weeks. On the last stretch, along River Road, he came upon the twelve hanged men, two of them dangling by their ankles with their heads jammed incongruously between their legs, just as Terry Einhorn had said. Vultures and crows were roosting on the corpses now, picking away at the flesh. Robert's presence barely disturbed their grisly operations. He tried throwing stones at one especially ugly vulture, but it returned quickly to perch on one of the purple-faced victims, using its beak to enlarge the hole where the nose used to be. The stench of death was overwhelming and Robert did not linger. It was a quarter mile farther to Bullock's place.

After inquiring at the mansion, Robert was directed to Bullock's landing across the road on the Hudson River. The landing consisted of a U-shaped wooden crib wharf and a small-goods warehouse in unpainted board and batten. Bullock had come down to dispatch his new trade vessel for Albany, thirty-seven miles downstream, with a cargo of new cider in barrels and several tons of grain: barley, corn, and oats. The boat was a sloop with the name *Sophie* painted on the transom in yellow and black. It carried a crew of six. Bullock was giving the manifest a last look before handing it back to his captain, Tom Soukey, one of four men who had been held in a hostage-and-ransom racket in Albany the previous summer before being rescued by Robert and a company of New Faith men.

"Tom," Robert said in greeting. "You're looking fit."

"I'm back at it," Tom said. "That's how much I love this river."

"Nice boat."

"It's a great improvement over the old girl," Tom said, referring to the *Elizabeth*, a much smaller catboat that had been their former trading vessel.

"Did you build her right here?" Robert asked Bullock.

"We found a man who used to run the boatyard up at Essex on Lake Champlain. Or rather, he found us."

"How fortunate."

"For us or for him?"

"Both, I guess."

A mate called down from halfway up the main mast saying that the halyard was clear. Tom Soukey said they were ready to go. "If we're not back in four days, send the boys down to fetch us home again," he added.

Tom hopped aboard. Two of his crew pushed off the wharf with gaffs while one raised a jib. Once they got clear of the landing, the mainsail went up with a great flapping of canvas. Robert and Bullock watched as the stately, tall-masted boat heaved downriver against the brilliant ochre of the foliage on the far shore.

"Tom and I played on a softball team in town years ago," Robert said, admiring the progress of the *Sophie*.

"Is that so?" Bullock said. "Why, that gives me an idea. How about you get a team of the townsmen together and play a team of my people? We could make it a regular thing. Maybe even get the farmers to put up a team, and the men up in Battenville. Pretty soon we'll have a league. Everyone would like it."

"I still have my old glove," Robert said. "I'm sure there are some aluminum bats kicking around town. But what do we do for a ball?"

"I'll have the ladies here stitch one up," Bullock said.

"I bet those New Faith boys could field a pretty good team, too."

Bullock made a face. "I don't know. Those Southern rednecks have a special gene for baseball. They might wipe up the floor with us."

"It'd force us to raise the caliber of our play."

Bullock sighed. "There's something about them I just don't like," he said. "But I suppose you're right. Is that what you came over to see me about? Softball?"

"No, that was your idea, Stephen. I came to see you about those bodies hanging along River Road."

"Quite a spectacle, isn't it?"

"I've had some complaints about it."

"I suppose you heard we were invaded the other night."

"I did."

"We came very close to being murdered. In our own bedroom."

"I heard."

"I killed three of them myself. Kind of amazed I still had it in me."

"Would you consider cutting them down now?"

"Absolutely not. They're just getting ripe."

"Stephen, this isn't the fourteenth century."

"It's not our mom and dad's America, either. I intend to keep them strung up until they rot out of their nooses."

"That's just plain morbid."

"If there are any more out there like them, looking to rape and pillage, I want them to see how things work around here."

"It looks like lynch law. You're supposed to be the magistrate."

"Believe me, justice has been served."

"What do I tell the folks back in town?"

"Tell them to steer clear of River Road for a month or so," Bullock said.

"I doubt they'll want to come down here and play softball with all these bodies rotting."

"Well, it's getting late in the year anyway," Bullock said. "There's no point in rushing anything. Let's aim for next spring on this softball league idea. But I suggest you start organizing it now. Talk it up. See if the farmers and the others want to get in on it."

FIFTY-FIVE

At midafternoon, Perry Talisker hunkered behind an ancient stone wall at the margin of the woods and caught sight of the big cat pronking for mice in a blueberry flat behind an abandoned farm below Todd Hill. The farmhouse, in the distance, was a roofless charred ruin. The barns lay fallen in heaps covered with brambles and Virginia creeper. Poplars dotted the old cornfields and pastures. It thrilled Perry to see nature triumph over the residues of man, even while it quickened his desire to strike back at God and his creations. He put down his field glasses and swung the Marlin rifle off his shoulder. He could get the cat in his sights, but at more than three hundred yards, lacking telescopics, and with the wind gusting, he decided to hold back the shot. The cat probably had a feeding range of ten square miles or more, and a missed shot might send him to another part of the county.

Perry felt lightheaded, having not taken a meal in two days. He was content with the notion that his duties in this life were winding down, and except for this final obligation, he felt the weightless delight of being untethered at last from the things of the world. Yet as his existence worked toward merging with the ethers of time and space, he felt the beauty of the earth ever more keenly. Watching the big panther pounce playfully in the blueberry scrub, Perry imagined the joy it felt in its muscles and nerves. The way its flesh rippled under its reddish brown coat, it looked well-fed, as though it had enjoyed a summer of kills and feasts. More than once, he wished he were the big cat.

The cat kept at it for a good half hour, stopping twice to eat something less than a mouthful. The North American mountain lion was known to like crickets and grasshoppers, too, though its

regular fare was the white-tailed deer. Then something Perry Talisker could not hear caused the big cat to stop pouncing and hold
its head high at attention. It blinked ostentatiously, then slunk away
in high grass the same color as its fur. Perry slung his rifle back over
his shoulder and left his rocky lair in pursuit.

FIFTY-SIX

Brother Jobe and his comrades entered the city of Glens Falls from the south along old Route 9, a desolate highway strip of plundered building shells, broken signs, and empty parking lots, across the sagging bridge over the famous falls itself into the city center. They left the mule, the wagon, and its blanket-shrouded contents in front of a three-story building that advertised itself as HOTEL AND MEALS. The sun had just set behind the rooftops, casting the deserted sidewalks into dispiriting shadow.

"This here's a hurtin' burg," Seth muttered, looking up and down Glen Street, as they entered the building. A single candle burned in a glass chimney at the registration counter. It failed to make the lobby, with its cast-off sofas and threadbare easy chairs, more cheerful. Behind the counter stood a half wall of wooden checkerboard fretwork with an opening to what looked like an empty dining room. No cooking aromas were perceptible at this hour. On the counter stood a miniature reproduction of the Liberty Bell, complete with crack, and a toy brass hammer for striking it. Elam hit it three times.

"To think that I spent my honeymoon in the Mandalay Bay, Las Vegas," Seth remarked. "Lord have mercy. Must have been ten pretty gals at the front desk. Bellmen everywhere."

"I guess the excitement is over there now," Brother Jobe said.

"Except for the tarantulas and the Gila monsters," Elam added.

"It was doggone nice," Seth said.

Distant footsteps caught their attention. They seemed to go on forever. Eventually, a potato-faced man about forty emerged from the gloom of the dining room and bustled behind the counter. His white shirt had been washed so many times the collar was almost frayed off.

"If you got yourself a halfway pretty gal to sit this here desk, I bet your business would pick up smartly," Seth said.

"Nothing we do here will pick up business," the desk clerk said matter-of-factly.

"That's not exactly forward-looking," Seth said.

"No, but it's the nature of these times. Nice to have you with us all the same. How can I help you?"

Brother Jobe engaged two rooms, one for himself, and one for Seth and Elam.

"You serving meals these days?" Brother Jobe inquired.

"We could fix your party some supper. Eggs and potatoes okay?"

"Got any meat?"

"Not that I know of. Got a nice cabbage soup."

"Is there any other place to eat in this town?"

"Nothing like a proper restaurant of the old-time sort."

"You got any cheese to go in them eggs?"

"We're a little shy of cheese just now. Business has been slow."

"We got some of our own you could put in," Elam said.

"We can do that," the clerk said.

"Let's do that, then," Brother Jobe said. "Just don't go charging us extra for it."

"This is an upright establishment," the clerk said. "I detect that you're not from around here."

"We're from Virginia."

"Really? How's things down there?"

"I couldn't tell you. We ain't been there for several years."

"Oh? What brings you up our way, then?"

"Couple of matters. Can you tell me who the law is hereabouts?"

"The law here got killed last night."

"How's that?"

"Murdered in a card game by a young bandit, name of Billy Bones."

"You don't say? The one who styles himself the 'singing bandit'?"

"That'd be Billy. You know of him?"

"I heard about him."

"Well, he's an infamous character, I'll tell you, and hardly twenty years old. When he isn't out robbing people on the roads, he hangs his hat at a certain house in town where ladies ply an ancient trade, if you know what I mean."

"That's a pretty way to put it," Seth said.

"Billy, he had quite a time last night," the clerk continued. "Killed our town manager, name of Luke Bliss, and two of his men. Then he went back to the house and killed one of the ladies—only it wasn't a lady."

"Is that some kind of riddle?"

"It was one of those men that like to dress up like a lady. This fellow was Billy's, uh, consort, I'm told. Billy was drunk, of course, and hot-blooded from having just killed three men—by hand with a long knife, I'm told. There was another quarrel and another left dead, I'm told."

"You're an oft-told fellow," Brother Jobe observed.

"And correctly informed, I think you'll find," the clerk said, bristling visibly. "News does come our way, being at the center of things. Anyway, I don't think Billy will be hanging his hat around here anymore."

"That's an awful lot of excitement for such a quiet town," Seth said.

"It's just extra heartache and hardship for us," the clerk said. "We can't stand much more."

"Do you know if this bandit had a boy with him?"

"Why, yes. I heard he had a little traveling companion, a protégé, he called him."

The three New Faith men swapped glances all around.

"Do you know what happened to this child?" Brother Jobe asked. "Is he still over at that house?"

"No, Billy snatched him out of there and they left town together, I'm told."

"Do you know when they skipped town?"

"Crack of dawn, I heard. They're long gone."

"Lord," Elam said.

"Good riddance, I say. You men have horses, I presume."

"Yes."

"You can put them away up the block at Efraim's. What was it you wanted the law for, anyway?"

"You see that wagon yonder?" Brother Jobe said, pointing.

"Yessir."

"There's a body under that blanket. We found it along the road up in the highlands. I have a suspicion that it was killed by this selfsame Billy Bones."

"Goodness gracious. How do you figure that?"

"We've been tracking him for some days now."

"Are you fellows some kind of policemen yourselves?"

"No, we're Jesus men."

The desk clerk cocked his head.

"Do you know the Lord?" Brother Jobe asked.

"I tried it," the clerk said. "Didn't work for me."

"Do you want to try again?"

"Not really. What do you plan to do with that body in the wagon?"

"I don't rightly know," Brother Jobe said. "I did want to inquire if anyone hereabouts had made a complaint about a missing person, but I see now there's no real law here."

"Was there anything on this poor soul with a name on it?"

"His pockets were turned out. Alls we know, he was just the humble driver of that there rig, toting a load of onions."

"You going to just leave him out there overnight?"

"Why? You think somebody might steal him?"

"No. It's just nasty, is all."

"There ain't much we can do about him now," Elam said, "unless you want us to bring him inside with us."

"Don't do that," the clerk said. "It's almost Halloween."

"What's that have to do with anything?" Brother Jobe asked.

"It's when the dead walk, they say."

FIFTY-SEVEN

The Reverend Loren Holder made a series of pastoral calls on his way back to Union Grove—the Galloway farm in South Hebron, the Callie Farm in Adamsville, and Temple Merton's orchard on Coot Hill—some of the more far-flung members of his congregation, who showed up in church on Christmas, and rarely otherwise. Among other things, none of them had seen any sign of Dr. Copeland's son, Jasper, over the week past.

"Why did he run away?" Temple Merton asked.

"He was despondent because his dog got killed by a horse."

"Children take that hard."

Temple Merton gave Loren a pint of a fine apple brandy he called Goose Island Lightning, and Loren enjoyed some of it on the next leg of his afternoon ride. It amplified his revived sense of well-being in a world of wonder. The beauty of the twilight sky almost brought tears of gratitude to his eyes, and he began to reflect on his recent relations with the Deity. A few red streaks remained in the sky when Loren came upon the hamlet of Argyle and saw a light burning in the old brick store that constituted all that remained of the little settlement's business district. At least two hours of his journey home remained and he was hungry. He tied Lucky to a post, hung a feedbag with a handful of oats off his mount's ears, and went inside.

The long room was dim in front. Articles of crude tinware hung from the ceiling. Shelves containing jars of sauerkraut, preserved fruit, and other common comestibles lined one side of the store, wooden bins of grain and dried beans the other. Baskets displaying fresh fruits and vegetables were deployed in a row on the floor. In the center was a display of small sheet-metal woodstoves assembled from scrap and also various articles of salvaged furniture from every period up to the last gasp of chain-store bargain shopping. Behind all the clutter, Loren saw Miles English seated behind a rear counter with his feet up and his chair balanced on two legs. He was cleaning his fingernails with a drop-point blade knife that seemed rather awkwardly oversize for the task.

"Help you?" he asked in a way that suggested he was more interested in keeping Loren at bay than actually helping him.

"Evening."

"I'm about to close. What do you want?"

"I won't bother you long."

"I won't be bothered period."

By this time Loren had completed the journey down the deep room from the front door to the counter. It did not escape him that the man behind the counter had a head that looked conspicuously small for his body, like a chicken's. He was sure the man had never set foot in his church.

"Are you upset about something?" Loren asked.

"If I am, it's none of your goddamn business."

Loren shifted his weight, attempting to measure exactly how hungry he was in relation to his distaste for the storekeeper's effrontery. He decided to proceed in the interest of his hunger rather than his pride.

"Have you got any baked goods?" he asked.

"There ain't a whole lot to bake with these days. Unless you like cornmeal."

"Corn bread would be fine."

"Don't have any."

"What have you got?"

"What you see down there," English said, pointing his knife at the baskets on the floor. "There's turnips, potatoes, butternut squash, onions, apples, pears, and black walnuts."

"Those black walnuts are in the shell," Loren said.

"So they are."

"Got any unshelled?"

"I guess I don't."

"It's a messy job shelling them."

"That's why I don't do it."

"Got any sausage or jerked meat?"

English shook his head, looking at Loren as if he were a mental defective.

"Okay," Loren said, "you can just give me two pounds each of apples and pears and I'll be on my way."

English grudgingly set down his chair, grabbed a tin pail, and sauntered around the counter past Loren. He brought the pailful of apples and pears back to the counter, weighed out both, and dumped them back onto the counter.

"I don't have any sacks," he told Loren.

"That's okay. I'll put them in my pockets."

Loren put the apples in one pocket of his coat and the pears in the other.

"You got real coin?" Miles English asked.

"Yes, I do."

"Two silver dimes will do it then."

"You don't seem to like the storekeeping business very much," Loren ventured as he fished the money from his leather pouch.

"I don't."

"Maybe you should find another line of work."

"Like what?"

"What are you good at?"

"Driving truck."

"I guess that's out now."

"Sad to say it is. Anyway, I hope the next thing out is you. I'd like to close."

"Maybe things'll pick up around here."

"Why do you give a damn?"

"Just being polite."

"Good night, mister."

Loren walked most of the way down the long aisle toward the front before he remembered something and turned around.

"Hey," he called to English.

"What now?"

"I'm looking for a boy."

English hesitated a moment before he replied: "Labor or sport?"

The words electrified Loren as he recalled what the doctor had said that rainy night about a shopkeeper in Argyle whom he suspected was trafficking in boys.

"Labor," Loren said.

English hesitated again before speaking. "I hope you got five dollars, silver."

"I do."

"Let me see it."

Loren walked all the way back up to the counter. He counted out five dollars in pre-1965 silver U.S. quarters and dimes.

"Wait here," English said.

As he waited, Loren struggled to imagine what he was getting into. In a few minutes, English returned with a boy in tow, holding him by his shirt collar. Loren was alarmed at the boy's appearance: obviously underfed, unwashed, and suffering with lice. His legs were closely hobbled with hemp rope.

"You go with this man now," English said to the boy, loudly, as if he were deaf or extremely stupid. "Go ahead, take him."

"That all there is to it?" Loren said.

"I don't have formal adoption papers, if that's what you mean."

"What's his name?"

"Ask him," English said.

"Come on, son," Loren said. The boy shuffled toward the front of the store, glancing back repeatedly over his shoulder. By the time they got out the door, the boy was heaped in sobs and shuddering. Loren himself trembled as he took the feedbag off Lucky and unhitched him. He cut the hobbles off the child's legs with his pocketknife, hoisted him onto Lucky, and led the horse south down old Route 40 in the light of a persimmon moon that hung a few degrees above Indian Hill. The boy's sobs only grew more energetic as they proceeded past the last few houses in the hamlet. There the countryside began in earnest. By the time Loren halted

Lucky under the shelter of a white oak tree down the road, the boy was hysterical. Loren repeatedly asked him his name, but the boy just sobbed and wailed. He decided that the only practical thing to do was wait until the boy exhausted himself, which took a quarter of an hour.

Meanwhile, Loren stood beside Lucky and pared an apple into sections and ate them. When he was finished with the apple, he started in on a pear. Eventually the boy came out of himself. For a few minutes, he merely sat in the saddle with snot dripping down his face, staring into the horse's neck. Loren held a section of pear up for the boy. He snatched it out of Loren's hand and ate it ravenously. Loren proffered one piece of pear after another, then fed him another apple, then cut up another pear for the boy.

"What's your name?" Loren asked.

"Jack," the boy finally said.

"How old are you?"

"Eight."

"Listen to me, Jack. I'm the minister down in Union Grove and the appointed constable, too. I'm going to help you find your folks and get you home."

"My folks are dead," the boy said.

"Where are you from?"

"Sandgate, Vermont." The boy started weeping again, but without his previous hysteria.

"It's going to be all right," Loren said.

"My brother Roy's back there."

"In Sandgate?"

"No. Where we just come from."

Loren glanced back up the road toward Argyle. The distant whitewashed houses shone spectrally in the moonlight.

"All right. I'll go back and get him."

"There's others, too."

"How many?"

"Three. And one that's dead."

"Are you sure he's dead?"

"Yes."

"Where did he keep you?"

"A barn."

"Back of the store?"

"I think so. In a hole under it."

The boy started hyperventilating again. Loren put a big hand on his neck and squeezed it.

"Look at me, Jack. I'm going back there to get them. Can you stay here and wait with my horse."

"No!"

"You'll be fine."

"Don't leave me here!"

Loren rummaged in the pannier behind the saddle until he found what he was looking for: the Smith and Wesson automatic that the doctor had given him. It was chambered for nine-millimeter Luger ammunition. The clip was filled with original factory cartridges from the old times, not reloads. The doctor himself hadn't fired it in a decade, though he kept it cleaned and oiled. Loren stuck it in his waistband.

"Okay, Jack, you can come with me. Here's what we're going to do. . . ."

Loren explained his plan to the boy while he tethered Lucky to a blowdown behind the oak tree. Then he and the boy stole back toward the hamlet, careful to stay within the shadows. They slipped through the yard of the darkened house next door to the brick store and crept around to a gray barn thirty yards behind the store. A candle was glowing in an upper rear window of the store building.

"Is this the barn where he kept you?"

"I think so."

"Does he live up there?"

"I don't know."

"You stay here out of the moonlight. Don't come out until I call your name."

The boy nodded.

Loren located the safety switch of his pistol in the moonlight and clicked it off. A wooden stairway sprawled up the back of the brick building to a door on the second floor. Loren climbed it carefully to keep the treads from creaking. It took him ten minutes. He could see Jack's face watching him anxiously below, at the edge of the shadows beside the barn. At the top of the stairs he pressed his ear to the door. He heard nothing. He wondered if the storekeeper had a wife or a companion, and he was not altogether sure what he would do with her if there was one. Despite the growing chill, he felt himself sweating through his shirt. He heard what sounded like chair legs scuffing against the floor, followed by footsteps. The glow of the candlelight faded in the window beside the door as the footsteps diminished. He tried to snatch a glimpse within through the window beside the door. It appeared to be a sparely furnished kitchen with no one in it.

He tried the doorknob and it turned easily, soundlessly. He pushed the door inward, an inch at a time. Soon he was standing in the small kitchen. A candle flickered somewhere farther down a narrow hallway. A jar of some amber liquid, whiskey or brandy, sat on the kitchen table along with a stack of old magazines. Loren could see that they were ancient pornography magazines of a kind that seemed to cater to men who preferred children. He heard some grunts and a cough from down the hall. He drew the pistol and held the barrel pointed up beside his ear, with his finger along the side of the trigger guard, as his father had taught him years ago at the Diamond Point Rod and Gun Club in Lake George. He proceeded into the hallway with agonizing slowness. Candlelight issued from a door ten feet down the hall, along with grunts and other noises that suggested the labors of solitary sexual activity. Loren drew in several breaths to oxygenate his brain and turned in the doorway to discover Miles English in a full suit of long underwear with the fly open and his generative member in his hand.

The storekeeper blinked at him breathlessly.

"What are you doing here?" he asked.

"Put your pecker away and get up."

English hoisted himself out of his bed.

"Turn around, back to me."

"You going to whack me on the head?"

"No," Loren said, seizing a fistful of the storekeeper's collar and twisting it until it impinged on his airway. "Okay, turn slowly and march into the hallway."

Rather than go out the way he came in, Loren took English down the interior stairway that led to the back of the store on the first floor.

"You sell rope?" Loren asked.

"No," English said.

Loren rapped him on the side of his head with the pistol.

"Is your memory improving?" he said.

"No."

"Really? How'd you tie that boy's legs up?"

English didn't reply.

Loren hit him again, harder.

"All right! All right! You said you weren't going to hit me."

"I changed my mind. Where's the rope?"

"On that shelf there."

Loren saw it in the moonlight that streamed through a transom window above the rear door, a fat coil of good quarter-inch hemp.

"Kneel down."

"You going to execute me?"

"No. Do what I say."

English jabbed an elbow into Loren's liver and attempted to squirm away. Loren smacked him in the face with the flat of his gun. English howled. Loren hit him again and slammed him against a wall of storage drawers.

"What's the matter with you?" he said.

"You knocked my front teeth out," English hissed.

"I meant to jam them down your throat."

"Why don't you just kill me?"

"Because I'm not like you. On your knees."

Loren flung him clear of the wall. English fell on his knees. Loren shoved him flat onto his stomach with a boot to his back.

"Hands behind you," Loren said.

He retrieved the coil of rope and cut three lengths of it while standing with one foot on the back of English's neck. He proceeded to tie the storekeeper's hands tightly together, hobble his ankles, and run a length of cord between his hands and his hobbles to secure him. When he was done, he picked up the smaller man and stood him on his feet. His chin was a smudge of blood.

"You comfortable?" Loren asked.

"What do you care?"

"You try my Christian patience, you know that? Do you sell matches?"

"Drawer under the counter."

Loren shoved him into the store proper, where he found a dozen crudely made splint matches in a bundle in the drawer. Loren put the matches and a candle in his pocket and stuck the pistol back in his waistband.

"Where'd you put that silver I paid you?"

The storekeeper stared balefully at Loren.

"You can't afford to lose more teeth."

"Under the counter," English said, spitting a gob of blood onto the floor.

Loren dragged him to the counter. The storekeeper directed him to a small gray stoneware crock with coins in it, a bit more than the $5.20 that Loren had paid for the boy and the fruit. Finally, he shoved English toward the back door and outside into the moonlight. They were halfway to the gray barn when Jack ran out of the shadows.

"I was afraid," the boy said.

"It's all right now. Do you know how to light a candle?"

"Yessir. I don't got any."

"There's one in my pocket and some matches. Reach in and take them."

It was darker inside the barn. Loren told Jack to light the candle.

"Where do you keep the boys?"

English mumbled.

Loren wheeled him around and smacked him repeatedly about the face and head with the flat of his hand. "You're starting to piss me off," he said.

English pointed to a spot on the floor beside an empty grain bin. The trapdoor was plainly discernable in the candlelight. It was secured with a crude oak bar latch and a three-inch cotter pin. Loren told Jack how to get the latch off. The boy opened the trapdoor and called down into the hole. Soon, three other boys warily emerged from the darkness, blinking against the candlelight. A terrible odor wafted out of the hole.

"I'm taking you boys out of here," Loren said.

They began crying and wailing.

"He's our friend," Jack told them.

Loren told English to lie down in an empty horse stall and threw the old gravity latch. He asked Jack to give him the candle and ventured down a rickety stairway that was little more than a ladder into the chamber under the floor. It was about twelve feet square, not deep enough for Loren to stand up straight in, though the boys had been able to. The stench was overpowering. A filthy old mattress was shoved against one wall. Several buckets filled with waste stood randomly about. There were no other furnishings. The place was nothing more than a hole. In the far corner, the body of a small boy sat on his haunches with his knuckles scraping the floor and his head sunk between his knees. Loren searched the cold skin on his neck for the carotid artery. There was no pulse. A centipede crawled out of the boy's ear and Loren shrank back to the ladder.

Up in the barn again, he gave the candle back to Jack, retrieved Miles English from the horse stall and told him to sit down on the edge of the trap hole.

"Can you feel the ladder with your feet?"

"Yeah."

"Go down there and look at what you've done."

"I know what I done."

Loren shoved him down into the hole. He heard him land with a thud on the floor.

"I'll be back to get you in due course," Loren growled into the hole. Then he shut the trapdoor, closed the oak bar latch, and replaced the cotter pin. The other boys had stopped wailing and crying. Loren got down on one knee, told them to gather round, and explained how they were going to steal out of town back to where Lucky was tied up just off the road.

"Did God send you?" one of the boys asked.

"I don't know," Loren said. "When we get where we're going tonight, I'll ask him."

Fifty-eight

Billy Bones stood on the road in the slanted orange evening light admiring Barbara Maglie's house and gardens.

"You hungry?" he asked Jasper.

Jasper shrugged his shoulders.

"Well, I am," Billy said. "This is a nice house. I think we could beg a meal here, no problem. You just keep your mouth shut and follow my lead. Understand?"

Jasper nodded.

"All right. Let's go."

Billy hid his pistol and his brush knife in his shoulder sack and went to the back door with Jasper. He peered through the window and craned his head around trying to take in the interior.

"It's real nice," he whispered, and then rapped on the door.

When Barbara opened it, Billy recoiled at the sight of her, so powerful was the impression her beauty made on him. Yet, unable to read the expression on her face, he stood gaping dumbly.

"What do you want?" she asked.

"Uh, ma'am," Billy said. "Me and my little brother are on our way to Granville, where we have some people. We lost our mom and dad to a fever over in Fonda. I wonder if you might give us a meal and a place to sleep. We came a long way today."

Barbara stared intently at Jasper.

"He don't talk, ma'am," Billy said. "His head was squarshed at a tender age by a falling tree limb, poor thing."

"You can sleep in the hayloft out there," she said, pointing to the barn. "No candles or smoking. I can't have you burning down my barn."

"We won't burn nothing, ma'am, I swear."

"I'll leave some food out here on the step for you. You can eat it on the porch out front. Go settle in and come back for your food."

"We can't pay nothing," Billy said.

"I'm not asking you to pay."

"You're a very kind lady. Say, if the man of the house wants a few chores out of us in the morning, just ask. We'll stack cords, clean windows, whatever needs doing. And then maybe we can get a breakfast, too."

"I'd prefer it if you get an early start tomorrow and be gone," she said, withdrawing inside and shutting the door in their faces.

"Maybe she ain't as nice as I thought," Billy muttered. "But she sure is pretty. Come on, let's have a look at the accommodations."

Jasper followed Billy into the barn and up a ladder into the loft.

The hay was loose and green and there was plenty of it, stuffed into the loft with an airspace above for good keeping. Billy swung off his shoulder bag and flopped backward into the hay.

"Ah, isn't that soft and lovely?" he said. "Try it."

Jasper reclined warily into the hay a few yards away.

"Lookit," Billy said, "you can burrow right in like a groundhog. We'll sleep warm and nice in here tonight. I bet she don't have any husband, though."

"How do you know?"

"Shut up! Didn't I tell you not to talk? She thinks you're a goddamn mute. I was just musing to myself. I don't know that I've seen a prettier lady lately. She's old enough to be my ma. But guess what? She ain't."

Barbara's voice could be heard outside calling them to come and get their supper.

Billy and Jasper found a splint basket on the step to the kitchen door. They took it around to the front porch and settled into two slat-back chairs with the basket on the floor between them. Billy fished out items one at a time and inspected each in the declining violet light. There was a jar of pickles, a chunk of cheese, six hard-boiled eggs, as many raw carrots, squares of corn bread, a bowl of warm mashed potatoes, two small oatcakes studded with nuts, a jar of sumac-and-honey punch, and a couple of apples.

"I'm sick of apples, tell you the truth," Billy said. He attacked the mashed potatoes. "Mmmm. They're all buttery," he said with a full mouth. "She's something, that lady. Better save an egg for your breakfast." Billy cut the chunk of cheese in two pieces, one obviously larger than the other, and told Jasper to take the smaller one.

Jasper bolted two of the eggs, a piece of cheese, the corn bread, and his oatcake.

By the time Billy passed him the bowl of mashed potatoes there were a few scant forkfuls left.

"Sorry about that," Billy said. "I couldn't stop myself. Hate to pull rank on you, but the master goes before the protégé. You can have my carrots. Hand me that pickle jar."

They were finished in a matter of minutes except for two of the eggs, a few pickles, and a fragment of corn bread.

"It ain't much for breakfast," Billy said with a burp. "Maybe we can winkle a little more out of her before we leave tomorrow. Put everything in the basket. We'll take it up to the loft so the animals don't steal it."

Back in the barn, Billy told Jasper to go up in the loft while he remained below, rummaging in the empty stalls. He followed in a matter of minutes with a coil of rope.

"What's that for?" Jasper said.

"You talking again?"

"No."

"Then shut up. I'm going to tie your leg to my wrist so you can't run off on me. You think Billy Bones is a moron? Sit down there and hold your leg up for me."

Billy tied at least half a dozen complicated-looking knots and hitches at Jasper's end of the rope, leaving about eight feet between them.

"Don't even try untying yourself. Billy Bones sleeps like a goddamn cat. I can tell when a mouse is cleaning its whiskers from twenty yards away."

Billy proceeded to burrow into the hay and Jasper dug out a nest for himself close by. He lay still in his hay cave for a long while, waiting for Billy to stop shifting around and jerking the cord between them. He determined that he was going to try to pick the knots out no matter what Billy said. The worst that would happen, he reasoned, would be a beating, and having to stay with Billy was worse than that. As he waited, the last streaks of twilight yielded to the rising moon. It shone silvery through the open loading door and was attended by a chill breeze. Jasper curled up in his nest, drawing up his leg so he could feel the train of knots. He found the short end of the rope and traced it back to where it entered the knots and began to pick and pull on them.

"What'd I tell you?" Billy said, a muffled voice within the hay.

Jasper stopped picking at the knots and lay still again, thinking that he would wait longer this time, until he was sure Billy was asleep. But it had been such a long and wearying day, and they had walked fifteen miles, and sleep began to gather him in as if he were a tiny bug that had been drawn into the web of a great spider, a spider that curiously had the face of the lady who had given them this place to sleep. And then he was asleep.

FIFTY-NINE

Since the disappearance of Jasper Copeland, Ned Allison had taken to adventuring with Darren McWhinnie, who was two years older but full of fun and mischief in a way that was absent in the more inward Jasper. It was Darren who came to the Allison house with interesting news just as Ned finished an early supper. He waited until he got Ned outside to tell him.

"There's bodies hanging from the trees down by River Road," Darren said.

"What? Did you see them?"

"No. But I heard my dad talking to Mr. Einhorn. Mr. Bullock hanged them."

"What for?"

"Busting into his house, I think."

"Who were they?"

"Just common pickers and roving riffraff. Two of them have their heads cut off."

"What?"

"Old Mr. Bullock chopped them off with a Japanese sword. How do you like that?"

"How'd he hang them from a tree when they don't have any heads?"

"You'll love this. From their ankles!"

"Jesus!"

"It gets better. He jammed their cutoff heads between their legs."

"Who said that?"

"Mr. Einhorn. I heard it. And Robert Earle went down to ask Bullock to take them down and he wouldn't do it."

"We have to go see them."

"We can go see them tomorrow."

"Let's go now while there's some light. I never saw anyone with a cutoff head."

"We can't go now. There's something else going on."

"What?"

"The doc is over at the cemetery with some of those Faith men. They're digging up a grave."

"Which grave?"

"I don't know. They're at it right now. Let's go over and watch."

"This is going to be some Halloween."

"Mr. Einhorn wants to cancel it."

"What? You can't cancel Halloween. It's a holiday."

"He wants to cancel trick or treat. Him and other men. My dad among them."

"Why?"

"Out of respect to the doc and Jasper and all."

"But what's the doc doing digging up a grave?"

"I don't know. Let's go watch."

"Something bad is going on around here."

"It's that time of year. People are only doing what comes naturally."

SIXTY

The Reverend Loren Holder led the four boys down Route 40, past ever more familiar land forms and landmarks as they came closer to Union Grove—Crone Hill, whose rocky outcrops seemed to compose the face of an old woman in the moonlight; the old Agway agency with its ghostly chemical storage tanks and abandoned offices; the ruins of the Town and Country Diner, shining like a silvery space vehicle, its windows broken, furnishings looted, and parking lot overgrown with thistles and milkweed.

Loren carried Jack on his shoulders while the oldest boy walked beside him and the two others rode Lucky. They'd made short work of the remaining apples and pears. Loren made an effort to conduct a friendly, bantering interrogation of the boys, with the dual purpose of finding out something about them and occupying their minds on the tedious journey back to town. It was obvious to him that all the boys were in poor physical condition and beaten down in spirit.

"I'm the minister of the Congregational church in Union Grove," he told them, "and the appointed town constable. I'm going to try to get you home, if that's possible, or see to it that you're properly taken care of if it's not."

Jack's brother, Roy, age nine, said that following the death of their parents in June, they had walked from Sandgate, Vermont, to the village of Shushan, New York, where they were taken in by an uncle, one Otto Singletree, a drinker who could barely farm and resented having to provide for them. One day toward the end of summer he marched them to Argyle and sold them to the store-keeper, whose name they never did learn. Otherwise, Roy said, he knew that his mother had a brother, Uncle Dick, in a faraway place called San Diego. He was married to Aunt Shelly, and they had several children who were his cousins, but Roy had never gone to visit them, indeed had never met them, and had no idea what their address was.

"I don't even know what they look like," Roy said. "Did you ever go to San Diego?"

"Many many years ago," Loren said. "It's in California."

"What's California?" Roy asked.

Sandgate, he learned, did not have a school.

The boys riding Lucky were Paul Byrd, age eight, and Jesse, five, who appeared dazed and did not seem to know his surname. Paul's home was in a place called West Nyack. He didn't know where that was, exactly. Loren knew it was right off the old New York State Thruway, near the Tappan Zee Bridge, less than an hour from New York City. Paul said he and his parents left their home in a great hurry one night late that spring. He remembered houses on fire. They walked for days, slept in the woods, stopped to stay with people on a farm for a while, then walked some more. They moved into a tent in a place with many tents. Nobody knew anybody. Days went by and nobody did anything. Nights, grown-ups sat around fires talking, singing, telling jokes. He liked that. The food came in pouches. It was very tasty. Then a lot of men swept through the place knocking down the tents, shooting and clubbing people. He remembered grown-ups and other children lying lifeless in the dust. There was a lot of confusion, fire. He became separated from his mother and father. He ran for his life into the nearby woods and hid there. In the morning, he saw that the tent city was a scene of smoldering desolation. Everyone who remained was dead. He waited in the woods all day, growing horribly thirsty. Eventually he came out of the woods and searched the tent city for his mother and father. He looked at all the bodies and couldn't find them. He found some containers filled with water and packages of food and went back to the woods to sleep and spent another day searching among the bodies. Again he returned to the woods. He thought that if he stayed in the vicinity, his parents might come back and look for him. They didn't. He repeated this cycle of searching and hiding several days more until the bodies started to stink and bloat and the animals started to come around and eat them. The wild dogs terrified him. He realized that he couldn't stay there anymore. He walked away and followed the big river. He came to a town where a man invited him onto a boat. The man gave him a big bowl of barley and some milk. He sailed on the boat with the man, whose name was Frank. Frank made him do things. He refused to say what they were. Just things. They came to another river town on a hill where Frank turned him over to another man, whose name he never learned. The man had a wagon with other boys. They were all taken around to farms to pick fruit and vegetables. Their legs were tied together so they couldn't run away. They would go from one farm to another, picking tomatoes, squash, apples. At night the boys slept in the wagon, roped together and locked with chains. Finally, he was turned over to the man who stuck him in the hole under the barn with Jack, Roy, Jesse, and Mark, the boy who had died sometime in the past week.

Jesse, Paul explained, had told them he didn't know how he ended up in the hole under the barn. He didn't talk much.

"How do I know you're not going to take us to some other terrible place?" Paul asked.

Loren hesitated.

"After what you've been through, I wouldn't expect you to trust anybody," he said. "The world is not full of bad people. Your mothers and fathers were not bad people. I'm not a bad man. When we get where we're going, you'll find yourself among good people who will take care of you."

SIXTY-ONE

Jasper woke up to the sound of screams coming from the house. He tried scrambling out of his hay cave but the rope on his left ankle jerked tight when he did. It baffled him for a moment that Billy Bones had not awakened instantly and set upon him. He tugged against the rope again, which did not yield an inch, and he wondered if Billy had miraculously died in his sleep. Then he traced the rope to its other end and discovered it was tied around a queen post that supported the barn roof. With moonlight flooding the loft through the open loading door, he spied Billy's shoulder bag in the hay. He dove for it and groped around inside until he found his hunting knife. The screams from the house continued, seeming to rip the fabric of the night.

Jasper sliced the rope off his ankle and climbed down the ladder to the ground floor. He ran to the back steps of the house where the lady had left their food earlier. The door was ajar and he could see that the jamb was splintered near the knob where Billy had pried the door open. He ventured inside and traced the screams in the dim interior through the kitchen and down a hallway to a bedroom on the first floor. Billy was on the bed, on top of the lady, with his pants down around his ankles and his hips pumping. The woman struggled underneath him as she screamed, batting at his head with her fists. He brandished his pistol over her, threatening to smash her face.

"Get off her!" Jasper screamed.

Billy cranked his torso around and, eyes bulging with malice, leveled the pistol directly at Jasper.

"Get out of here, boy, or I'll blow your damn head off!"

"Help me!" the lady screamed. "Please, help me!"

Jasper ran straight into the room at Billy with his knife raised high and brought it down at an angle, slashing Billy's gun arm. The pistol flew out of his hand and bounced off a chest of drawers.

"You stabbed me, you crazy little shit!"

Jasper plunged his knife down again into a soft place between Billy's shoulder blade and his spine. Billy torqued his body around, struggling to avoid the blade, and hoisted his bloody arm in a posture of defense while Jasper brought his knife down again into a hollow at the base of his neck. Both Billy and the woman screamed. Now the blood really began spurting all over the room, black in the stark moonlight, as Jasper had severed Billy's carotid artery. Billy struggled desperately to get off the woman and claw his way toward Jasper. In the effort, he blurted out, "You've killed me!" and then collapsed in a heap just off the foot of the bed, with his ankles tangled up in his pants, and his head down near the floor, bleeding out into a puddle that spread darkly on the varnished pine planks. Curiously, perhaps because his head was upside down, he seemed to have a smile on his lips, as if he found satisfaction in the manner of his departure from this world. His last words, muttered at Jasper looming above him, were "Look who's a murderer now. . . ." And then the last vapors of his life rattled out of him, and his cheek squashed against the floorboards as the rest of his body slumped off the bed and fell with a thud.

Instinctively, Jasper and the lady rushed toward each other, the lady enfolding Jasper in her arms as they both trembled and gasped. They remained frozen together for minutes, not speaking, eyes riveted to the other side of the room where Billy's twisted body lay half hidden and utterly still at the foot of the bed, and the pool of black blood continued to spread across the floor, until their breathing returned to normal, and the lady felt the knife still clutched in Jasper's hand, and he allowed her to wrest it out of his fingers.

"Stay here," she said.

She stepped around the chest of drawers and reached for a robe hanging from the closet door. It was only then, watching her move across the room in the moonlight, her flesh like a silver liquid, that Jasper was startled by her nakedness. And then she was covered up. She returned and took him by the hand, led him gingerly around the bed, around the pool of black blood on the floor, and into the hall, where she pressed her back up against the wall just across from the bedroom door and slid down to sit on the floor with Jasper held tight under her arm beside her. Together they sat watching Billy Bones for a long time, until the moon rose above the sash of the window it had been shining through.

"I think he's dead," Barbara said eventually.

"I think so, too," Jasper said.

"You can talk?"

"Yes."

"He said you couldn't."

"That was just one of his lies."

"Who was he?"

"A bandit and a murderer. Billy Bones was his name."

"What were you doing with him?"

"He wouldn't let me get away. It was all a mistake."

"Who are you?"

"I'm nobody."

"You're the doctor's boy, aren't you? From Union Grove."

"How'd you know that?"

"They were here, looking for you."

"Who?"

"Your father."

"When?"

"Some days ago."

"Who else?"

"A friend. A man named Robert."

"Robert Earle."

"Yes, Robert Earle."

"I've done terrible things," Jasper said. "I can't go home."

"Yes, you can. You must."

"I can't. I have a place I can go to in Glens Falls."

Jasper tried to get up but Barbara held on to him tightly.

"Don't go now. Please. It's night. There are wild animals out there. Wolves. Big cats. You can't go out there on the roads by yourself at night."

Jasper yielded and slid down against her again.

"Stay until morning, at least," Barbara said. "Please. I'll need help to get his body out of here."

"Where are you going to take him?"

"Into the woods. We have to bury him."

They sat quietly a while longer, watching Billy Bones's inert corpse. His eyes remained open, unblinking.

"Why did you attack him like that?" she asked. "He could have killed you."

"I had to stop him. He killed people. He would have killed you."

"But he pointed his gun right at you."

"The gun was empty."

"What?"

"The metal part you shove in that holds the bullets. He never had one. He just hit people with it. He killed a man up in the hills, a wagon driver, trying to rob him. He smashed his head over and over with the gun and the man died. I was there. I saw it. He killed the he-she at the house in Glens Falls."

Jasper burst into tears and buried his face against Barbara. He cried for a long time. She let him cry himself into exhaustion. They remained against the wall until they both fell asleep, well past midnight, when the moon had arced clear across the sky and begun disappearing behind the treetops on the other side of the house.

SIXTY-TWO

The doctor sat in his ladder-back chair and took another pull on the bottle of pear brandy while he gazed across the dank spring-house at the corpse of Shawn Watling, dead more than five months now, shot to death on a hot and dusty afternoon at the old town landfill, where he had gone with Robert Earle to buy a few pounds of roofing nails from the Wayne Karp gang, who ran the place as a retail salvage yard. The circumstances remained murky to those not present at the incident. Robert Earle had conveyed Shawn's body back to town in a cart, and it was his word against about a dozen of the Karptown men as to how the young man happened to get half of his face blown off.

So enormous were the forces of rage and despair roiling inside the doctor this night nearing Halloween that he wanted to obliterate his consciousness. He didn't want to do it inside the house, where his wife, Jeanette, and daughter, Dinah, would have to suffer it, or even in his office where someone might come looking for him. His tortured, convoluted thoughts prompted him to do his drinking in the company of the corpse, his only suitable companion at this time, he believed.

He had carried out the first part of Magistrate Stephen Bullock's writ to exhume the body from its resting place in the cemetery with the help of three New Faith brothers, who actually did the hard work of digging up the coffin. They conveyed it to the doctor's place in a horse cart, removed the corpse from the coffin—an odious task—and arranged it in the springhouse with its head on a wood block on the long table that had hours earlier been occupied by an array of winter squashes and onions. A dozen hams, which the doctor sometimes received as payment for services, hung dimly up in the rafters gathering protective mold. The shelves were lined with glass jars of vegetables and preserved fruit, some of it also payment for services. Stoneware crocks of sauerkraut stood on the floor along the fieldstone wall. A beeswax candle in a tin saucer guttered at the end of the long table, inches from the corpse's moldy boot heels.

The doctor lifted the bottle again, hesitating a moment as he wondered whether he had imagined some slight movement in the corpse's facial expression—such as it was. The fragment of the jawbone that remained hung from a shriveled tendril of ligament. The eyes and surrounding flesh had dissolved into the sockets, and various organisms of the soil had bloomed within the coffin and eaten down most of the nose. The doctor managed to ignore the vivid stink of decomposition, as he had learned to do years earlier during a rotation in pathology.

"What's next?" the doctor thought he heard the corpse say. He had known Shawn Watling since the dead man was a teenage boy, had treated him for one thing and another, had delivered his daughter, Sarah, seven years ago, and knew his voice. The doctor lowered the bottle, squinting at the corpse, who seemed strangely now to have assumed the very look of Shawn Watling when alive, that is, a perceived representation of it.

"What happens next to me?" the corpse seemed to speak again.

"Postmortem examination," the doctor said.

"Are you going to cut me open?"

"Afraid so. Bullock ordered it."

"It isn't pretty in there."

"I'm well aware."

"Can you give me a little something to ease the pain?"

"You won't need anything."

"Says you." The corpse appeared to laugh.

The doctor blinked, raised the bottle to his lips again, and tipped his head back. The powerful liquor transpired through his stomach lining and soon roared in his veins.

"I have to search for the bullets that killed you," the doctor said.

"You'll find a couple of 206 grain .41 caliber hollowpoints in there," the corpse said. "One in my neck up against the C2 vertabrae.

Another way up in the parietal lobe of my brain, or the miserable jelly that remains of it."

"I still have to go through with it," the doctor said.

"I don't hold it against you, Doc. Cheers."

The doctor stared at the corpse in the dim, flickering light. He was strangely relieved to have someone to talk to. The room and everything in it rotated slightly.

"I'm drunk," the doctor said.

"You're worried about your boy."

"I'm worried sick and crazy," the doctor said.

"He's in a lot of trouble," the corpse said. "But he's a good boy."

"He was never anything but a good boy," the doctor said, and tears began to pool in his eyes. He hoisted the bottle again but paused to rest the butt of it on his thigh. "I couldn't save his pup. I couldn't. There was nothing I could do." The doctor sank his chin down into his chest and began quietly blubbering.

"Your boy's been through an ordeal," the corpse said.

"Where is he?"

"He's up north."

"Up north where?"

"In the north end of the county."

"Where exactly?"

"You don't need to know."

"Of course I do."

"He's coming back to you."

"When?"

"Soon. He's got one more tribulation."

"What is it?"

"No point telling you. He has to go through it alone. The way we all go through this life."

"What good are you?"

"That's a helluva question, Doc."

"You're a useless piece of rotten meat."

"I'll try to not take that personally."

"Go to hell."

"I know you only say that because you feel helpless," the corpse said. "In life, you liked me."

"You should tell me where he is, goddamn you."

"He'll be home soon enough. He'll be changed, but he'll be home."

"Changed how?"

"Not a child anymore."

"What's that mean?"

"I'm so weary—"

"Goddamn you."

"Goddamn me? I'm beyond that now," the corpse said. The appearance of life went out of it and it settled back into mute stillness.

The doctor tried to raise the bottle to his lips again, but the effort defeated him. His eyes rolled up in his head, he listed to the left, fell off the ladder-back chair, and crashed to the floor unconscious.

Sixty-three

Jane Ann, in her nightclothes and robe, rushed down the front porch steps of the big rectory in the lustrous moonlight as Loren helped Paul and Jesse down off Lucky.

"Look what I found," Loren said.

Jane Ann knelt down in the maple leaves and the boys naturally gravitated around her. She wanted to embrace them, but Loren warned her about the lice. He gave her a very abridged version of the rescue story, who they were, and their situation, while Jane Ann looked them over one at a time, turning them this way and that, attempting to determine if any of the boys had an immediate problem that would require an urgent trip to see Dr. Copeland. She couldn't see much, even under the nearly full moon. They all seemed able to stand on their own and had few obvious sores or injuries. But the temperature had dropped and their breath hung on the still air in silver clouds; they wasted no more time getting inside the warm rectory. Throughout, the boys hardly spoke, so undone were they with fatigue, trauma, and malnutrition, and merely obeyed anything they were told to do.

When Loren returned from putting Lucky away in Tom Allison's barn down Van Buren Street, he brought in two of the largest pots from the church's community room, filled them with water, and put them on the stove to warm. Meanwhile Jane Ann had cooked a big batch of scrambled eggs with pieces of hard sausage and carved a leftover corn bread into blocks for the boys to eat with a tub of butter, a three-pound chunk of Mr. Schmidt's Center Falls brick cheese, and glasses of that same farmer's milk. They ate as much as hard-working grown men and with the same kind of fierce concentration, even little Jesse.

When they were finished with their meal, Loren took each boy into his study, where he placed a chair on a bedsheet that was spread on the floor, and cut his hair as closely to the scalp as possible without shaving it altogether. He rubbed sunflower seed oil on their scalps and their eyelashes to suffocate the remaining lice. Jane Ann brought each boy into the bathroom, where she rubbed vinegar onto their scalps to loosen the gluelike substance that kept nits attached to what remained of the hair shafts. Loren took the sheet with all its hair clippings outside in a bundle to his burn pile. Then Jane Ann bathed the boys one at a time, scrubbing them with strong soap. Loren waited outside the bathroom to apply another dose of oil to each boy's head and give him something to wear to bed in the way of an old T-shirt or some other article from the church's impressive collection of donated clothing.

Finally they brought the boys upstairs and put the two Singletree brothers in the room that had been their own boy's room up until the day he left Union Grove. The room had a set of bunk beds. Paul and little Jesse were installed for the night in a double bed in another room that years before had been reserved for sojourning relatives and out-of-town guests—two categories of visitors lately made obsolete by circumstances. That they were being cared for, bathed, fed good food, and shown to comfortable beds seemed enough to reassure them that they were finally safe in good hands. Loren and Jane Ann took turns saying good night to the boys, telling them again that an effort would be made to find their parents or relatives, and that they would be looked after in any case. The boys fell asleep within seconds of crawling under the blankets. Then Loren and Jane Ann retired to their own bedroom. He gave her a more rounded version of his discovery and rescue of the boys from the dungeon behind the Argyle store and of his doings with Miles English, their captor, and of the boys' probable destiny: to remain in Union Grove, perhaps with them, or with other families willing to take them in. Loren and Jane Ann clung together closely in bed as he told her all this. He felt her physical presence in a way that he had not for years, and she sensed his feeling her, and each perceived the other in the fullness of the moment, and then a wondrous thing occurred.

In the aftermath Jane Ann held on to his broad chest as if it were a life raft in a tumultuous strait between two unknown shores. Her eyes remained wide open, as if struggling to comprehend something that might reveal itself in the moving shadows of the naked tree branches, cast by the moonlight through the windows, that played over the walls.

"What's happened to you?" she asked.

"I've changed."

"But how?"

He hesitated. "I found a witch," he said. "And she put a spell on me."

Something in his voice convinced her that it was not necessary to ask if he was kidding. Instead she asked, "Have you changed? Or is the whole world changing around us?"

"Both, I think."

Sixty-four

As dawn broke over Glens Falls, Brother Jobe woke up in his hotel room with sharper pains in his abdomen than anything he had felt in the days preceding. Despite the window being open and his labored breath coming out in a frosty fog, he sweated into his bedclothes, and the damp made him shiver. It galled him additionally that he'd made himself go hungry the whole day before and now his gut hurt worse than ever. He managed to pull himself out of bed and knocked on the door of the adjoining room. Seth answered it in his long drawers, scratching.

"What's up, BJ? You don't look so good."

"I'm low. I got the cancer or something."

"Cancer?"

"Cancer of the guts. It killed my daddy. I must have it, too. You got to bring me back."

"Uh. . . . Okay."

"And I mean right away. If I'm going to die, it's going to be amongst my own. Prepare that wagon for me. I can't take a mule now."

"What do you want to do with our dead man?"

"Guess I'll ride with the sumbitch until we find a suitable place to bury him. Get your lazy rear end out of the rack, Elam!"

Elam rolled over, blinking.

"BJ ain't feeling so good," Seth explained.

"Go fetch our mounts from what's-his-name," Brother Jobe told Seth. "I ain't in no mood to linger or dawdle."

"What about all them onions?"

"Leave them on the sidewalk for folks or something. O Lord, I never felt nothing like this before."

They borrowed a grain scuttle from Efraim, the livery owner, and shoveled all but a few pounds of the onions onto the sidewalk in front of the hotel, a gift to the town of Glens Falls. Soon the horses were hitched onto the wagon and they were under way, Seth driving, with two saddles stashed beside him. Brother Jobe lay in the cargo box under several blankets on a mattress purchased hastily from the hotel, with the bundled remains of the dead man with him for company. Elam rode Atlas behind the wagon to keep an eye on Brother Jobe and distract him from his torment with conversation.

Leaving town, with Brother Jobe croaking in pain from the jolts of the wagon, they again crossed the ancient bridge over the town's eponymous waterfall where the Hudson River leaped sixty feet down on its run from the Adirondack wilderness below Mount Marcy. There was a great whirlpool beneath the bridge.

"Maybe we should dispose of the body here," Seth said over his shoulder. "Commit his soul to the watery depths and all."

"That ain't right," Brother Jobe said. "And you know it."

"He stinks something awful."

"If I can stand it back here, you can too."

"We're more worried about you than him," Elam chimed in.

"My daddy lived like this for months before it took him." Brother Jobe winced as the wheels bounced over a loose chunk of concrete. "O Lord have mercy!"

A few miles east of there, beyond the last traces of small-town suburbia, they came upon an overgrown rural cemetery. Brother Jobe directed them to stop and bury the remains of the onion-wagon man.

"I hate to tell you this, but we ain't got no shovels," Seth said.

"What happened to that shovel you took all them onions off here with?"

"I give it back to the man at the stable before we left."

"You mean to tell me we left home without no shovels?"

"We didn't expect to be burying folks all up and down the county."

"What are you going to bury me with if the Lord snatches me before we make it home?"

"You said your daddy lived for months after he got the cancer."

"Well, I ain't him. And besides, they had hospitals back then. They doused him with enough chemicals to put down the weeds on a hundred acres of goldurned cotton."

"I say we just leave him under a tree somewheres, nice and peaceful," Elam said. "I don't think it's doing you good to lie there with it."

"He's our brother now. We ain't chucking him aside like a banana peel."

Elam was beginning to wonder if Brother Jobe's illness was affecting his mind, but he didn't want to argue.

"All right, then, gee your team back up, Seth," Elam said.

They went five miles more and the road grew steeper as it ascended into the Gavottes. Brother Jobe appeared to be slipping out of consciousness at times. In one of the intervals when he lay quietly laboring in his agony, Seth said it would help the horses make it into the highlands if they could lighten the load.

"It's either the saddles or you-know-who."

"I say we hold the five-minute funeral."

"I'm with you. It ain't doing anybody no good to ride him around."

They halted in their journey and found a suitable place for the dead man, still bundled up in Seth's blanket, in a grove of tamarack trees. They piled a cairn of loose granite stones over him to discourage the wild animals from getting to him and spoke a very few words over his grave.

"Lord, please hallow the ground where we leave these mortal remains," Elam intoned over the cairn, with his hat upon his heart and Seth standing beside him likewise, while Brother Jobe groaned in the wagon. "He hath no marker but was some poor mother's son and perhaps some poor son's father, and maybe some good woman's husband, and if he was not all those things he was his own soul, at least. Take him home in your keeping, ye who alone knows his name, amen."

"Okay, we done it," Seth said. "Let's get out of here."

Over in the wagon, Brother Jobe groaned again.

SIXTY-FIVE

Barbara Maglie was shocked at first to wake up in a bed with the boy. She had taken him into one of the other bedrooms very late in the night and locked him in a protective embrace while he slept. But Barbara could not find sleep. Worry consumed her for hours. She didn't know how to persuade the boy to return to his home and his family, when he was bent on going to Glens Falls. She would offer to ride him down to Union Grove in her own one-horse trap, she thought, but would he come willingly? She doubted it. She might have to journey down to Union Grove by herself to inform the doctor and his comrades to go to Glens Falls and search for the boy there.

This acid swirl of worry dissolved sometime before daylight gathered in the eaves. Sleep finally found her and when she did wake up—because Jasper was trying to pry her hands off him—she recalled the dire events of the evening before while a sharp conviction of the boy's immediate destiny flashed through her mind, spooling out as colorfully as cinema used to. She saw that indeed he would set out for Glens Falls but some circumstance would cause him to return to her house. The intimation was powerful enough to persuade her that it was inevitable, and she resigned herself to it.

"Please help me get the body out of the house," she said. "Then you can go if you must."

"I'll help you," he said.

So the two of them rose out of bed in the gray morning and proceeded to remove Billy Bones from the house without ceremony. His twisted body was stiffened in rigor mortis. Barbara pulled up and fastened his trousers for the sake of decorum, then asked Jasper to take a leg and help pull him outside. Doing so, they left a long smudge of coagulated blood down the hall and through the kitchen, and Billy's head bounced audibly on the steps as they dragged him out the door. They dragged him down a path past the outhouse, through the yellowing high grass beyond the paddock where Barbara's brindle horse grazed oblivious to them, and behind the pasture where her cow, Sonya, stood waiting to be taken to the barn and milked. They penetrated the margin of the woods there and deposited Billy between two locust trees.

"Help me get the shovels," Barbara said, and Jasper dutifully accompanied her to a toolshed attached to the barn. She handed him a long-handled shovel and took a garden spade for herself, and they walked back toward the woods. "Who was he?" she asked.

"I don't really know," Jasper said.

"You were his companion."

"Only for a few days and nights. He tried to rob me when I first came upon him."

"Why did you join up with him?"

"He made me. He wouldn't let me go. He kept calling me his pro . . . pro . . ."

"Protégé?"

"Yes. I tried to get away from him but he caught me and said he'd kill me. He meant it, too. He killed three people that I know of during the time I was with him, maybe others, too. I didn't have any part of it—" Jasper broke down sobbing again. Barbara gathered him in her arms.

"No one will blame you for his crimes," she said.

"How do you know?"

The truth was she didn't know. She knew the law had become a flimsy thing in these new times, but she also knew that people acted in concert in the absence of the law, when they felt strongly enough about something, and that justice and the law were not always the same thing.

"You're just a child," she finally said.

They walked silently the rest of the way back to the locust glade in the margin of the woods. Barbara spaded out the top layer of leaves and weeds, and then they took turns digging out the grave with the long-handled shovel. When they had gone down less than three feet, she said, "That's enough." They dragged Billy's body into the hole, where his body deployed itself rigid and twisted, his dead eyes staring blindly up, and his mouth open as if caught in a smart remark. Of course his expression did not change as Barbara dumped the first shovelful of earth on his face. She did the remaining work while Jasper stood by, wiping tears from his eyes with his sleeve. Soon, she had the body covered up.

She took Jasper back to the house and fed him a breakfast of fried potatoes and eggs, resigned to what she knew about his fate, which she did not reveal to him because he would not understand it, and it wouldn't change anything.

"Do you need help cleaning up the mess?" he asked, when he was finished with his breakfast.

"No. I'll take care of it."

"Can I go now, then?"

"Yes."

"I'm sorry about what happened here."

"I know. It's not your fault."

"Please don't tell anybody."

"I won't."

"I don't think anyone will come looking for him," Jasper said. "Nobody cared about him."

"I understand."

"You're a very kind lady."

"Thank you. You're a good boy. I see the light of love in you."

Jasper made a pained face, as if he couldn't imagine such a thing.

"Maybe we'll meet again some day," he said.

"I know we will," she said.

She gave him three hard-boiled eggs, a wedge of cheese, and a slab of corn bread wrapped up in a kerchief, and kissed him on the forehead. He went to fetch his backpack out of the barn and set out to make his way over the highlands toward Glens Falls, with the visage of Robin centered in his mind as a totem to ward off the frightening memories of his recent misadventures and his fears about the journey ahead.

He had gone four miles that gray morning, feeling lighter and less burdened by the mile, imagining his career in the distant town and the friend who waited for him. He was not altogether sure of the way, but he followed a route that took him ever higher through the Gavottes, knowing that eventually he would descend back into the Hudson Valley. On a forgotten byway called Shine Creek Road, he entered into a rocky defile where the road twisted severely in its effort to traverse the ridgeline. He rounded the curve of the road and heard a high-pitched cry, as of a baby stuck with a pin, and ran his eyes up the jutting rocks until, in amazement, they fastened on the sight of a big golden catamount perched down on its haunches ten feet above him, its mouth wide open and fangs in bold display. In the long moment of recognition that this was something apart from anything he had seen in his childhood story-books, Jasper became a statue. He locked eyes with the creature and saw in their red brilliance the odd apparition of his own death.

SIXTY-SIX

Perry Talisker woke up on the summit of Wilmot Hill, the highest point in the Gavottes, enveloped in a fog bank. The fog reminded him emphatically of his position in the transit between life and death. He greeted the morning with a solemn joy that his final trial was at hand and he was fully prepared for it. He had left the darkness of night and darkness in general behind, along with its agents and principalities, and knew he would never be troubled by them again. The fog that blanketed his bivouac on Wilmot Hill was a vapor of angels, heralding the Great Thing that awaited him on this last day of his life on earth. Even his profound loneliness had become an exultation.

He left his campsite without breakfast—indeed, he had not taken a meal for days—and an animal instinct guided him down from the summit, out of the fog cloud, onto a barren hillside of rocky scree, below which the forest seemed to spread endlessly in a golden tapestry, with no sign of man along the vast panorama. He was beyond the cares of man now. He knew that his destiny lay below, that he was closing on it, and that it would reveal itself shortly. A bright confidence unbounded by the leaden tropes of memory or need lured him down into the golden woods, with the rifle slung over his shoulder, gliding effortlessly through the understory, over blowdown and rill, in pursuit of his own transcendent becoming.

Hours later, he emerged from the rapture of the forest at a place just short of where Shine Creek Road entered the defile over the Gavottes. He stepped lightly uphill on the road with his senses on fire, in thrall to his own animal instinct. His breathing and his heartbeat quickened, and when he rounded a bend where the road cut a cleft between two scarps of ancient uplifted rocks, he was struck more by the beauty of leaves fluttering soundlessly on the breezeless air than the fraught frozen stances of the crouching cat up on the rockpile and the boy below.

Jasper did not hear Perry Talisker come up behind him so much as smell him—a vibrant stink like the rectified essence of the woods itself. Jasper thought it was the cat. The big cat snarled and sank deeper into its haunches. Perry swung the rifle off his back and shouldered it in a single deft movement. But when he pulled the trigger, the only report was a dull metallic click. He shoved down the lever and the next bullet failed to enter the chamber properly. By then, the cat was in the air with all four limbs extended against the sky. In that timeless interval, Perry flung away the rifle, drew a knife from his belt, and turned the eight-inch blade upward so that it entered the cat's heart at the exact moment the cat closed its jaws on his head. As they fell to the earth, the back of Perry's skull dashed against a jagged chunk of broken pavement, and the force of the fall drove the shard of asphalt deep into his brain stem. Both the cat and the man quivered a few moments while life struggled out of them.

Jasper, who had recoiled in the event and fallen over, lay goggle-eyed on the road's dusty shoulder beneath the wall of rock with his own pulse pounding in his ears and the air scintillated with death. He remained motionless for a long time, afraid to do more than breathe while he studied the mute vignette of cat and man a few scant yards away. It was a long while before he was satisfied that the cat was dead, and the man beneath him, as well. A pool of blood had poured out of the cat's heart and joined with a pool of blood that came out of the man's brain, and flowed in a single rivulet off the crown of the road into the yellow weeds of the roadside. So absorbed was he in his study of cat and man that he did not register the sound of the wagon struggling up the road from the west until it had crested the ridge.

SIXTY-SEVEN

Coming over the crest of the hill, Brothers Seth and Elam spied Jasper right away and swapped knowing glances. Elam gave heel to Atlas just as Jasper pulled himself up and attempted to run away. Because the defile was walled-in, he could not run into the woods. Elam caught up to him, dismounted fluidly, and seized the boy by his clothing, while Seth followed in the wagon.

"You're the doctor's boy," Elam said.

Jasper did not reply. He recognized the men, not so much by their faces as by the costume of the New Faith order and their extraordinary size, like giants out of folklore.

"That's him," Seth said, ratcheting up the hand brake and jumping down from the driver's box. "I'm sure of it."

"We've been looking for you," Elam said.

"Where all have you been?" Seth asked.

"You know who we are, don't you?" Elam said, squatting down to the boy's level.

Jasper's terror was so overwhelming, he was unable to speak, let alone come up with a credible lie. He nodded his head.

"We're bound to bring you back to Union Grove," Elam said. "I'd prefer to not have to tie you up. We've got a long road ahead. Maybe two days' travel. What do you say?"

"Please don't tie me up," Jasper croaked.

Meanwhile, Seth's attention was distracted by what he'd noticed up along the rock wall. He marched fifty yards back up the road to where Perry Talisker lay beneath the body of the dead mountain lion. He squatted down to marvel at them.

"Woo-wee, will you look at this!"

Elam let go of Jasper's sweatshirt and hitched the mule's reins to the wagon. He and the boy walked together up to where Seth squatted beside the bodies.

"Lord have mercy," Elam said as Seth pried the animal's jaws open to free Perry Talisker's head. Then he put both hands around the cat's hindquarters and dragged its body off to the side. Elam kneeled beside the dead man and drew down his eyelids.

"Were you with him?" he asked Jasper.

"No."

"We had information that you were traveling with someone."

"Not him."

"How'd you come to be with him here now?"

"I don't know."

"How could you not know?"

"He was just there."

"Just there?" Seth said. "He come out of nowhere?"

"Yes." Jasper said. "He saved my life."

"But you don't know him?"

"I know him," Jasper said.

Elam and Seth swapped glances again.

"You're confusing me, son," Elam said.

"I know him from town."

"Who is he?"

"The hermit," Jasper said. "He lives in a shack by the river."

"So that's the hermit," Seth said. "We heard about him. You weren't with him all this time, you say?"

"No."

"He's a long way from home, isn't he?"

Just then, Brother Jobe gave out a groan from down in the wagon.

Jasper had been unaware that there was someone lying in the cargo box. Now that he was uphill of it, he could see someone swaddled under a quilt down there. Another groan, this one elongated, brought both the men to their feet.

"Who's that?" Jasper asked.

"That's the boss," Seth said. "Something's laid him low all of a sudden. Cancer of the guts, he says."

"We were up this way searching for you, son," Elam said. "This sickness come over him last night."

"I'd like to skin out that panther awfully much," Seth said.

"We're not toting any stinking pelt all the way home," Elam said. "You'll have to come back for it, if you can get leave to do so."

They dragged the bodies of the man and the cat to the side of the road, arranged them side by side, like sweethearts, and hurriedly covered them with rocks from the loose ones at the base of the scarp. They enlisted Jasper to help. Elam was about to speak a few sparse words over the hermit's body when Brother Jobe gave out a yet more desperate cry below. The men slapped the dust off their hands and hurried down to him and the wagon. Jasper followed.

"You all right, BJ?" Seth asked.

"No, I ain't all right."

"We found what we were looking for," Elam said. "Lookit here."

He grasped Jasper around the midsection and hoisted him up like a shoat so that Brother Jobe could inspect him from where he lay.

"I'll be jiggered."

"It's him all right," Seth said.

"You boys better get me down to his daddy as fast as you can," Brother Jobe said, gasping between his words. "I need a doctor."

Seth climbed back in the driver's box. Elam lifted Jasper into the saddle on Atlas, mounted up behind him, and tossed the boy's backpack in the wagon box. They rode behind the wagon to keep an eye on Brother Jobe, who seemed to come in and out of consciousness as they made their way down the road from the elevations. After an hour, Seth halted his team and climbed down to take a leak. Brother Jobe lay groaning in the wagon, turning his head from side to side and sweating heavily, though it was fifty-four degrees at two o'clock in the afternoon. Elam and Jasper remained in the saddle while Seth emptied his bladder at the side of the road.

"I think I know what's wrong with him," Jasper said.

"How would you know what's wrong with him?" Elam said.

"My father is the doctor."

"And you're but a child."

"I'm a child who knows doctoring."

"What do you know of doctoring?"

"I've assisted my father with patients since I was eight years old."

"That so?"

"Including surgeries."

"He says he's got the cancer."

"I don't think so."

"What ails him, then?"

"Set me down to examine him and I'll tell you for sure."

"Can't you tell from up here?"

"I'll know for sure if you set me down."

"Don't even think of running off," Elam said.

Seth had finished relieving himself and was buttoning up as he walked back to the wagon. Elam hoisted Jasper out of the saddle and lowered him down to the road.

"What's up now?" Seth asked.

"The boy's going to have a look at BJ."

Seth made a skeptical face.

"He thinks he knows what's ailing him," Elam said.

"How would he know?"

"He says he's been helping the doc with patients since he was eight."

"You think we ought to let him?"

Elam hesitated a moment, glanced right and left, and nibbled his lip. "Yes, I do," he said.

In the meantime, Jasper had climbed up the running board into the cargo box of the wagon. Brother Jobe lay on his mattress in a state of tentative consciousness, muttering fragments of Bible patter, imagined commands to subordinates, and sundry disconnected words. His eyes opened for moments and then closed again as he babbled.

"I'm going to examine you, sir," Jasper told him.

Brother Jobe did not respond.

Jasper pressed the back of his hand to Brother Jobe's damp brow, pressed his ear against his chest to listen to his heart and lungs, and took his pulse at both the wrist and the neck.

"Now I'm going to loosen your trousers and touch your abdomen," Jasper said. He undid several buttons and drew out Brother Jobe's shirttails so that his generous belly was exposed. With his fingertips overlapping each other, as he had watched his father do many times, he pressed on a spot about one-third of the distance diagonally between the crest of the hip bone and the belly button. Though the pressure was gentle, Brother Jobe gave forth a howl. Satisfied, Jasper lowered the shirttails back over Brother Jobe's belly but left the trousers unbuttoned to relieve the pressure on his belly. Then he climbed out of the box and stood between Seth and Elam.

"Brother Jobe has got acute appendicitis," he told them.

"What makes you think that?" Seth said.

"You can tell by pressing on a spot. It's called McBurney's point."

"How do you know that?"

"I've done it with my father."

"You sure?"

"Yessir. It's this spot here." Jasper showed them on his own abdomen.

"What's it mean?" Elam said.

"He needs an appendectomy."

Seth flinched. "You mean, like, an operation?"

"Yessir."

"Well, we got to get him down there to your father."

"I don't think there's time for that," Jasper said, looking up at Elam. "Didn't you say we're more than a day from Union Grove?"

"Yes," Elam said.

"Maybe we might hurry it up more," Seth said.

"We can't jostle him all to heck—that can't be good," Elam said, looking to Jasper.

"That wouldn't be good," Jasper said.

"You sure it's the appendix?" Seth said.

"I'm pretty sure," Jasper said.

"Are we fools to look to a child for medical advice?" Seth said, drilling his eyes into Jasper's.

Jasper shrugged.

"One way or another, it's going to be coming on nightfall in a few hours," Elam said.

"I say let's see if we can hurry it up a little," Seth said.

"All right," Elam said and extended his hand down to Jasper to hoist him back into the saddle.

Seth climbed aboard his wagon and geed up his team. But trying to drive faster on the broken road, with its fissures, potholes, and loose chunks of pavement, only made the wagon bounce around more violently, which caused Brother Jobe to cry out louder and more frequently. After fifteen minutes of it, Seth brought the team to a halt again. This time Elam dismounted and went over to Seth and had words with him out of earshot of Jasper, who remained in the saddle. Then they both came over and stood at the mule's withers, looking up at Jasper.

"Just how much time does he have, anyways?" Seth asked.

"Twelve hours, maybe," Jasper said.

"What's going on in there?"

"Inside Brother Jobe?"

"Yes. How does this sickness work?"

"It's an infection. There's this little sac that comes out of the bowel. It fills with pus and it can burst. Then the infection spreads in the abdominal cavity and that's generally what will kill a person."

The two men exchanged looks of alarm.

"What are you saying here, son?"

"He could die from this," Jasper said.

"Unless he gets an operation," Seth said.

"Yessir."

"But we don't have time to get down to your father who would do the operation."

"Probably not," Jasper said.

"So he's going to die, then."

"He doesn't have to die," Jasper said.

"How can that be if he don't get the operation?"

"I can do the operation," Jasper said.

The two men glanced at each other again in utter incredulity.

"You can do it?" Seth said. "How's that possible?"

"I've done it with my father."

"How many times?"

"I don't know. Five, at least."

"And that makes you qualified?"

"I'm not qualified," Jasper said. "But I know what to do. Do you know how to do it?"

"'Course I don't," Seth said.

"How about you, sir?" Jasper asked Elam.

He made a face and shook his head.

"I can't guarantee it'll come out okay," Jasper said. "But it's probably the only thing that will keep him from dying."

Elam took Seth by the elbow and dragged him about ten yards forward, where they consulted privately again. Of the two, Seth appeared particularly exercised, making large gestures of exasperation. Then they returned to Jasper.

"This here's a very grave matter," Elam said. "The question is, how can you do an operation out here on the road, with night coming, and alls we have is a few candles, and you don't even have proper instruments, nor barely enough water to even boil a knife in. What in heck are we talking about here, son?"

"I know a place we can go," Jasper said. "It's a fine clean house, not far from here. A very kind woman lives there and I believe she can help us."

"Is that so?" Seth said.

"Yes."

"How do you know this?"

"I was there last night."

The two men both appeared to search the treetops for guidance.

"How far is it?" Elam asked.

"We can get there by dark," Jasper said.

"Lord," Seth said, returning to his seat on the wagon. "If this is a bad dream I'd appreciate it if you could wake me up now."

They lost no more time getting under way again, nor did anyone say another word until they arrived at their destination about two hours later.

Sixty-eight

Barbara Maglie came out of her barn with a milk pail at the sound of the horses and the wagon. She stopped for a moment in the gray twilight, set down the pail, and then, seeing Jasper up in the saddle with Elam, hurried over to them.

"We've got a very sick man here, ma'am," Elam said. "We'd like to bring him into your house, if you don't mind."

Barbara nodded her head. Elam swung off of Atlas and Seth stepped down from his seat in the wagon. The two of them wrangled Brother Jobe, mattress and all, out of the wagon box, brought him into the kitchen, and set him on the floor for the moment. Barbara and Jasper followed behind. Then the two men took Barbara across the big room and spoke to her in low tones while Jasper remained standing beside Brother Jobe's boot heels. Barbara nodded as they spoke, but more than a couple of times she shot a worried glance across the room at Jasper, who merely shifted his weight from one foot to the other. When they were done huddling, the three grown-ups stepped over to Jasper.

"Can you really do this surgery?" Barbara asked.

"Yes, ma'am," he said.

"On your own, without your father?"

He hesitated, then nodded.

"It could kill him, you know," she said.

"I know," Jasper said. "But without it he'll surely die."

The three adults looked to one another to give the go-ahead.

"Can you tell us exactly what to do to help you?" Barbara asked.

"Yes."

"Then let's get started, son," Elam said.

"I'll go settle the animals in," Seth said. He hurried out. Elam and Barbara watched him leave and turned back to Jasper.

"Clear off that long table by the stove," Jasper said. "We'll put him up there. Get as many lamps and candlesticks and stands as you can. I'll need a mirror to focus the light. You have to fire up the stove and boil several pots of water. Have you got any strong liquor?"

"Yes," Barbara said. "Apple brandy."

"We have some whiskey somewheres in our gear," Elam said. "You going to knock him out with it?"

"No, it's to kill germs," Jasper said. "Do you know when Brother Jobe last ate anything."

"He didn't have supper with us," Elam said. "Said he wasn't hungry. And I'm sure he didn't have breakfast, neither."

"Good."

Brother Jobe cried out from his mattress. Only the word *Jesus* was comprehensible.

"I wish we had some opium," Jasper said.

Elam looked at the boy askance.

"I have some opium," Barbara said.

"Black gum?"

"Yes. I have other herbals, too."

"Which ones?"

"What do you want?"

"Monkshood."

"I have it."

"Can you pull a tuber and crush out the juice?"

"Yes."

"What's that for?" Elam asked.

"Numbs tissues," Jasper said. "I need three bean-size lumps of black opium as soon as possible." He turned to Elam. "Mister, you'll have to put this opium up his rear end."

"What!"

"It gets absorbed through the bowels," Jasper said.

"Can't you just put it in his mouth?"

"He could choke on it, or it could make him vomit and he'll choke on his vomit."

"I don't know as it's right to—"

"Please, sir, just do what I say."

Elam made a sour face.

"I'll need instruments," Jasper said. "Do you have a razor?"

"I have a straight razor," Elam said.

"Can you strop it up real sharp?"

"Of course."

"I need a very sharp, fine pair of scissors."

"I have several," Barbara said.

"Do you have a curved needle?"

"Yes, my lamp-shade needle."

"Silk thread?"

"Yes."

"Have you got any musical instruments with strings? A fiddle or something?"

"I have a guitar," Barbara said.

"What kind of strings?"

"Gut."

"Real gut or the old kind."

"Real gut."

"Cut off the highest string."

"What for?"

"I have to stitch something inside him. It dissolves in the body after a week or so. I'll need something that you can fire up red-hot on the coals. Something with a metal tip. A tool."

"What's that for?"

"To burn the places where we cut the appendix. It stops the bleeding into the cavity."

"I have some screwdrivers," Barbara said.

"Good. By any chance do you have a hemostat?"

"What's that?"

"It's a little forceps that clamps shut."

"You mean one of these?" Barbara rummaged in a kitchen drawer and found one, a Kelly mosquito.

"How'd you happen to have that?" Elam asked.

"In the old times, we used them for smoking dope," she said.

THE WITCH OF HEBRON 307

"Oh, 'course, well . . . ," Elam said.

"I could use a small needle-nose pliers, too," Jasper continued.

"I've got a tool box."

"Tweezers?"

"I have different ones."

"Have you got any sponges?"

"Yes. Little natural ones."

"You'll have to boil them. Do you have one of those things with a bulb at the end for squirting a roast chicken?"

"Yes."

"Have you got salt?"

"Plenty."

"Make a salt solution with some of the boiled water and put it aside to cool."

"Okay."

"Now go ahead and get that opium ready, ma'am. It takes a good half hour to start working, and please put the water on to boil."

Elam set about fetching lamps and candle stands and arranging them around the long table. Barbara put water on and prepared the opium suppositories. She and Elam removed Brother Jobe's boots and trousers and, with Jasper watching, rolled him onto his left side.

"Would you mind doing the honors, ma'am?" Elam asked. "I don't know as he'd ever forgive me for touching him up there."

"Spread his cheeks for me," she said. She put the bean-size pellets of opium gum in place without ceremony. Elam rolled Brother Jobe onto his back again while Barbara went to scrub her hands.

"Soak your fingertips in that brandy when you're done, ma'am," Jasper said.

By that time Seth returned from feeding and bedding down the horses. He and Elam hoisted Brother Jobe onto the table. Elam went to the barn to fetch his razor out of his pannier. Jasper asked Seth to remove the rest of Brother Jobe's clothing. The heat from the cookstove had made that part of the kitchen very comfortable. Brother Jobe's fervid restlessness was clearly subsiding under the influence of the opium. Barbara returned with various tools and went about shredding a monkshood root with a box grater. She pounded it in a mortar, added some brandy, and strained a brownish fluid into a bowl. Elam stropped his razor on his belt and then dropped it in the pot of boiling water with the other tools and instruments. Jasper found a footstool that would allow him to work on Brother Jobe at a comfortable level. Then he fetched a side table from the front parlor to hold instruments. Finally, he told Seth to heat up several screwdriver tips through the grate of the cookstove's firebox.

"You have to get them red-hot," Jasper said.

"Yessir," Seth said.

"Ma'am, do you have some kind of a clean nightshirt I can put on?" Jasper asked. "I can't do this in dirty clothes." She bustled away and returned with a long white cotton T-shirt displaying cartoon black-and-white Holstein cows, the logo of a bygone ice-cream manufacturer.

Jasper took it around the corner into the hallway and discarded his overalls and sweatshirt. When he came back, he told the three adults to roll up their sleeves, wash their hands up past their elbows, and douse them in brandy. When they had finished, he did likewise. He asked Barbara to fish the various tools and instruments out of the boiling water and set them on a clean white towel on the side table. He noticed that she used a set of kitchen tongs, and he said he could use it as a retractor when the time came. Next, he had Barbara cut a hole in a clean bedsheet about twelve inches across. He positioned it over Brother Jobe's lower abdomen to frame a surgical field.

"Sir," Jasper said to Elam. "I'm going to ask you to turn that mirror to shine the light on where I'm working, okay?"

"Yessir, son," Elam said, and began experimenting with it until he had focused a nice bright spot in the field.

"I'm ready to begin," Jasper said, and took several deep breaths.

"Can we say a prayer?" Seth asked.

"I wish you would," Jasper said.

"O Lord of mercies and miracles, please guide this boy's hand surely and fortify the spirit of our boss and brother in his hour of need, amen."

"Amen," they all said.

"Ma'am, will you please swab down the field with alcohol," Jasper said, and she did. "Now, will you hand me that razor. . . ."

In the eyes of the adults present, Jasper worked with stunning speed and economy. He made a three-inch diagonal incision through McBurney's point, carved past a layer of blubber, found the external obliques, and sectioned through them to the internals. He retracted the incision with the tongs, asked Barbara to hold them in place, and entered the abdominal cavity proper. Along the surgical pathway, he swabbed the exposed tissues with the tincture of monkshood and explored the area inside the peritoneum with the tip of the hemostat until he found the pouch of the cecum at the base of the ascending colon. There, with a deft flip of the steel tip, he exposed the appendix. It was inflamed—as red as a sumac leaf—but intact. The fluid within the abdominal cavity was clear. He called for the length of catgut, made a slip loop, and tied a ligature near the stump of the appendix, then drew it tight, repeated it twice more, and clamped the hemostat ahead of it. Next, he took up a pair of fine embroidery scissors and attacked the appendix with a series of cuts between the last two ligatures. With each cut, he called to Seth for a screwdriver with a red-hot tip and cauterized the tissue at the site, vaporizing the escaping pus and sealing the wound. Then he unclamped the stump of the appendix and used the hemostat to lift it out of Brother Jobe's body and deposit it in a little saucer on the table, where it lay like an angry red worm.

"Lord above," Seth said. "Is that the miserable bugger itself?"

"Yessir," Jasper said.

"I be dog."

"Ma'am, would you wipe my forehead, please?" Jasper said.

She did. He told Seth to take her place at the retractor and asked Barbara to fill the baster with salt water. He laved the saline solution into the abdominal cavity and then suctioned it out with the baster, repeating the procedure twice more, until he was satisfied that there were no visible shreds of infected tissue swimming there. He dribbled a little whiskey around the ligatures on what was now the stump of the appendix, withdrew the tongs to rejoin the obliques and close the abdominal cavity, and sewed the wound closed with the silk thread and the lamp-shade needle held in a pair of needle-nosed pliers. Finally, he swabbed the stitches with more whiskey. Barbara had cut another sheet into long bandages. Seth helped lift Brother Jobe's trunk so she could wind the bandage around him and secure it with safety pins. When this was concluded, all three of the grown-ups turned their gaze to Jasper.

"That's it," he said. He wobbled a moment on his footstool and then crumpled in a heap on the floor, unconscious.

SIXTY-NINE

Loren brought the four boys over to the doctor's office right after breakfast to have them checked out. The doctor looked rumpled, his clothes slept-in, his eyes red-rimmed. Loren gave him an abbreviated version of the incident at Argyle and said he was both glad and sorry that Jasper was not among them—glad that Jasper had not fallen into the hands of Miles English but very sorry that the boy was still missing.

"I think he's going to be all right," the doctor said.

"How do you mean?" Loren said.

"It's hard to explain. I've had a vision, I guess you could call it. You think I'm nuts, don't you."

"Not at all," Loren said. "We can't account for everything."

"It goes against my training, of course."

"Do you want to tell me about this vision?"

The doctor hesitated. Loren noticed that his hands were trembling.

"I think I had a conversation with a ghost," the doctor said. "How nuts is that?"

"Well, it's that time of year. Who was it the ghost of?"

"Shawn Watling."

This time, Loren stopped to puzzle and reflect.

"Why him?" he asked.

"His body is over there in the springhouse. Bullock had him dug up."

"What for?"

"To settle the issue of what killed him, I guess."

"We know what killed him."

"Bullock wants it signed and sealed."

Loren glanced at the springhouse. It looked like a mausoleum.

"And you think the corpse communicated with you?" he said.

"I was pretty drunk."

"What did it say?"

"It told me Jas was coming home soon." A tear leaked out of the doctor's left eye, and he leaned in closer to Loren in order to whisper. "I've got to stop this drinking," he said. "Can you help me?"

"Yes," Loren said. "I can help you."

Aside from their nutritional problems and ringworm, the doctor pronounced the four orphans healthy. Little Jesse, however, seemed to have a mental problem. He was less than completely responsive to verbal promptings. The doctor told Loren to pay him special attention and report what he observed in the days ahead. When they were gone, the doctor had no other patients. Wishing to get away from the temptation of the several kinds of alcohol around his office, he decided to take advantage of the cool and brilliant weather and go for a walk out to the Battenkill. But he was intercepted by Robert Earle before he could even get out to the street in front of his house.

"Are you on your way to see a patient?" Robert asked.

"No, just a walk. Clear my head."

"Mind if I walk with you a ways?"

"Sure."

They set out toward the east edge of town, past the Union-Wayland Mill, where the community laundry was under construction, then out the east end of town, past the abandoned Walgreen's drugstore building and the empty Cumberland Farms convenience store.

"A bunch of the men wanted me to cancel Halloween on account of Jasper," Robert said. "I didn't think it was a good idea."

"I understand."

"I just want you to know it wasn't out of disrespect. I saw it as a question of community morale."

"Of course," the doctor said. "Life has to go on. When Ed Hardie's wife died of tetanus last year around this time, everything went on as usual."

"The adults are still having their ball upstairs at the old town hall," Robert said. "I'll be playing with the band."

"I hope everybody has a swell time."

"Our thoughts will still be with you and your boy and the family."

"Of course."

They walked silently for a while, past the remnants of Kmart.

"I hear you've dug up Shawn Watling's body," Robert said.

"Bullock issued a writ. I got some of the Jesus boys to do the actual digging."

"What do you suppose he's up to?"

"He wants some kind of legal proceeding. To settle the matter."

"Why now, I wonder."

"I suppose he's finally taking his duties seriously."

Seventy

It seemed to Stephen Bullock that his wife had come to the breakfast table from her morning bath in turbulent spirits. She slapped butter on her spelt crumpet rather aggressively, he thought, as if she wished to teach it a lesson, and she pushed her scrambled eggs this way and that way with seemingly no intention of actually eating them.

"Something on your mind?" Bullock asked.

Sophie's shoulders drooped and she put down her fork. "Won't you cut those bodies down?" she said. "I can smell them from the bedroom now. And they get worse by the day."

"Good," Bullock said. "They'll make all the more of an impression on the bad guys."

"And who are these hypothetical bad guys?"

"You know. Men like them. Pickers, bandits, vagabonds. People who would rob us, harm us."

"Can't you just put up a sign that says 'Trespassers will be shot' or something?"

"They'd laugh at it. Before cutting our throats."

"Well, I have to say that living with the constant stench of death is extremely unpleasant."

"I find it a piquant reminder of how delicate our situation is here," he said. "And how blessed we are."

Bullock reached for his wife's hand, but she rapped his knuckle with the fork.

"Oh, darling," he said. "Don't go all soft on me now."

SEVENTY-ONE

Barbara had had the men move Brother Jobe carefully into her own bedroom, and she brought the little fainting couch up close by the bed to lie near him and monitor his condition. He came to in the hours before dawn. He called for water, and she helped raise his head while he sipped from a tonic she had made, composed of tincture of opium and cannabis, with whiskey for flavor.

"Oh, Lord, my guts hurt," he groaned.

"This will make you feel better," she said. "Drink some more."

"Tastes horrible," he said.

"You'll appreciate the effect."

Brother Jobe blinked at her in the candlelight.

"What all happened to me and who all are you?"

"You were very sick. You've had surgery."

"You the doctor?"

"No."

"This a hospital?"

"No."

"This a dream?"

"No."

"Well, you seem real enough, anyways, I suppose," Brother Jobe said. Then his eyes narrowed in concentration. "I can see inside of you, you know. Lots of interesting colors in there."

"I think you and I have a few things in common," she said.

Soon, the potion allowed him to subside again in peaceful sleep.

He was resting comfortably without a fever when the men got up with the sun. Barbara apprised them of Brother Jobe's progress and they were satisfied when they looked in on him resting in the big bed. They put the sweat-stained hotel mattress out on the front porch and retrieved a basket of eggs from Barbara's chicken house. She had bacon frying and a pan of corn bread working in the oven by the time they got back from turning their animals out in her paddock. They got a greater surprise when she filled two steaming mugs from a pot on the stove.

"Why, this here tastes like coffee!" Seth said.

"It is coffee."

"I be dog. How'd you get that?"

"People bring me things," she said.

"How's that, ma'am?"

"Born lucky," she said, leaning against the counter and sipping from her own coffee mug. "What happens with the boy now?"

"I'm going to send him back to town with Seth," Elam said. "I'll stay here, if you don't mind, until our boss is ready to go home."

"I could use a man's help around here for a day or two," she said.

"It'll be my pleasure, ma'am," Elam said.

Barbara took the corn bread out of the oven and refilled Elam's cup. She'd washed out Jasper's sweatshirt and overalls and hung them above the hot cookstove to dry while the men finished their breakfast.

"The boy's been through a lot," she said.

"I expect he has."

"He's afraid to go home."

"I expect things will go all right with him from here on," Elam said.

"I think they will," she said.

"There's been some bad blood between them. But the boss owes him a debt of gratitude."

"He owes that boy his life," Barbara said.

Jasper woke to the murmur of voices downstairs, conscious that he was not in his own keeping and uncertain where he stood with the New Faith men who were now his keepers. In the meantime, a sense of duty prompted him to look in on Brother Jobe, who was asleep again, but unmistakably alive. Jasper took his pulse, felt for a temperature, pressed his ear against the patient's chest to listen, and was satisfied that his condition was stable. He followed the breakfast aromas to the kitchen, still wearing the T-shirt with the cows on it. Elam had gone to the outhouse and Seth could be seen outside throwing a saddle on Atlas. When Barbara told him that Seth was going to ride him back to town, Jasper seemed resigned, yet peaceful. He had never tasted coffee, and she gave him a mug of it, well-creamed, to wash down with his eggs. His clothing was still warm when he changed back into it.

Just before they departed, Barbara took Jasper aside while Seth waited atop the mule. "I'm very proud of you," she told the boy.

He searched the ground with his eyes, and she lifted his chin up with a long slender finger.

"I did what I was taught to do," he said.

"Things have changed for you in ways that you may not understand just now," she said. "You might feel uncomfortable with it for a while. But you're growing into yourself, and you will fit yourself perfectly when you do."

Jasper nodded, though he was not altogether sure what she meant.

"Be patient with your father," Barbara added. "He's suffered."

"How do you know?"

"I can tell things."

"Are you a witch?"

"What do you think?"

"I think you know some magic."

"Tonight's Halloween," she said. "Did you know that?"

"No. I've lost track of the days."

"And it's a full moon, too. A good time for a boy to return to his family and his people. Thank you for everything you've done."

She kissed him good-bye and squeezed him, and then she helped boost him up into the saddle in front of Seth.

The two made excellent time in fine, crisp weather, trotting smoothly on some of the long flats where the road followed Mourning Creek, then Black Creek, and then the Battenkill on the way into Union Grove. At one of the farms along the way, the hired men and their wives had set up plank tables in an orchard and were holding a harvest feast, drinking and laughing. One of the woman plucked a banjo and sang a song about the devil being in the corn. They fed Seth and Jasper a lunch of roasted goat, cider, and squash pudding. The rest of the way, Seth entertained Jasper with tales of adventure as a soldier in the Holy Land War, of his missions, shoot-outs, rescues, and ambushes, and his flight in an airplane to the hospital in Germany with a piece of shrapnel the size of a jackknife blade in his thigh.

Eventually they arrived at a place in their journey where the landscape was no longer a mere composition of random hills and valleys but a disposition of things achingly familiar to the boy— the old steel railroad bridge over the Battenkill, the back side of Pumpkin Hill, glowing like a heap of folded gold fabric in the slanting late-day sun, the white steeple of the Congregational church. Even the shell of the old ruined Kmart strip mall had a comforting, familiar look. The boy's brain was effervescent with emotion as they entered town. Several women had been enjoying the late-day sunshine in front of Einhorn's store. They turned and stared as Seth and the boy rode past. Then one waved excitedly when she recognized Jasper, and turned to inform the others, whose mouths opened and faces lit up. Townsmen returning on foot from their work on the surrounding farms recognized the boy and looked up at him on the big mule with guarded curiosity. Seth rode Atlas right up the drive between the house and the doctor's office in the rear. First Jeanette came out of the house, with little Dinah trailing, and then the doctor stepped out the door to his office, blinking in the low sun. Seth lowered Jasper out of the saddle and down into their waiting arms, where parents and children became one tearful, pulsing organism for a while.

"That's some young man you got there," Seth said. "I'll be seeing you around, junior." He reined out his mount and headed up Van Buren Street toward his own people, as goblins, ghosts, pirates, and princesses made their way from house to house with their begging baskets, thrilling in the onset of night.

SEVENTY-TWO

The family had supper of Jeanette Copeland's chicken braised in cider, a recipe from her native town of Evreux in Normandy. Nobody knew what to say, and Jasper himself ate silently. Before the meal ended, neighbors began appearing at the door to pay their respects and offer good tidings for Jasper's return and to catch a glimpse of the boy. Children in costumes also came calling, Jasper's schoolmates and friends, disguised as ghosts and witches, begging for treats and also angling to see the object of so much town mystery, speculation, and gossip.

Jeanette was in charge of politely fending off the well-wishers with her charming European manners, giving out popcorn balls to satisfy the goblins, while Jasper and the doctor retreated to the doctor's study, where the doctor struggled to overcome his craving for a drink and endured the strange stoical silence of his son. He deliberately chose not to light a candle so that he and his boy would not be visible through the window to anyone coming up to the house from the street, and anyway the moonlight was sufficient.

"When will you feel able to tell me what happened to you?" he asked.

The boy shrugged and sighed.

"Nobody's going to punish you. I just want you to resume your regular life."

Jasper looked up at his father. "I want to be a doctor," he said.

"You can be a doctor. I always thought you would be."

"I don't want to go to school anymore."

"You should go to school."

"I just want to see patients with you."

"You can do both. You can go to school in the mornings and see patients with me after."

The boy turned his gaze out the window, where costumed figures moved along the moonlit street laughing and shrieking.

"I performed an emergency appendectomy on Brother Jobe last night," Jasper said.

His father fumbled with his mug of peppermint tea.

"You mean, like, in a dream?" he said.

"No," Jasper said, still peering into the moonstruck street. The silence between them was so oppressive that the doctor's hand started to tremble again.

"You really did it?"

"Yes."

"Maybe you can tell me how on earth that came to be," the doctor said.

Jasper told his father how the New Faith men had caught up with him, how Brother Jobe lay ailing in the wagon, how he examined him and reached a diagnosis. He described the procedure in precise clinical detail, the place where it was conducted, and the woman who lived there, and gave an account of the patient's postoperative condition.

"I know that woman," the doctor said. "I know that place."

"I'll never forget her," Jasper said, but he offered nothing more about the events that preceded that night, or where he had been, or with whom.

The doctor had a peculiar feeling that he was sitting with a person he hardly knew anymore, someone like a distant colleague from an earlier time in life instead of the child who had been his own boy not so many days ago. They sat in silence for many minutes more, clutching their mugs of tea, watching the spectacle of Halloween darkly through the window. The children Jasper had grown up with skipped, ran, and laughed as they went from house to house.

"Aren't you going to tell me why you ran off in the first place?" the doctor eventually asked. "And what else happened to you out there?"

"Death was everywhere," Jasper said.

The doctor waited for the boy to elaborate, and was chilled when he didn't.

SEVENTY-THREE

Later that evening, up on the third floor of the old town hall—a grand room that, in the 150-odd years of its existence, had hosted everything from political meetings to boxing matches to community theater extravaganzas—the annual Halloween levee, or ball, got under way. A heightened spirit of festivity filled the big room, with its beautiful coffered ceiling on which the signs of the zodiac had been painted long ago. Candles burned along the walls in a dozen sconces and on stands up on the small proscenium stage where the six members of the string band tuned their instruments, but the candles were outshone by the moon streaming though the tall arched windows. The news had crackled rapidly across town that the doctor's son had returned to town unharmed, thanks to Brother Jobe's rangers, but little else was known about his misadventure or about the fate of the hermit, Perry Talisker, who was thought by some to have abducted him.

Tables were laid with savories and confections, pumpkin and apple puddings, nut cakes, jam cakes, meringues and fondants. Felix Holyrood supplied ciders of several kinds, and Carl Schmidt brought a ten-gallon keg of his strong dark ale, and the men and women, fathers and mothers, of Union Grove came costumed as astronauts and scuba divers and hippies and football players and all types of characters who no longer existed, leaving their younger children at home in the keeping of their older children, who had returned from their rounds. The grown-ups ate and danced and laughed and flirted until the moon swung above the windows and hung at the zenith of its transit above the town.

Along about the middle of the evening, Stephen Bullock appeared in the old town hall, having ridden alone from the farm on one of his big Hanoverian geldings. He had enjoyed the contents of a silver flask filled with his own whiskey on the ride, and he wobbled slightly as he entered the festive scene. When the musicians went on a break, he navigated to the beverage table, where Robert Earle was refilling his glass with strong sparkling cider.

"You came a long way," Robert observed.

"Beautiful night out there on the road. Full moon and all."

"Don't your people put on their own levee?"

"Of course. I showed my face. But I think they're more comfortable when I'm not around. If you know what I mean."

"I think I get it," Robert said.

"Just so you know," Bullock said, "I cut down those miserable bastards along River Road and buried them."

"What made you change your mind?"

"I'm henpecked."

"Well, we appreciate it here in town, whatever motivated you. I understand you ordered Jerry to dig up Shawn Watling's body."

"Indeed I did," Bullock said. "It's like the night of the living dead around here, isn't it? I'll be glad when Halloween is over."

"Isn't it a little late to start a proceeding over Shawn?"

"The mills of the law grind slowly, Robert. Why?"

"You know I'm in an awkward position, Stephen."

"What were you thinking when you took that young woman into your household?"

"I was thinking she needed someone to look after her and that there was a child involved. Are you saying you disapprove?"

"No."

"Am I a suspect?"

"Not as far as I know," Bullock said. "I don't even have Jerry's report yet."

"Do I become a suspect after that?"

"Let's just take this one step at a time, shall we?"

"We both know who did this."

"You were the only witness, Robert. Apart from Wayne Karp and his thugs."

"I mean, is there any question?"

"There are always questions where the law is concerned," Bullock said. "Anyway, you and those Jesus boys were so hot for me to take up my duties as magistrate. Well, I'm taking them up."

Robert replied only with a steely gaze, as if he were struggling to take measure of Stephen Bullock and piece him together like a diabolically complex puzzle. Perhaps it was something about Halloween, he thought, or the strong drink, but the man he had known pretty well for more than a decade took on a fiendish glow in the flickering candlelight.

"I've got to check the set list with the boys," Robert said. "Excuse me."

"You fellows sound better than ever. Too bad the recording industry is dead and gone. Break a leg."

SEVENTY-FOUR

Two days later, Brother Jobe returned to Union Grove with Brother Elam. The pair journeyed in fine brisk November weather, under a deep blue cloudless sky, Brother Jobe bundled comfortably on the hotel mattress in the cargo box of the onion wagon, propped up against a saddle to enjoy the sweeping views of the landscape as they went along. The leaves had mostly fallen from the trees, but the pastures remained vividly green, and the cultivated places—the crop fields, orchards—looked lovingly groomed by caring hands in preparation for their long winter sleep. The air was filled with enticing aromas—hams smoking, apple butter in the kettle, a whiff of things baking here and there, the piquant stink of autumn rot where the road took them through the stretches of woodland, and always the reassuring smell of the horses.

Brother Jobe didn't talk much with Elam along the way. His customary compulsion to gab was suspended. He felt so at peace with himself and with the world that he had to view his sudden illness as a kind of gift. If nothing else, it was the first time in years that he had stopped having to be in charge of things and other people for a while.

The company of someone like Barbara Maglie was not something he would have known outside of the extraordinary event of his sudden illness in strange surroundings, and he was not a little amazed at how much he enjoyed her. They couldn't have come from more different backgrounds, yet they were so much alike in spirit they could finish each other's sentences after a couple of days together. She was in every other way an embodiment of what his parents had warned him about in fast Yankee city women, but he couldn't help smiling to think back on the movements of her body, her striking costumes, her lovely silver hair, her expressive long-fingered hands, her goddesslike face, and her voice, like a certain kind of fiddle music played slowly in the lower registers. He was sure he would see her again, and, indeed, as the wagon trundled along, her visage seemed superimposed in his imagination over the lovely vistas of the autumn fields and sky. And then there was the question of the boy.

When, late that day, he returned to his people in the old Union Grove high school, among the first things he did was dispatch a message to the doctor, requesting a visit from him to evaluate his recovery, with an added request that might as well have been a demand to bring the boy with him. He sent Brother Asa to fetch them in the early evening for the short ride across town. The boy had maintained his strange stoical calm since returning, and his demeanor unnerved his father and mother, who continued to have the impression of harboring a stranger in their house.

"Will you let me stay in the room when you examine him?" was all Jasper said to his father on the short trip over.

"All right," the doctor said.

Brother Asa dropped them off at the front entrance of the old school where Brother Boaz met them and escorted them inside to Brother Jobe's suite of rooms.

"Close the door, please," Brother Jobe said, propped up in bed with account books in his lap. He followed the visitors over the top of his reading glasses with a severe look. Brother Boaz withdrew and shut the door, leaving the doctor and Jasper triangulated with Brother Jobe.

"That boy of yours carved me up like a Christmas turkey," Brother Jobe said. "Probably lucky he come along and done it, too," he added, and the severe look transformed itself into something more forbearing. "Anyway, here I am, still amongst the living, and no more aching guts. I never did have a bellyache like that before. Tell you the truth, it was a goldurned miracle they found him when they did. I'm mighty grateful. And I never did get a chance to say thank you, son."

The doctor glanced at Jasper, who returned the look without betraying any particular emotion.

"Mind giving me a once-over, doc?" Brother Jobe said.

"Sure," the doctor said. "Would you come out of the blankets and lift your nightshirt.

The doctor took Brother Jobe's temperature, his pulse, listened to his heart and lungs, removed the cloth dressing on his abdomen, and peered closely at the sutures between his hip and his belly button.

"Nice work, Jas," he said, looking over to the boy, who remained in place across the room. "I'll take out these stitches in a few days," he said to Brother Jobe. "The wound looks clean and is healing nicely."

"I had a peach of a nurse."

"I think I know her."

"A woman like that give a man reason to live," Brother Jobe said. "If you know what I mean."

The doctor smiled uncomfortably. "You should take it very easy for a couple of weeks," he said. "You don't want the slightest risk of infection. Stay away from livestock, especially. Anything gets to feeling funny, you send for me right away."

"I'll do that. I'm going to pay you, too. And the boy in particular."

The doctor did not pursue the subject. It only made him more uncomfortable.

"But would you mind leaving the two of us alone for a minute?" Brother Jobe said to him, readjusting his nightshirt and bedclothes. "Me and your boy got some bidness don't concern you."

The doctor hesitated a moment, then blew out a sigh and shrugged his shoulders.

"I guess so," he said, shooting Jasper a glance. He left the room, shutting the door behind him.

"Come over and sit in this here chair beside the bed, son," Brother Jobe said.

Jasper moved tentatively toward the chair and sat down.

"Been quite a time for you out there, at large in the county, hasn't it?"

Jasper shifted in his seat but said nothing.

"Fell into some interesting company. Seen some interesting things."

Jasper remained silent. A big clock on a chest of drawers ticked noisily.

"Anyways, you done me the greatest turn a fellow human being can do for another. I wonder what you got to say for yourself. Speak to me, son."

Jasper hesitated and something caught in his throat when he spoke. "I did what I was taught to do," he said.

"Yes, and you done it first-rate, too. I'm surely grateful. But the fact remains that you killed my horse."

For the first time in days, Jasper betrayed emotion. His mouth twitched, his pupils contracted, his breathing went shallow and short, the color left his face, and he shifted uncomfortably in his seat.

"What do you got to say about it?"

Jasper didn't know what to say. He was sure that saying he was sorry was not adequate.

"He was a fine horse, a brave and good-natured animal," Brother Jobe said. "He was only defending himself when he reared up on that dog of yours that was running around his legs, barking and snapping and carrying on. He was as much a friend of mine as that dog was a friend of yours."

Jasper could no longer restrain his tears.

"What I want to know is, how'd you kill him?"

Jasper began to weep loudly and shook his head.

"Tell me, boy!"

The doctor opened the door and intruded in the room.

"Get out of here!" Brother Jobe boomed and fixed his gaze on the doctor's. As their eyes locked, the doctor turned helplessly and withdrew from the room as if obeying a command he had no power to resist.

"You ain't answered my question, boy," Brother Jobe growled at Jasper. "Look at me!"

Jasper just sank deeper within himself.

Brother Jobe leaned forward and seized Jasper's face in one hand and positioned his own reddening face close to the boy's so they could not avoid each other's eyes. Then he raised an index finger to the outside corner of his right eye and drilled his gaze into Jasper's.

"I'm amongst your own mind now, son," Brother Jobe said. "Can you feel me in there?"

"Yes," Jasper said.

"You going to do like I say?"

"Yes."

"Answer my questions?"

"Yes."

"How'd you kill my horse?"

"Opium."

"Must have been a lot."

"Enough to kill a horse," Jasper said.

"I know you're not trying to be funny."

"I'm not."

Brother Jobe relaxed his grip on Jasper's face and dropped his hand, but remained very close.

"I'll tell you something private," he said. "If a horse killed my dog when I was a boy, I might have felt exactly like you did. Thing is, we didn't have no horses when I was a boy. It was all cars. But if a car done it, I'd'a poured Karo syrup in the ding-danged gas tank or something."

Jasper only blinked in reply.

"You got your mind in a dark place, son. I'ma do something about that just like you brought my body back from the darkness. I can see all kind of things that have happened to you in the days just past. I know who you been with and what all has been done in your presence and your own actions in it. You ain't ever going to lose those memories, but your mind's going to be different with it. Like something you read in a storybook. You going back to being a boy for a while. You going to leave that darkness behind. You hear what I'm saying?"

"Yes."

"You ain't going to be afraid or sad no more. You going to feel the love and goodness of this world. You going to be happy in your home and family. You going to be a boy again and grow into yourself like a natural man will. Hear what I'm saying?"

"Yes."

"The only thing you ain't going to remember is this here little talk we just had, at least the way it was. You going to tell your daddy that I just gave you some Jesus and said that you was a good boy and thanks for doing what you done for me and all like that. Hear?"

"Yes."

"All right then. I'm going to leave you to your own mind now when I'm done counting backwards from five."

Brother Jobe counted. Jasper blinked again and turned to look at the door.

"You can be on your way now, son. Thanks again."

Jasper nodded and smiled. Then he leaned in close and whispered to Brother Jobe, "Want to know something funny?"

"Sure."

"People think you're the devil."

Brother Jobe laughed, a high, creaking sound, like a door opening.

"Only on Halloween, son." he said. "And it's done gone for this year, thank the Lord. Rest of the time I'm just a sawed-off ugly old cracker with a few tricks up my sleeve. Get along now."

Jasper got up and found his father out in the hall. The doctor detected something different in the boy's demeanor. His shoulders seemed less rounded and a light was back in his face that had been missing since his return.

"What was that about?" the doctor asked.

"Just some Jesus and thanks and all," the boy said. "Is this a school night?"

"Yes," the doctor said. "It's Wednesday."

"Good," the boy said. "Let's go home."

EPILOGUE

Two days after Brother Jobe's return, Brother Seth rode his blue roan, Ollie, back into the highlands west of Hebron and found the bodies of the panther and Perry Talisker where they'd been left under a rock pile beside the road. He skinned the panther and conveyed the hermit's body a quarter mile down the road below the rocky defile to a place in the woods where he dug a proper grave and buried him, allowing a few minutes for recitation of the Twenty-third Psalm: "*The Lord is my shepherd; I shall not want. . . .*" On his way home he stopped at Barbara Maglie's cottage, hoping to find a good hot meal, but he arrived just as another man, a prosperous-looking stranger of about forty from Arlington, Vermont, was unloading several large hams from a horse cart in her dooryard drive. She recognized Seth with a smile but did not invite him to stop. Seth tipped his hat and smiled back. Then he rode home to Union Grove, making do with the ration of corn bread, cheese, and pickles that he had packed that morning.

The Reverend Loren Holder returned to the village of Argyle with Robert Earle and Tom Allison to bring Miles English to the jail in the old Union Grove town hall, where he would await the disposition of his case for trafficking in children and other charges. Stephen Bullock had issued the necessary writs and was all for mounting a prosecution. But Miles English saved everybody the trouble. He had hanged himself from a floor joist in the dank cell under the stable behind his store, using the rope he had been bound with to accomplish it, in a space too low to even stand in comfortably. His knees barely scraped the floor where he hung. Loren, Robert, and Tom brought his body to the Argyle cemetery, along with the little body of the dead boy, and committed them both to the earth. The boys that Loren had liberated from Miles English could not be returned to their families, since they had none left, so they took up happy residence with Loren and Jane Ann. The youngest of them, Jesse, proved to be deaf, not mentally defective or ill, and began a tutelage in signed speech with the town polymath, Andrew Pendergast.

The evening before Thanksgiving, Brother Elam appeared at the door of the doctor's house with a two-month-old puppy tucked under the collar flap of his long wool coat. He asked for the doctor's boy, and the doctor invited him to step in because it was sleeting out and near freezing and they were running the woodstoves now. The big ex-soldier entered the front hall, a figure so intimidating that little Dinah shrank up the stairs at the sight of him. When Jasper came in from the kitchen, where he'd been shelling butternuts for his mother, it took him a moment to see the little dog sheltered in Elam's coat.

"The boss thinks this might be a good home for her," Elam said. "He says you'll be able to feed her and care for her."

Jasper looked to his father.

"Yes, we will," the doctor said.

Elam took the twelve-pound puppy out of his coat and handed him to Jasper, who backed into the seat of a wing chair, holding her in his arms.

"What's her name?" Jasper asked.

"She don't have one," Elam said. "We got three more where she come from and we didn't want the little ones getting too attached. You call her whatever you like."

"I'm going to call her Robin," Jasper said. "Tell Brother Jobe."

"I'll let him know," Elam said.

As the population had declined in this corner of the place still thought of as the United States, the coyotes had interbred with the eastern timber wolves migrating down from Canada until a very robust breed of carnivores ran the hills of Washington County in regular circulating packs, electrifying those who heard their keening cries in the cold, lengthening nights. One of those nights between Thanksgiving and Christmas of the year that concerns us, a pack ventured onto the property of Barbara Maglie in the rural township of Hebron. She was inside, warmly entertaining a visiting planter from Sunderland, Vermont, with scallops of pork—which he had brought with him—sautéed with sage and plenty of butter. She was unaware of the wolves digging into the shallow grave of Billy Bones two hundred yards away. His body was very much intact due to the generally cold weather that followed his interment, but it had ripened nicely. The wolves removed him from his place of retirement and scattered his remains where no one would ever find them.

In the months and years to come, the story of the outlaw Billy Bones entered into local legend. His image was as colorful as his true persona had been in the world but tilted somewhat to a more benign, friendly view, as is often the case in the folkloric afterlife of psychopathic killers, who are remembered more fondly than they deserve to be. One of his surviving victims had even recorded a few stanzas of the bandit's infamous ballad, to which many more would be added by others over the years to come. His ghost was said to haunt the roads and byways of the county, particularly the highlands between Hebron and the old city of Glens Falls and especially around Halloween, the time of year when he was reputedly slain by a rival who was jealous for the affections of a woman, a silver-haired beauty who was either a prostitute or a witch, depending on the version of the tale.